THE TREES HAVE EYES

HORROR STORIES

HAUNTED HOUSE
PUBLISHING

PUBLISHING

Copyright © 2018
Haunted House Publishing
TobiasWade.Com

The Trees Have Eyes
Cover by: Taylor Tate

CONTENTS

BILL OWENS III

By Jesse Clark

MY NAME IS "BILL" OWENS III, AND IN THIS JOURNAL I publish stories of those who've encountered supernatural, paranormal, bizarre and otherwise unexplainable phenomena, benevolent or malevolent or benign, and who feel they can't turn anywhere else but need to be listened to. You may do with this information what you will.

TAP. Tap. Tap. Tap. Tap.

Robert Billings is rapping a light beat on the floor with his foot. It is a nervous tick, as he'll explain, and throughout the course of this conversation, save for two occasions where he excuses himself briefly, that tick will cease only a single time. To calm himself he smokes too, and once he's got his cigarette he lifts the pack and

1

produces one for me; I decline. Then I set up the recording device and place that on the little table next to my chair, and turn it on.

"You know what's a fact?" he says.

"What's that?"

"Started smokin' the same day the foot-jitter started." He places the cigarette between his teeth and lights it after a failed attempt, puffs on it and coughs. "Ain't that somethin'? Same damn day."

"That have something to do with why I'm here?"

He nods a bit. "Ain't no doubt about that."

I write this down, and without looking up say, "So you were an outdoorsman, right?"

"Yessir. Never was one for cities. Closer I can get to nature the closer I am to God; why I chose to live out this way." He nods up and over to the window. From there a rolling hill can be seen on which this house is built. At the bottom of its slope it is consumed by woods and surrounded, some miles off, by the eastern Appalachians (although those can hardly be seen from the living room). He takes a long drag on his cigarette. "Started hiking when I was, what, seventeen? Eighteen, maybe? Late high school years, somewhere around then. Loved it too. Started climbing after that, and diving. Wish I could still get out there and do that stuff. But, y'know how it goes."

"The march of time."

He nods. "The march of time. Yessir."

Throughout all of this I notice but do not mention the fact that his "foot-jitter" has subsided. Talk of nature calms him. The next topic will not.

"And in our phone call you said it was... caving, right?

I remember you saying that was your 'final frontier,' is that right?"

The jitter resumes. *Tap. Tap. Tap. Tap. Tap.*

"A-yep. I was around twenty-seven, twenty-eight, realized I didn't just like the outdoors for the sake of it. I liked the thrill, too, you know? *Not danger*, really, but, uh..." he trails off and swirls his hand in the air while he struggles to find the words

"The adrenaline rush."

He snaps his fingers. *"The adrenaline rush.* Yes. The excitement. A little danger, I guess." He laughs. I smile.

"So how experienced were you when it happened?"

"Intermediate. I'd been doin' spelunking for a year or two at the time, give or take. Mostly in big, safe places, y'know—Carlsbad, Natural Bridge. Places folks go to a lot. Realized the uh, the novelty wore off after a while. It was fun, still, but—"

"...But not thrilling."

"Bingo. Can't be properly thrilling if it's been done before. Way I see it, anyway." He takes another drag that finishes his cigarette, and without hesitation produces, lights, and starts on a second. By the time our talk is concluded he'll have finished what was left of the pack. "You thirsty?" he says. "Got some Billing's Brew in the fridge."

"You brew your own beer?"

"Keeps me busy." He doesn't wait for my response; he gets up with the cigarette between his teeth and moves into the kitchen, and a moment later he is back with two glasses filled with a thick stout. I take a sip, hold in a retch, and place it down. He downs a third of his glass in a

3

single gulp. "Tryin' to get the uh, the local farmer's market to sell this stuff. But there's all sorts of licensing shit I gotta work through."

I steer the conversation back to the matter at hand. "So you said 'it can't be thrilling if it's been done.' So I'm guessing you started exploring caves that were... not as well known."

Tap. Tap. Tap. Tap. Tap.

"Few of 'em were named. Most weren't. Means I an' whoever it was I was with got to name 'em, which was a neat privilege. Usually just combined our names to make it easy. Billings-Adams. Billings-Baldwin-Francis-Pucker. Most of 'em were small things, too. Little, one, two chamber holes in the mountainside. Tall enough to crouch in, maybe deep enough to lose sunlight, but not much bigger than that." There is a pause before he adds, "But then there was Baldwin-Billings." And his foot-jitter begins again, and with speed. Tap-tap-tap-tap-tap-tap-tap. When he takes another sip of his beer this causes him to spill a bit of it on his shirt. He dabs lazily at the stain; under his breath he mumbles, "Hell."

"'Baldwin-Billings,'" I say. "That one on a map?"

He shakes his head no. "An' I hope it stays that way."

"So how'd you find it?"

"My guide was a caving vet named John Baldwin. Met up with him on a previous hike and he tells me about this place he'd found all on his lonesome. Said he hadn't had a chance to explore the place yet—at least not past the second chamber or so—and he invites me. An' let me tell you this—a place that's both unexplored and worth exploring? That's a rare combination indeed. So I jumped at the chance. We get there, we park a good mile, mile an' a half out, give or take, march up the mountain slope, an' there it is. Just a little humble hole between two trees. Had to squeeze our way in."

"No wonder it went under the radar."

"For as long as it did, anyway. So in we go, an' like most of the places I'd been in up to that point, it was real damn small. You know, we had to crouch in there, and for a minute I thought I got myself conned, or something. Like, 'why the hell did he bring me here? There ain't nothin' special about this.'"

To avoid looking rude I force myself to swallow a third of my beer.

"That ready for prime time, you think?"

"What's that?"

"The drink. You think I could sell it?"

"Uh, yeah! Yeah, it's real good. Real strong." After a pause I say, "So the cave was small?"

"Well, at first, yeah. But that's when he turns on his flashlight and points over to the, uh, northern, north-western side of the cave, roundabouts, an' there's a little gap there. Little cut in the rock that you could shimmy through. So he gets to work doin' that, starts callin' out stuff he sees, you know, 'bend your knee around this rock, gotta duck a bit, twist your arm to get past this.' Stuff like that. An' before I get inside I'm thinkin', hey, man, you know—I liked spelunking for the quiet, the adrenaline, the exploring. But I don't like tight spaces. No, sir. If anything I like nature because it's the opposite of tight spaces: wild, free air. Claustrophobia's for high rises."

"You'd never run into any tight caves?"

5

"Well, I had, but like I said—the ones that weren't well mapped out, where I knew what I was gettin' into, were so damn small, y'know, that even if there was a little squeezing required, or crawlin' or something, you could usually see the other side. An' usually that was it. But this —it was just blackness in there. Didn't know how far back it all went." He finishes his beer and wipes his mouth with the back of his hand. "But I'd already come that far, you know? So I suck it up, and I go in, an' I'm workin' real damn hard to not panic, you know—slow my breathing, trying to stay nice and relaxed. An' he's callin' out obstacles an' I'm doin' what he says. Get through it just fine. Figure hell, I did that. Had to squeeze and duck and twist, but I got through. Can't get much worse."

"Might as well keep going at that point."

He nods and finishes his second cigarette, and dumps its ashes in an overflowing tray. Then he lights his third. "Went on like that for a while. Place really was bigger than anywhere else I'd been that hadn't been mapped out. Longer at least, not so much tall or wide. But it kept goin' an' goin.' Started losin' track of time. Lost track of how far in we were. When you're workin' that hard—an' boy it is hard work, lemme tell ya—stuff like that just gets away from you."

"So when did things start to go wrong?"

His foot-jitter picks up its pace again. *Tap-tap-tap-tap-tap-tap-tap.*

"We found a pond. Eventually we get to a little precipice; overlooks a big drop-off. Over to the side of that is a small pond. Ain't no life in it that I can see. Might not've even been deep enough to dive in. But I fill up my bottle at the pond before we start the descent, an' I drink it. But then John yells at me not to; tries to wrestle it out of my hands, I'm confused an' struggle back, and—and down he goes."

"Into the pond?"

"Over the precipice."

"God."

"Yeah." There's a beat of silence while he collects his thoughts. Then he says, "Nasty fall, too. Big slab he was standin' on weren't as stable as it looked. It cracks, it slides, he goes down. Then I try to lean over to see if I can't help him back up, and I go down too. Along with the rest of the rock."

"How'd you survive?"

"Ain't sure. I was pretty damn banged up; I'll tell you that much." He bites his cigarette, half-turns in his seat and lifts his shirt to reveal a jagged scar that runs nearly the full length of his right side.

"You see that?" he says. "Cracked three ribs, later found out. Had to wear one o' them corset things for a few months. Felt like a real man in that." He starts to chuckle.

But then I say, "What happened to John?", and the laughter dies, and he lowers his shirt.

"Couldn't find him." He flicks ash in the tray. "Dunno how long I was out, but when I came to he was nowhere to be found. Had to dig out of the rubble myself. Called out for him, searched for him in the mess, you know—to see if he was buried. Nothing. Which meant he'd wandered off without me. So add bein' real pissed off on top of every other damn thing."

7

"Did you look for him?"

He shrugs. "At that point I didn't give a damn what happened to the man. I just wanted to find a way out." He begins a fresh cigarette—his fourth, by my count—and he says, "So I just wandered off into the cave. Didn't know where I was goin.' Didn't know if there even was another exit, you know? But it's not like there were any way out from where I was. So off I went. Walked for, God—I don't know how long. Hours an' hours, easily."

"Can't imagine you were equipped for that."

"Had two granola bars. Ate those. Had a bit of trail mix. Ate that. Finished my water; never did find another pond to fill it in. Luckily the place opened up after that, though—tight corridors became hallways; little rooms you couldn't stand in without bangin' your head were now chambers, y'know, that you could hear your echo in. But I couldn't find John for the life of me. At least not before things started gettin' weird."

"In what way?"

He relights his cigarette and gives me a smug side-look as he does it. Then he says, "Found writing."

I blink. "You saw writing? Is that what you said?"

"Yessir."

"In English?"

He shakes his head no. "Wasn't any language I could identify, y'know, but it looked old. Ancient, even—almost like those, uh—Egyptian cuneiform things, like—"

"Hieroglyphs."

"What?"

"Egyptians wrote in hieroglyphs. Picture-words. Cuneiform was Sumerian."

8

"Well, whatever it was, it was bizarre. Somehow—an' this is gonna sound insane—I didn't know what the writing said, like in a translatable way, but I got the gist of it. An' I don't know how. Don't make any sense at all."

"What was that gist?"

All at once he becomes visibly distressed. He fidgets, and adjusts himself in his seat. Then he says, "It wasn't specific. Wasn't like it was describin' death an' mayhem' or anything. It was like... here. I'll put it this way: you know when you're a kid, an' you're afraid of the dark but you don't know why? You see that uh, like an open closet at night, or look down in the basement from the top of the stairs, or somethin? You're six, eight years old. What do you do?"

"You picture the boogeyman."

"Right! Right, but why?"

I shrug. "I would imagine because the brain wants to put a face on what it doesn't know. So it fills in the blank with possibilities that reflect your emotional state. Tries to justify the fear."

"Good, good—now get rid of all that. You strip away the zombie, strip away the vampire, you know, the boogeyman—an' what do you have? What's left behind it all?"

"Naked, contextless, faceless dread. I guess."

He snaps his fingers and leans back in his seat. "Exactly. Exactly. I didn't read those words—hell, I didn't even look at 'em directly—but when I was runnin' through the cave it was like they were just puttin' exactly that shit in my brain somehow. Like it cut out the middle-man, y'know—took out the reading, took out me inter-

9

preting the words, took out the ideas behind the words. There are just words—coverin' the floor, the walls, the ceiling, all of it—an' then there's that shit in my head. How'd you put it? Naked dread?"

I nod. "Like it… quantified death, or fear—and found a way to invoke that in you. Without you having to read it. That's fascinating."

"Fascinating to hear about, maybe. Bein' there it'll drive you mad, I'll tell you what," he says. "At that point it was less about escaping the cave, y'know, an' more about escaping the words. It was torture, Bill. Truly, it was. Mental torture, psychological torture, spiritual—whatever you want to call it. I'd have much rather died alone—starved to death or suffocated in some godforsaken corner of that damn cave—than have to keep on enduring it. It was getting worse as I went, too."

"How so, exactly?"

He pats out the ash. "Cave got darker as I went in. Don't know how—ain't like there'd been sunlight for as many hours or days as it'd been. But still; got darker an' darker. Flashlight was less an' less effective. I thought the batteries were dyin' so I fumbled around an' swapped 'em out with my reserve pair. But it didn't help. I couldn't see my hand in front of my face, you know. That kind of dark. Gets right in there in your bones. It's intimate. An' the words—I don't know. I got more an' more aware of 'em. An' what they were puttin' in here." He taps his temple with his right hand. "Then other shit started happenin.'" He clears his throat and this rolls over into a whooping cough; he puts it out with a swig of beer. Then he says, "I started leavin' the cave."

"I don't follow."

"I just... I was in the cave, an' it got darker, an' then, even though I could still feel the walls of the cave—the rocks, the floor, y'know—I started seein' other stuff. Like layered on top of it, like another dimension. Can't explain it any more than the words, but that's the feelin' I got. Like I was in the cave, but part of me was somewhere else."

"What did this... new place look like?"

"Like a hallway. Smooth surfaces. Smooth walls, smooth floor. An' I know it weren't part of the cave cause if there's one thing you learn spendin' your life outdoors it's that nature don't make right angles, you know? An' if by some act of God it does, it sure as hell don't make multiple ones all right next to each other. No, this place? This place was man-built. Or somethin' built." After a drag on his cigarette he adds, nonchalantly and as if it were a minor detail, "An' there were pictures on the walls."

"Really?"

"Yessir."

"Of...?"

He sets the cigarette in his teeth and he says, "It was the cuneiform from before, but—"

"Hieroglyphs."

"Hieroglyphs, whatever—but they were alive. Moving. Writhing. Squirming. I felt like somehow they had depth to 'em. An' I realized that, you know—wherever I was, this new plane, this new dimension—it was a much realer existence than the one we're in now. Everything was so much deeper, so much more real. Everything here, y'know—" He picks up his empty glass and turns it over in his hands without purpose, "It's like it was just a thin summary of that place. Somehow I'd stumbled right on through, I guess you'd call it the Veil—an' I was in the real world. The one behind the illusion. I don't know."

"Did this... more real version of the hieroglyphs provide you any insight into their nature? Any deeper understanding beyond an emotional response?"

"Sure. Sure, they did. That dread started gettin' its own context, a little bit. Somethin' that's still alien, y'know, but it started feelin' more focused. An' the further down the hallway I went, the more focused it got."

He put the glass down and stared at it for a bit, lost in thought and his own wordless musings. Then he said, "Anyway. Finally got to the end of the hallway. Words were behind me; guess they'd served their purpose, or whatever. An' at the end there was a staircase. Massive, mighty flight o' stairs, stretched off to the left an' right as far as I could see. Stretched down so far there wasn't nothin' but blackness there. Don't know what was at the bottom. Don't know if anything was at the bottom, really. But I saw what was in the middle of that place."

After an extended pause, in which he assembles the words, during which the tap-tap-tapping of his foot gets faster, he says, "It was... a creature. A demon, or something. Maybe worse. An'—oh, God. God, it was—it was this mighty, massive thing, size of a planet, it felt like—just watching me from the mist; from the shadows. An' I couldn't get away from it. I couldn't run, I couldn't turn around. No matter where in the cave I went. Every single fuckin' step I took brought me closer to it. Realized, y'know, that I was still in the cave, an' no matter where I ran in that place it had no effect on where I was in this—this real world. Like some kind of uh, like a computer game character, you know? You can move around in that fake world all you want. But you ain't never gonna leave the living room."

"What did it look like? The creature, I mean?"

Taptaptaptaptaptaptaptaptaptaptap...

"Didn't look like anything that's ever been alive here, I'll tell you that much. It was—God, it was almost like a reptile, y'know? Maybe just a little bit; just a vaguely reptilian-thing, vaguely deer-like too, an' shaped like a jellyfish, almost, since it didn't have, y'know—a head or arms or anything you'd recognize as a body part. It was just this hideous mass, bigger than the moon, an' covered in rot and what looked like tree bark, and bones. I thought I saw old, like, rock formations dangling from it, too." He gestures to his chin and to his arms as if something is hanging from them. "Stalactites an' stalagmites, all the stuff you heard of in school—dangling pillars of rock—were a part of this thing, or an extension of it, I don't know. But it was old. Ancient; an' not like, Roman ancient but truly otherworldly, before-time-itself kind of ancient." He pauses for a bit to collect himself. Then he says, "Then it, uh—it spoke to me, Bill."

"The... demon spoke to you?"

He puts his head in his hands and rocks back and forth and trembles; this time his whole body joins in it. And he nods. "It spoke the same language as the words. An' I couldn't translate it for you if I tried. Human language, I don't know—it ain't better or worse, it's just different. We explain this world. The fake world. You know? Like we got a word for cup. Beer. TV." He nods at his television. "But that language explains, I don't know— the essence. The Deep. The true, naked reality behind the Veil. An' somehow I just knew what it meant when it spoke."

"What did it mean?"

A tear rolled down his cheek and he groaned pitifully.

"It was... it was calling me, Bill. It wasn't sayin' my name, y'know, but it was callin' me. The me behind the skin; the me behind the flesh, behind the bones. Oh, God. God, God. It was like a thousand dead voices at once, just singin' in this rolling, echoing, gravelly fuckin' dead language. An'—an' then I was just... I was with it. Next to it. Part of it. I looked behind me an' I saw the stairs way, way off, you know—like as far away as the sun is from earth. Don't know how long it took me to get there. Don't know if time or space even had any meaning in that place at all. I was just gettin' closer to it, an' somehow—for some reason—I didn't care. I wasn't scared. Weren't upset, or happy, or anything. I was me, y'know, but without the flesh or emotions. Everything was stripped away; I was just a floating, naked soul."

"What happened when you reached it?"

"I started comin' back a bit, weirdly. Started gettin' feelings like, you know, this ain't right, somethin's wrong, this ain't real, it can't be. Yadda yadda. Started as just a little trickle of normal thoughts, y'know, like I was still in there somewhere, fightin' to get out. An' I start to resist, an' it pulls me in closer, an' I fight some more."

By now Robert is staring off at nowhere in particular

at all; he is every inch as thoroughly wrapped in the tale as I am.

"Then it—it says somethin' like… blood. Or, or sacrifice, or somethin'—that's the closest English word for what it meant. Maybe it was all the same thing in that language, I don't know. But I got the impression I could only escape if I gave it life."

"If you gave it life? Like allowed it to kill you, or…?"

"That, or some other life." There is a brief pause before he adds, "An' I realized that, y'know—that's what this thing was. This place wasn't the reality behind the illusion at all, but the opposite of reality. An' this thing is the opposite of life. That's the only way I can describe it. The opposite of life. The thing on the Other Side. An' only after realizin' that, an' fightin' like hell, did it start to lose its grip on me. An' the cave started to come back, and the light, an'—an', oh, God." He breaks down but manages, "I didn't mean to do it, I didn't—I didn't know. I didn't know. Oh, God, no, no, no."

I sit up straight. "What? Do what?"

After a moment he holds up his trembling hands as if he hasn't washed the stains of blood from them in all these years. "It was John," he says. "It was… he'd been calling me an' I couldn't, I didn't know, I didn't—"

"John… was the demon?"

He shakes his head. "No, no—when I came outta that damned place I was back up by the pond, an' John was—he was dead. Beaten into the ground, dead. Broken nose, bloody, bruised. Disemboweled. An' my hands hurt, an' I knew—I just knew—that it hadn't been hours or days or weeks or however long. We hadn't even fallen over the edge like I thought. It'd been no time at all. John had been saying, 'No, no, don't drink that! Don't drink the water here, you don't know what's in it!' An' he grabbed my arm, an' I just—I beat him to death, Bill. I killed him."

Robert begins weeping again, tearlessly and heavily; he drops the cigarette and grabs his head and bunches up his hair between his fingers and rocks back and forth. "No, no, no, no. I'm sorry. I'm sorry, I didn't—"

Only after a long time has passed does he sigh loudly and sit back. Then he wipes his nose with the back of his hand, and grabs the pack and dumps the last cigarette from it into the palm of his hand. This comforts him to a small degree. He lights it.

I say, "I'm sorry, Robert."

"Yeah, well. What's done is done, right?" His voice is shaking. But he takes a long drag and produces a cloud that fills the air above his head and lifts away. Then he pats the ash into the bowl. "Took John's keys after that," he says. "Brought a rock down on his head, tossed him over the edge. Found my way out eventually, you know. Drove to a gas station, got a pack, drove home, called the police an' smoked the whole damn thing while I waited for 'em. Thought I was goin' to prison, you know? But when they got there I told 'em John died in a caving accident. Tripped an' fell right over the edge; weren't nothin' I could do. An' they saw I wasn't in no shape to be a killer, y'know? So they let me be. Left me there to stew in my fuckin' filth an' in my misery." He looks at the floor. "I don't know. Dunno if they ever did find him down there. Spent, God—better part of a year, maybe more—worryin' someone would find my handprints on his neck an' I'd be

16

gettin' a knock on the door. But I never did get that knock. An' by the time I was able to sleep normally again —live well enough with the nightmares—all the stress had produced this here foot-jitter." He nods down. Tap-tap-tap-tap-tap-tap-tap. "An' it ain't ever left me since; that was some twenty years back this May."

I consider all this for a time, and finish my beer while we sit in silence. Then I say, "So... do you think it was the pond water that did it? Put you in a hallucination, made you attack John?"

He snorts. "Thought about that," he says. "But how'd I get the broken ribs?"

"So it wasn't an illusion at all, then."

"Maybe not."

"I do have to ask, though—I get the impression you've bottled this up for a while. While tell me now?"

"Because I'm almost out of time," he says. "Like you said earlier. The march of time. Thought I'd get it off my chest before I went to the Deep."

I blink. "You think you're going back to that place?"

"Hell, Bill. Been seein' the place real vivid like in my dreams lately, y'know?" He pats the last of the ash into the bowl, and laces together his fingers and places his hands across his stomach. "Fact of the matter is, it's where we all go at the end. To join our bones with the Pit."

ISOLATION CABIN

By H.G. Gravy

IT WOULDN'T BE DIFFICULT TO LIST WHO WAS STANDING OUT there among the trees in the middle of the blizzard. Their names and blood types were etched into my brain forever like a hall of shame. They scratch against the wood and windows of the cabin and pound against the door. I dare not allow them inside. Their horrible accusations moaned through the crackled and dried lips of the dead.

I tell myself over and over again:

They're dead. They can't be here. They're dead. They can't be here.

It's a desperate cling to the sanity and logic of the real world. Out there in the forest, rationality, logic, and reality were self-deceiving words devoid of any meaning. There was only madness in denying the truth of what I heard out there.

"Why did you let me die? I was only nine. You should have saved me..."

Emma Brighton. O Positive.

Attempting to avoid a collision with a drunk driver, Emma's father swerved their family's vehicle into the breakdown lane and then lost control of it. Her mother and father were killed on impact when the car wrapped itself around a tree. Emergency services required the use of hydraulic tools to remove Emma from the wreckage. Losing precious time in the process of getting Emma to the hospital, there was nothing I could do to save her life despite all my years of experience and training. I tried to keep her heart pumping for as long as I could, but there was just too much damage to her little body.

She never regained consciousness. I'd never heard her speak, cry, or laugh. Her final moments were nothing but memories of chaos, pain, and fear. I remember wishing I could have comforted her while she passed. No one should ever leave this world so violently.

Tonight, I hear her voice taunting me outside the cabin.

"Why did you let me die? I was only nine. You should have saved me."

Emma's voice is the loudest among the other dozens I heard. Many I recognized. Others, like dark magic, I could see pictures in my mind's eye of their faces and remember them.

Donald Slater. A Positive.

"You can't save anyone, can you? Just give it up!"

The first person to die on me. Heart attack.

Lindsay Gravat. O Negative.

Gunshot wound to the chest.

"My husband tried to kill me, but it looks like you finished the job for him. What did I ever do to you?"

The cabin rumbled with the hammering of ghostly fists upon its outside. The chorus of the dead moaned louder in their deafening voices. There was no escape from the onslaught. They continued crawling out from behind trees and through the snow-covered path up the driveway. The blizzard would not halt their progress.

Mary Grant. B Positive.

Blood clot.

"I'll never get to know my daughter because of you."

I pleaded for little Emma to forgive me. I told her I tried my best. There was nothing anyone could have done to save her life or anyone else's. I begged the dead to realize I'm only human. I asked forgiveness for my failures.

My apologies and justifications meant nothing to them. The dead have no room for forgiveness. They care nothing for the anguish or sorrow of the living.

With the last ounce of strength inside me, I shouted for them to stop and took the pistol from the dinner table into my hand. The voices stopped. There was silence again for the first time since I'd arrived at the cabin.

The voices of the dead then whispered to each other and then in unison they chanted: *"You failed us. Do it. You failed us. Do it."*

There was something seductive in their chanting. It was an invitation with open arms. It was atonement and forgiveness. I raised the gun from my side and placed the barrel into my mouth. My lips wrapped around the cold metal. It touched the back of my throat, and I gagged.

The taunts intensified in their fury. The voices came from everywhere all at once. Men, women, and children. I could feel their icy whispers in my ears and down the side of my neck. My finger trembled on the trigger.

One pull is all I needed, and the warmth of divine peace would forever be mine.

The chanting stopped, but I could still feel them surrounding me. The pounding against the cabin ceased. The wind muted too. All the world went silent and lied in wait. The pistol had warmed in my mouth. My finger danced on the trigger. I was terrified of killing myself, yet I wanted nothing more than to free myself of the guilt and the faces of the damned which haunted all my waking moments.

I didn't want to disappoint the dead again. I lost them in life and wanted to please them with my death. They wanted my soul to join them in their eternal damnation.

My finger stopped dancing on the trigger. I held it steady now. The gun felt warm in my mouth now. Its metallic taste reminded me of blood. I wondered if I'd eternally have the taste of blood and bullets in my mouth when I joined those outside the cabin in the afterlife. The idea of it gave me pause once more, and without a second thought, I pulled the gun from my mouth and set it on the dinner table like I'd done each of the previous nights.

If the dead wanted me to die, they were going to have to do it themselves. I charged to the front door and pulled it wide open to find the blizzard had placed several feet of snow there. Jumping through the soft powder and landing at the bottom of the steps, I readied my pistol and aimed it in both directions searching for those who haunted me.

Once again, there was no one there in the pitch-black darkness.

The chill of winter burned my face with its wind. The light from inside the cabin only stretched a few feet, and all I could see is the thick snow which continued to fall from the sky. Fearing for my life, I returned to the warmth of the cabin and shut the door behind me.

I leant against the door and fell to the ground, releasing the pistol from my hand and letting it drop to the floor.

"They're dead. They can't be here," I told myself. *"They're dead. They can't be here."*

The doorknob rattled and the scratching against the door and windows began again.

"You should have saved me! You let me die!"

"You failed us! Join us!"

WORLD'S OLDEST TREE

By Tobias Wade

"Just because you can't see them doesn't mean they aren't real."

"How do you know?"

"Because you can feel them when they're close," I said. "The goosebumps on your skin even though it's not cold. The way the air tastes, and the dry lump in your throat. That's how they let you know they're about to strike."

"How do you get away?"

"No one ever has. You get about ten minutes after you notice them before they force themselves inside you. Then it's all over. Wait—did you feel something? Clara look at your arms! You've already got the goosebumps!"

My sister squirmed, thrashing against the seatbelt which suddenly looked like it was squeezing the breath out of her frail body. Her skin was bone-white, although that was hardly surprising since she never went outside.

"Mark stop scaring your sister," mom clucked from the passenger seat. "We're almost there, just hold on."

"Moooooom I can feel them!" Clara howled.

I was doing my best to softly blow air on her from the corner of my mouth without her noticing it was me.

"Ghosts aren't real, Clara. You're twelve-years old—you should know better by now," my dad said without turning. It had been a long drive for all of us, and he was gripping the wheel so tightly it looked like he was ready to swerve off the road and camp in the first ditch we found.

"See? I told you." Clara crossed her arms in an infuriating display of smugness.

"Then how come dad's mouth didn't move when he said that?"

I'm almost ashamed to admit how much pleasure I got from her double-take. Almost. Then came the rapid, aggressive burst of tapping on the window and Clara actually shrieked. I couldn't stop laughing as dad rolled down the window.

"Camping registration?" the park ranger asked, face shadowed by his wide-brimmed hat. He glanced disinterestedly into the back seats to catch Clara giggling and smacking me. She wasn't strong enough for it to hurt, and I was laughing so I didn't bother defending myself. Mom looked tired, but peaceful.

"Thank God. I thought we'd never get here." Dad handed the man an email printout.

"Long drive, huh? Where you folks from?" the ranger asked.

"California. I tried to tell them we have our own

forests, but Clara was heart-set on seeing the great quaking aspen."

"Welcome to Utah then. You won't be disappointed. Did you kids know that the Pando is the oldest and biggest life form on the planet?"

"I did!" Clara raised her hand, flailing it around like an eager student. "Although each tree is only about 120 years old, they're all connected to the same root network which has been alive for over 80,000 years, stretching over 105 acres."

"Just 80,000?" The park ranger smirked. "I've heard it's more like a million. We're not sure exactly, but there's a good chance the Pando was alive before the first human being walked the earth. Pretty incredible, huh?"

"Yep! I wish I could live that long." Mom and dad exchanged furtive glances.

"It's not about how long you live." Mom's voice cracked, and she had to take a long breath before she restarted. "It's about what you do with the time that you have. And I for one am grateful for every second we get to spend together as a family." Dad squeezed mom's hand. It must have been hard too, because their interlocked fingers were trembling. The uncomfortable silence which followed only lasted a moment before the park ranger handed us a pass and waved us on our way.

It's no secret that my sister is sick. Mom and dad don't like to talk about it, so I didn't know exactly what it was. She spent a lot of time in the hospital though, which seemed stupid to me because she was always weaker going out than she was going in. I've asked her about it before, but she just shrugged and said, 'they'll figure it out.' I didn't like the way her face looked when she said it, so I didn't ask again. Seeing her scared like that wasn't any fun.

It was almost dark when we got to the campsite. I helped dad setting up the tent while mom unpacked the car. Clara just sat on a log and stared at the sunset, which seemed really unfair to me, but it's not like she'd be much help anyway. The light was weird here—even after the sun went down it didn't really get dark. The twilight felt like it went on for hours, and the air was so quiet that time must have frozen. I was half-hoping Clara would pick up on the weird atmosphere and start believing in my ghosts again, but I think she'd forgotten all about them. Maybe she was never even afraid in the first place, only putting on a show for my amusement.

"Can you hear them?" she asked when I went over to call her for dinner.

"Who?"

"The trees. They've been waiting for me for a long time."

I didn't buy it. She was just trying to creep me out as revenge. "What are they saying?" I asked anyway.

Clara's pale skin glowed in the enduring twilight, almost as white as her eerie smile. "It doesn't speak with words. It's more like feelings. Images. Ideas. The 'Trembling Giant' is angry. Slow, purposeful, smoldering, anger, like a glacier carving a hole in a mountain range. And it needs me to set it loose."

I wish she wouldn't smile like that. "Dinner's ready, come on." I turned back toward the fire in a hurry, not wanting to give her the satisfaction of seeing me shudder.

Glancing back over my shoulder, I could still see the glow of her little teeth piercing the gathering dusk.

The next day was miserable and dull. I wanted to go out hiking and explore the forest, but Clara was too tired and mom insisted we didn't leave her behind. The whole point of this trip was to spend time together as a family, she said, so we were just going to do activities that we all could enjoy. So there we were, surrounded by spectacular natural beauty with adventure and discovery hidden behind every tree, while we sat in the dirt whittling sticks. Singing songs. Weaving baskets, watching the world drip by one excruciating second at a time.

"The baskets are fun! Look how nice your sister's is turning out."

"Can I make a really big one?" I asked.

"Of course! You can make whatever you want."

"Okay I'm going to weave a coffin then. You can just bury me wherever."

"Don't even joke about that," my father grunted.

"Or better yet, I'll make one for Clara. If she's too sick to do anything fun then she might as well--"

"Mark!" Mom that time. I'd crossed a line and I knew it, but I didn't care. I was bored out of my mind. I missed my computer and my friends. I hated all this lovey-dovey family time. They always took her side about everything and gave her whatever she asked for, but if I ever wanted something I was just being selfish.

"I'm going to be in the woods if anyone needs me. As if."

I heard mom start to chase me for a second, but dad stopped her to interject: "Stay close, okay? Don't get lost."

Getting lost didn't seem like such a bad option at the moment. White-barked giants stretching as far as I could see, with mazes of fallen trees and branches that I could use to build forts. Lush grass and ferns to run through, craggy rocks to climb, meandering streams to jump—I can't believe the rest of them sat eight hours in the car just so they could keep sitting around here. I marveled at the natural grandeur as I walked, mesmerized by the idea that this huge forest was all a single living thing. I decided to dig with a stick to get a look at the connected roots, but the ground was hard and the going was slow.

This would have been a lot easier if I'd had some help. When Clara and I were little, we used to do everything together. She was like my sidekick, always enthusiastically following me around leaping to attention whenever I had a mission for her. What was the point of playing games with yourself when no one was there to celebrate your victories or mourn your defeats?

My frustration at the futility of the digging was quickly mounting, but I used that feeling as fuel to ram the stick down even harder. Out of breath, sweating and aching, I thrust the stick so hard that it snapped in two. I don't know why that made me so angry, but it did. I dropped to my hands and knees and started digging with my fingers, hurling rocks and dirt clods around me in every direction. My fingers were accumulating cuts and scrapes, and I was about to give up when my hand suddenly broke through a thick clump of roots to reveal a hole in the ground.

Dirt and pebbles rained down the hole to disappear in the darkness below. It must have been deep too, because even with my ear to the ground I couldn't hear anything land. Unwilling to return and admit defeat, I spent the next few hours widening the hole and trying to find a way to climb down. By around noon I was so filthy that I was practically indistinguishable from the earth I churned through. My fingers were bleeding in places, and the beating sun frowned down with disdain at my efforts. None of that mattered though, because I'd opened the hole wide enough to slip inside the yawning darkness.

I climbed down the network of roots which were matted as densely as a net. My phone's flashlight prodded the darkness like a needle in an elephant, utterly underwhelming in the massive space I suddenly found myself within. The hidden cave was a converging point for the tendrils from the innumerable trees, which joined together here into larger roots, merging in turn to weave great networked tapestries which dwarfed the thin trees above the ground. I continued climbing downward along the widening roots, tempted to hide down here all day and freak out my family.

Below the cave, my route terminated in a small circular space, not much larger than my own body. It felt like being on the inside of an egg: completely encapsulated by the roots which were matted so densely now that they formed an impenetrable wall of wood. It was so quiet down here that I could hear my heart throbbing in my ears, my labored breathing a hurricane which fractured the stillness.

"Can you hear them?" my sister had asked last night, wide-eyed and serious.

Up above under the wide open sky with my family

eating dinner? That question was child's play. But here in this hidden kingdom under the earth? I placed my hand on a massive column and felt what she was talking about. This could have been growing before humans existed. It could have been touched by forgotten Gods or aliens who walked the Earth before history began. Or perhaps the Earth itself was living through these mighty pillars, lying dormant but for the quiet seething anger which slowly burned through the millennium.

The root was warm to the touch, and as I felt it, it was unmistakably feeling me in return. The unnerving sensation of a sound too deep for my ears to register was silently screaming around me. The feeling became more intense the longer I held on. I saw fire in my mind's eye, running in infernal rivers from the depths of the world to drown the cities which infested the land like festering rot on clean skin. The root was getting hotter under my touch, and as much as I tried to clear my head, the thoughts returned—the decaying towers, the teaming crowds aimlessly running, the rivers of blood which flowed down crumbling streets.

I ripped my hand away and let go, panting for breath. This was better than ghosts. This was real. And all I could think about was showing it to Clara and watching her freak. I scrambled back up the roots, pulling myself hand-over-hand onto the surface to run the whole way back to the campsite.

"What in the world—" my mother started.

"Where's Clara? I want to show her something."

"She went to lie down for a little while. How did you get so filthy?"

But I didn't wait. I sprang into her tent, practically dragging her to her feet while my parents protested from behind.

"Just for a second, okay? You can sleep anytime, but this is what we're here for."

"Mark don't you dare bother her—"

"It's okay, mom," Clara said, dragging herself out to flinch beneath the sun. "I'm here to spend time with Mark too, right?"

There it was again. Mom and dad holding hands, clenching so tightly they shook. That didn't matter though. All I could think about was Clara's face when I showed her my secret discovery. Our parents offered to come with us, but I figured that would destroy the whole fun of the secret. I was pleasantly surprised that Clara was so willing to go—it seems like she didn't want to do anything anymore.

"You heard it too," she said the moment we were alone.

"Not heard. Felt."

"This isn't a trick, right? You're not just making fun of me because I believe it?"

"When have I ever tried to trick you?" I put on my best facade of shocked-innocence. She snickered.

"How about when you wrote 'soap flavor' on the ice-cream box so you wouldn't have to share?"

"That's an isolated incident."

"Or when you told me the cactus had soft spines like cat's fur?"

"I didn't think you'd just slap it."

She laughed again, and we walked on in silence for a bit. She was obviously struggling, but she was just as obvi-

31

ously making an effort to hide it, so I didn't say anything. It wasn't much farther anyway.

"Up there, right around that grove. Anyway if I trick you so much, then how come you still believe me?"

She shrugged, catching my eyes for a second before turning to look where I was pointing. "I guess I don't know how many more chances I'll have to be tricked. I want to make the most of it while I still can."

I didn't know how to respond to that, so I kept walking.

"That's why we're here. You know that, right?" she asked.

I kept staring straight ahead.

"This might be our last chance for the whole family to be together before I..."

"It's over here," I interrupted, squatting down beside the hole. I expected her to say something sarcastic or to complain.

"Give me a hand, okay?" She didn't even hesitate. Feet first, she began lowering herself down. I helped keep her steady while she climbed. I kept my eyes on our hands so I didn't have to look at her face. I fully understood what she was saying, and I didn't want her to say more. I didn't start climbing after her until her feet had touched the cave floor.

"You're right. It's stronger down here," she said.

"You haven't seen anything yet. Come on."

I continued leading to the point where the roots terminated in the enclosed root-egg. There wasn't enough room for both of us to fit in the perfect nest, so I helped her climb in while I waited in the larger cave. Her fingers grazed the roots in silent reverence, hand jerking back from their warmth. That little smile glinted in the darkness, stretching into a euphoric grin as she touched the wood again to massage it.

"You feel it?" I asked. I knew she did, but I had to ask anyway because the silence was so heavy down here.

She simply smiled and closed her eyes. The sound of my rushing blood filled my ears again. I had to keep talking.

"What made you think it was calling for you?"

She wasn't the one who answered though. It was that scream again, too deep to hear, but I felt the echo in every vibrating root. It came from everywhere—all the mighty forest bellowing in silence, all the unknown depths of the roots, all resonating with a single, persistent, throb. Even outside of the egg I could start to feel the colossal intent seep into my mind. Incessant, irrepressible thoughts, so vivid I might as well be seeing them with my eyes. Imagery of burning rivers bubbling up from the Earth to exhaust themselves in the open air, leaving behind an abyss so deep that it must pierce through the core of the planet.

"Clara? What's going on? What do you see?" Even shining my light in my face, I could barely see it. All was fire and the bellowing howl, mounting in pitch just enough for me to actually hear the low rumble like an earthquake.

"Clara you have to get out of there. Something is going to happen."

"I know. I'm making it happen." The voice sounded so small and distant next to the enveloping presence. "We

33

both need each other. I need its enduring life, and it needs a body to guide its will."

"Clara where are you? Quick, grab my hand!" I fumbled to reach down to her, but the visions were too intense for me to see straight. My raw hands kept butting up against the roots.

"Tell mom and dad that I didn't die. That I'll never die."

Why couldn't I find the opening? I'd been standing right over it a moment ago.

"Tell them I'll be with them in the forest, even if they think themselves alone."

It took me going down on my belly to finally realize what had happened. It wasn't that I couldn't find the hole —it's that the hole didn't exist anymore. The roots had moved, fully sealing Clara inside the earth.

"Clara! Can you hear me? Clara get out!"

"I am out, Mark." The reply was so faint. "No more tricks between us. You're the one who should be running."

I'm not proud of the fact that I ran, scrambling back up the roots to pull myself onto the surface. Some might call it cowardice, but I know the certainty in her voice and I trusted her more than I trusted myself in that moment. Even above the ground I could still feel the silent scream, so low and powerful that my entire body vibrated. Panting for breath on the surface, I started to scream with everything my ragged lungs would allow. I don't know how long this went on for, but by the time I stopped, the forest was silent again.

The earth wasn't shaking. The visions had cleared. All except for the hint of Clara's face outlined in the bark of an aspen tree.

FACES IN THE WOODS

By JP Carver

My wife wanted us to get out of the city, I did not. I have no true love of nature, nor do I enjoy the allergies that seem to attack me the moment I step into something more than just grass. But I could never say no to her and so I packed up my things, my work, my projects, and drove out to the Poconos.

I could feel unease the moment I passed the sign announcing that we were entering Pike County. I'm not one prone to listening to just a feeling, but I wanted to turn around. I even stopped at a gas station and tried to talk Elise into heading back home.

"We could stay inside and just enjoy our time together. I don't see why we have to come out here."

She smiled gently at me, patiently. "I know you get this itch whenever we go somewhere that isn't surrounded by buildings and a Starbucks just down the road, but please?

Just this once, for me? I need to get out of all the... noise. It's just for the weekend, honey. Besides, you could use the time away too."

She touched her hand to my face, the pad of her fingers soft and feather-like on my skin. I couldn't help but relent. She always affected me in that way. I sighed, nodded and undid my seat belt. "Fine, I'll do it. For you. Right now, though, I'm aching for a Baby Ruth and a soda, you want anything?"

Elise shook her head, her short hair bouncing against her cheeks. She smiled as she spoke. "No, I'll just steal some of your soda if I get thirsty."

I chuckled. "Nothing new there. Be back in a bit."

The bell above the door rang and I looked up to it. It had been a long time since I had heard an actual bell in a convenience store, but there it was. I smirked and slowly walked forward, my eyes scanning the store. There was a different layout for each store you entered even while named the same. The candy aisle was on the other side of the place and I made a beeline to it.

I took two Baby Ruths out of the cardboard box as I was sure Elise would want half of mine, might as well get her one too. I went to the back of the store and stared through the glass doors. When did there become six different kinds of coke? As I tried to decide between them, a conversation from over by the Slurpee machines made its way to me.

"Joe has been seeing shit up there for years. I don't blame him, when you're alone all day and night you're bound to see something just so you're not bored."

"I dunno, this time he seems pretty damn sure. He says he even got pictures. Says it was those bitch—or birch things we use to tell stories about." I turned to see the two men who were talking. Rough and tumble looking, maybe loggers, or just your run-of-the-mill hunters. The older and shorter of the two adjusted his cameo hat as he stifled his laugh.

"Then he can send it on to some college and then they can put his ass in some hospital for the crazy."

"Don't have to be a dick, Don," the second man said and picked up his drink from the shelf of the machine. "I'm just saying what he told me. That's all."

I furrowed my brow at the conversation but didn't spend much time thinking about it. There was always some urban legend stirring about in rural towns.

I went to the cashier and handed him a ten. He tried to start a conversation but I just nodded along without really responding. He gave me my change and I headed out into the parking lot and stopped dead in my tracks.

At the passenger side of my car stood one of the men from the store. Don. He smiled at Elise, a shit-eating grin if I ever saw one. I could see her laughing at something and felt my blood start to boil. I stalked over to the car, opened the door, tossed the soda and the Babes on the seat, and placed my forearms on the cool metal of the roof.

"Can I help you?" I didn't even try to hide the anger and Don noticed.

"No sir, just the lady here asked for some directions." His bushy brows fell down over his eyes slightly. I bent down to take a quick look at Elise and she glared at me through the window. I glared back for a moment before I stood straight.

"Right, well I'm sure my wife and I can find our way." I didn't wait for a response before I sat down into my seat, and cursed as I felt the Babe Ruths squish under me. I pulled them out, tossed them at the console and started the car. The soda had found its way to the floor and I fought with it trying to get my foot on the gas without it under the pedal or under my foot.

"Keith, what's wrong?" I looked over to her as I shifted the car into reverse, but said nothing. I clenched my jaw and backed the car out, partly hoping that Donnie boy found his way behind me. Sadly, I made it out of the parking lot without a cameo cap on my back bumper.

Elise didn't talk to me again as after ten years of being together she learned my moods well enough. I knew that I shouldn't be mad, or acted the way I had, but the anger sat in my head like an old friend. For years I had worked on getting a handle on it, at the urging of Elise. Sometimes though, especially when she talked to some other guy, I felt it rise up.

I munched on one of the candy bars as I stared out the windshield, looking for a sign.

"What was the name of the place again?" I asked and used my tongue to pick out a peanut that had lodged itself between my teeth.

"Miller's Lodge." The coldness in her voice made me turn and I found her leaning against the door, her head against the window. I could see from the reflection that her eyes were turned to the trees that sped past. The rest of the drive was very quiet.

We got to the cabin; it laid deep in the trees with a twisting driveway that probably came close to half a mile up a steep hill. The car barely made it up. I had to admit the view could almost be called worthy of coming for, but I still felt outside my comfort zone and it did little to ease my temper. Little would, and knowing that made me even angrier.

Grudgingly I took our suitcases into the cabin, carrying them all at once which wasn't the brightest idea I'd ever had. I pulled my shoulder, which was just more annoyance. I swore and dropped them off in the bedroom. Elise stood behind me when I turned around. Obviously her own anger had started to grow.

"This is how it's going to be? You're gonna be a raging prick the entire trip?"

"Sure, a trip that I didn't even want to come on. Waste of money and fucking time."

She held up a hand and walked down the hall. "I had hoped you'd calm the hell down by leaving work for a bit. Guess that's too much to expect."

The front door slammed.

"Goddammit." With a heavy sigh I sat down on the bed andflopped back to stare at the wood ceiling. She was right and that didn't anger me. I was being a raging prick and over what? Some old guy talking to her? For a time, I tried to think of when my life had turned into this nightmare. I never would have guessed that I'd be who I am, an angry and stressed-out man; a shadow of the man I had once been. The man she fell in love with.

Click-clack

The noise came from outside, and I turned my gaze to

the wall. Sounded like wood smacking on wood. I didn't know enough to say if it was unusual, but the sound had been oddly close. I pushed the thought aside and got up. It was probably nothing.

Elise sat on the porch swing, her head turned to the trees in front of the cabin. Her brow was down, arms crossed and the corner of her mouth twitched just a little. She had her own temper which made mine seem pale in comparison, probably because she only got mad for a reason.

"Elise?" I said and took a step forward, as cautious as a bomb tech. She acknowledged me with a flick of her eyes in my direction. "Look, I'm sorry."

"Sure."

"No, really. You're right. I have no excuse, just... everything is stressing me out and you know I don't do well with that. How can I make it up to you?"

She turned to me, still angry but I could tell it was by force of will now. "You could start be not acting like a jerk. There was no reason for you be like that at the gas station. None. Do you really think I'd drop my panties for some eighty-year-old mountain man, Keith? Do you not trust me anymore or something?"

"I do—I mean I didn't think that at all—"

"Then why did you flip?" She bit the inside of her bottom lip for a moment and then shook her head. "I just... I don't feel like I know you anymore. You're a damn firecracker with a fuse that changes length by the hour."

"It had nothing to do with you. I just came out, feeling like I didn't want to be there and it annoyed me that he was there. I'm sorry."

"We need to do something about this, I can't... I won't live on the edge of a knife with you." She stood and came to me, her hands laying on my shoulders. "I love you, but I'm not going to be your screaming match partner. I'm tired of it, Keith. I understand that work is crazy, it's why I wanted to come out here. This wasn't for me, it was for you."

I nodded. "And I appreciate that, I do. I'll try to keep myself on a tighter leash. That foul mood is gone."

"Is it?" She asked and tilted her head up to me. "Because if it isn't I'm gonna kick your ass out into the woods for the weekend."

"I believe it." We kissed, a mix of sorry and caring. For the moment there was a patch covering the problem, but I knew it would take more than that for her to forgive me completely. For now, we could move on.

The rest of the evening went fairly well, dinner was microwaved meals that we ate in front of the fireplace, talking and laughing like we did when we first started dating. My work was forgotten, my stress gone; it was just me and Elise.

But while sitting there I heard the click-clack of wood hitting wood nearby. Elise heard it too this time and we both got up and went to the window. Clouds blocked the moon, making it impossible to see anything in the darkness of the forest. We sat there, listening to the bangs that went on for what seemed like an hour before they finally stopped.

"What does that?" I broke the silence first and looked to Elise. She shook her head. "I mean, is there an animal that does that kind of stuff?"

"I don't know. I can't think of one. You locked the doors, right? The car too?"

"You think someone is out there?"

She shrugged, rubbing her arms. "I don't know, Keith. There could be, or it's miles away and someone is just throwing stuff around. Sound acts weird out here sometimes."

We went to bed soon after, Elise falling asleep quickly in my arms, but I didn't feel quite so safe. It started up again about an hour after she fell asleep. Clack-crack. More wood breaking. I quietly slipped from beside her and went to the window.

The trees were only a few yards out from the cabin and I could see nothing but silhouettes in the darkness. The sounds seemed to rubber band back and forth, and I finally opened the window and stuck my head outside to try to hear better.

The sounds stopped as soon as I opened the window. The night was quiet and still, as if everything had just stopped at the sight of me. I stood at the window and watched the darkness for about fifteen minutes until I noticed something.

At first, I thought it was a play of moonlight on some bush, but then it moved. A face so white that it looked like it emitted its own glow. It moved from bush to bush, always facing me.

It continued moving farther and farther back into the trees, its movement spider-like—disjointed but quick. Eyes that were black holes watched me the entire time until it slipped beneath a low branch of a tree and disappeared. A few moments later the click-clack sounded once more and it was quiet again.

I stood there, staring out into the trees, frozen in place. My brain kept coming up with ways to explain it away, but nothing seemed to really fit. Every time I blinked I saw that blank white face. It looked like a mask. That was what finally got me away from the window. Someone was messing with us. I slammed the window and went into the living room where I brooded until day broke through the windows.

"What are you doing out here?" Elise asked with a yawn. "You feeling all right?"

"No, I'm not." I sniffed in anger and then looked over. "Someone was outside the cabin last night."

Her eyes widened. "Who?"

I shrugged. "Hell, if I know, but they were wearing a mask. I bet they're the ones making that damn noise too." I stood and went to one of our bags and removed the handgun that was buried underneath my clothes. I had decided to wait until she was up before I went out looking for the bastard.

"Keith, what are you going to do with that?"

"What does it look like?" I threw my jacket on and headed out the door. To be honest I didn't know what I was going to do. I just needed to do something—anything —because that damn mask spooked me. I went down the steps and rounded the cabin. Elise appeared at a window in the back.

"Don't do anything stupid, all right? It was probably just a joke."

"You hear me laughing?" I said and went to the bushes.

"Hey, assholes!" I called out into the woods. "Come out here, let's have a good laugh at what happened last night."

No sound came other than Elise slamming the window. I looked back to see her glaring at me through the glass. I turned back to the woods and stepped in.

I walked for some time, until I could barely make out the path I was taking. I stopped next to a large tree and rested against it. The only sounds were birds and cicadas chirping into the sunny morning. I stayed there listening for a while for anything that could lead me to discover what happened last night. After twenty or so minutes I gave up and started heading back; that's when the smell hit me.

It wafted from somewhere farther in the undergrowth. It's a hard smell to describe, but if you ever got a whiff of spoiled milk that would probably be pretty close to the stench. I don't know why I decided to investigate, but on I went through the underbrush until my boots sank into some kind of muck. I looked down and recoiled at the sight.

At one point the muck had been the back half of a deer. The front half looked almost completely intact, while even the bones in the back looked almost like... noodles. I had never seen anything like it and was so engrossed that I didn't hear the footsteps behind me until a hand touched my shoulder.

I jumped back and had the gun out of my holster as I struggled to my feet. On the other end of the gun was a man I had seen before. Don. He had a shotgun cradled in his arm and had his other hand in the air.

"Whoa there, son, no harm coming from me."

"What—what are you doing out here?"

He cocked his head. "You're that ass from the gas station, ain't ya?"

"You stalking us now?"

"Christ you city shits are nuts. Naw, I ain't stalking you. Mind if I put my hands down?" I nodded slowly and he dropped them with a sigh. "We're out here looking for a friend of mine."

"We?"

"Yea, bunch of buddies and me. Joe didn't show up last night for our weekly poker game. Ain't picking up the phone either so—shit, what happened to that poor bastard?" He had turned as he spoke and saw the deer soup I had come across. "Jesus, you do that?"

"What? No, I just found it."

He eyed me for a moment and then turned completely toward me. "What you doing out here?"

"What business is it of yours?"

"Whatever, buddy. You see Joe? He's a heavy guy, gut out to here." He motioned out a foot or so. "Got a big black beard too."

"He also big on scaring vacationers?"

"What you on about?"

"Saw someone outside my window last night in the bushes. Came out to see if I could find out who it was."

"Naw, Joe stays out of the woods at night lately. Been seeing shit." Don crouched down and stabbed at the muck with the tip of his shotgun. "Maybe he weren't going nuts. Never seen anything like this."

"This is insane. Your buddy was skulking around my

cabin last night wearing a white mask. He probably did this too. What is wrong with you people?"

"Now listen here, I don't know what happened to you—"

"Yo! Don!" a faint voice called, followed by a high-pitched whistle. "Come 'ere!"

Don looked back at me. "That's Tanner, must've found something. I suggest you go on back to your wife and stay out of the woods for now."

"I'm going with you."

"Like hell—"

"I want to know what's going on, plus it can't hurt to have an extra set of eyes to look if he really is missing."

"You just want to shoot him." Don said with a chuckle and then shrugged. "Feel like doing that too, so whatever. Come if you want, just don't get lost. I'm Don by the by."

"Keith."

He nodded and I followed him through the woods. He whistled every few minutes and Tanner replied back. Using that we found ourselves in front of... well, it's hard to describe. A shrine is the best way to put it, made of wood and vines; it towered above us and spanned three large trees. The branches and logs made a shape between the trees, but nothing I recognized. In front of the trees was something that looked like a cave, propped up with more wood, as if someone dug it out. The smell of rot and mold was almost overpowering.

"What the hell is this?" I asked. I was answered with a shrug.

"Hell, if I know, it weren't here a few weeks ago. Joe and me were out for spring gobbler and came right along this trail," Tanner said as he skirted the edge of the hole. "You ever see anything like this, Don?"

"Heard stories from the old folks, but nah, never seen this crap before."

"What kind of stories?" I asked and swallowed dryly. This was feeling less and less like a prank, but at the same time I didn't know what else it could be.

"Just stories, you know? Campfire bullshit. They say there are things that live out here, make tunnels and such under the entire forest. Called them Birch faces or some shit. But this... this gotta be a prank. It's too close to what they used to say, even down to the rotted smell."

"You think your buddy did this?"

"Joe has the discipline of a toddler, he wouldn't spend the time for even half this work." He looked once more at the cave and the trees and then turned to Tanner. "Come on, let's keep looking. We can report this to the rangers after we find Joe."

I followed them as we rounded the structure and headed off deeper into the woods. After a few yards something crunched under Tanner's boot and he stooped to pick it up. It was a camera.

"Don't Joe have one like this?" Tanner said turning the grey digital camera over in his hands. "Battery is dead."

"Looks like his. Must be in the right place. Joe? Joooe?" Don called and we started to spread out calling for Joe. We were a few yards apart when the ground beneath me gave way with a loud crack. I hit the ground and laid there, the wind knocked out of me.

I was in a tunnel. Everything around me was a dim grey with only a few feet in either direction bathed in light. I stood and looked up, the hole I fell through feet above me, just out of reach. I swore.

"Yo, Keith you all right?" I looked up to see Don's silhouette looking down. "Tanner, get—Tanner?" He moved away from the hole.

"What's going on?" A scream ripped through the woods and echoed through the tunnel. I shivered as if the sound itself held a chill. Something else moved in the tunnels now, a distant thump and catching sound. "Don, get the fuck back here."

"Something took Tanner." He said as he reappeared, his face turning from side to side. "I don't know what it was... he was here and now—"

"I don't care if it was fucking Santa. Get me out of here."

"Shit—How?"

"Find a goddamn log or something." I called and pressed myself against the tunnel wall. Something wet and sticky bled through my jacket and I stepped away and looked at it. The walls themselves were covered in slime and it was starting to burn my skin. I tore off my jacket and shirt in a hurry, tossing them into the tunnel. It still burned but not nearly as bad.

"Don—Don, how we doing on that log? Keep talking so I know you're out there." I called and felt air move around me, as if something large was very close.

"There ain't nothing here, Keith. Fuck, I can go get help."

"I won't be here when you get back. Stick your gun down here, might be enough to grab onto. Unload the fucker first." A few moments passed and then he reappeared at the top of the hole. He stuck the gun down and I grabbed the two barrels as movement in the shadows caught my attention.

There was a white mask just at the edge of the sunlight. In the next moment I felt a quick, sharp pain rush across my leg as Don pulled and I climbed. In seconds I was back in the brush of the woods, panting and staring up at a blue sky.

"Holy shit." Don said and I looked down, between me and him was torn pants and a leg that looked like someone had taken a very large knife to it. Blood gushed down my leg and into the grass. I didn't feel any pain, which I figured was a bad thing. "What the hell is going on?"

"Get me up, we need to go."

"What about Joe and Tanner?"

"Fuck both of them. Hurry and help me up." He did so and then reloaded his gun. We started out of the woods, me limping and being held up by Don. Behind us came a low rumble, as if something was running across stone or other hard ground. I didn't dare look, but Don did and he stumbled. He fired once behind us and practically dragged me the rest of the way out of the woods.

We landed in the grass behind the cabin. Don got up, leaving me there, and ran off toward the main road. I cursed him as I struggled to my feet.

"Keith?" Elise called from the deck. "I heard gunshots, what the hell was that guy doing—" She gasped and rushed down the wooded steps on the side. "What the hell happened to you?"

"Help me get in the car."

"But—"

"Please... we can't stay here." She stared at me, eyes wide and searching and then nodded. We made it to the car, and she drove us away from the cabin. We passed something on the road as we headed down... something that looked like yellow vomit and a shotgun.

We never went back for our stuff. We never leave the city now and I still have nightmares of that mask—of those Birch faces as Don called them.

CROSSES IN THE FIELD

By JP Carver

"JESUS SAVES." GOING THROUGH MOST COUNTRY AREAS OF Pennsylvania it's likely you'll see at least one of these signs and they are almost always accompanied by a cross. Some are more elaborate, large steel crosses painted in red, blue, and yellow, while others are two planks nailed together on a tree in haste. They always bought up the same question in me when I saw them... why?

I get that people are religious and want to share the word of God with everyone they can, but they always seem so out of place, especially the larger crosses. You have to wonder what kind of person would take the time to haul and put in place these crosses in the middle of nowhere. It just seemed like a lot of work to write "Jesus Saves" on a plank of wood in a place like this.

As with many things in life, it should have been left as a curiosity. It was late fall, the point of the year when all but the most stubborn leaves littered the ground. I was in my teens and bored out of my mind, whiling away a Saturday afternoon in my room playing some console game. I was also a bit annoyed because my best friend was stuck going to some recital for his sister, so there wasn't much to do.

Luckily, my cousin came over and saved me from my boredom. She only lived a few miles away and my mom and hers saw each other at least once a month since my cousin's dad had died. It really tore up their family and while my cousin tried to hide her pain, I could see she still wasn't over it.

She knocked on my door a little after two in the afternoon.

"What?" I called lazily and didn't even bother to turn to the door as it opened.

"Why are you in here? It's a crazy nice day outside," she said as she flopped on my bed. "You better not tell me you've been inside all day, Kevin."

"If I was? It's not a big deal, Ashley," I said, putting the same accusing tone to her name as she did. I paused the game and looked back to her. "Besides, if it's so great outside why did you come over?"

She shrugged and picked up a book from my nightstand. She started to page through it and lost my place. I glared at her but she didn't notice.

"What? Can't I want to come see my favorite cousin? Besides, with Cassie camping with her family there isn't anyone to really hang out with."

"Cassie went camping?" I asked with a bit too much surprise in my voice, which she picked up on. She tossed the book aside and sat up. She narrowed her eyes at me with a sly smile.

"Yes, why so interested in what my friend is up to?" I turned back to the TV and tried to ignore her. She threw her arms around my neck and pulled me back. "Are you into her? I knew you had a thing for her."

I tried to shrug her off but she just tightened her hold. "Leave me alone."

"Oh, don't be like that. I can set you up with her."

"She's single?"

Ashley shrugged. "She might be... she might not be. I'll see what I can do." She dropped back down on the bed. "I'm bored."

"Join the club."

"I wouldn't join any club that had you in it."

"You're such a bitch to me," I said and then cursed as I died in the game.

"Only 'cause we're family. Where are all your little buddies?"

"Why, want me to set you up with one of them?" I laughed when she kicked the back of my chair.

"No, but you said you guys were building a fort up in the woods. I wanna see it."

I shook my head. "We haven't got much done on it, it's just a bunch of sticks and rotting logs right now."

"So?" She stood up and moved in front of the TV. "I'm not sitting here watching you suck at a video game all afternoon. Let's go see it."

I sighed. There was never any arguing with her and if we didn't go she'd make my day hell just because. I saved and turned off the game.

"Fine, but it's like fifteen minutes to get there through the field."

"I'm game, let's go."

We told our moms that we were going for a walk and left out the back door. Our backyard butted up against a cornfield, and beyond that was a forest. My friends and I were always in the trees, playing games and building stuff. Our newest project was a large fort that we were trying to get done for the summer so we could hang out and drink far from any parents.

Ashley and I walked across the leftover roots of corn stalks and did our best not to break our ankles as we went. She stopped as I turned toward the edge of the field to head to our fort.

"What's that?" she asked and pointed toward the highway that ran alongside the field.

I looked over and saw what she was pointing at. There were three crosses in front of a circle of brush and trees. They looked like they were made of steel tubes and each was a different color. They hadn't been there the day before and I told Ashley the same.

"There's no way someone put those things up that quickly."

I shrugged. "Maybe the farmer did it, he's a big church goer. Come on, you want to see the fort or not?"

She took a few steps toward the crosses and turned back to me. "Let's go check them out."

"They're just crosses, what is there to check out?"

She started to walk away. "I dunno, but I see these things all over the place, I bet it has a 'Jesus Saves' sign on it."

"How much does he save?" I said with a smile.

"Don't be dumb."

"You're no fun." I followed her over to the crosses. They were even larger up close and seemed to tower over everything. They drew long shadows over us and I felt a shiver rush up my spine. Beyond them the thicket laid shadow so dark that I couldn't see anything beyond the first few trees. But I could hear movement and I stopped Ashley from getting closer.

It sounded like birds were fluttering around inside the cropping of trees. Ashley and I took a step back as the sound grew with each passing second. Then, it stopped, and the sound of small things thumping to the ground reached us.

"What the hell is that?" Ashley asked and she grabbed hold of my arm as if she was worried I'd run off without her. I couldn't say that she was wrong. Everything in me said to run, but I stayed. I waited.

Branches cracked and snapped slowly. Something came toward the edge, closer to where Ashley and I stood.

"Kevin..."

"Shush," I said and moved back a step. The snapping stopped and Ashley's nails dug into my arm. I looked over to see that her eyes were so wide that they looked like they'd pop out any moment. I followed her gaze to the tree line and felt my heart skip. There was a face of sticks in the shadows between the trees.

"Dad...?" Ashley asked and made a step forward. "Is it really you?"

"I've been waiting for you..." a voice said from the

face, but nothing moved. "You've taken so long to find me that I had almost given up hope."

"But… you died, dad. I saw you…"

"And now I'm back. Didn't you read the sign? Jesus saves, sweetheart."

"Ash, stop." I reached out to grab her arm but she swatted my hand away. "It's just a bunch of branches."

"It's not," she said and turned to me, tears were making wet trails down her cheeks. "It's him."

"Yes, it's me. I need your help, sweetheart. You need to get me out of here before something terrible happens." She continued toward the edge of the trees. She walked between the steel crosses and paused there. Branch-like vines slithered from the trees and slowly made their way toward her, but she didn't seem to notice. She was too focused on the face of sticks.

I finally found the strength to move and ran to her. The vines reared back and then shot forward with such speed that I could barely see them move. I reached Ashley just as they hit; one pierced her shoulder and I felt another rake across my back.

The voice cursed at me as I pulled Ashley back. I laid her down and broke off the piece of vine that was trying to pull her back in. It said some of the vilest things I had ever heard in my life, but I ignored it and focused on my cousin.

"Are you all right?" I asked and she just looked at me listlessly. I put pressure on the hole in her shoulder, but there was so much blood. I removed my jacket and pushed it against the wound, and she didn't even flinch.

She looked out of it, as if her mind was somewhere else entirely.

"Ash, come on, we need to get you help."

"Leave me."

"Ash—"

"Leave me, my dad is here."

I moved so that she had to look at me. "Your dad is dead, Ash. I'm sorry, but he is and that thing in the trees is not your dad."

"You don't know that—"

"Ooh, is that Kevin?" I froze at the sound of the voice and slowly turned to look back to the trees. Another face had appeared, this one far more human-like and one I knew well: it was Cassie. "Ashley didn't tell me she'd be bringing you. I hope she didn't tell you anything I said about you."

"What the hell are you?"

"Someone who can bring you all the pleasures this world has to offer." She licked her lips and then grinned. "Why don't you come over here so I can show you?"

"You're not human," I said and turned to Ashley. She was staring at me. "It's not human. What do you see next to your dad?"

She sat up and looked to the trees and then at the crosses. "It's a wooden face made of sticks."

"It looks like Cassie to me."

Ashley gave me a disbelieving look. "There's no way—"

"Oh, stop talking to her and come have some fun with me in these trees. The darkness is just the right place for us to explore each other," the head said.

"We need to get you to a doctor and get away from here."

"A doctor? We could play doctor if you want, Kevin. Come on. Let the girl see her dad a bit longer and we can do what everyone our age is doing anyway."

"Why don't you come to me?" I said and looked back to the trees. The way it talked pissed me off, but Cassie just smiled.

"Remove the crosses and I will gladly do so."

"You're stuck there," I said and grinned. Cassie did the same.

"For now, but we know you now. We know both of you. At some point these crosses will come down and we will find you and we will feast on you." Cassie started to laugh and so did the wooden face beside her.

"Why is he laughing like that? He never laughed like that..." Ashley said, her eyes locked on the wooden face. "This doesn't make any sense."

"No, it doesn't. What the hell do you want from us?"

"Freedom. Let us free and we shall leave you alone."

I looked at the crosses in front of the trees. I looked at the sign that stated that Jesus Saves and I felt a heavy weight in my chest. I turned back to Ashley. She sat staring at the faces and I knew if we stayed she would try to go see her dad again.

I picked up Ashley and stumbled away from the trees. She put up a small fight, but the pain of her shoulder was enough that she stopped after a few yards. I wanted to put as much distance between me and that wooden face as I could.

It took a lot to explain what happened to Ash and I

don't think my aunt bought much of our story, but after that moment things were back to normal.

Then Ashley went missing. She went for a walk one day after school and then just never came back. We all looked for her along with the police, but we didn't find a trace of her. I knew where she went, but it took a long time to work up the courage to go and see.

Her face appeared between the trees when I was a few yards away, then more of her appeared until she stood behind the bars of the crosses, vines holding her up.

"I've been waiting for you."

"Why'd you do it?" I asked, knowing I wouldn't get a real answer. Ashley was gone.

"To see my father. You should come too, I can see all my dead family here and our grandparents say hi."

I nodded with a small chuckle and bit back the tears that threatened to overwhelm me. She should have never gone back. I took a few steps to her, wanting so much to bring her into a hug, but knew that it wouldn't change a thing. I stopped and reached into my pocket.

"You shouldn't have taken Ashley from us," I said and took out a lighter. It took a few flicks for it to light. "We already lost too much."

"Cute lighter, Kevin. Come on, we haven't lost anything, you can come and see. Everyone is inside." She moved back and reached into the thicket where she pushed back branches to show a golden light that bled from the depths.

"No, thanks for the offer." I reached down and tore a handful of dried grass that grew up around the crosses. I crushed it together and then lit it. The flames burn brightly, the grass curling as it turned black. I dropped it to the rest of the dry glass and watched it catch. The flames traveled toward the thicket and slowly began to burn into the wood.

Ashley just stood and watched, a small smile on her lips. "You think it's so simple..." I said nothing as she turned her gaze to me. "We'll still be here, even if you burn down everything. We'll be here, waiting until we are free again."

"Maybe, but at least you won't trap anyone else for a while."

"Don't be so sure," she said and grinned. She turned and walked into the thicket and disappeared into the trees. I stood and watched the smoke travel up toward the sky as the fire started to crackle and the golden light was replaced with an orange glow. I looked at the crosses and understood then what they were for.

They were a fence, a gate of some sort. I still don't know who put them there, but whoever they were they did the world a service...but just how many places are like that thicket in the field?

I REMEMBER FIREFLIES

By JP Carver

I REMEMBER FIREFLIES. I REMEMBER HUMID HEAT THAT made it impossible to sweat. I remember small ponds and freezing water.

I don't remember how my best friend died.

At thirteen I already had my personality pretty well set. I was a rebel without a cause, a pain in the ass girl who ran her mouth and thought she knew far more than all those around her. In some ways I did, but that didn't make me very popular among the other girls in my neighborhood.

I didn't care, most of them would rather sit inside reading glamour magazines and spreading nasty rumors anyway. I much preferred getting dirty and exploring.

Luckily, I found a like-minded, if a bit quiet, friend in Scott Mowbray. He was the typical nerd back then, liked his Gameboy more than talking to other people. Which meant most people ignored him or beat him up. He took it in stride but I knew it bothered him.

It didn't help that he was pale and skinny and wore glasses with such strong lenses that his eyes looked comically huge at certain angles. But he was cool, he wasn't afraid to try anything when we explored. He would go through streams first, test vines for swinging, and jump off ledges without a second thought.

But I really can't remember how he died.

The night before my memory fails me we were in our treehouse and staring through a torn blue tarp at the stars. I wasn't supposed to be there because, for some reason, if a boy and a girl are in the same place by themselves something sexual is gonna happen. Mostly adults just thought that. We were best friends, nothing more.

We were also neighbors and sneaking out of my first floor window was an easy task. Scott didn't have it as good, nearly killed himself climbing down the rain gutter. But we did this most nights during the summer, just to get away.

"You see Mars?" he asked. We were lying beside each other on a turned-over van chair that we got from the scrap yard. "The little reddish dot there?"

"Yeah, cool."

He chuckled. "Okay, Kells, what's going on?"

I narrowed my eyes at the sky as he stared at the side of my face. I was annoyed that night. I got in a fight with both my parents over some rumor another girl in the neighborhood started. I was tired of being the scapegoat. "Nothing, why?"

"Because you've been bitchy all day."

"Well, according to most people I am a bitch so..."

"Oh, stop that crap." He swatted my arm. "Come on, Kelly, spill."

"You ever think about just... I don't know, staying here?"

"Where else would we go?"

I shook my head and sat up. He turned his gaze to me, eyes squinted and dancing over me. "I mean, just be away from it all... for a while at least."

He shrugged and turned back to the stars above. "All the time, but where are we going to go?"

"I don't know. I hate it here."

"Sorry I'm such a bore."

I scoffed and flopped back down on the chair. "You're the only thing keeping me sane. Let's leave."

He just laughed. I wasn't joking. I wanted to get out of the neighborhood, away from all the parents and kids who hated my guts. I wanted an escape but he had a point... we had nowhere to go.

"We could go camping," he said after a few minutes of silence. "I mean, we could leave for a bit. There's that pond in the woods, it's far enough away that no one would probably stumble in on us, but close enough in case you try to kill me." He grinned.

"Sounds like you thought all this out."

"Got to always have an escape plan when I'm around you."

"Asshole."

"We all got them."

"Yours just stinks more than others."

We made plans, told lies to our parents, and met on

the trail that we had forged back in the fall. It was mostly overgrown, but the trail still showed through the brush. I went first as I was a bit taller than Scott and could see over the bushes. We walked for what felt like an hour. The sun was heavy on our backs and the air felt like a blanket, so it was one of our less fun hikes. Scott had to take three breaks before we found ourselves at the pond.

The pond was fed by a steam and the water was mostly clear. It was deep enough that the water would reach just over my waist, which was just perfect to relax in if you could stand the ice-cold water and the odd small fish getting a bit friendly with your underwear.

When we first found it we spent almost two weeks there, building dams to bring the water higher and Scott tried to warm the water using heated rocks. Didn't work out that well, but we had fun.

We set our tent up a few feet from the water's edge and then settled down to cook hotdogs over a fire. The day turned to evening and the forest became colder. We huddled against each other under a blanket and watched the flames, enjoying our first night of freedom from it all.

"Wow..." Scott said and I jerked awake from the slight doze I had fallen into.

"What?"

"Look at all of them."

I lazily looked up and then gave a small gasp. It was like a light show in front of us. Fireflies of all different colors danced between the trees and above the water. The way they blinked to each other was almost magical.

"I wish I had my camera," I said after a few minutes.

"Yeah... you hear it too, right?" I looked over to see him gently swaying back and forth. "It's nice."

"What are you talking about?"

"The music they make. It's lovely."

"Okay, I think it's time we get to bed if you're going to be this nuts." I stood and held my hand out to him. When he didn't even look over I flicked his head. "Let's go. I'm tired already."

"You go on ahead, I'll be in later."

"You sound like my dad. Come on, I won't be able to sleep with you out here."

"I'm not a kid."

I laughed. "We're both kids. Don't make me drag you into the tent, I'll do it."

"I think I agree with everyone else right now, you are a bit of a bitch." He stood slowly, his eyes never leaving the dance of light.

I picked up the bucket that was beside the tent and went down to the lake to fill it so I could put the fire out. I bent down and then froze with the bucket just above the lake. I noticed something then in the reflection of the pond. A... person stood on the other bank. But it was strange, tall and thin and seemed to be watching me.

I jerked my head up and looked at the other side. Nothing was there. "Scott...?"

"Hm?"

"Did you see something over there?" I pointed to the tree line and looked back at him. "Something standing there?"

He shook his head. "No, but that music stopped. Are you sure you didn't hear it?"

"Maybe we should head home." I stood with the bucket full and dumped it on the fading fire. "What do you think?"

"What, are you scared, Kells?"

I swallowed my pride and nodded. "What if I am?"

He looked up as if ready to make a joke and then his face almost blanked. "Sorry. There's nothing here to be scared of. Besides, there is no way in hell we're walking back in the dark. We'd totally get lost."

"Yeah... but I know I saw something and you said you were hearing music and—"

"I hear shit all the time. Don't mind me. Come on, we'll be fine. We are more likely to get hit by a crashing 747 than having to worry about someone being out here."

"So our choices are creepy person or flaming wreckage?"

"It's all about the odds." He grinned and pushed up his glasses. He went to the tent and unzipped the front. He slipped in and the lantern inside turned on and the hazy light from it drowned the fireflies out a bit. I watched them dance for a few more seconds before following Scott into the tent.

We talked for a bit. Then Scott read, and I quickly fell asleep.

I woke in the morning, freezing. I sat up to see my sleeping bag was bunched up at my feet and Scott's bag was empty. There was also a film of water along the grey bottom of the tent... and my clothes were soaked through. I thought maybe the pond had risen in the night, but the water was only on my side, as if I had gone for a swim and didn't dry off.

My teeth chattered as I unzipped the flaps to the tent and looked out at the pond. Only it wasn't a pond anymore, just a hole in the ground. I stood there for a moment, not seeing what was there, and slowly it sunk in. All the water was gone. The little stream had dried up and the bottom of the pond was... black.

I moved closer and realized that it wasn't only black, it was brown and orange and it wasn't just a color. The entire pond was covered in dead fireflies. They were stacked on top of each other, dead insects over every rock and pebble.

In the middle was a mound of something; it was covered as well, but I didn't need to guess what it could be, a memory that I could not fully grasp gave enough of a hint.

"Scott?" I called and nothing came from the mound. I could feel tears burn in my eyes as I slid down, the fireflies crunching under me and streaking me in their blood. "Scott, please don't let that be you."

The mound wasn't moving at all. My hands shook as I started to swipe away the fireflies and then I froze. Fabric the same color of Scott's shirt showed. My heart felt like it stopped and my breathing hitched. Then time seemed to return to normal and I dropped to my knees while uncovering the rest.

Scott laid in fetal position, his glasses broken and skewed on his face. His mouth was open, but a smile was frozen on his face even though his eyes were wide in what I could only guess was fear. I gingerly touched his cheek and his skin felt like paper. He was gone.

I stayed beside him for hours, just staring at his face,

trying to remember what could have happened. That's when I heard what sounded like music; it was far off in the forest, echoing off trees. I stood and looked around, trying to find its source, but by the time I had turned completely around the music stopped and the birds filled in the silence. It must have been what Scott had been talking about.

I still can't remember everything. The only thing I distinctly remember from the entire night was an itching in the back of my skull, a dam that seemed to hold back any memory.

That dam is slowly breaking, though, and I'm remembering bits and pieces of it. That night I hadn't imagined the shadow on the other side of the pond. Scott hadn't imagined the music.

My newest memory is the dark form of a woman standing on the water in front of us as fireflies danced around her, and telling us that we are still wanted. Needed. That she could only take one for now.

I remember holding Scott under the water. I remember him struggling. But did he die then? Did I kill him? I don't think I want to know.

Maybe some dams are best left alone, no matter what they hold back.

TONGUE'S BONDAGE

By Patrick McGrail

I LOVED THE WAY HER TITS BOUNCED WHEN SHE LAUGHED.

She knew it, too. That's why Zenia drew her jacket more tightly around her chest as she guffawed at Steve's joke. She didn't look at me, but she knew where my eyes had wandered.

She had always known.

Covering her chest had been a new development, of course. God, the subtle things have a way of stinging so much more.

Brenda was sitting on Steve's lap. His fingers were gently grazing her hand, stopping occasionally to fondle the newly-placed ring on her finger.

Zenia and I sat on opposite sides of the campfire. She and I had agreed that the four of us would still be able to spend time together, and that things would not be weird.

I mean, of course I went along with it. Anything less would have meant cutting Zenia out of my life entirely.

I couldn't bear the thought.

"Okay, Barry," Zenia shot in my direction. My heart fluttered and I felt nausea at the same time. "Tell us the one about that damn Nighttime Clown."

I cleared my throat and began. Maybe it would impress her.

"Okay, this wasn't told to me as a campfire story—my cousin Lenny says it happened to a family in his hometown." Obligatory snickers. "Hey, I'm just letting you know the source. I'm a man of my word."

Zenia was listening. Good.

"There was a married couple, relatively young but still together long enough to have two kids. A boy and a girl, like elementary school age. White picket fence, 1913 Craftsman bungalow. Happy family all around." I paused for effect, letting the crackling fire dominate the soundscape. The dwindling sun was finally beginning to burn out from the summertime Idaho sky.

"The couple gets woken up in the middle of the night, like 3:30 a.m., by a knock on the door. Thing is, it's their fucking bedroom door. It scares the shit out of both of them, because their kids never knock on the door if they need something—they just kind of walk in. Not so good for their sex life, but whatever."

Brenda grinned and nuzzled her head into Barry's neck. Zenia acted like she didn't notice.

I cleared my throat again. "So this knocking ends, and the twisting of the doorknob begins. The couple, they grab each other and don't know what to do, because the

70

door is the only way out and they're on the second floor. It opens, and there's this silhouette standing in the frame. It's got a pointy hat with a fuzzy bobble on top, and they realized that it's a goddam clown."

It was almost too dark to see Brenda shudder.

"So the clown slowly points to his right, lowers his hand, then turns and points to his left. They don't know what the fuck to do, so they just hold each other and tremble.

"And that's when some sort of rope creeps across the bed and entwines them like a goddamn snake. The wife is pulled away from the husband, and she starts to scream, but the thing gags her mouth. The husband reaches over to try and help her, but he gets bound and gagged by the rope, too. And whatever is holding them in place fucking pulls them into a standing position."

I tried to see if I was getting to Zenia. She had heard this story before. It had gotten to her before.

Now she was in the dark.

"Whatever is holding them in place is both warm and wet. That's when they realize why the clown is silent. His tongue is protruding from of his mouth, and has wrapped around them both like a snake."

"Ick," came Brenda's voice, but she was otherwise silent.

"The couple wants to get to their son and daughter, because the whole family is clearly in danger. But they can't move, and the clown keeps pointing to the left and then the right. They each realize at the same time that he's asking them to choose one of their children. They squirm, they shake, they try to get free, but the tongue, it

71

only pulls them tighter. It keeps them there for like an hour.

"Finally, the husband looks at the wife, and he nods. She starts to cry, but she doesn't try to stop him. He wiggles a solitary finger free from the tongue's bondage, and he points to the right—the boy's bedroom—he's the older one.

"So the tongue slackens immediately, and rolls back toward the clown silhouette like a measuring tape getting rolled up. They get out of bed and sprint to the boy's room, but he's already gone. The clown is gone, too, with no trace of him anywhere. The daughter, she's safe, she's only like four years old, but the police never find any sign of the son.

"Of course, the cops never saw the big, floppy shoe prints. The mom and dad had cleaned them off the ceiling before calling anyone."

I let the fire speak for all of us after that.

"Well on that lovely note, I'm off to bed," Barry offered cheerfully. He stood and lifted Brenda playfully with him. They trotted off to their tent, hands held and eyes locked the entire time.

Zenia stood and faced me; I reciprocated the action.

It was uncomfortable.

"Hey, Zenia," I began, using an entirely different tone from the one I'd employed while telling the story, "if you want—I know that you always did like sharing a tent when we went camping—"

"Thank you. But I won't be doing that." She paused, and I could tell that she was sad that I'd asked. "Good

72

night." I heard her walk away, but it was far too dark to see her go.

I HAD to get up and pee. It really pisses me off to think just how much my dick controls my decisions.

The moon was shining brightly when I emerged from the tent flaps.

And something wasn't right.

A figure was silhouetted against the trees, not twenty feet away.

"Zenia?" I whisper-shouted. The shadow did not react. "Barry? Brenda?"

Something was just so fucking wrong about the way it refused all body language after my speech. I wondered for a fleeting moment if it was even a person at all.

Then I noticed the hat.

It was perfectly conical with a small sphere at the top. I felt sick.

I hadn't been aware of how silent the forest had gotten until I heard the creeping. Twigs snapped as a long, thin, invisible object wormed its way along the ground by my side. It stayed low as it inched behind me and began to form a circle.

Panic set in. I looked to the right, where Barry and Brenda were sleeping in one tent. I turned to the left, and stared longingly to the spot where Zenia slept alone.

The creeping on the ground grew closer.

I lifted a trembling finger, and pointed left.

Whatever had been crawling along the ground

whizzed loudly around me and quickly disappeared. I blinked, and could see no figure in front of me.

I began breathing normally again.

Now don't judge me for what I did next.

Whether or not I had imagined the whole thing, I didn't want to awaken Zenia to find out the truth.

I went back to sleep, andlet the morning decide.

WE NEVER FOUND ZENIA. No one did.

I may be a coward. But I believed I was making the right choice when I brushed away all of the footprints leading into and out of her tent.

They were far too large.

CALIFORNIA DREAMING

By J.D. McGregor

NATALIA KNELT ON THE MATTRESS AND LOOKED UP through the sunroof. The natural light of a night's sky filled with stars shined through onto her face.

I pulled the last of the worn grey curtains over the back windows of the van and collapsed down flat against the mattress. I folded the pillow in half and let my neck sink in. While I lay flat on the bed, I watched my girl-friend gaze above.

It seemed her anger, in full heat less than twenty-five minutes earlier, had subsided. The tired lines that stretched across her cheeks and forehead were gone. She didn't like that I hadn't arranged for a proper campsite that evening. She made that very clear from the moment she discovered the fact.

My eyes fell from her head and down to her body. I admired the slender curves and her back arched neatly above her calves. I adored every bit of her figure. It was still the fleeting body only a woman less than twenty-two could possess.

I was content things just the way they were. Watching her childlike curiosity towards stars shining more brightly now than they would above the city lights was all I needed. But, when I yawned for the first time, she treated me to a little more.

Her arms stretched as far as the confines of the campervan would allow. She reeled her neck back so far I thought she may catch me as a silent observer. She reached for the straps of her white tank top and slid them down her shoulders before pulling the shirt off. She sighed in relief before reaching back and unhooking the straps of her bra. She fell onto her back and pulled her ripped denim shorts over her legs lifted in the air. Soon, she was under the blankets and beside me, naked and relaxed.

I took the last sips of my beer and rolled it gently off the mattress and onto the floor. The cold brew had been exactly what I needed after a day of driving through the desert. I found myself incredibly grateful and fortunate having decided to pull the van over where I did.

It was the only night of our road trip vacation that I decided not to book a campsite for us to park the van overnight. From Eugene all the way down to San Diego, I had carefully devised a route for us to follow. We had followed it religiously up until that night. Every day had us seeing something new, whether it be a city, national park or coastal paradise. And each night carried the promise of a sure place to park and sleep.

I decided to do things differently that night. Just to see what it's like if you just parked somewhere. How big of a deal could it really have been? We were only three nights from dropping the van off and were driving the open roads running through Joshua Tree National Park. Nobody was going around patrolling for people camping overnight where they shouldn't be.

Of course, Natalia didn't see things the same way. She protested and sulked until the moment I pulled into the closed gas station parking lot (though its sign was still lit) and what looked to be an abandoned general store beside it.

There was another van parked there already. Three people sat on lawn chairs outside its open trunk. I parked six spaces away from them (close, but not too close), and got out while Natalia stayed in the passenger seat in a silent protest against me.

As I got closer to the three guys sitting around the van, I realized they weren't speaking English. Their conversation was in some Asian language. When I got close enough to make their faces out, I figured they may have been Japanese.

Whoever they were, they seemed to understand me well enough. They nodded when I asked if we were allowed to park overnight. They looked to be doing the same thing themselves anyways. They also gave me a few bottles of water when I asked if they had any to spare. They even threw in two ice-cold Sapporos for good measure. I thanked them and headed back to the van, excited to be able to break good news to Natalia more than anything.

She drank her water down like a desert animal and we started getting the van ready for sleep. That's how we found ourselves there. Calm, under the covers, and parked in the middle of a California desert.

With what felt like my last bit of energy, I slipped off my boxers, (which I had worn for three straight days) off and threw them to the end of the bed. I rolled to my side and pressed myself against Natalia's body. Usually, I would have slid the undercover of the sunroof over to block out at any light before trying to sleep, but on that night, I was too exhausted to bother.

Being the only one driving through eight hours of desert terrain will do that to you, I figured. Though, Natalia didn't have the same excuse. She spent the early part of the day admiring the desert scenery from the air-conditioned van, and the later portion arguing with me.

But all of that was behind us. And I was happy for that. As I started to doze off, I thought about what a success our little road-trip vacation had been. My girlfriend of two years and I had gotten through nearly three weeks without any major argument or disruption. Just little conflicts that arise between with anyone in close proximity for long enough.

I wrapped my arms tightly around her just before I slipped away. She didn't make a sound, probably already sound asleep. It was a gentle embrace. As pleasant as could be.

I STARTED to dream and things changed very quickly. It

still involved embrace, although I was the one being held. There was nothing pleasant about it. Not in the slightest bit. I was being forced and held in a position that brought out only bitter agony.

And that's when I realized it. *Pain.* You don't feel pain in dreams. The moment anything bad happens to you, you wake up or you start dreaming about something else. As I slowly came to consciousness, and the realization of the pain I was in started to intensify, it became clear I wasn't a dreaming at all.

The weight was the first thing my mind competently processed. Something was on top of me. I wasn't exactly sure what it was, as I couldn't turn my head and look. But it was very heavy and very big. So much so in both respects that it had me pinned down, hardly able to breathe or move any limb.

There was one striking feature about the mass on top of me that stood out. It wasn't one solid piece. Rather, it was a collection of many smaller pieces. I felt them moving. Individual parts were either stacked or held together on top of me and they were moving. And the movement wasn't gentle. They thrashed out against each other.

As far as what I could see... The space I was in was lit only dimly. Less so than I remembered the back of the campervan under the starlight. But, the little illumination that was in there seemed natural. Like a little crack of bright daylight was allowed to sneak in somewhere.

Sometimes, the weight above me would shift and put me in an even more painful position. It would shift higher, and it would press down against my upper half.

That's when my neck and the left side of my face would press against the floor. After enough times of this happening, I could feel that it was wood I was on top of. Not one consistent piece, but many separate planks of it. They were moist. And when my vision finally cleared enough to get a decent enough view of the space, I could see that the boards of wood were weathered and splintered.

I tried to speak. My throat was so dry that the feeling of my Adam's Apple scraping against my throat hurt like heartburn. I coughed so dryly that dust (perhaps partially comprised of dead skin) shot out over the floor.

I thought back to those bottles of water those three men had given me. How carelessly I tossed them into the van after I thought it tasted funny -- like they had no value at all. I would have done anything to have them within my reach in that moment.

I coughed again and something clutched my arm as I did. It had nails that dug into my flesh, which then scraped down away from my wrist before releasing. If it hadn't happened, I may not have realized that for the entire time, my arm had been twisted far behind my back and mixed into the mass that struggled on top of me. More pain settled in after that realization. More pain than I had ever felt before.

I struggled to move again and this time felt I could go a little farther. I was able to slide up, more to the side of the mass than below it. I felt the thrashing grow stronger as I did, but I was able to work myself into a position where the weight wasn't so heavy. I finally took in full breaths of air. I sucked in as much oxygen as I could, knowing it very possible the weight could shift and I would find myself below it again.

I tried to keep pushing outwards, but there was something stopping me from moving far. Two lines of it ran against my thighs and the other over my abdomen. They were thick and coarse. Different stretches of the same rope lining. It had me bound to whatever trashing pieces I was up against. It was responsible for holding us all together.

I struggled against it in futility until I felt my ears ripple. Similar to the feeling you get after take-off when your ears adjust to the altitude. A dull ring rose and fell. Then, for the first time since finding myself wherever exactly that I was, I could hear.

Breathing and gasping. That's all that came through at first. It wasn't just the sound of my own desperate breaths. I could hear others in my immediate vicinity. There were many different breaths that took in oxygen at varying lengths and paces. All of them were coming from right behind me. All of them bound in by the same rope netting that I was.

The next thing I heard was the creaking. But that wasn't coming from me, or what I was tied up against. That came from the wooden floorboards we rested on. Not just there, but also from the lower parts of the walls as well. When I looked, I saw they weren't regular walls that stood at 90-degree angles, perpendicular to the floor. The shape of the room was curved. The walls rounded up from the floor and towards the ceiling forming a rounded "U-shape".

Thirst and desperation must have been well set in by

that point, because I swore the whole place moved up and down.

I wriggled my fingers as best as I could and they met the soft, sweaty flesh of something living. Someone groaned from a space that didn't feel very far away. I thought I heard someone say something, but I couldn't have been sure. My attention was diverted elsewhere.

The crack of light was growing bigger. More details of the room came into focus. Creaking started. This time it was lighter softer and farther away. The sound of a door opening.

Light filled the room so much it was blinding. I had to blink in rapid succession to protect my eyes. Footsteps sounded and moved towards us. Shadows cut into the light.

Men spoke in a foreign language that was distinctly familiar. They sounded angry, like they were in some kind of argument.

Something pulled and tensed the ropes that bound us. Me, and whatever (or whoever) else I was tied too, slid a foot closer to the light before stopping. The bare skin of my stomach and thighs scraped under the weight and against the splintered floor. I winced and screamed out in pain until we were pulled again.

And for a little while, that's how we moved.

Slowly.

Painfully.

The floor started to incline as we got closer to the light. The collective groaning misery grew with each pull. By the time we were almost completely out of the darkness, I started to make out the appendages. Arms, legs, faces. All of which that I didn't recognize were in the mass. I had been tied to a group of people. Perhaps ten or more in total.

Finally, we were pulled up completely into the daylight. And we were a long way from the desert parking lot where I remembered falling asleep.

My one wish, for water, was granted. But not in the way that I had hoped. I saw that water surrounded us from all sides. None of it possible to drink. We were on the deck of a boat sailing the ocean. Not a massive cruise ship, but something closer to a tugboat. The sea was below us maybe twenty-five feet down.

My body was situated as such that I could see to the rear of the boat. Over boxes and scattered fishing nets, I was pretty sure I could see a coastline. It slowly disappeared in the distance.

The men started yelling in the language I couldn't understand again. It still sounded as if they were very angry with each other. But it couldn't have been so intense, because sometimes I would hear them laugh. One would yell something louder than all the others, and then all of them would laugh.

Footsteps separated from the group and surrounded us. Again, the ropes pinning me to everyone else were tightened as I felt us get hoisted up. My head dangled out of the net, just above the deck that smelled like fish as they carried us. I could see us getting closer to the edge.

I wondered exactly how it was that I had found myself in that position. How had I comfortably fallen asleep with my skin warm and pressed against Natalia in the back of the campervan, and now found myself on a boat tied to a bunch of people I didn't know? Who were these people anyways? Were they campers just like me? Had they fallen in deep with the sharks and pissed the wrong people off? What exactly had I (or any of them) done to deserve any of this?

Above all else, I wanted to know where exactly Natalia was. Perhaps she was free of the netted clutches that currently had me ensnared. Every bit of me wanted to believe that was true. Even, I thought, I would have preferred if she was the reason that I was in that net. Even if she was the one to blame, it would be better than her being tied up along with me. Anything was better than her being part of that nightmare.

The net was pulled up on the railing of the ship. In the cold ocean wind, we teeter-tottered to each side. Only because of the grips of the yelling men were we staying on the boat at all. Below us, I could see the white of the water rippling as the hull of the ship cut into the ocean.

Someone yelled something louder than all the others. And all at once, they let go. The mass turned in the air as we started our free-fall towards the water. I thought I heard someone laughing one last time as we went over. But it was quickly drowned out in the screaming of everyone that I was tied against.

We hit the side of the boat on the way down. Whoever was unlucky enough to be at that part of the net was surely injured terribly, if not killed. It bounced us further from the ship and spun us faster than we already had been. I was close to hitting it myself on the recoil. I could feel the rope around my abdomen stretch as it caught on a rusty screw of the ship's exterior.

We were only in the air for a little while longer. Before hitting the water, I was sure I heard one desperate scream standing out from all the others. Unmistakably, it was Natalia's. The worst thing I've ever heard.

We slammed against the water and a great splash fired up around us. Whoever was on the bottom as we landed surely met a similar fate as whoever struck the side of the boat.

The screaming intensified as we bobbed up on the surface of the ocean before starting a steady sink. It only lasted for a short period. It was soon muffled by the ocean water pouring into everyone's mouths as we were submerged completely.

When the screaming stopped, the struggling really started. I felt people kicking, scratching, and doing whatever they could to try and get out. It was all hopeless of course. Save for one person.

Myself.

I saw that the rope was completely torn where it had caught the side of the boat. My middle part was almost completely free. It seemed possible that I could get myself out. And the force generated from the struggle above me was helping. I was being pushed out of the little hole by all the desperate people tied behind me.

My right arm came loose. I utilized it immediately to pull the torn pieces of rope aside. It opened a little further.

I looked up and through the bubbles surrounding us as we sank. I could see the bottom of the boat. It was moving quickly away from us. Slowly, it was getting smaller as we sunk deeper into the cool depths of the ocean.

I was desperate for a breath. It wouldn't be long before I started swallowing gulp after gulp of seawater. I pulled the rope a little more and now had enough space to move my legs. One after the other, I pulled them out of the net.

Once my lower half was free, it was easy. I pushed off from the chest of whoever was tied against me, and again, I felt someone claw at my arm as I pulled away.

For the first time since I had fallen asleep in the back of that van, I was completely free.

My lungs were desperate for air. As was everyone else as I could see. Some were already swallowing mouthfuls of water. None of them looked like they had been able to move much. The thrashing started to weaken.

I looked them all over, desperately searching. Right near the top, I finally saw her. Natalia was hardly moving. Five layers of the rope netting were holding her in place. She managed to get an arm out. Her hand grasped at the ocean water as if she was trying to grab it for some kind of leverage.

I swam over to her, now taking in little bits of water when my mouth forced itself open. She saw me as I came in front of her. I looked back and tried desperately to pull the ropes. But it was no use. She was naked and completely constricted. Her eyes looked terribly sad.

The mass had all but stilled at that point. Nobody thrashed anymore, and the descent into the ocean depths was gentle. I could feel the water getting colder and deeper. The increasing pressure pushed harder against my ears.

I wasn't going to give up on her. That's what I thought.

I would rather have died down there than swim back up alone. And that's fully what I fully intended to do.

The funny thing was, my natural survival -instinct didn't agree. In fact, it had already started moving ahead with its own plan. Because, almost without my control, I had kicked off the mass as it sunk and launched myself back towards the surface which then seemed so far away.

I swam in as straight of a line as I could manage. My lungs exhaled any little bit of air that was still inside them. My ears popped, and I started swallowing mouthfuls of water. My vision blurred again and I almost couldn't see the surface by the time I finally emerged.

I coughed up barrels of sea water while I tried to breathe. No breath I took in so desperately seemed enough. As I treaded there, struggling to calm myself, I saw the ship on the horizon. It had become a smaller on the horizons. But, it wasn't so far away that they wouldn't have been able to see me if they looked. Perhaps they would decide to turn around and come back.

Back on the shore, the brown cliff face seemed at an impossible distance. Only in my wildest dreams could a man nearly drowned swim that far.

When I finally caught my breath after all the chaos, I ducked my head back into the water. I spun around in circles, searching all over the blue. I was looking for what I already knew so was gone. I saw no net of drowning people. It was too far down by that point.

I screamed under the water as hard as I could. In hindsight, perhaps it was best that I did it this way. It's possible the boat could have heard me if I did above the surface.

It was helpless. As much as I hated to accept it, I

started my swim back towards shore, fully expecting to drown along the way. It would be the longest swim I would ever make. The most energy I could ever expend. A swim that was impossible to complete.

Yet, somehow, I made it.

By the time I reached the shore, I thought it was possible that I was dreaming again. Because there was no way I was on solid land again. If it were real, I would have drowned in the ocean just like everyone else thrown into the ocean alongside me.

As I crawled flat against the coarse sand and up to where the rock formation started, I felt the faintest flicker of hope.

If I was dreaming, that meant I would wake up in the desert in the back of a campervan. My sticky body would be pressed against Natalia. We would be safe and far away from the ocean.

Then, just as I had hoped, I woke up. It seemed like no time had passed at all. Sand was everywhere. But I was in no desert. My naked body was soaked and scratched all over. I heard the waves crash behind me and the water rise up against my toes before falling again. The brown cliff walls, towering over the beach lay in front of me.

It had been no dream.

SCARECROW

By J. Speziale

IT WAS EARLY WEDNESDAY MORNING. MY PHONE BUZZED on my bedside table.

2:30 AM

Dylan: Hey, I just parked my car, heading to the trail now.

Me: You're crazy man, how cold is it?

Dylan: Not bad actually. 30s. You gotta come out here soon! It's beautiful.

Me: Ha! We'll see in Spring when it warms up. Have fun man, and be careful.

Dylan: You know I'll be fine :)

My old college roommate, Dylan, lives just outside of Denver. Like most Colorado natives, he loves to camp. He's the crazy kind of camper who does it all year, even in December.

Whenever he goes to the mountains alone, I have him check in with me just in case.

I was surprised when he texted me again. He usually just sends me a text or two when he arrives, and when one when he leaves. Just so I know he is okay.

7:44 AM

Dylan: Dude... r u up?

Me: Yes sir, you okay?

Dylan: This is so weird. I woke up this morning, and there's someone else out here?

Me: On the mountain? Looks like you're not the only Winter camper.

Dylan: No... Not a camper. I can see them on the horizon, but they haven't moved. Like at all.

Me: What?

Dylan: I don't know it definitely looks like a person but, they haven't moved. They're probably 300 yards away —standing completely still.

Me: That's super creepy, Dylan. Keep me updated.

9:19 AM

Dylan: They still haven't moved. I made breakfast over the fire and acted like I didn't notice anything. I'm going check it out.

Me: Okay... lemme know. Maybe it's a stump or something?

9:33AM

Dylan: Dude...

Dylan: It's a fucking scarecrow.

Me: What? Like a farmer's scarecrow?

Dylan: Ya man, what other kind of scarecrows are there? Its clothes are weird though.

Me: Weird?

Dylan: The clothes are modern. Its wearing a nice black jacket and blue jeans. Its face is kind of scary looking. Burlap sack with black eyes and a stitched-on mouth. Why is this thing out here? I'm tempted to steal its jacket...

Dylan: I posted a picture of it online if you want to see what it looks like.

Me: Dylan, I'd leave it alone. Maybe it's some sort of conservation study or something? Like to see if bears will attack it? You might be on camera. And I know you have drugs on you...

Dylan: Ha! Good point. It's probably nothing. Speaking of drugs, it's about that time.

Me: Have fun! Haha.

I checked Dylan's picture of the scarecrow. He wasn't lying. It was terrifying. The hollow, black eyes and stitched frown gave it a sinister look. The clothes fit surprisingly well on the stuffed burlap body. The scarecrow stood about seven feet tall, supported by a large wooden cross staked in ground. It was strange, but I didn't think too much of it.

The chiming of my phone woke me up. Adjusting my eyes to the bright screen, I opened my phone to discover another text from Dylan.

3:33 AM

Dylan: Someone is outside my tent.

Me: Oh I'm sure. Come on man it's like 3 am here, you woke me up.

Dylan: Please this is serious! I can see their shadow.

Me: Call the police Dylan!

Dylan: No! I don't want to make any noise. They probably think I'm asleep. I have my knife. I'm texting inside my sleeping bag so they can't see the light from my screen.

Dylan: I thought I heard a noise and I woke up. I guess I didn't zip up my tent all the way, and I assumed it was the wind. But then I saw the silhouette.

Me: Should I call the police for you!? Where are you? Send me your latitude and longitude now!

Me: Dylan!!!!??? Please respond and drop a pin on my phone so I know where you are.

My heart was pounding. I paced around my room in the darkness in an attempt to come up with a plan. If I contacted Denver PD, I would have no idea what to tell them. My friend is camping somewhere outside of Denver and he thinks he's in trouble? If he was in actual danger, I didn't want to call his phone if he was pretending to be asleep. Maybe someone was just rummaging through his cooler, or maybe it was a bear?

The hours waiting to hear from him felt like days. Then, he finally called me.

6:56 AM

Me: Dylan! Are you okay!?

Dylan: I'm alright.

Me: Thanks for finally responding!!! I almost had a heart attack. Barely slept. I was going to call the police or ranger station but I still don't where you are.

Dylan: There's something weird though...the scarecrow is right outside my tent. Someone put it there last night while I was asleep. That's the shadow I saw. I don't like this at all.

Me: Go home Dylan, seriously. That's messed up even if it's a joke.

Dylan: I'm about four miles from my car. I'll text you when I get back to it. Also, I forgot to mention something.

Me: What?

Dylan: My hat was on top of the scarecrow this morning. Someone must have gotten into my tent last night while I was asleep, and put my hat on its head...

Me: You need to get out of there.

Dylan: I agree. I'll text you when I get back.

I was sitting down to breakfast when my phone chimed.

9:13 AM

Dylan: Oh shit....Someone slashed my tires.

Me: Please tell me you're calling the police.

Dylan: Hang on, I'm going to see how bad of shape the car is in, and yes I'm calling them.

Me: Alright let me know ASAP!

Me: What's going on?

Dylan: Will text later. Not safe.

Me: Dylan! Please let me know what's going on!

A few hours later, my phone rang:

Dylan: Alright, I have a second to catch you up, but I have to keep my voice low. This is so messed up dude. I don't know what to do. I don't want to be here. Also my iPhone is dying and I'm going to have to switch over to the shitty flip phone I use for work.

Me: Dylan, what do you mean by not safe?

Dylan: So I went to try and start my car, to get a quick charge on my iPhone, and see how bad the tires were. The engine wouldn't even turn over. I called the police and told them about the car, and that I was stuck. They transferred me to the ranger station to explain where I was for assistance. That's when it got weird.

Me: What do you mean?

Dylan: The ranger seemed pretty lax about it at first, saying things like "Where are you? Stay calm, we'll send help, just stay where you are, etc." Monotone voice like he's used to it. But then I mentioned the scarecrow... and the ranger was different...

Me: Different?

Dylan: He became really serious and panicked.

He proceeded to act out the conversation.

Ranger: "Did you say scarecrow?"

Dylan: "Yes sir"

Ranger: "I need you to listen to me carefully."

Dylan: "Okay"

Ranger: "I have some bad news. I'm in my truck now, and I was headed your way. The old bridge leading into your trail is partially collapsed and impassible. We're not sure how it happened, but we have emergency crews working on it now. I need you to start moving this instant. Right now you are at the north side of the mountain, and I need you to go to the south face. That's where we'll meet.Do you have a compass and map?"

Dylan: "Yes sir."

Ranger: "Good. All right, here is the exact point to meet." (He explained where to go.)

Ranger: "That's the exact point where I will meet you. DO NOT STAY WHERE YOU ARE! Get away from your car. Most importantly DO NOT hang around any of those scarecrows. Do you understand me? If you see any more, I want you to run as fast as you can away from it. Clear?"

Dylan: "Scarecrows? So there's multiple? How many are there?"

Ranger: "I need you to keep moving."

Dylan: "What's going on? Am I in danger? What does the scarecrow have to do with anything?"

Ranger: "Listen, just keep moving while the sun is up, and make as little noise as possible. Are you wearing bright clothing?"

Dylan: "Uhhh no I'm not. I have a dark brown coat and grey pants."

Ranger: "Good. Try and stay out of plain sight as much as possible. Move quickly, and call me if you see or hear anything unnatural."

Dylan: "Unnatural?"

Ranger: "You'll know. But only make phone calls if absolutely necessary. When night falls, stay warm and hidden. NO FIRES. If you hear anything in the night, DO NOT RUN. Stay as still and quiet as possible."

Dylan: "Wait—will you tell me what I should be looking for?"

Ranger: "Get moving south, NOW!"

Dylan: "Wait…I…"

Dylan: Then he just hung up.

Me: Where are you now?

Dylan: Moving south. There's creepy stuff going on.

Me: What do you mean?

Dylan: I walked by the spot where my campsite was last night. The scarecrow… it wasn't there.

Me: Just gone?

Dylan: Yes. Nothing at all.

Me: I... I'm so sorry you're going through this. My eyes are watering just reading your texts.

Dylan: I hate this, I just want to go home.

Me: You have to do what the ranger said, and we'll get you out of there. Do you have data on your work phone?

Dylan: No, just talk and text.

Me: Of course you don't. Plenty of battery?

Dylan: Yes, thank God.

I felt hopeless at this point. I wanted to help my friend, I just didn't know what else I could do besides wait for him to contact me.

3:03 PM

Dylan: I'm exhausted and scared as hell. Still making my way to the other trail on the south side to meet the ranger.

Me: Keep moving.

3:44 PM

Dylan: I see the scarecrow! The one from my camp. It's up in a tree. Wayyy up in a tree. Dude, fuck how did it get so high up there?

Me: Send me a picture!

Dylan: I can't get a good shot. It's so high up and this camera sucks. It's just hanging there, it looks like it's staring at me. I'm so freaked out and tired. Something is dripping off of it.

Me: Get away from it Dylan!

4:17 PM

Dylan: The sun's about to set. I'm going to find a place to sleep.

Me: Okay, please keep me updated!

Hours went by. I still hadn't heard from him. I decided it couldn't hurt to send a text.

11:07 PM

Me: Dylan? Are you okay? Text me back when you can. I don't want to waste your battery.

Dylan: It's getting closer.

Me: What is?

Dylan: Fuck...it's right next to me. I'm going to make a run for it. It's...it's too close.

Me: Please tell me you're okay! What is it!?

Me: Dylan? I'm going to call the police! What happened!?

Me: I called the police. They are looking for you at the south face. Where the ranger said he would meet you. Please, please, please tell me you made it.

Me: Dylan???

I spoke with the police, and they informed me they had a search party looking for Dylan. I couldn't take it. I wanted to be there for my friend. I assumed the worse. Then, around 3 a.m., my phone chimed. I had a voicemail from his phone. What I heard sent a chill down my spine. The sound of rustling wind and crunching of leaves burst through my phone's speaker for at least a minute. Then I heard what I feared the most, the ear-piercing screams of Dylan begging for his life. Then... silence.

That was the last I heard from him.

I immediately called the Denver authorities. In a state of shock, I was eventually able to explain all that I knew. I was transferred to the ranger's station, and they arranged for me to come to the station. I was on the next flight out.

After I got my luggage, I rented a small truck and

drove to the ranger station. As soon as I arrived, I was escorted to a back room. I assumed the man was the same ranger that had talked to Dylan. He was a lanky, disheveled man with shaggy, black hair and pale white skin. He reeked of smoke and looked like he hadn't slept in years. I sat down across from him. He placed his hat on the table, lit a cigarette, and spoke.

"We called you down here because, at first, we needed your phone as part of the investigation, but I'm afraid that is no longer necessary." His raspy voice was tattered and broken. His clothes shared the same features.

"What happened?" I asked quietly.

He took a drag from his cigarette and spoke.

"I'm sorry, but—I cannot discuss any details at the moment. You need to leave this to the professionals. We will do everything we can to find your friend."

Anger pulsed through my body.

"That's bullshit!" I said with tears welling in my eyes. I started to stand, only to have the ranger grab my wrist and motion for me to sit back down. He looked me in the eyes and spoke.

"I'm so sorry, but we cannot have civilians interfering. We need you to stay safe and out of the way."

I interrupted, "I got text messages from his phone right after I landed! Something happened to him!"

The ranger raised his voice.

"I know this is hard. We are looking into all possibilities, but we do not believe there has been any foul play. Teenagers in the area have been known to play pranks on lone campers. You are more than welcome to help us with reports. I know how hard it is to lose a friend..."

My anger started to peak. "Oh and these teenagers slash tires, and attack people!?"

He took another long drag from his cigarette before he responded. "I promise we are working night and day. I think the best thing to do is stay off the trails and be there for his family and—"

I couldn't even let him finish his sentence. I was too upset. I stormed out, and he didn't attempt to stop me. I knew that was all bullshit. What was he trying to keep from me? I had evidence that Dylan was being followed by someone or something. I went to the only place I was familiar with in the area... Dylan's apartment. I still remembered his door code from the last time I had visited. The world seemed quiet as I drove. I had never felt so alone.

The apartment was eerily quiet. I was overcome with feelings of fear and sadness. As soon as I saw a picture of Dylan in the kitchen, I couldn't help it. I had to cry. Eventually I collected myself, opened the fridge and pulled out a beer. I downed it in a few gulps. I needed to sit and think. As I got up to throw the empty beer away, I saw something in Dylan's kitchen. His Colorado map. I had forgotten all about it. Dylan used this large topographical map to keep track of all the places he trekked. The map was riddled with black thumbtacks and a few white ones. Dylan's method was simple. Black thumbtacks for the areas he had already explored, and white for his upcoming adventures. I wrote down the coordinates of the white markers. I searched through Dylan's apartment, and collected the remaining camping gear. I grabbed a wooden baseball bat from his closet as well.

I knew where to go.

I loaded the truck, tossing the supplies in the truck bed, and headed to the mountain. It was a long drive. I passed the old bridge on the way, and didn't notice any sign of recent construction.

Ten minutes later, I pulled up next to Dylan's car. It was eerie to see the yellow police tape wrapped tightly around the body of his white sedan. It made the situation all too real. As soon as I parked the pickup, I dropped a pin on my phone.

After what seemed like an eternity of hiking, I reached the point on the map that Dylan had marked, and I got to work setting up camp. Night began to fall. I constructed my tent and placed a sleeping bag inside. As soon the sun had set, I lit a large fire and quietly snuck away from the camp. I took cover in the trees about a hundred yards away, cracked open an energy drink, and kept my eyes glued on the tent.

Just as I started to nod off, I heard rustling in the leaves, but I chalked it up to the wildlife. I was exhausted, cold, and trying to stay awake. I downed my last bit of caffeine. Around 3 a.m. I saw something. Walking towards the tent. It was man. With a flashlight he started looking around my decoy camp site. He noticed no one was in the tent and illuminated the surrounding woods with his flashlight. The light flashed rapidly around the trees. Luckily he didn't see me. About twenty minutes later the man left and headed south. I followed. I took off my shoes in an attempt to walk as quietly as possible. I threw on a couple more pairs of wool socks from my backpack, and kept my distance. I continued to follow him, taking countless turns in the dark. The man appeared to be wandering, illuminating the ground in front of him as he walked.

He finally stopped near a pile of leaves—tripping on something beneath. The man started brushing away the leaves.

Then I saw his face… It was the park ranger. I almost called out to him, but covered my mouth at the last moment.

I saw what he had uncovered. There were doors under the pile—huge, metal cellar doors. A chain was fastened around the handles, and the doors led straight into the ground. He stopped to smoke a cigarette, pulled a notepad from his coat pocket, and scribbled something down. After he finished writing he started looking through a flip phone.

My head started to spin. There was no way...

I sent a text to Dylan's phone.

4:19 AM

Me: "Where is Dylan?"

The phone in the ranger's hand chimed a few seconds later.

THIS PIECE OF SHIT HAD DYLAN'S PHONE.

He read the text and whispered to himself, "I told you to leave it to the professionals," and put it back in his pocket. I wanted to kill him. Blinded by rage. He's started undoing the chains, making a lot of noise. I couldn't let him disappear from my sight. I was running out of time.

I gripped the cold, taped handle of the baseball bat, and quietly crept towards the unsuspecting park ranger. I felt like my body was moving without my control. Then…

I did it. I clubbed him in the skull with the bat. Right before he opened the doors, I swung as hard as I could. He fell to the ground and didn't move. The chain rested next to his bleeding temple.

He never heard me coming. I'll never forget the sound of the bat connecting. That dull thud and crack of solid wood smashing into bone. Sweat and blood misted in the air as he fell.

I caught my breath and made my way to the cellar doors. I wished I hadn't. It was the smell—a putrid stench of rotting of flesh—that hit me first. As soon as I saw the first human limb sticking out of the massive mound of corpses, I had to look away. My head was spinning, and my stomach turned over as I expelled what little food I had eaten that day.

I ran. I ran as fast as I could, fueled by fear.

Hours later I got back to Dylan's apartment.

I was still sweating and breathing heavily as I bought a plane ticket for the next flight home. I decided the best plan was to call the police when I landed. I just wanted to go home. My heart was pounding.

Everything felt surreal as adrenaline pulsed through my veins.

To my horror, red and blue lights flashed outside as a police car pulled up to Dylan's door. I had to try and keep my cool.

I stepped outside and met the officer halfway. I felt like I was going to vomit again.

He had seen me pull in, and stopped to investigate. As we were talking about Dylan's disappearance, the officer's radio receiver sounded. My heart pounded in my chest as I listened.

I couldn't believe what I was hearing. Some campers discovered a scarecrow—strung high in a tree, with a noose around its neck. The campers claimed dark liquid was seeping through its burlap skin, and it was wearing a park ranger's hat.

My thoughts began to race. I'd made a huge mistake. The ranger was just investigating a lead which led him to the cellar. He must have found Dylan's phone after I got those weird texts. But how did he get a key to the cellar? I... I acted so quickly. I hit him with the bat and ran.

What had I done? I just left him to die. And most importantly... that cellar? What the fuck was that? My head was spinning. My hands were shaking so much I nearly dropped my phone as I handed it to the officer. I told him everything. I fell to my knees on the curb, waiting for him to handcuff me. Instead, the officer excused himself, and went to his unmarked car to make a call. I couldn't help but notice a limp as he walked. He looked nervous as a small crowd of pedestrians gathered, drawn in by the red and blue lights. A short while later, the officer got out of his car, and walked over to me. I was still on the curb when he spoke:

"I just talked with the chief. We believe that you may be at risk. We do not want you to panic, but we need you to be safe. I am going to hold on to your phone for now. Any texts you receive are considered part of this investigation. You are not from Colorado, correct?"

I was confused. Was he not going to take me in? I had just confessed to assault.

"Uhh—no sir," I stuttered.

He spoke again.

"I need you to get in the car with me. You're not under arrest at the moment but we need to get some statements from you down at the station."

My heart pounded as I walked with him.

The ride was silent; I tried to talk but he cut me off. His tone changed drastically, taking me by surprise.

"Just stop talking. I was trying to keep this operation running smoothly and you just decided to fuck it all up."

I noticed we were driving further away from the city.

"Your friend told you too much."

"What?" I said in confusion.

He snapped at me. "I told you to be quiet. But you were too curious—decided to do some of your own investigating, didn't you? Jimmy, the ranger, told me what he could before he died. I could barely make out what he was telling me."

My adrenaline returned. I looked to the door handles, but knew they wouldn't open.

"You must have got him good. Was only conscious for a few minutes. Good riddance though, he was getting too soft. The rest of us were worried he might start talking. Said he didn't want to do this much longer."

I couldn't believe what I was hearing.

"You killed Dylan didn't you, and set up the scarecrows."

He laughed, "Hahaha, well I didn't kill your friend. I just help facilitate the deeds that must be done. We supply a food source to keep civilians safe."

"What the hell are you talking about!?" I demanded.

"Well she has to eat something! You don't want her coming down from the mountain, do you? Can't get rid of her either. Sacrifices must be made to ensure that the majority survive. You might call me a murderer, but I don't see it that way."

I froze as he continued, trying to make sense of what I was hearing.

"She's been eating more than usual. That's why we have a nice pile of meat down in that cellar. Homeless people, mostly. But I can't help it if she wants to pick off some lone campers."

"You're insane! What are you feeding people to?" I said. I reached towards my pocket, only to realize he still had my phone.

He laughed again.

"I can't have you running around telling the media. Could you imagine the chaos this would bring? All the victim's families wanting justice? Exposure and rock climbing accidents make much more sense."

I listened in horror.

We had been driving a while. I could tell we were getting close to the trail. A camper, walking a brown dog alongside the road, waved to us as we passed. I wished there was some way to tell him I was in danger. We continued the drive in silence. I was trying to comprehend the situation. When we got to the trail head, the officer parked the cruiser and got out. He drew his pistol, opened my door, and motioned for me to start walking.

The walk up the mountain was slow as he limped behind me.

"I'll tell you where to go. If you try anything, I'll put a

bullet in your head and throw you in that cellar with the others."

I quietly obeyed.

It was a long and silent walk up the trail. The cold air stung my face as we trekked along. Even in my panicked state, I knew we were in the same area as the cellar.

Finally, I spoke up. "Where are you taking me?"

"Her," he responded nonchalantly.

"What's her?" I asked.

"Not sure," he said in an annoyed tone.

I sighed. "If you're going to kill me, at least tell me what place we're going to."

"I can't tell you, because I don't know what she is. Clawed her way here from Hell is my guess," the officer snapped.

My legs grew weaker. I didn't ask any more questions. The sun was starting to set. The only sounds were the crunching of leaves and snaps of twigs beneath our feet. We took countless turns. The trail had turned to dense woods and uneven ground. I was exhausted.

I felt the officers pistol press against my back as he spoke, "Getting close. I'm glad I didn't have to drag your corpse all the way up here, hahaha."

I had already lost all track of time. What seemed like hours of hiking, finally ended. We stopped in front of a small pond, perfectly round. Something was wrong though. The water was black, and a thick layer of fog clouded the surface. It should have been frozen in this cold. Peeking just above the haze, I could see the heads of a hundred scarecrows lining the pond's perimeter. All were facing me—as though they had been waiting.

The officer began to speak again as he started building a fire.

"The routine started to wear on us. It was always the same: get the bodies, throw them in the cellar, write a bogus police report, contact the families. It got…stale. And she got tired of the easy meals. So we got a little more creative. Get the camper scared, get them moving in this direction. Let it hunt. It likes the trophies." He pointed lazily to the scarecrows. "When I saw your buddy's phone, I took it upon myself to get you down here. I thought it would be more of a challenge, but you basically turned yourself in."

I felt myself becoming more nauseous as I recalled the events that led me here.

Night fell, and the black pond began to stir.

"Won't she kill you too?" I asked.

"Likes 'em one at a time, whatever she can get to first," he responded.

I didn't want to know just how many cops and rangers were a part of this. I considered making a break for it, but I knew I would be gunned down. The officer kept his distance, with his gun pointed at me. He motioned for me to move closer to the pond. I hesitantly crept forward.

"Stand there, that's where I put her food."

The water began to churn as it surfaced. Black ripples formed small waves that splashed against the pond's edge. Its dark matted hair was the first feature to break the surface. I immediately smelled its damp, rotten flesh. I was frozen with fear as it moved in my direction and continued to ascend from the dark pool. I cannot fully describe what I saw. The hellish figure had risen from the inky depths and moved closer. It had a tall, thin, form with long hair descending from its skeletal head to the middle of its gaunt humanoid body.

In that moment I was sure of one thing—the creature did not belong on this Earth. As it moved closer, I found my body paralyzed with fear. I studied its face, and its hollow black eyes were a crude emulation of the scarecrow's.

I heard something behind me—the shuffling of leaves and a man's voice yelling in the distance. I turned around, only to see a large brown dog dragging a broken leash behind it. The canine walked cautiously as it eyed the officer and I with curious skepticism. A beam of light flashed before us, and a man carrying the other end of the leash appeared. The same man I had seen earlier on the road.

The man spoke. "Sorry guys...I've been chasing my dog forever. He broke off and started following your scent. Is uhh—?"

He saw it.

"What the... Wha...?"

I took advantage of the moment.

My survival instincts kicked in. The officer was distracted for only a few seconds, and I started running fast as I could, only to be outpaced by the frightened dog. I heard the first bullet fly by my ear. The second shot came soon after. I'll never forget the camper's scream as the bullet pierced his body. His agonizing voice echoed throughout the mountains. I never actually heard his screaming stop, it only grew quieter as I ran farther away from the pond.

I ran for hours, fueled by adrenaline and survival. I knew the officer couldn't keep up with me, and he had to make sure his new witness could not escape.

Eventually, I will attempt to work with the true authorities after I figure out how to tell them what I have seen without sounding insane. Right now I am trying to forget the sound of the man's screams, and the snapping of his bones.

PROJECT EREBUS

By J. Speziale

PROJECT EREBUS IS THE OFFICIAL NAME—AND I BELIEVE IT is the public's right to know of the creature that has entered our world.

My team and I do not have a title, but I would refer to us as "government contractors." Our primary objective is to study unexplainable phenomena and report back to the federal government. We set up wherever we are needed.

Our team currently resides inside an underground bunker just outside of Yellowstone National Park. You can search all you want, but I guarantee you will not be able to locate it. And it's better that you do not.

The location of the creature was discovered one year ago by local hikers—a young married couple. Their names have been removed from all public records. Since then, the government's focus has been on reinforcing the underground facility, containment of the creature, and studying it as much as possible.

The two hikers were led to the dwelling when they followed a trail of animal carcasses. The trail stretched several hundred yards and eventually led to a cave opening between two large pine trees. The hole was described as a perfect circle about ten feet in diameter.

The discovery was reported when the husband made a distress call to local park rangers. His wife claimed she smelled "the sweetest aroma" coming from inside the subterranean lair. As the husband attempted to remove her from the area, she reportedly become "violent and hysteric." Escaping from his grip, she sprinted to the hole, turned to smile at her partner, and gracefully fell backwards into the darkness of the cave.

The husband reportedly ran forward and heard his wife's body hit the cave floor after a few moments. It was a forty-foot drop from the cave's opening. The husband stated he heard the sound of hoarse laughter coming from the cave below. The woman's remains were never located.

When the feds were notified, we were called in to help with containment. We received an initial briefing that identified a horrifying creature dwelling in the cave. Thus began construction of the bunker and containment process.

The "creature" we have been dealing with is far more sinister in nature than anything I have ever seen or studied. My one solid conclusion is that the being is otherworldly. Whatever it is, it is invisible to all video recordings. Both digital and film. The live footage shows the cave as completely empty, and all recorded files are corrupted. We are unable to study it from a distance.

Containing the beast was nearly impossible. We eventually trapped it by sealing the entrance the aforementioned hiker fell in. Our team then drilled our own opening, and barricade it with a steel blast door.

There are only a few humans who have seen it with the naked eye. A retired captain known as Walsh was the first. It was my first day on project Erebus when we lost him. Equipped with his 9 mm sidearm, Walsh entered the cave around 6 a.m. on Monday morning, and the massive steel door was quickly shut behind him.

He immediately began to complain of the heat, claiming the temperature was unbearable. The facilities thermometer showed the cave at only 55 F. His complaints of the heat were followed by several minutes of silence.

Walsh's voice boomed out of the intercom speakers. "Let. Us. Out. How can you people be so blind?"

Looking at the monitor, we saw nothing but an empty cave. But Walsh could obviously see something. We spoke into the receiver.

"Walsh, what is it? Tell us what you see."

He hissed a response, "Worthless swine, all of you. Let. Us. Out."

Our team looked around in a state of confusion and panic.

Walsh was staring directly at the center of the cave as interior lights rapidly strobed. For a moment, the creature showed itself for the first time on film. I saw the outline of a dark, humanoid being sitting on the ground, cross-legged with one hand in the air, and the other resting at its side in the Baphomet pose.

Walsh began to move out of frame, back towards the entrance. The video feed cut out. Rapid whispers came through the speakers and sounded like a hundred voices in unison.

Our team sat in silence, waiting for something, anything. The silence was interrupted by three loud knocks from the other side of the steel blast door.

Our defense unit got into position, rifles aimed at the doors as it was opened. To our relief, a seemingly unharmed Walsh crossed the threshold and stood in the open doorway.

Our relief turned to horror.

It was his eyes. I can still picture them—the image forever burned in my mind. His eyes were a blank canvas of white—absent of irises and pupils. Two steady streams of blood ran from his tear ducts down his cheeks, creating two crimson puddles on the stone floor.

He just stood there, silent and unblinking. We were shocked, unsure of what to do or say.

He broke the silence again. "It can smell us... It's... hungry," he said in a whisper as he raised the pistol to his temple.

It wasn't the shot that frightened me the most, or the explosion of gore that painted the walls behind him. What horrified me the most was the massive, jet black, three-fingered hand that pulled Walsh's lifeless corpse back into the cave, just before the blast door was slammed shut. I will never forget the sound of his tearing flesh.

ALL RECORDS of Walsh were deleted. Even a personal email chain between us was erased without my consent or knowledge.

After the incident, nobody wanted to enter the cave. Many of us, myself included, tried to abandon the project. The officials told us that leaving the site would be considered treasonous and we would regret the decision.

The feds decided to send in one of their own. I do not know his real name, but they referred to him as "X." He was a middle-aged, muscular man with salt-and-pepper hair. By the way he carried himself, you could tell he was in charge and not to be messed with. Someone in the room described him as "unbreakable."

Before he went in, we concluded that looking at the creature with the naked eye was too risky. We sent X in with carbon fiber protective glasses equipped with impenetrable plexiglass lenses.

The blast doors opened, and X confidently walked inside.

As soon as the door closed, we lost audio. We repeatedly tried to reach him, only to be met with static. An hour passed, with no response. Panic grew in the facility as we waited, praying that we would not be chosen to go in after him.

Just before we lost hope, a fury of knocks and screams came from the other side.

We opened the door and a ghost-white X came crawling out. The "unbreakable man" was on the floor, screaming hysterically as he held his hands over his ears—

as if he was protecting them from an unbearable noise. He repeatedly screamed: "its name, it told me its name!"

Medical staff raced to his side attempting to settle him down. It was no use. He squirmed in agony until one of the doctors injected him with a sedative. It took five men to hold him still.

I never saw X again. But the story of what happened to him spread around like a disease. His ear drums had somehow been completely removed while inside the cave. The feds brought in their top psychiatrist to analyze X. With his loss of hearing, the doctor reverted to writing questions on a small notepad for him to read. During the session, X got up and whispered the name of the creature into her ear.

It is on record that the second X whispered the name, he instantly lost the ability to speak, and the psychiatrist appeared to enter a trance state. Both were found dead the next day, hanging from the rafters of their individual rooms.

From the evidence we have gathered, the creature seems to be stealing human senses: the hiker's sense of smell, Walsh's sight, and X's hearing.

The reason I am telling this story to the world is because I genuinely believe it is too late. Three more caves have been discovered, all with ten-foot openings and a trail of dead animals leading to them. We have no idea how many more there are.

SISTER

By J. Speziale

I WAS HAPPY TO ACCEPT MY GRANDMOTHER'S CHORE—
cleaning out the small, tin-roof cabin on her property.
Growing up, my sister Annie and I would play there all
the time. I have always cherished those memories. This
weekend was the anniversary of her death; I couldn't
believe it had already been five years.

I pulled down the long gravel drive of grandmother's
rural home. As I made my way to the door, it swung open.
My grandmother and uncle stepped out with luggage in
hand. They were headed to the city to visit my parents, as
this time of the year was understandably difficult for
them. We talked for a moment, avoiding the morbid
subject on our minds. My uncle's fidgeting indicated his
desire to hit the road. Eventually, we said our quiet
goodbyes.

"Don't clean too much," my uncle said as he sat in down in the driver's seat. "Just needs a little tidying up."

I smiled softly and closed his door.

As they drove away, I inhaled the fresh country air. A flood of childhood memories consumed my mind as I made my way to the cabin. It was a two-mile hike through woods and pasture to the cabin. After what seemed like an eternity it was in sight. I smiled as I stared at the simple structure, feeling like I had just run into an old friend. As I climbed the hill and made my way to the porch I heard the low rumble of thunder in the distance.

The wooden door creaked open, and I was greeted with the distinct smells of dust and cedar. The cabin is simple: the front door enters into the kitchen, there is a small wood-burning stove, ice box, and a wooden table stands in the middle of the room. The kitchen leads into a small sitting room complete with wicker furniture, red area rug, and fireplace in the corner.

Pale yellow sunlight filled the room through dirt-stained windows.

To my surprise, my uncle left a good lot of supplies. Plenty of food, lanterns, and a hot plate for cooking. My grandmother mentioned that he had been sleeping here a lot. He and my aunt didn't have the strongest marriage. I got to work, wandering around the cabin cleaning off all of the surfaces. As I made my way back towards the entrance, I noticed something different. A painting—a large painting, placed in front of a window near the door. I studied it for a few moments. It depicted an exact landscape rendition of the pond directly behind the actual window.

I was confused as to why it was blocking the window. The painting was a perfect fit, covering the entire window.

Tap tap tap tap tap tap tap tap

Rain pounded the tin roof.

BOOOOOOMMMMM

A flash of lightning and bolt of thunder made me jump. The lightning illuminated the cabin, revealing something in the painting I hadn't seen before. I went in for a closer look, and stared at the pond.

There was something there—a small, round, black smudge slightly sticking out of the water in an unnatural way. Different in color and shape from the other rocks depicted in the painting. I placed two fingers on the canvas.

It was still wet.

Confused, I studied at the dark liquid. I felt uneasy. I was curious to know who painted the mysterious picture, and why this particular out-of-place rock was still wet.

BOOOOOOMMMMM

Another strike of lightning made me jump back in fright.

I gathered myself, and looked back.

The black smudge was bigger and more defined. I shined my flashlight on the dark, wet spot. It was then I realized it was not a painting of a rock at all… it was a head—a human head, breaking the surface of the water. Dark wet hair covered its face.

I backed away. Phone in hand, I was tempted to call my grandmother and ask her who painted it, and why they felt the need to include a surfacing human head in the pond. I decided it was too late to bother her. I retreated to the sitting room, built a fire, and poured some bourbon in an attempt to get my mind off of the oddity. The image was disturbing, and the thunderstorm wasn't making it much better. I covered the painting with a sheet before returning to the fire and booze.

Just as I began to nod off for the night, a violent knocking jolted me awake.

BANG BANG BANG BANG

I froze.

BANG BANG BANG BANG A voice screeched my name from the other side of the front door.

Eddieeeee

Eddieeeee

The voice was unnatural, scratchy, and broken. Like someone who hadn't spoken in years.

Paralyzed by fear, I pulled out my phone. No service.

BANG BANG BANG

Letttt me innnn Eddddd-iieeeeee

I started to shake.

I grabbed the bottle of bourbon by the neck as a makeshift weapon, praying the old latch-lock would hold off whatever was on the other side.

I waited, unsure of what to do.

Then… it stopped. The voice, the knocking, all of it.

I couldn't sleep that night. I sat on the floor until the pale morning sunlight crept into the cabin.

Cautiously, I opened the door, and crept outside. To my relief, I was alone.

I ran back to my grandmother's house, and gave her a call. As we spoke, I contemplated telling her of the previous night's events. I am not sure why, but I didn't. I couldn't. The last thing I wanted to do was scare the sweet elderly woman. We spoke for a few more minutes.

I sat for an hour and reflected on the previous night. There couldn't have been anyone there. Not this far out in the middle of nowhere. The storm was noisy. I must have imagined it, scaring myself like a child.

I made my way back to the cabin, after grabbing the old Russian rifle from my grandmother's closet... just in case.

I spent the majority of the day cleaning the floors, sifting through my uncles useless junk. I kept the painting covered with the white sheet. The sun set and the rain started again. I lit a few lanterns and sat down to dinner. I looked back at the sheet. Near the center was a small, dark, dot. I got up to investigate. Wet paint was beginning to seep through. I concluded that there must be a hole in the window causing a leak and making the paint run. Without hesitation, I took the painting down. It weighed a ton.

Once on the floor, I looked at the window. I jumped back in fright, and nearly collapsed.

Something was standing at the edge of the pond. With dirty, wet, dark hair covering its face. Torn and filthy clothes hung loosely from its skeletal frame, starting straight at me. I stepped out onto the old wooden porch, rifle in hand.

"WHAT DO YOU WANT!?" I yelled over the heavy rain pounding the tin roof.

It stepped forward.

"I WILL SHOOT, DON'T MOVE"

The creature continued.

"I SWEAR!"

It continued its slow and determined pace towards me.

CRACKKKKKKKKK

The old rifle rang out, and the bullet soared through its torso.

Unaffected, it continued forward, just a few yards in front of me.

Tears streaming down my face, I worked the bolt and loaded my next round.

CRACKKKKKKK

The bullet soared right though its head. As if it was made of air. The creature remained unharmed as the bullet splashed in the pond behind it. I sat, defeated, knowing now there was nothing I could do. Pleading with this hideous nightmare to leave me, attempting to cope with my remaining sanity.

It walked straight past me.

The smell of rot and damp moss filled my nose as it passed.

It entered in the living room of the cabin, leaving black, thick, oily foot prints in its wake. The creature and stood on the rug. Dripping black water into the fabric.

Head down, it stared intently at the rug, for what seemed like an eternity. After a few moments, I attempted to speak and it looked right at me.

I gasped as I stared at a grisly, haunting apparition of my deceased older sibling.

My sister's cold white eyes stared straight into mine, with a look of recognition and fear.

Then... she vanished, and I lost consciousness.

I woke up on the floor the following morning. The first light of dawn filled the room. Within an instant, I remembered the terrifying events of the prior evening. I rushed over to the rug. Still damp and dark in the spot where she had stood. The pungent, rotten smell lingered in the room.

I pulled back the rug. Directly below the dark spot were brand new floorboards, crooked and loose. I grabbed a crow bar and uprooted loose flooring, revealing a makeshift storage space dug into the earth. Inside was a small black duffel bag. A bag which contents changed everything. After rummaging through the bag I realized it belonged to my uncle. I ran back to my car and drove to the nearest police station.

A detective and I sat and discussed the contents of his duffel: numerous pictures of my sister, a lock of her hair, his incriminating diary of twisted entries, expressing his love for his own niece; and finally, brake lines and hoses. Lines and hoses that belonged to her car.

Lines and hoses that explain the police report of my sisters accident five years ago. Stating:

"Victim's vehicle contained excessively corroded brake lines, failure to properly brake likely the cause of the accident."

The evidence put him in prison for life.

As for the paining, it currently hangs in my home. No wet spots or human heads. A beautiful painting created by my sister, just a few months before her death.

RAIN

By J. Speziale

I SAT DOWN ON MY COUCH WHILE MY COFFEE BREWED IN kitchen. I turned on the TV and propped my feet up on the table. My phone buzzed. I grabbed it, stared at the screen, and froze.

I had a new voicemail from my wife. This didn't make any sense. She had been presumed dead for over a year.

After ten minutes of trying to comprehend the situation, I played it.

"Hey it's me! It's so beautiful up here! I just got settled in. I cannot wait until you see the cabin. Love you!"

I played it again. My head was spinning, and my stomach turned.

Last year, my wife and I planned to spend a romantic weekend in the mountains. I had something come up at work, so I told her to go ahead without me, and I would meet her the next day. She ran into a bad storm on the way. The police told me they found her car in the river the next morning. She never made it to the cabin, and her body was never recovered.

This didn't make any sense. Why was I receiving the message now? And it sounded like she had in fact made it to our cabin that day.

My phone chimed again, and another message came through.

"I hope everything is okay. Why aren't you answering my calls? It's been storming non-stop here. Oh, by the way, I think the roof is leaking. There was a puddle on the kitchen floor. But… it's weird—there's nothing dripping from the ceiling above it. I don't really understand that. Oh well, that's your job! I miss you. I'll talk to you later, and please answer my calls next time!"

My whole world felt like it was crashing down. I jumped to my feet and began pacing around my living room. The voice was unmistakably hers. Was it possible to receive messages over a year later? I had the phone company deactivate her number after her passing. I tried to call her.

Nothing.

My phone chimed again. Tears welled up in my eyes. I hadn't heard her voice in so long.

"Seriously why are you not calling me back!? I'm starting to get worried. My phone says it has a good signal. I tried to drive into town today but the bridge is flooded. I don't think these storms are ever going to stop! Also, I'm starting to get scared… I think it's just because I'm by myself—but a flash of lightning illuminated the outside, and it looked like a woman was standing at the window. I know there's no one else out here, but it freaked me out. I think my eyes are playing tricks on me. I just wish you were here. PLEASE, PLEASE call me back."

I played the message again, then tried her phone. No answer. I felt like I was going crazy. I considered telling a friend what was going on, but I couldn't bring myself to do it.

With no particular plan, I loaded my car, and headed towards the cabin. I hadn't been there since the accident. It was a four-hour drive. I would be able to get there right at sunset.

On my way, my phone chimed again. Another message.

"PLEASE tell me you are coming up! Why aren't you answering!? I am officially freaking out. The bridge is still flooded, and I can't get out of here. I tried the sheriff's department but no one answered. The phone just kept ringing. Remember how I thought I saw a woman at the window last night? I went outside this morning and there were prints of bare feet leading up to the window. I followed them into the woods. They stopped at this huge rectangular hole, right in the middle of the ground. I'm really scared. I'm going back to the cabin and locking myself in."

My heart and mind were racing. I was getting closer, and the sun was starting to go down. I accelerated my car and tore through the back roads. Dark rainclouds formed overhead. I looked at the clock. I still wasn't making as good of time as I hoped. I was an hour out, and the sun had set. Large raindrops splashed against my windshield.

My phone chimed again.

I could hear a storm in the background. My wife's voice was a mixture of sobs and whispers.

"She's... here... in the hallway. The woman from the window. She's just standing there, soaked in water and mud. I don't know how she got in? I'm in the bedroom, I can see her through the gap in the door. Oh my God, what do I do? She's getting closer. The whole cabin smells like death. Please help me.... Please."

THE MESSAGE ENDED THERE. My heart felt like it was going to explode. Nothing made any sense.

I came to the bridge. Although the rain had stopped, the water was still too high—I pulled over and waded through the murky stream. The bridge was just a quarter mile from the cabin. I sprinted the rest of the way.

When the cabin came into view, uneasiness washed over me.

I burst through the front door and yelled my wife's name, tears streaming down my face. The floor was covered in sporadic splotches of black water. The putrid smell of rotten flesh made me gag. I tried the lights—they weren't working. I clicked on my flashlight and searched everywhere, screaming my wife's name.

As I circled back to the front door, I noticed footprints leading out of cabin and onto the porch. I followed them from the front lawn all the way into the dense woods. The tracks were fresh in the soft mud. I continued to scream my wife's name as I searched. The prints came to an abrupt end at the edge of a deep hole in the ground. Twigs snapped in the distance as my heart began to beat out of my chest. The air was unnaturally still and my instincts begged me to leave. I trekked back to the cabin, over-whelmed with the feeling of being followed. I opened the front door, walked into the kitchen, and fell to my knees. I pounded my fists into the hardwood floors, and as I looked up, a bolt of lightning flashed.

I looked towards the illuminated window—my stare met the dead, hollow eyes of a woman covered in mud and rain. Decaying skin hung from her skeletal remains.

That's when I lost consciousness.

Dim, morning light flooded the cabin. I awoke, confused and sore. My phone lit up, and I read the notif-ication on the screen.

1 New Voicemail.

I held my breath as I listened to my wife's voice whisper through the small speaker. "Why did you leave me in the woods last night? We were finally together and it felt so good to be near you. It's time to sleep my love... go with her... she will return for you...soon."

CHILDREN OF THE FOREST

By Tara A. Devlin

WHEN YOU HEAR THE FOREST TALKING, YOU SHOULD HEED its call. I didn't, and I paid the price for my ignorance.

I was hiking with my husband Chris when he suggested we go off the beaten track.

"Come on, it'll be fun. Nothing ventured, nothing gained!"

I rolled my eyes. "Only those who have never actually lost anything would say something so stupid."

"Are you calling me stupid?"

"No, I'm calling what you said stupid. I'm calling you a moron."

"Well, this moron wants to do a little exploring. What do you say?"

We went hiking often, at least once or twice a month. We went all over the country, but it was our first time at this particular mountain. The forest was deep, and the guide said that parts of it were impenetrable. Signs littered the track informing hikers that help would have trouble reaching them in time if people injure themselves, warning them not to leave the trail under any circumstances. That just made Chris even more determined.

"Sure, why not?"

Birds sang and insects chirped. The forest was alive, and as the sun beat down on it, it seemed to breathe. The leaves rustled, and the branches swayed. In and out. In and out. Small creatures scurried underfoot. Birds fluttered in the trees above.

Chris smiled and led the way, like a child on his first school trip. His lust for life and living each day to the fullest was what attracted me to him in the first place, and five years of marriage hadn't dampened the spirit that drove him forward. He was difficult to keep up with at times, but that was part of the fun.

"What are you going to do if we get lost out here?" I asked his sweaty back, pushing through the trees ahead of me. I had no idea where we were going, so I sure hoped he did.

"Maybe we can become hermits and live off the land!" He turned back and smiled at me. I wasn't sure if he was joking or not. It was hard to tell sometimes.

"You can live off the land, maybe. Me, I need a toilet. A shower. Plumbing. Warm, delicious, processed food. A bed with a blanket I can bury myself in. You can sleep in the dirt with all the animal poop and bugs."

"You make it sound so unappealing."

The trees swallowed us, leading us further and further in. The sun was high above, but it was becoming more difficult to tell where it was. The trees grew higher and more dense. Every few steps something scurried away in the brush, upset at our intrusion upon its land. The insects got louder, almost deafening. It was easy to see why hikers often lost their way out here.

"Let's have a little bet," Chris called back. "If we get lost, you get to pick where we go for the rest of the year. How about that?"

I laughed. "If we get lost out here, we're probably going to stay lost, if you know what I mean, so that's not gonna matter."

Chris raised his eyebrows with a sly smile. "How do you know that wasn't my intention in the first place?"

He stopped and put his hands on my waist, pulling me in close. I slapped him across the shoulder and he kissed me on the nose.

"You never know, if you play your cards right..." he whispered in my ear. I scoffed and pushed him away.

"Maybe we should get lost so I don't have to listen to your awful lines for the rest of my life."

"Oh you'd still have to listen to them," he replied. "Just for a shorter time, I'd imagine."

"Exactly," I agreed. He kissed me again and pushed forward. My hands stung from the scratches of hundreds of tiny tree branches. Occasionally one nicked my face and drew blood. I was going to come out looking like I was on the wrong end of a knife fight, if we managed to find our way back at all.

An hour into our walk off the hiking path the forest suddenly fell silent. Chris noticed it as well; he turned to look back at me, an eyebrow raised.

"You noticed too, huh?"

"It's like everything just up and died at once," he said. "Weird."

The leaves no longer rustled in the trees. The forest floor was silent and unmoving. Not a single bird called out, nor a single insect chirped. The forest was silent. The forest was dead.

"Do you think we should go back?" I asked. The hairs on the back of my neck stood up. I didn't like this at all. It wasn't right for a forest that, until 10 seconds earlier, had been alive and full of life to suddenly fall so quiet. So still. So empty.

There was movement up ahead.

"Hey, did you see that?" Chris took off running, not waiting for my reply.

"Chris, wait!" I ran after him, trying not to lose him as he zig-zagged through the trees. Branches clawed at my face and snagged my ankles. It took everything I had to keep upright and not lose sight of him.

"Wait, come back!" Chris screamed.

"Why are we running?" I was struggling to breathe, and the words came out ragged and hoarse.

"He was bleeding! The kid was bleeding!"

"Kid?" There was no way a kid could be all the way out here, certainly not by themselves. Chris ran, never once losing step. I fell farther behind and pain burned throughout my side.

"Chris?"

I could no longer see him. Just like that, he was gone.

"Chris?!"

Panic set in. Why did I agree to let him drag me out

here? I was in the middle of nowhere, off the track that specifically said 'enter at your own risk,' my phone had no reception, and I couldn't even tell which way was back anymore.

"When I find you I'm going to kick your ass so hard you'll wish you never came back!" I screamed. "Get back here!"

The forest was silent. I listened, but not a single thing moved, not even the leaves in the wind. I hugged myself, trying to calm the beating of my heart. Just think it through. Chris went that way—at least I thought he did— so if I went in the same direction I'd come across some sign of him sooner or later. Or I could stand in the same spot all day, slowly going insane. I couldn't go back without Chris, so it was a no-brainer. I started walking.

Dry leaves crackled under my feet. They were the only sounds in a forest that five minutes ago was buzzing with life. The temperature dropped as I pressed forward, and the trees above became so thick it was difficult to tell what time of day it was. My watch told me it was still afternoon, but my surroundings suggested otherwise.

"Chris, where are you?"

There was no reply. I couldn't tell how long I'd been walking for. Minutes? Hours? Everything looked the same. But then, as though I'd stepped over an invisible threshold, I heard it. Whispers. Above me, below me, all around me. Something scuttled over my feet and I fell back in horror. I almost forgot what life looked like, so long had passed without sound or sight of it. It was a spider, a rather large one, but it passed on without a fuss.

A shadow moved through the trees.

"Hey, wait!"

I took off after it, leaping over stones and ducking under branches. The noises of the forest got louder. Birds. Insects. Beasts. Whispering. Rustling. Scurrying.

Laughter.

I stopped, my hands on my knees as I tried to catch my breath. My skin burned from a thousand scratches as my lungs struggled to keep up. It was too fast. I couldn't match it, let alone catch up. The laughter intensified, closing in on me.

"Who are you?! What do you want?!"

A rotten stench pierced my nostrils, like meat left in the sun too long, or the noxious gas of a dirty swamp. It was hot. Too hot. It was off-putting after the coolness of the trees just prior. Sweat poured off my face and hit the dirt below. I took out my phone, but as I went to press the home button it went flying. A boy, no older than seven or eight-years-old, had snatched it from my hand and fled into the trees. The whispers and laughter intensified.

I ran after him. He looked back, a smile lighting up his childlike features, and then he was gone. I took off my jacket, the heat becoming unbearable. The stink of the forest invaded my nostrils, and I realized that I was well and truly lost. They lured Chris away from me. Now they were toying with me.

"Please," I called out. "I just want to find my husband. I don't want to disturb-" I tried to gather my thoughts, tried to understand the situation, "—whatever it is you're doing here. You can keep the phone. Hell, take my bag. Take all of it. It's yours. Just please. My husband. Chris. Take me to him. Let us go."

They had him. I knew it in my heart, I just didn't know why.

The forest fell silent. All the things it had been trying to tell me, its warnings, its admonitions, its mirth, its joy, its sadness and its pain, all of it fell silent.

A boy stepped forth, different to the one who stole my phone. His hair was ragged, his clothes torn and muddy. There was sadness in his eyes, but also something else. Fear?

"This is no place for adults."

"I'm sorry?"

"You shouldn't be here. Go."

He was tall and lean, perhaps thirteen or fourteen. By the looks of him, he'd never had a proper meal or bath in his life.

"Go, while you still can."

"What do you mean?"

I was tired and confused. His words weren't making any sense. He looked me over for a moment, thinking.

"You should still have some time, ma'am. Leave, before it's too late."

I ran over and grabbed him by the shoulders. He didn't flinch, didn't run. Just looked at me with those sad, fearful eyes.

"Before what's too late? What's going on? Where's Chris?"

"It's the forest, ma'am."

A shadow ran through the trees to my side.

"It takes us all, eventually."

A shadow ran in the distance, past the boy.

"Only the children are safe. The forest protects its children."

There was a scream in the distance. It was more animal than man.

"Sounds like it's too late for him now. You really should go."

I ran in the direction of the sound. The boy yelled at my back but his words were drowned out by the growing panic in my head. Fear pushed me forward. Fear that there was some truth to the boy's words and fear that the knot in my gut wasn't lying. The scream was Chris, and he was in trouble.

There was a small clearing ahead.

"Chris?"

I stopped, unable to comprehend the sight before me. There was a man, hunched over, tearing into the carcass of a rotting animal. I gagged, the smell so putrid it was difficult to breathe. He looked up at my voice before returning to his meal. I took a tentative step forward.

"Hey, it's me. It's me."

He didn't reply.

"Chris. Sweetie."

His clothes were torn and bloodied. There were scratches all over his face and arms, and he was covered in dirt and dried up blood. He tore into the rotten flesh again, and it was all I could do not to throw up. I reached a hand towards his shoulder.

"Let's go."

He growled and snapped at my hand. I fell over in the mud, landing hard on my tailbone.

"Ma'am, I told you."

I jumped, turning at the boy's voice behind me.

"The forest protects its children."

Several stepped out of the shadows. One held my phone. Another had his arm in a makeshift sling, stained red with blood. There were boys and girls of all ages, but the one talking to me was the oldest of all.

"Adults can't be here. You need to go now while you can. It's too late for him."

I clawed my way to my feet and fell before the boy. There was a roar to my left, and the boy turned to face it. That wasn't Chris.

"What's going on? I don't understand. What happened to my husband? What's going on here? Tell me!"

"I don't have much longer left myself. My time is coming."

He turned from the roar and looked me straight in the eyes.

"You cannot save him now."

He grabbed my shoulder and squeezed.

"You should have left when I told you to."

He squeezed harder. I flinched under his surprising strength as his voice lowered to a growl.

"It's coming."

The children took a few steps back. They looked up at the boy in awe, with almost reverence in their eyes. A few jumped and clapped.

"It's time! It's time!"

He grabbed my other shoulder and squeezed so tight I thought my bones might crumble beneath his touch. He leaned forward, his back arching into the air as a groan of pain tore through his throat. The children grew even more excited. The pain in my shoulders, the humidity pushing down through the trees and the putrid smell in the air made me woozy. Chris continued tearing at the animal behind me, oblivious to what was going on.

The boy raised his head to look at me and I recoiled in horror. His eyes were yellow, almost cat-like, while his teeth pushed out of his gums into long, white fangs.

"This is what happens," he spat out. "It takes us boys faster, but make no mistake..." He paused, struggling to breathe. I tried to shake free of his grasp, but he was too strong. "You will be next."

I broke free of his grasp and fell backwards into the mud. He was on me in an instant, eying me like prey.

"Of course, it can't take you if there's nothing left to take."

He tore into my shoulder, fangs piercing through the flesh and clamping down on bone. I screamed as the children roared with laughter. It was not the first time they'd seen this. One of their own turned into a beast of the forest. A beast that fed on missing hikers. Their turn would come too, one day. When they were no longer children. When the forest was done nurturing them. When they were on the cusp of adulthood. It raised them for that long, and then they became a part of it. One of the beasts that kept the ecosystem running. Kept the forest protected. Allowed it to survive in a time where man's presence extended everywhere and touched everything.

But not here.

I tried to throw the boy off—although he was no longer a boy, apparently—but he was too strong. His fangs tore through my upper arm as his claws pushed me farther into the mud and for a moment, just a moment, I closed my eyes and waited for it to end. I said my good-byes to Chris, whatever might be left of him, as he chewed on dead animal flesh behind me. I waited for the darkness to claim me. We would just be two more missing hikers. They might mount a search party, but they wouldn't find anything. They never did. That's why there were signs. Signs we ignored. We had no-one to blame but ourselves.

Darkness never came though. There was a roar, and I opened my eyes to see Chris barreling into the boy, sending them both sprawling in the mud. I scrambled to my feet as the children ran off screaming. I picked up my phone, abandoned in the mud, as blood poured down my arm. Chris didn't look back. He didn't stop to tell me to run, he didn't stop to tell me he loved me. He didn't stop to tell me that I won the bet, that I could choose where we went for the next year. That he was sorry for dragging us out here in the first place. I didn't know if he even knew I was there. But he ripped into the boy, not yet fully trans-formed into a beast of the forest, and their screams attracted more of them. The forest sprang to life as they closed in from all corners. I couldn't be here when they arrived.

I ran. Tears streaked my mud-stained cheeks and mingled with the blood coating my neck and arm and shoulder. I ran without knowing where I was going, without knowing if I'd even make it. Chris was gone; the forest claimed men faster. I would be next unless I got out.

I ran for what felt like hours, far longer than it took me to get in. Then, finally, when the forest fell silent around me, I knew I was safe. I was out of the beasts' territory. They wouldn't follow me out here.

I wandered until nightfall when some fellow hikers found me. I was delirious and dehydrated, and raving about monsters, they said. They never found Chris's body, but I knew the truth. When you hear the forest talking, you should heed its call. I didn't, and I paid the price for my ignorance. We should have listened to the signs. We should have listened to the forest. I can still hear it at night when I close my eyes and wait for sleep to take me. Calling me back. Inviting me to return to its warm embrace.

WHAT LURKS IN NIGHTFALL FOREST

By Tara A. Devlin

PEOPLE LIKE TO WARN YOU ABOUT THE DANGERS OF NATURE when you go camping, but that's not what you should be afraid of. Not exactly.

I went camping with my girlfriend in a place called Nightfall Forest. As you might expect from the name, it was a dark, foreboding place, with areas where the trees grew so thick that very little sunlight got through their overgrown branches. Lacey, my girlfriend and a biologist-in-training, wanted to study the ecosystem of a particular area of the forest known for its unique fungi and bacteria. A break from work sounded great so I agreed to tag along.

She moved out to set up her instruments as I set up camp not too far from the river. It was cool, a gentle breeze blowing over the camp as I hammered the last nails into the soil below. I had to admit it was nice.

Nobody screaming at me about deadlines, no phones ringing every few minutes to complain about a product I had no part in making, no cars honking at traffic or neighbors yelling loudly over the noise of their TVs. Nothing but the sound of the wind through the trees, the trickle of water over rocks, and a few birds that I couldn't quite spot in the dense foliage above.

"What are you smiling at?" Lacey walked over and sat down beside me on a half-rotten log. It creaked under our combined weight.

"I was smiling?"

"You were."

"Just enjoying the quiet and solitude, I guess."

"It really is nice out here, isn't it?" She grabbed my hand and kissed the knuckles. "Don't worry, you can get back to your keyboard tapping and smog-infested city in just a few short days."

That night we cooked a fish Lacey had caught over the fire she built and it struck me how little I knew of surviving in the wilderness. I was a city boy, born and bred. This was foreign land to me. We made love for the first time under the stars, at least, what little of them shone through the trees above us, and then retired to the tent. I was beat.

It was around 2 a.m. when a sound outside woke me up. Dry leaves crackled and branches snapped. I looked over and Lacey was gone, and for a brief moment I panicked. Something had taken her. A wild animal had come in and was dragging her away right this very second. A crazy old hermit was living in the woods and he had abducted her as penance for trespassing on his land.

Endless scenarios ran through my mind as a shadow appeared at the front of the tent.

'This is it,' I thought. 'This is where the crazy old hermit comes to murder me and rip out my liver for tomorrow's breakfast.'

The zipper began to rise, slowly. Each metal tooth it ran over reverberated through the tent, throughout my soul. Inch by inch it rose, getting stuck on something halfway. It was too dark to see. I fumbled around for something, anything I could use to defend myself. All I could find was my pillow. All the tools were outside. God, what an idiot I was. The zipper broke free of its snag and rose again, edging closer and closer to my impending doom.

I grabbed the pillow and swallowed. At the very least I could confuse the intruder and escape into the forest. If it was too dark for me to see that meant it was too dark for them to see as well.

I braced myself. Three. Two. O—

"Jesus, you scared me!" It was Lacey.

"That's my line! What the hell are you doing?"

"I had to pee."

"Did you have to pull the zip to the tent like a serial killer?"

"I didn't want to wake you."

"Too late, I'm awake! Fuck me. I thought I was about to lose my liver."

"Your liver? What?" Lacey got into her sleeping bag and fluffed up her pillow.

"Never mind. Well, now that I'm awake I'm gonna go pee too."

"Have fun!"

I made my way out into the darkness. Crickets chirped and the trickle of water over rocks continued unabated. It was both unnerving and soothing at the same time.

I finished my business and as I turned to return to the tent I froze. I wasn't alone. This wasn't Lacey trying to sneak her way back into the tent without waking me. There was someone standing in the trees, just a few meters away. It was too dark to see anything but a vague outline, but there was no mistaking it. There was a person, right there. I could pick up a rock and hit them with it. Did they see me? I couldn't tell which direction the person was facing. They were just standing there, like a statue.

I stood still, waiting to see if the figure would make a move. I was sure it could hear the beating of my heart in my chest. Why wasn't it moving?

There was a cry in the distance. We both turned towards the sound, and then the figure looked at me, its eyes glinting in the darkness before it took off running. I scrambled for the tent and yanked the zipper down as hard as I could, forcing it as it got stuck several times.

"What are you doing?" Lacey asked, rubbing her eyes. I put a shaky finger to my lips and crawled into my sleeping bag. We waited, listening. There was another cry, fainter this time, and then silence. The thing was gone.

"There was someone out there," I whispered, unable to hide the fear in my voice. Lacey sat up.

"What do you mean, someone out there? Who?"

I shook my head. "There was a cry... a scream... something... and then they took off."

I left out the part about the eyes. No need to worry her

or make her think I was insane. I was a city boy, she would put it down to my unfamiliarity with the woods and not take me seriously. Camping virgin or not, the thing I saw... it wasn't human.

Morning came without a wink of sleep and Lacey went off to check her instruments.

"Don't you want some breakfast?" I called out.

"I'll eat later!"

The forest felt cold. Unwelcoming. Like eyes were watching me from every corner. I stood up, thinking to join Lacey as she did her rounds, but then it dawned on me that I had no idea where she was. I was setting up camp when she put out her stuff.

I was alone.

I made my way over to the trees where I saw the figure the night before. There were footprints in the mud, leading in the same direction the figure ran off. I didn't imagine it. I followed them for a few meters before they disappeared. It wasn't that the mud ended, the footprints just... stopped.

I needed to think of an excuse before Lacey got back so we could get out of here. She could call me a chicken all she wanted, at least I would be a living chicken. But as the morning went on, there was no sign of her. I tried my hand at fishing, but all it brought was frustration and even more time to think. I tried to set up booby traps around the camp, but I was no boy scout. I didn't know the first thing about setting up a snare. Mud squelched under my feet and twigs snapped. How on earth did someone get so close to our camp without us hearing them? I couldn't take two steps without alerting half the forest.

Several hours passed with no sign of Lacey. I bit my nails and wore a path in the grass beside our tent. Our phones were off and unable to receive reception out here, regardless. I knew the way back to the car, but that was it. If I went looking for Lacey, chances were I'd get lost myself and be in even more trouble. But then a scream drew me from my thoughts.

"Lacey?"

I took off running. Getting lost didn't matter if Lacey ended up dead or injured instead. I pushed my way through the trees, branches scraping at my arms and face. There was another scream, to my left. I turned, sliding in the mud before picking up speed again. The thing I saw outside the tent, it had her. It was all I could think. I slipped and fell several times, covering myself in mud, and then I heard a third scream, this time to my right.

It was playing with me. I fell to my knees, exhausted. I had no idea where I was, no idea how to get back, no idea where Lacey was or even if she was okay. It had lured me out here, away from the camp, and now it could do as it pleased with Lacey. It was all I could think of, rational or otherwise. Lacey. I had to save Lacey.

I stood up and ran in the direction I came from. At least, the direction I thought I came from. Panic was settling in and the forest looked the same no matter how far I ran. I could have been running in circles for all I knew. Maybe I was.

My heart jumped into my throat. Footprints. I found footprints. If I followed them back I could reach the campsite. I didn't miss a beat as I leapt over rocks and branches. It would have been beautiful if I wasn't scared shitless. Then something moved in front of me, and I was on my back in the mud.

"Lacey?"

She looked at me, confused.

"What are you doing?"

I extracted myself from the muck and grabbed her by the shoulders. "That's my line! Are you okay? I heard screams!"

Her brow furrowed.

"I didn't hear anything. Are you sure you're okay?"

My head pounded. My chest ached. My brain was clouded with fear and confusion.

"You didn't hear those screams just before? They were loud enough that I heard them from camp. I thought it was you!"

At that she smiled.

"Aww, you're so sweet. But I was just checking my instruments. I didn't hear anything at all."

"Really?"

She nodded. "You're probably just tired. You didn't get much sleep last night after all."

"Maybe." A sleepless night wasn't new to me, but it didn't explain why I heard someone screaming when she didn't.

"Come on, let's go back to camp. I'll whip up a lunch special of canned beans and filtered river water!"

I attempted a smile that never quite reached my lips and followed her back. The forest was quiet. Too quiet. My nerves refused to settle down.

We ate lunch in silence. My muddy clothes hung by the tent and all I could think was that I didn't want to be out here any longer. Camping wasn't for me. We were supposed to stay a few more days, but I wasn't sure if I could make it through the next night.

"Lacey."

"Yeah?" she asked, stuffing her face with beans like she'd never eaten a meal before in her life.

"I want to get out of here."

"You wanna go for a walk or something?"

"No, out of here. Entirely. I want to go home."

She snickered. "Now you're just being silly. We just got here and I haven't finished my recordings."

I felt bad, but I couldn't do it.

"Please."

She looked at me. "You're serious?"

"I am."

She considered it and then sighed. "Is this about the screams?"

I shook my head. "It's not just that. And I know you didn't see them, but I saw someone last night. Right there, by the trees. I don't like this place. It's dangerous. Who's to say that tonight they won't return and murder us for real? I know you wanted to do some research, but that research isn't going to be any good if we're both dead. I don't like this place. I just don't. I want to go home. Please."

She finished her plate of beans and set it down on the log beside her.

"You owe me, you know. Big time."

I couldn't hide the smile from my face. "Anything at all! You name it!"

"Yeah, well, first I have to go and get all my gear, I

suppose. One day's worth of results is better than nothing. And you, sir, get to break the tent down and put everything away."

"Not a problem, it'll be done before you know it!" My spirits lifted. No doubt she'd give me shit the entire way home, but I could deal with that, because we would be alive and we would be safe. That was all that mattered.

I gathered up our gear in record time and was waiting when Lacey returned. We loaded up, I said an internal 'fuck you, hope to never see you again!' to the forest and we went on our way.

"Did you manage to get anything from your tests?" I tried to make conversation as we walked so I wouldn't have to think about how creepy the forest was. The sun was setting and it would be dark soon. I hated winter. Early nights sucked.

"Not very much, no. But it's fine. I can come out here some other time by myself."

I scratched my nose and avoided looking at her. This was the right thing to do. I wasn't imagining things. I wasn't.

"I'm sorry. I know you were looking forward to this trip."

"Look, if you're gonna mope the whole way home, just stop that shit right now. I agreed to go back with you, didn't I?"

She did, yes.

"Now stop fussing over it."

"Sorry…"

We walked in silence. The closer we got to the car the more the forest sprang to life. Birds sang, insects chirped, and various creatures scuttled around the forest floor. The sound of several large animals stomping through the brush caught my attention, but I couldn't find them. As long as we didn't get in their way, we would be fine. The sun disappeared behind the horizon, but the car was in sight. Just a few more meters and we'd—

"Josh!"

Lacey, a few steps ahead of me, stopped dead in her tracks. She turned to look at me in the gloom of dusk, her expression unreadable. Lacey's voice called out my name. Only Lacey, standing in front of me, wasn't the one who called it. It came from the trees to our right.

"What the fuck?"

"We need to go, now," Lacey said. She didn't wait for an answer and picked up the pace towards the car.

"Josh, wait!"

Something came running out of the trees. It was Lacey.

"What the fuck?"

Lacey, the original Lacey, turned around. There were two of them, looking right at me.

"What. The. Fuck?"

Lacey, the other Lacey, was disheveled and covered in mud. I took a step back as she ran towards me.

"Josh, it's me!"

My eyes flickered back and forth between the two of them and my back pressed into a tree.

"I went out to pee last night and something grabbed me! That thing isn't me!"

I didn't know what to believe. Other than the mud and messy hair, they were the mirror image of each other.

"I don't know what that thing is, but I can tell you that when I went out to pee last night I most certainly wasn't grabbed." The non-messy Lacey looked at me, her eyes wide. "And yes, I agree. We really should get out of here now."

The messy Lacey turned and jumped before I could say a word. The two Laceys fell in the mud, scratching and punching and kicking. I ran over, grabbed the nearest one and pulled her off. There was a growl, deep in the forest. I swallowed. That wasn't a deer. There was no time for this. It was getting darker and colder by the second.

I turned to the Lacey on my right. "What did I get for my fifth birthday?"

"A red matchbox car," she said without hesitation. I turned to the Lacey on my left, pushing herself up out of the mud.

"What did I want but did not get for my birthday last year?"

"A rainbow cake with buttercream frosting," she said, flicking the mud off the front of her pants. Both were correct. The red matchbox car was the pride of my childhood and it still sat on my dresser at home. Only Lacey knew about the cake I wanted last year but, due to a mistake at the bakery, never got.

This was insane.

"I don't know what the fuck is going on here, but I can't be the only one who heard that growl just now."

Lacey, both Laceys, looked at me. A second later it was on us. A featureless man, like something molded out of clay, ran for the other Lacey. Its eyes glinted in the darkness and it barreled into her at full speed, sending them tumbling to the ground. A scream barely had time to escape my lips before it was all over; the clay man ripped out her throat.

Lacey, the other one beside me, screamed. The yellow eyes turned towards her, then looked at me. A mistake was made. There weren't supposed to be two Laceys. Something fucked up the process. The clay man grabbed my wrist and began to change before me. It grew taller, matching my height. The watch on my arm began to form on his. The bare chest morphed into my shirt and jacket. Its blank face... became mine.

Lacey screamed again. I pulled the creature away from her and we fell, hitting the ground hard. Mud clouded my vision. Mud. So much mud. It was on everything, working its way into every crease and crevice in my body. I extracted my limbs and swung for the thing with my face. It grunted and grabbed my hair, pulling me back down. It pinned me to the ground and as it adjusted to bear its full weight down on me I lifted my knee. I kicked with all my might, sending other-me tumbling to the ground. I grabbed Lacey's hand and ran blindly for the car.

"Get back here!" the man yelled with my voice. I ran as fast as I could. No turning back. "Hey, don't leave me here!"

I fumbled for the keys in my pocket. The car was just ahead. Lacey was dead. Was this my Lacey? There was no time to think about it. I pressed the button on the keys, relief flooding through me as I heard the familiar beep signifying the car was unlocked. I ran for the driver's side while Lacey ran for the other. Our things could be replaced, but our lives could not.

I saw myself running for the car as I put the key in the ignition. Even more frightening than seeing another Lacey in front of me was seeing myself. It was a perfect copy; it even ran with heavy feet just like I did. The engine roared to life as the no-longer-clay version of myself jumped on the front of the car. Lacey had her head in her hands, crying. I threw the car into reverse and watched as I went flying into the parking lot. I sped off, visions of myself running like a crazed Terminator with a limp in the rear-view mirror burning into my mind.

Lacey said nothing as we drove the empty roads home. We both watched her, or at least another version of her, die before our very eyes. But which Lacey was it? Did she even know herself? And now there was another version of me running around somewhere out there too.

Both Laceys truly believed they were the original. It keeps me up at night sometimes, wondering. I've never seen anything to doubt that the Lacey sleeping beside me isn't the one I first met when we were seventeen-year-old and stupid kids with too much time on our hands, but I had seen it in their eyes when they argued. They both believed they were the one and only "true" Lacey. They both had the same memories. The same features. The same scars. The same feelings and emotions.

Somewhere out there is another version of me. Did he return to the woods, lost and confused, or is he figuring out his next move? Waiting for the right moment to get rid of the imposter inhabiting his house, sleeping in his bed and making love to his girlfriend?

Sometimes I wonder though. In the quiet of the night when the world is asleep. Am I really me? If we both have the same memories, if we both believe ourselves to be the one and only true version, how do I know that I'm the original? Even if he does come to kill me and take my place, how will I ever know?

I won't. And that's the thing that worries me the most.

FOREST OF DOLLS

By Tara A. Devlin

"Oh my god, what is that?"

Kenny pointed to something in the distance. I squinted, trying to focus my eyes on the dark spot beyond the trees. He ran off before I could say anything.

"Hey!"

"Holy shit, check this out!"

I caught up with him, stepping around a rather large puddle of mud, and stopped in my tracks when I saw it.

"Oh, gross."

It was a doll, burnt in several places and missing its eyes and legs. The empty eye sockets were filled with twigs.

"Who would do such a thing?"

Kenny was looking at something else though.

"Look, there are more!"

I followed him through the trees. So much for our peaceful camping trip.

"Jesus..." he muttered, stopping underneath a veritable forest of mutilated dolls. They hung from several trees, ropes around their necks like nooses. They were in various states of decay, missing legs, arms and faces. Again, twigs were stuffed into the holes and cracks.

"Ewwww gross!" A spider scurried out of the doll closest to my head. "I've seen enough, let's get back to the others."

"Worried they'll be thinking we're up to something lewd out here?" Kenny grinned. I rolled my eyes.

"You wish." Something caught my attention out the corner of my eye. "What was that?"

"What was what?"

"That." I pointed. "Something moved, over there."

"It's just the wind," Kenny said, pulling a twig out of one of the dolls. "What the hell are these things, anyway? Oh, eww, what the fuck?"

Kenny dropped the stick and wiped his hands on his jeans. "That's not okay."

"What?" I asked.

"There was something wet on it." He sniffed his fingers. "Blood?"

"We really should get back now," I urged.

"I concur," Kenny agreed.

We picked up the pace. A soft rain fell through the trees. It was not going to be a comfortable night.

"It was probably some crazy old lady that hung them up." Kenny was trying to convince himself more than me.

"She lost her daughter in an accident or something, and then she moved out to the woods to live alone, and then—"

"Kenny."

He looked at me.

"What?"

I pointed through the trees to our right.

"No. No way. Is that—"

Four bodies were hanging from a tree a few meters away, surrounded by dolls. But these bodies were real. They swayed gently in the breeze.

"Are they…?"

"I think so."

Twigs were shoved into their empty eye sockets. One body was wearing a suit, another gaudy leggings. One was missing a leg entirely, and the other had a tattoo covering most of one arm. What on earth were they doing out here? Who were they?

"We need to tell the others. We gotta get out of here."

"I'll see if I can get them down or something first. You get the others." Kenny was climbing the tree before I could protest. There was no time to waste. I ran.

I reached camp and explained to the others what we had seen.

"You saw dead bodies hanging from a tree?" Frank asked.

"And a forest of dolls?" Shay confirmed.

"You could think of better excuses than that if you just wanted some alone time. Where is Kenny, anyway? Was it that good, huh?" Ellie poked a few more sticks into the fire.

They didn't believe me. I grabbed Ellie's hand and dragged her to her feet.

"Hey, what are you—"

"Come on."

Shay ran to catch up with us, Frank hot on her heels. The rain falling through the trees covered the forest in a mist that made it difficult to see where we were going.

Suddenly Ellie screamed and brushed furiously at her face.

"What was that? What was that?"

It was one of the dolls.

"We're close. It's just over there. Hey, Kenny! Are you there? I brought the others!"

Ellie grabbed my arm like her life depended on it. We moved through the trees, stepping around and then through the mud. Nobody said a word. The forest was silent but for the sound of rain on the leaves. I couldn't hear any signs of Kenny.

I stopped. My heart began pounding furiously in my chest.

"Oh my god." Shay covered her mouth in surprise. Ellie gripped my arm even tighter. Frank moved towards the bodies and poked the guy in the suit with a stick. He swung back and forth in the rain, hitting the lady in the leggings and the guy with the tattoo.

"Jesus, they're dead all right."

"Hey, are you okay?" Shay was looking at me, my mouth opening and closing like a fish out of water.

"T-there's more of them," I stammered.

"What?"

"There's more…"

157

There were several new bodies, swaying in the rain. I looked up higher and gasped.

Kenny swung from the branches high above us, twigs shoved into his bleeding eyes.

DON'T STOP ON ROUTE 33

By Blair Daniels

THERE'S A STRETCH OF ROUTE 33 THAT GOES OVER Shenandoah Mountain. It's one of the most beautiful roads in the country—some parts cling to the side of the mountain, with gorgeous view of the valley below. Others snake through deep, lush forest, scattered with deer and all kinds of wildlife.

But, if you ever see a car broken down on the side of it—

Don't you dare stop.

Connor and I first saw it on the way to his parents' house one evening. A silver Accord, parked askew in the grass. The flashers were on, blinking in the blue dusk. And stuck in the back window was a piece of paper, scrawled with the words HELP! BROKE DOWN.

But Connor didn't slow down.

"Police patrol the area all the time," he said, swerving around it. "They'll be just fine."

I scoffed. "Oh, no, I know what this is about." I crossed my arms over my chest and glared at him. "Getting to your parents on time is more important than helping out someone who's stranded on the side of the road. That's it, isn't it?!"

"No. As I just said, Vee—if they actually need help, they'll flag down an officer."

"Why are you being so terrible?! They broke down! They need our help!"

"If they really broke down, Vee," he said, yanking the steering wheel, "why did they just pull out behind us?"

I turned to the mirror.

No—Two white lights, swinging onto the road.

Thud.

I was thrown back in my seat, as Connor put the pedal to the floor. We flew through the darkness; branches scraped at the car, and the wind howled.

"I knew we should've waited 'til morning," he muttered under his breath.

"Connor, what—"

"Bad people hang 'round here at night." His voice was barely audible over the roar of the car. "Dad's always talking about 'em, but I never believed him. Thought they were tall tales, you know, to scare me into not taking this road. It's a dangerous road, with the curves and all."

"Bad people? What do you mean?" The headlights disappeared behind a bend. "Like cults? Or serial killers? Or—"

"Maybe both," he said. "Just know all the victims are

160

found the same way: in the middle of the woods, completely naked, with slashes across their throats."

I shuddered, and my mind began to race. *What if they catch up with us? What if they get us? What if—*

But then I saw it.

A narrow road, splitting off from the right side of the highway, climbing up into the forest.

I glanced in the mirror. The headlights hadn't reappeared yet.

"Turn, there!" I said. "And then cut the lights. They'll pass us right up."

Connor hesitated. "I don't even know where that goes," he said. "Didn't even think there was an exit for another twenty miles, at least."

"Just turn!"

He jerked the steering wheel. The seatbelt cut into my chest, as we veered off, braked to a stop.

And then waited for the Accord to pass. Two, five, then ten minutes.

But they never came.

"Did we lose them?"

"Must have," he said. "Let's go." The car rumbled to life. He turned sharply towards the trees, then backed up—

A shadow caught in the headlights.

Silver metal and glass.

The Accord.

Lights off, still and silent, parked right behind us.

I screamed. Connor cursed under his breath. We swerved back onto the road, heading deeper into the forest. "If this is a dead end, then—"

Thunk!

We went flying. Dirt and trees and sky all whirled together. I shut my eyes, screaming, clinging to the door.

We hit the tree with a loud crunch.

"Veronica!"

"I'm fine," I groaned. "Just hit my head, but—"

Crunch!

I whipped around.

Crunch!

The Accord was ramming into us, over and over.

"Get out!" Connor yelled.

I swung the door open, and tumbled out of the car. We stumbled through the forest, back in the direction of 33. Branches clawed at my arms; rocks bit into my feet. Tears were running down my face, and it took everything in me to silence my sobs. "I can't do this," I heaved. "I can't—"

Slam.

I whipped around. Someone was stepping out of the Accord—a tall, pale figure with wild hair, illuminated in the flickering light of our dying headlights.

"Where is it?!" Connor huffed. "Where's 33?! We didn't drive that far away. Where the hell is it?!"

But he was right.

There were only branches, dirt, darkness.

Route 33 was gone.

It was as if the forest had swallowed us up, and severed us completely from the outside world. Behind us, the figure advanced, the sharp crunch of footsteps echoing off the trees.

"I'm so sorry," Connor said, his voice faltering.

But then I saw it. A light—smeared and blurry through my tears, shining through the trees like a beacon of hope.

We stumbled towards it. The trees got sparser; the underbrush grew thicker. Patches of blue sky peeked through the branches.

"Oh, thank God!" I gasped.

It was a flashlight.

And beyond it—

The uniform of a police officer.

Unfortunately, by the time we led the officer back to our car, the silver Accord was gone.

But, fortunately, Route 33 didn't actually disappear. We must've just gotten disoriented in the darkness. She told us it's very common for people to get lost in these woods, even during the daytime.

After filing various paperwork, she safely drove us to my in-laws' house. The four of us had a great dinner, too much dessert, and lots of laughs. "Want to take a walk?" I asked Connor, after things had settled down. "I think I need to walk off all that ice cream."

"Sure," he said, taking my hand.

We took a short walk around the block. It was fully dark, now, and the stars twinkled high above. A cool breeze came in from the west, fluttering through my hair.

And in the moonlight, something glinted across the street.

"Connor! Look!" I grabbed his arm.

"No—"

Parked on the street was a dented, silver Accord.

THE WALL IN GRANDPA'S BACKYARD

By Blair Daniels

"NEVER GO OVER THE WALL." MY GRANDPA SAT IN THE rocking chair, massaging his bad ankle through mud-stained jeans. "This isn't the safest area of Florida. Especially at night."

"Okay."

"Also, be careful with that. You could take your eye out."

See, that's why my nine-year-old self didn't take him seriously. He was always warning me about various "dangerous" things. *Don't swim in the deep end of the pool; you could drown. Don't run so fast; you could trip and break your neck.*

So when—one night—I heard a voice on the other side of the wall, I wasn't scared.

I had been playing alone in the backyard, sitting in the grass between the orange trees, when I heard it. A woman's voice, low and soft, echoing over the concrete wall at the end of the backyard.

"Hello?"

Being the curious kid I was, I immediately ran over to it. I wouldn't climb over—even though I didn't believe Grandpa, I didn't want to make him mad—but there was no harm in taking a peek, right?

I stepped up on the old stone fountain, reached for the top of the wall, and hoisted myself up. And then I peered down.

Underneath the intertwining oak branches and Spanish moss was only darkness. I squinted, trying to make sense of the shadows flitting across the dirt floor. Maybe I had imagined it—

"Hello?"

The voice rang out in the darkness, up through the trees.

"Hello!" I called back.

I heard a rustling sound, and the soft thump of footsteps. "Who's there?"

"Amanda," I called down.

"I'm Elizabeth." The shadows shifted, but I still couldn't quite make out the figure below. "And I need your help, Amanda."

"Sure! I can help!"

"I'm thirsty," she said. The wind picked up, and the branches swayed, scattering the shadows below. "So very thirsty."

"I'll get you some water!" I said, without second thought.

"Oh, that would be so wonderful, Amanda."

I jumped down, scampered inside, and fished a bottle of water from the fridge. Grandpa didn't even notice; he was watching some boring World War II movie on TV, rubbing his bad ankle all the while.

I stepped back up onto the fountain. "I got you some water," I called. "Do you want me to throw it down?"

"Oh, well... it might hit me. Maybe you can come down and give it to me?"

I paused. The warm Florida air blew over my face, and there was a strange smell: sour, like when Dad's meat freezer in the basement broke a few years ago. "I can't. I'm not supposed to go over the wall."

I was met with awkward silence.

"Hello?"

"Please, I'm so thirsty," the voice said, again.

I looked at the rough concrete. Maybe I could pull myself up a bit, reach down, and hand her the bottle of water? I swung a leg up over the wall, and with a grunt, pulled myself into a sitting position.

Slowly, I leaned down, and reached my hand through the canopy of branches.

But nothing took the bottle of water.

"Hello?"

Silence. Not even a footstep, or a rustle, from the underbrush below.

"Hel—"

Something yanked my ankle.

Hard.

I jerked forward. The water fell to the ground with a sickening splat. My hands flew out, gripping the edge of the wall—

Ch-ch-ch-ch.

A chittering sound, almost insect-like, emanated from the underbrush. Large, dark figures emerged from the shadows, swarming towards me in jerky motions. I screamed, holding on to the wall for dear life, but my fingers were slipping—

"Amanda!"

Two rough, strong hands grabbed my shoulders. In one motion, they yanked me back over the wall.

"What did I tell you?" Grandpa shouted. "Never go over the wall!"

"But there was a woman," I said, through sobs, "and she said—"

"No buts!" He dragged me back inside, and sat me down on the couch. "No matter what you heard—what you think you heard..." He propped my leg up on the ottoman. An angry red mark had appeared—the imprint of four long fingers and a thumb.

Fingers so long, they wrapped around the entire circumference of my ankle, and then some.

"Grandpa, what were those things?"

He didn't reply.

Instead, he slowly rolled up his pant leg.

There was a white, shining scar—

Of long fingers wrapped around his ankle.

PATTERNS IN THE BARK

By Blair Daniels

HAVE YOU EVER SEEN A BUNNY IN THE CLOUDS? OR A FACE on the moon? Or a creepy grin in that dried-up splatter of tomato sauce on the kitchen floor?

That's pareidolia.

Our brain sees faces in random patterns. Call it evolution, insanity, or whatever you like—but it's an instinct ingrained in all of us, from the very day we were born.

And that's exactly what happened when I found myself staring at a birch tree, waiting for Jake to finish up his lunch.

"Jake! Look!" I said, pointing to one of the black marks on the white trunk. "Doesn't that look just like an eye?"

"Not really."

"What? It's totally an eye! There's the pupil, and the eyelid—"

"Looks more like a bird to me," he said, through a

mouthful of tuna. "Or a bat. The wings, the round little body. Those points could even be fangs!" He grinned. "Maybe it's a vampire bat."

I rolled my eyes. "It's totally *not* a vampire bat."

See, that's the thing about pareidolia. Everyone sees something different; it's like a Rorschach test. While you see a cute kitty on your morning toast, your boyfriend sees the perfect likeness of Alice Cooper.

"I'm done," Jake said, crunching up the paper bag and throwing it in his backpack. "Let's go."

We continued to hike up the hill. The birch trees surrounded us, the pale trunks contrasting sharply with the yellow leaves of autumn. And the black eyes etched into the bark seemed to multiply, the deeper into the forest we got.

"Shouldn't we be heading back?" I asked, as I applied more bug spray. "It's nearly four—the sun's going to set soon."

"Aw, come on, don't be a party pooper. Just a little further." He took out the pamphlet, and fluttered it in my face. "I want to see this kickass waterfall."

But it took at least thirty minutes for us to find the waterfall. And when we did, we were both disappointed; the recent dry spell had reduced it to little more than a trickle. "It was worth it," Jake said, trying to convince himself more than me. "Totally worth it. It's beautiful, isn't it, Teresa?"

"Really beautiful," I replied, rolling my eyes behind his back.

After a tedious five minutes of taking photos, we finally turned around. My legs ached, and I scratched wildly at a bump on my arm; but at least we would be back soon. As we stumbled down the hill, the eyes seemed to watch our every move.

"Woah, wait a second," he said, stopping dead on the trail.

I groaned. "Jake, come on. We need to get home." It was nearly five-thirty, now, and the forest darkened with every passing minute.

"Look at that tree."

I looked up, and squinted in the shadows. Among the sea of white and black and orange, nothing looked amiss. "What are you talking about?" I said, glancing from tree to tree. "I don't see any—"

No.

There, a few feet off the trail, was a pure-white birch tree. All the black markings were gone: no eyes, no birds, no bats.

"Maybe it's like, an albino birch tree or something?" I said, ignoring the chill down my spine.

"Then how come we didn't see it on the way up?"

"I mean—I was looking at the ground most of the time. I didn't want to trip. There are so many rocks, and—"

My eyes flicked back to the trees, and I faltered.

Now *several* of the birch trees were white.

"Jake?"

We both gasped.

Before our eyes, the black markings wriggled and twitched. They scuttled down the trunks, across the forest floor.

Towards us.

"No, no, no," Jake whispered.

A low chittering burst through the darkness. The *crunch* of leaves, the *snap* of twigs, and a sickening clicking sound.

"Run!" I screamed.

But I already felt the prick of their legs on my ankles. The touch of their smooth, round bodies; the itch of their long antennae swishing against my calves.

We ran as fast as we could.

The chittering grew louder, into a shrill scream. *Don't turn around,* I thought, an intense itch flaring up my legs. *Just focus on running. Focus. Focus—*

Eeeeeeeee!

I turned around.

The insects—or whatever they were—had coalesced into a dark shape. Wriggling, writhing, twisting in the gray shadows of the forest. A shape with wobbly legs. A throbbing chest. A lumpy head.

A human shape.

Around us, the trees paled, as more of the things spilled out into the trail. "Just keep running," I huffed. *Just. Keep. Running.* But the image of them crawling up my legs, under my shorts, and all over my body, didn't budge.

"Are we almost there?" I shouted.

"I—I don't know!"

The trail was now a shifting, rippling mess of black. And the shape... it was growing larger by the second.

But then I remembered.

"Wait, Jake! The bugspray!"

I reached into my backpack, pulled out the aerosol can—

And aimed at the ground.

Pzzzzzzssshhh!

Shrill squeals in response. The black sea parted, and we ran for our lives.

It felt like hours had passed when we were finally out of the woods, huffing and puffing in the dying sunlight. "What were those things?" I said, collapsing against the hood of the car. "Beetles? Or…"

Jake shook his head. "Let's just get out of here."

We dove into the car. I thrust the keys into ignition.

And through the windshield, in the shadows of the forest, I could just make out the figure. As we pulled out, it turned its head—watching us.

I mean, it didn't *really* look like a person.

But pareidolia is a powerful thing.

THE FOREST: A VIDEO GAME

By Blair Daniels

"CAN WE PLAY A GAME?"

"Which one? Minecraft, or—"

"The one we got at the garage sale."

Oh. That game. The one with the badly-drawn trees on the cover, that was hanging out in the FREE bin at the end of the sale.

But a boring game is better than one of Peter's tantrums, so I popped the CD in.

And waited.

And waited, and waited, and waited.

Finally, the scene loaded—but it wasn't pretty. We were standing in the middle of what appeared to be a forest. The trees, which were identical clones of each other, had leaves that stuck together in big, stiff clumps. A low-resolution dirt texture was mapped to the ground, and the render distance was terrible—beyond a few steps, it was all just black.

And then the webcam light went on.

Was this some kind of virtual reality game, where it was recording our movements, or something? Either way, I didn't really want the camera recording us, and—

Suddenly, it blinked off.

I shrugged, and turned to Peter. "Where should we go first?"

"Right! Right!"

I jiggled the mouse, so we were facing right, and pressed W.

We walked through the virtual forest. But as the minutes went by, everything stayed the same. The same weird trees, the same dirt, even the same rocks—two small ones and a big one, flitting by every ten seconds. I was just starting to get bored, when the dirt fell away, and the world beyond was pitch black.

"Whoops! The game broke, buddy."

"No, it didn't!" he said, grabbing the laptop from me. He marched the character forward, and as the trees faded back into view, I realized we had just been standing on top of a really big hill.

"Hey, it's like the woods behind our house. You know, when we go down the hill, and then there's the stream and the boulder?"

"You mean the butt rock?"

"Peter, don't call it that. That boulder has been there for hundreds of years; it's a relic that reminds us of how time is fleeting, and—"

"But it looks like a butt."

I groaned, and took the computer back.

I could only see a few steps ahead of me as I stumbled down the hill. But slowly, the trees started to thin a bit, and the ground began to level out.

And then I saw it.

A stream, snaking across my path.

And behind it—

The vague outline of something large and round.

I mashed down on the W key. The scene bounced as my character jogged toward. Peter was squealing with delight, but I wasn't listening. Because I knew.

I stopped, and there it was: a large boulder, with a huge crack running down the middle.

The butt rock.

My heart started to pound. The mouse slipped under my fingertips.

"How'd it do that? So cool!" Peter said, grinning from ear to ear.

I circled around it, just to be sure. But it was identical to the boulder in our backyard, down to the very last pixelated lichen. I walked around it again, and again, until I was dizzy. It must be coincidence, right? There was no way—

"What's that?" Peter asked.

"What's what?" I said, trying to hide the quaver in my voice.

"That dark thing."

"That's the crack in the rock."

"No, the thing sticking out of the crack."

He was right; there was something sticking out of the crack, small and dark, near the forest floor. I walked closer to the boulder and panned the camera down.

Stubby things, stained dark red.

It couldn't be, but they looked just like…

Toes.

Snap. I closed the laptop, and jumped out of my seat.

"No! I want to keep playing!" He clung to my arm. "Please?"

"This game isn't appropriate—"

He started screaming. "You never let me play anything fun! Never ever ever!" He got up and stomped on the floor. "Let me play!"

"Peter, this isn't—"

"Let me play!"

I slowly opened the laptop, and held up my hands in surrender. "Okay, okay." I grabbed the mouse, turned the character around, and started in the opposite direction. Back up the hill, back into the ugly, uniform forest.

Except, this time, it wasn't so uniform.

The trees grew thin. The ground faded from dirt to grass. The rocks grew smaller and smaller.

And the distance wasn't black anymore.

There was light, golden and bright, shining through the trees.

My heart sank. I pounded the W key, running closer, hoping it wasn't what I thought it was…

A house came into view. A small colonial, tan with green shutters, with a fire pit on the patio, and a toy truck in the grass… All rendered into pixelated, blocky forms.

I crept towards the window. Slowly, shapes faded into

view from behind the virtual glass. A person, seated at a table, next to a smaller figure—a little boy...

"Dad?" Peter's eyes were no longer on the computer screen.

"Who's that in the window?"

BOTTOMLESS PIT

By Blair Daniels

"Are we there yet?"

My legs burned. My bites itched. Cory had promised an interesting hike, but so far, the most interesting thing I had seen was a woman wearing sunglasses in the shade. Oh, and a squirrel falling out of a tree. So I was about to abandon them—take my chances with the bears and the moose and whatever the hell else was out here—when Cory replied:

"We're here."

"Finally," I groaned. "This better be good, because—"

My breath caught in my throat.

We were standing on the cusp of a huge pit. A thin fence circled it, covered with signs that read DANGER and NO TRESPASSING. Vegetation crept up to the edge and spilled over into the darkness, like some kind of grassy waterfall. And an unfortunate tree grew at the edge, its exposed roots stretching towards the bottom.

If there even was a bottom.

"What is it? A sinkhole?"

"Beats me," he replied, pacing around the fence. "All I know is, locals call it the Pit of Endless Darkness."

"Oooooh, so spooky," Kat mocked.

"How deep does it go?" I asked.

"Who knows?" Kat shrugged. "And who cares?"

Cory got out his phone. "If we throw something in, I can time how long it takes to reach the bottom. And then, using kinematics, we can calculate—"

"You're such a nerd, Cory," she said, rolling her eyes.

"No, let's do it," I said, reaching into my pocket. I pulled out a water bottle, and chucked it. With a soft rush, it fell down into the pit.

Kat leaned against the fence, peering down into the darkness.

But she leaned a little too far.

Snap!

The fence gave way.

Kate tumbled forward—arms outstretched, face frozen in surprise.

And then she screamed.

And screamed, and screamed, and screamed.

Cory and I lunged forward. But it was too late—her scream was echoing up the pit, fading with every second.

And then silence.

No *smack*, no *clunk*, no *thud*. Just the chittering of the birds above, and the rush of the soft breeze.

"Kat!" I yelled, trembling.

179

"No," Cory said, his voice cut with sobs. "No, no, no! Kat!"

I stumbled away from the fence and collapsed in the soft grass, sobbing. I pulled out my phone, started to dial 911; but I knew, deep down, there was no saving her.

But then I heard it.

A noise—

Shrill, high-pitched, reverberating through the trees about a dozen yards away.

Cory and I stared at each other.

And then we ran as fast as we could, the branches snapping beneath our feet. "Kat!" we yelled, as the sound grew louder. "Kat !"

There she was.

Lying on the ground, caked with dirt and dust, facing away from us.

As we approached, she tilted her head up towards the sky. "I'm okay!" she called up, her hands cupped around her mouth. "Cory, Jen, I'm okay! I'm at the bottom!"

"Kat?" Cory asked, stepping towards her carefully.

"Yes! I'm okay!" she yelled, her face still tilted towards the sky. Then she stretched her arms out, groping at the dirt. "Dammit, I can't see a thing. So dark down here."

"Kat—"

Wobbling, she pulled herself up.

Then she turned in our direction.

Cory stumbled back.

"No," I choked out.

Her eyes—

They were completely gone.

THE LIGHTS IN THE WOODS

By Blair Daniels

OUR TRIP TO VERMONT WAS *NOT* GOING AS PLANNED.

Instead of spending the night in a quaint little bed-and-breakfast, like I'd hoped, we were sleeping in the car. On a desolate road in the middle of East Jabib. On one of the coldest nights of the year.

"I just didn't think—"

"That hotels would be booked solid on the Saturday after Christmas?" I snapped.

"Nicole, come on. This was supposed to be fun."

No, you idiot. This was supposed to be a last-ditch attempt to save our marriage.

"Look, we'll sleep here in the car, and in the morning we'll get one of those mushroom omelets you like at the diner in town." He leaned the seat back, hitting me squarely in the elbow. "Goodnight, Nicole. I love you."

I mumbled a response. Then I lay across the backseat, pulled the covers over me, and stared out the window.

If I wasn't so mad at him, I might've enjoyed it. We were parked on a narrow road, smack-dab in the middle of nowhere, surrounded by forest and the stars. In the distance, five amber lights glowed, all in a line—probably streetlights from the town.

No, wait—

There weren't five.

There were six.

Huh, that's odd. I could've sworn there were only five.

I shrugged, lay my head on the armrest, and closed my eyes.

I JOLTED AWAKE.

The crick in my neck ached. The car was freezing cold. All was quiet, save for the sporadic hoots of an owl and Brandon's snores.

Oh, sure, *he* was sleeping peacefully.

I glanced out the window. It was totally dark outside; the amber lights had been turned off. *That's weird. Usually streetlights stay on—don't they?* I thought. *Or maybe sometimes they go off... oh, I don't know.* I reached for my water bottle, in the cup holder up front.

Huh?

Through the windshield, there they were—the seven amber lights, shining even more brightly than before.

I glanced back to my window. Pitch black. To the

182

windshield. Lights on. Back and forth, over and over, but it was clear. The lights were on.

But then—

Why couldn't I see them through my window?

I leaned in close. No—there was *some* light coming in, through the top and upper corners of the window. But the middle was still black—a dark silhouette, that looked kind of like…

A person?

No, there was no way.

But then I blinked—

And it moved.

I jumped back. "Brandon!"

He snorted, and mumbled "what?"

"There's someone out there!"

"Probably just a raccoon…"

"No, Brandon, this is serious! Turn on the car!"

"Okay, okay, easy!" I heard the click of the keys, the rumble of the engine. The headlights blinked on, flashing the forest with white light. I pointed to the window. "Brandon, look, someone is—"

"I don't see anything."

I turned to the window, ready to shout him down—

Nobody was there.

I began to laugh—a nervous laugh of relief. "Oh, I can't believe that. I actually thought someone was standing at the window, staring in. I must have been dreaming! Oh, what a…"

The car lurched forward.

"Uh, Brandon? What are you doing?"

"We've got to get out of here," he said, his voice shaking.

"What are you talking about?"

"Look at the window, Nicole!" he yelled.

There, in the middle of the window, was a patch of fog.

Not on the rest of the glass. Just in one, small, circular area.

Almost as if—

Someone had fogged it up with their breath.

"No, no, no..." Shaking, I climbed into the passenger seat.

We shot down the dark road. The shadows rolled across the trees, across the deep footprints in the snow. And the amber lights seemed brighter, closer—were we driving towards them? There were more of them, too... at least a dozen.

"Don't worry," Brandon said. "Whoever's out there— I'll protect you."

The anger bubbled up. And suddenly, the reason I couldn't stand him anymore—the reason our marriage was failing, that I had buried deep inside myself—shot out. "You'll protect me? Like you protected me on 4th Avenue?"

"Are you still mad about that?"

"Of course I'm still mad about it. You ran, Brandon. There was a gun against my ribs—I thought I was going to die—and you. Ran. Away."

"I was getting help."

"And what if he shot me, huh? You would've just let me bleed out on the sidewalk, alone?" There were at least twenty of the lights now—some so bright, they looked as if they'd cross the forest's threshold any second.

But if they were streetlamps...

How come I didn't see any roads?

"But he didn't shoot. And he wasn't going to." Brandon took a deep breath in through his nostrils. "You know, it was your fault for wearing one of those expensive Kate-whatever purses! That's the whole reason he targeted us!"

"Really, Brandon? You're going to blame *me* for being mugged?! You were a coward, and you know it!"

"I wasn't a coward, I was just being logical—"

The car screeched to a stop.

A branch lay straight across the road. Or—it was more like a small tree, that someone had ripped straight out of the ground.

My heart stopped. "They blocked us in?!"

Brandon jerked the steering wheel, and started to turn the car around—

No.

Two people had come out of the forest, and were standing behind the car. Each one was holding a pole, and at the top there was something orange, light, flickering—

"Are those... jack o'lanterns?" Brandon said.

To call them jack o'lanterns was an understatement. Atop the poles were fleshy orange things, carved with faces, but they were far scarier than any jack o'lanterns I had ever seen. One had the face of a man, contorted in pain, mouth wide open in a scream. The other was even worse: a grinning woman, with pointed teeth and flickering yellow eyes.

They weren't streetlamps at all.

The two figures marched forward, towards the car. As I glanced at the forest, I saw more of the amber lights coming towards us, shining through the tangled trees. Several... dozens... no, many more than that. Some far away, just orange dots among the murky shadows; others right upon us, floating over the asphalt. And some dark figures, slithering through the underbrush, not holding a lantern of any sort.

"Just drive over it!"

"No. We'll get a flat. Then we'll really be stuck." He unclicked his seatbelt. "I'm going out there."

"Are you insane?!" I screamed. The low hum of a chant came through the windows, muffled and low. "There are dozens—maybe hundreds—"

"I got to prove to you I'm not a coward, though," he said, with a sad smile.

"Brandon, no—"

Slam.

He stepped out into the darkness. As soon as he did, the figures froze. They seemed to stare at him, heads tilting towards him, though I couldn't make out their faces in the dim light.

He grabbed the base of the branch, and tugged on it with all his might. It slid towards him, opening up a small spot of road.

That's when something like a shiver rippled through the crowd. And then, all at once, they started racing towards him.

"No," I screamed, pounding the glass.

"Go!" Brandon yelled. They were closing in—just a few feet from him, now. "Drive!"

I shook my head.

"Nicole, please!" One of the men grabbed him by the shoulders, and pulled him towards the darkness. A few more paced towards the car, their jack o'lanterns floating inches from the window.

No—not jack o'lanterns.

Or, at least—

Not the kind made out of pumpkins.

"Drive!" Brandon screamed, as they pulled him into the forest.

I jumped into the driver's seat, and put my foot to the floor.

WE BURIED AN EMPTY CASKET.

They never found the body. And sometimes I think it's better that way. Something tells me that the body wouldn't have been... recognizable. And seeing the man I love, broken up like that, would break my heart all over again.

And if he's still alive...

Well, that means he became one of them.

And that's even worse.

So, please, take it from me. If you're driving on a desolate, wooded road, and you see some orange lights through the trees—

Say a prayer for Brandon Wright.

Then get the hell out of there.

BLIZZARD WARNING

By Blair Daniels

"THE STORM IS GETTING WORSE. DO NOT GO OUTSIDE under any circumstances. If you need assistance, dial 911."

I plopped down on the couch with a bottle of wine. "We certainly picked the right time for a honeymoon, huh? We're going to be snowed in for days."

"I don't mind," Daniel said, with a wink.

I rolled my eyes. "No, seriously! I picked this cabin for the view. Pines for miles, with herds of deer and wild turkey. Now it's just—this." I gestured to the window. It was all white, save for the fuzzy gray outline of a few trees.

"Come on, it'll be a funny story to tell our—"

Crack.

A sharp crackle of static on the radio, followed by the announcer's hurried voice—

"Close all curtains and blinds. I repeat, close all curtains and blinds."

I shot a glance at Daniel. He shrugged back.

"If you have any windows without blinds—including cellar windows, glass insets on front doors, and mail slots —cover them with a sheet."

"That's weird."

"I bet it's because of snow blindness," Daniel said, pouring himself a glass. "You know, they don't want anyone looking out their window, and getting blinded by the sun reflecting off the snow." He stood up, and slowly lowered the blinds, until we were left in shadowy darkness.

"I'll turn on the lights," I said, flicking the switch.

Click.

Darkness.

"The power's out?! No wonder it's so cold in here! And how are we supposed to watch *Game of Thrones?* Or charge our phones? Or—"

"Rebecca, it's okay. Here, sit, and drink the rest of your wine. I'm going to find some matches; then I'm going to chuck that stupid radio out into the snow, and we're going to sit in front of a roaring fire. Okay?"

"Okay, fine."

He disappeared into the kitchen.

The light through the blinds was fading now, and the room was steadily getting colder. The wooden bear in the corner—that I thought was cute and rustic—now looked like some sort of monster. And the antlers hanging from the walls looked no better than sharpened spikes, ready to impale anyone who dared to walk by. "Hurry back," I called, pulling the blanket up to my neck. "It's cold without you here."

"One final warning." The announcer's voice came over the radio, muddied with static. "Do not go outside—do not open the door—no matter what you hear. And don't—"

Static.

I grabbed the radio, shook it, and sighed. "The reception's gone!"

"Good!" he called back. "And I think I found some matches!"

I clicked the dial forward.

A cheery voice came on, clear as day.

"We are handing out free supplies at the edge of the forest on Maple Street. Bottled water, canned food, blankets, and battery packs."

Daniel rushed back in with the matches, looking confused. "Wait—I thought they said—"

I turned up the volume.

"Come out and get yours as soon as you can. There is limited supply."

The firelight flickered across the cabin. The shadows jittered and jumped, as if they were alive. The chill settled in, and I pulled the blanket tightly around me.

"So every phone number goes to voicemail. Including my mom's, and she always wants to talk to me." I swirled the dregs of wine in my glass. "And there's no mention of anything on the news. Where does that leave us?"

"Stranded?" Daniel said, with a dry laugh. "Dead?"

"Daniel!"

"Kidding, kidding! Here, let me see if I can find anything online about it." He pulled out his phone. The blue glow contrasted sharply with the fire. "Instead of looking on news sites, I'm going to just Google with wild abandon. Let's see... 'Minnesota'... 'radio broadcast'... 'put sheets over windows'... ugh, page loading, we're down to 3G."

The fire crackled and hissed.

"Aha!" he said, thrusting the phone in my face. I took it and began to read.

QUEENOFTHENORTH89

Hey, anybody in C___, Minnesota? We just got a really weird radio broadcast. They told us to lock up and shut our blinds, but now other broadcasts are saying to come out and get supplies on Maple Street. Anyone know what this is about?

CrazyCatGuy

The second one's fake. It's been playing on repeat, on every local station in range, for the past six hours.

EXCALIBRRR

Guys, I did a lot of research, and a similar thing happened back in the '70s. YOU WILL BE OKAY, if you follow these rules:

Don't look at them. Don't let them see you.

Even if you're camping in a tent, or sleeping in your

car, you can survive. Just be sure to cover any windows and apertures with something opaque.

Keep all pets (and other animals, even livestock) inside. Don't put out the garbage. Don't light a fire. They can smell the smoke from miles away.

DANIEL and I looked at each other.

And then at the roaring fire.

THUD.

I jolted awake.

The blanket was tangled around my feet. My neck ached, and my hands were cold as ice. The cabin was pitch-black now, save for the dying embers in the fireplace.

"Daniel?"

He only snored in response.

"Daniel!"

"What? "

Thud.

"Did you hear that?"

"Probably just a branch, or something. Don't worry about it."

Thud! Thud, thud, thud!

The thuds echoed across the cabin, coming from every direction—even the roof. Daniel jolted awake, threw on his glasses, and sprung off the sofa.

"What the hell—"

Thump! Thump!

A sharp knock at the door.

"Hey, open up!"

A man's voice, loud and clear through the silence of the blizzard, coming from the other side of the front door.

"Police! Open up!"

Daniel stood up, and hesitantly stepped towards the door.

"What are you doing?!" I hissed.

"It's the police, Rebecca."

"It's a trap!" I leapt up and chased after him, as he slowly walked down the hall—away from the fire, away from the warmth. "They said don't open the door for any reason, remember?!"

He stood in front of the door, frozen.

A shadow fell across the sheet we had pinned up. At a first glance, it looked like the silhouette of a normal person—a normal policeman. But the longer I stared at it, the stranger it looked. The neck was just a hair too short, the legs too long; and the head was cocked at an unnatural angle.

"Police! Open up!"

"We have to let him in," Daniel said, staring at the covered window.

Staring, staring...

At the corner of the window, where part of the sheet had come undone.

I darted in front of him. "Do not open that door! It's not the police! It's them—whatever they are!"

"Rebecca, it's the police!"

He darted his hand under my arm, past my waist—

And yanked the door open.

"No!" I screamed.

For a moment, time froze.

The silence of the blizzard filled the cabin. Wayward flakes floated in, landing softly on the wooden floor. Daniel stood still as a statue, right on the threshold, gazing into the storm.

He let them in.

There's no coming back from this, no way to save us now. We're going to die, right here, before our marriage has even begun.

But then I had an idea.

I leapt up, and in one, violent motion—

Smacked the glasses right off his face.

Clack.

As the glasses fell from his face, the scales fell from his eyes. His expression turned from apathy to terror. He grabbed the edge of the door, and with all his might, pushed it shut.

Or tried to.

"Shut it! Shut it!" I screamed.

"I can't!" he yelled. "It's pushing back! I'm not strong enough—

Crash!

The sound of breaking glass, from deep inside the cabin.

"It's too late!" I screamed, tugging at his arm. "They're inside!"

"Close your eyes!" he yelled.

"What are you doing?!"

"Just trust me!"

Creeaaak! Thump, thump, thump!

I heard the door fly open—and the sound of rapid, heavy footsteps.

Daniel grabbed my wrist and yanked me forward. I felt the wooden bear poke at me, the antlers scrape against me.

Ting, ting.

The jingle of keys.

And then I was yanked out into the cold. The flakes stung my face, my ankles burned in the snow. I stumbled through it, crying and terrified, but pushed forward, until I felt the familiar leather seats under my hands.

"I got you," Daniel said, hoisting me into the car.

Slam.

The engine rumbled underneath me. The car jerked forward, and then swerved unto the road. "Good thing we have four-wheel-drive," he said. "Oh, and you can open your eyes now."

"But—won't I see them?"

"I don't see any on the road," he said.

I opened my eyes.

The scene wasn't much different from the dark of my eyelids, save for the headlights. Black trees flanked the road, stretching up towards the starless sky. A myriad of snowflakes glittered in the light, hovering in the branches, as if miraculously suspended in mid-air. No—not snowflakes.

Eyes. Hundreds of eyes, watching us from the treetops.

Thump. Thump.

Shadows dropped from the trees, like raindrops falling

from the sky. The car lurched forward, flying over the blanket of snow.

"They're in the road!" I screamed.

"What? Where?!"

"Everywhere! Can't you see them?!"

"Of course I can't see them! I can barely even see where we're going! You took my glasses, remember?!"

The shadows came closer, flitting into the headlights' beams. I closed my eyes tightly shut. *We're safe, I thought. We're in a car. Protected by layers of glass and steel.* Even that Excalibur guy on the internet said you're safe in a car.

The car swerved again.

But that's if they haven't already seen you.

The car swerved violently. My head glanced off the window. The engine roared, as Daniel muttered under his breath, "come on, come on..."

"Why are we slowing down?!"

"I don't know!" Daniel said, his voice starting to quaver. "Everything's working fine. I don't think the snow is deep enough to stop us—"

Rrrrr-rrr-rrrr!—the sound of wheels, spinning against the snow.

"I think *they're* stopping us."

Even with my eyes closed, I could feel them. Their eyes, that glittered in the headlights like the freshly-fallen snow. Their silhouettes, that were little more than shadows, or wisps of smoke. And—after they killed us—their new forms, shaped into eerie, uncanny versions of us.

Tap-tap-tap.

They were at the glass, now. How long did we have

until they broke through, just like they did in the cabin? Minutes? Seconds?

The wheels stopped spinning. *Click.* Daniel shifted into park.

"What are you doing?"

"I have an idea."

I opened my eyes, shielding my gaze from the forest with my hand. Daniel reached into his pocket, and pulled out the book of matches.

Fzzzssshhh.

He struck the match. The flame fizzled and glowed, and small wisps of black smoke floated towards the ceiling.

"Wait—isn't that going to attract more of them?"

"Exactly," he whispered.

No.

My heart began to pound.

I trusted him. I let him pull me across the snow. Pull me into the car. Pull me to my death, trapped here as they closed in.

The man sitting with me, here in the car...

It wasn't Daniel.

It was one of *them.*

"What did you do to Daniel?! You killed him, didn't you?!"

"What are you talking about?!"

"You're leading them right to us! You said so yourself!"

"Not leading them to us! Leading them to this." He took a piece of paper from the glove box, crumpled it, and held it to the match. The flames crawled over it, curling the edges of the paper. "I'm going to throw this out the window. Hopefully they'll follow it."

"...Oh." I shook my head. "Wait, that makes no sense. Won't the wind extinguish it?"

"You got a better idea?"

The metal groaned and screeched, as they worked to pull it apart. The *tap-tap-taps* echoed across the glass, like the ticks of a clock.

He rolled down the window. In my peripheral vision, I saw the orange ball piercing the darkness; heard the movements of the creatures, thumping over the car, over the snow—

Eeeeeeeeeeeee!

A shrill screech.

And, involuntarily—I looked up. The figures weren't running towards the fire. They were running away.

In seconds, the silence of the forest returned. Snow slowly drifted to the ground. The trees were still as statues. And the branches above were dark—no glittering, white eyes.

"They're afraid of fire," was all he could choke out.

After holding him for what felt like an eternity, I realized how little sense that made. "But wait. That Excalibur guy on the message board said that they were attracted to fire—attracted to the smoke. Why would he say that?"

"I guess he didn't know. Or—" My voice faltered as the realization sunk in, "—maybe he saw one of them. Maybe he was speaking for them."

"But then why would he tell everyone to stay inside and cover their windows, too?"

"Maybe being trapped inside our houses, waiting out the storm, is exactly what they wanted."

Daniel looked at me, his eyes wide in the darkness. "What are you saying?"

"I'm saying that maybe... the second radio message was the one we should have believed."

We raced back to the car. I thrust the keys into ignition, and the car rumbled to life.

"We're going to Maple Street."

WHEN WE TURNED onto Maple Street, a strange sight greeted us.

A small house sat on the edge of the forest. It was surrounded by dozens of small fires, their trails of smoke merging into one large pillar that reached up towards the sky. Several people stood in the yard, and a few started pointing to us as we approached.

As we entered, a black-haired woman ran over to us. "Stand over here to the side, please. We need to test you first." She picked up her handheld radio. "Two more just arrived, Mark."

"Test us?"

"We need to make sure you aren't compromised, ma'am."

We awkwardly stood in the yard, the fire hot against our backs. "Maybe this was a bad idea," Daniel whispered. "Are we sure that—"

"Hey there!" A burly man walked over to us, wearing an ill-fitting flannel shirt with a rip across the chest. He slipped a flashlight out of his pocket, shined it in our eyes, and then called over: "Hey, Nancy, they're good!"

She motioned for us to come inside. "Make yourselves at home. Eat some dinner, take supplies—we have plenty. Not many have come by... we were too late in intercepting the alert, it seems."

"What are they? In the forest?" Daniel asked.

"Are we safe here?" I added.

She didn't reply. Instead, she led us to a table of sandwiches, and hurried away.

Daniel and I took food and joined one of the emptier tables. Across from us sat a teenager, chin resting on her hand, pushing the coleslaw on her plate in circles.

"Why won't they tell us anything?" I said to Daniel, my voice low.

"And how did they set this up so fast?" Daniel said. "Firewood, an external generator for power, tons of food —it's almost like this has happened before, and they were ready."

"It did happen before."

We looked up. The teenager was staring at us, smiling like a child divulging a secret. "My dad told me it happened back in the seventies, and they've been prepared ever since."

"That's what that Excalibur guy on the internet said," Daniel said. "I guess there was *some* truth in his words."

I nodded. "So—uh—what *are* they?" I asked, a little too loudly. From across the hall, Mark shot us a disapproving look.

"I've heard the name 'ice shadows' thrown around," she replied, shrugging. "But who knows what they really are?

Shape-shifters, phantoms, demons... We had one outside our bedroom window, talking in my mom's voice, telling Dad she wanted to get back together. Saved him in a nick of time."

"What I don't understand," Daniel started, "is why the first alert told us to cover our windows. Don't they *want* us to see them?"

"Oh, that's because of the sunlight. It burns them right up, just like the fires do. Same reason they come out in the blizzard." She lowered her voice further, and glanced around the room. "They want to be safe in your house. Because after... they want to live in it. Breed in it. Make it their own little den. And then do it to the next house, and the next, until they've taken over the entire town—"

"Kendra, that's enough." Mark clapped a hand on her shoulder. "She likes to tell tall tales, this one. Sorry if it caused you any trouble."

"Dad! Were you *eavesdropping?!*" She sighed, and rose from the seat.

Mark removed his hand. The shirt shifted, and the rip pulled open, exposing some of his chest.

Underneath it was a tattoo.

A tattoo of a sword, stuck in stone.

Of Excalibur.

No way. As they made their way from the table, I turned to Daniel. "He's one of them."

"What are you talking about?"

"He's the Excalibur guy! The guy who said they're attracted to fire, who *lied* on that message board. Didn't you see the tattoo?"

"But he can't be one of the ice shadows. We're surrounded by fire."

"He isn't. He's just under the influence of one." I stood up, and scanned the room. Wait—

Where had he gone? Kendra was standing by the food table—arms crossed, leaning against the wall. But she was alone, and there was no trace of dear old Dad.

"Kendra! Where's your dad?" I said, running up to her.

"No idea.

"This is really important—"

"We think he may be compromised," Daniel said, immediately.

"What?! No. Absolutely not." The anger flared, and her voice grew to a shout. "I saved him. He was going to look out the window, but I stopped him! Just in time!"

I opened my mouth to respond—but movement from the window caught my eye.

Outside, the orange glow had faded. Where fires once stood, there were only dark shadows of ash. Over one of the remaining fires hovered a figure, holding something large and metal.

A bucket.

Hisssss!

Water splashed over the fire. It sputtered, sparked, and faded to nothing.

And then the shadows at the forest's edge began to close in. Shifting and swirling, racing to the house. One leapt forward, mouth stretching larger and larger by the second—

"They're coming!" I shouted. "He put out the fires! They're coming!"

In one swooping motion, it engulfed Mark in black smoke.

As quickly as it happened, the smoke dissipated. Mark stood stiffly by the fire, his head hanging to one side. Then he began walking towards the house, his feet moving mechanically across the snow. They bounded after him, following him, their faces—

Daniel yanked the curtains shut.

The silence of the house grew into a roar of chaos. Footsteps thundered, plates crashed, people screamed.

And a strangely familiar sound joined the din—

Tap, tap, tap.

They were here.

And we were in chaos. Running, shoving, screaming. We were all going to die here, in this hut, if someone didn't take the lead...

"Follow me!" I shouted.

I raced to the basement door. The thumps of footsteps followed me, shaking the staircase.

The damp air blew over our faces, dusty and stale. *Click.* A lightbulb flicked on overhead, and we were all bathed in a dim, yellow glow.

"What's the plan?" Daniel said to me.

"We'll wait here until morning," I said, hanging my sweater over the tiny window. "The storm will be gone, and the sun will be out."

"Yeah, unless they get to us before then," Kendra interjected, her voice oddly monotonous. And why was her head tilted like that? "You saw what they did to Dad."

"Trust me," I said. "This will work. I promise."

But now others had overheard, and panic rippled

across the room. "Tha' woman is right," someone called out from the gray shadows of the basement. "If they get in upstairs, they'll easily break down this ol' door. And then, we're trapped here, like pigs ready for slaughter."

"They won't break down the door. They can break through glass, sure—but not a solid wooden door."

"Rebecca, if they can stop a car," Daniel whispered, his face hidden in the shadows, "don't you think they can break down a door?"

Another voice jumped in, coming from the silhouette of an old woman. Her back was strangely crooked, and her eyes glittered in the dim light. "We're sitting ducks. We need to go back upstairs!"

"Yes! We have to go back upstairs—"

"Absolutely!"

No.

They must have seen the shadows.

All of them.

"We need to stay here! It's the only place we're safe!" I screamed. "Don't you get it?!"

A silence filled the room.

Then Kendra lifted her arm—

And pointed straight at me.

"She saw them, didn't she?"

Daniel stared at me—tears welling in his eyes, glinting off the dim light. "I thought I pulled the curtain in time. But I—I must've been too late."

Someone grabbed my arms. Another thrust my face under the light. Kendra bent over me, her face contorted in a frown.

"Her pupils aren't contracting with the light."

I pulled and wriggled. "I'm just trying to help! To save you all! Let me go!"

Click. The door opened, and I was carried up the staircase. "Wait—where are you taking her?!" Daniel yelled behind me. "You can't do this! There's a way to break the trance, isn't there? She did it with me! Took off my glasses, and—"

"Sure, if you wanna cut out her eyes so she ain't seein' no more," the man holding me spat.

"Daniel! Don't let them take me! Please—"

Thump.

MY EYES FLUTTERED OPEN.

Pitch black.

No. Those men must've thrown me in the forest. And I'm here, in the darkness, with the ice shadows. My heart started to race. *Am I one of them, now? A flitting, demonic shadow, with glittering white eyes?*

No. Wait. The last thing I remember was someone talking about cutting my eyes out.

I began to panic. *I don't have eyes anymore. That's what they did—no, no, no—*

A sliver of light appeared. And the door creaked open.

"How are you feeling?"

"Daniel!" I tried to stand up, and failed.

"Sorry about that," he said. I looked down; thick rope wrapped around my body, tying me to the chair. "They were going to throw you outside the house, but I... uh...

persuaded them to lock you here instead." He rubbed his knuckles.

"Is everyone okay?"

"Yeah. Except for Kendra's dad." He bent down, and began working on the knots. "The sun came up a few hours ago, and it looks like the shadows are gone."

"But what about... everything—"

Kendra poked her head in. "The people want to talk to you," she said to Daniel. "Oh, Rebecca, you're okay!"

"I am," I said, smiling at her. "Wait—what people?"

"Some official-looking people. They drove in this morning, said they'll be 'cleansing' the area. I think that black-haired woman is one of them." The rope unraveled, and I stood. "Anyway, let's get you downstairs. We got bagels."

I held took his hand, and we made our way down to the kitchen.

LATER THAT AFTERNOON, we drove the six hours back home. We spent the rest of our honeymoon indoors—catching up on sleep, rest, and quality time. Life has been pretty uneventful since then, and we've been having a fantastic time.

Except that, sometimes, when I look out the window late at night I see two glittering eyes in the forest behind our house.

And I have the urge to open the door.

HOW TO RESURRECT A SISTER

By Blair Daniels

WARNING

If the ritual is not performed correctly, serious side effects may occur. For example, you might bring the body back, but not the soul.

Like Pet Sematary? I shuddered, lit the candles, and began to read.

"O, Name of Deceased—uh, Natalie Wysocki—hear my call."

The trees rattled; the shadows shook over the forest floor.

"Come out, from the depths of the dead."

With a strong gust of wind, several leaves blew across the dirt, and into the ravine.

"Come forward, into the land of the living."

Her death was my fault. I brought her out here. I just thought a hike would be a good distraction from our mother's recent death. But she ran ahead of me, peered into the ravine. And leaned over a little too far…

One of the candles blew out. I struck a match, and set it to the wick; it flickered, fluttered, and then went out again.

Now say, in your own words, a message to the deceased, imploring him or her to join you.

I had written down a million things that I wanted to say. But in the end, all of them were too formal, too stiff. So I cleared my throat, sat up straighter, and said what came to mind.

"Natalie, please come home. I love you. And I want you to know that I forgive you, for…"

For what? There were too many things to name. Stealing my Barbies at seven. Stealing my boyfriends at seventeen. Lying to our mom constantly, telling her everything was my fault. She was the kind of person that, when everyone told me she's in a better place…

I didn't quite believe them.

"Natalie, I forgive you for everything."

Everything—yes, even that.

When you visited Mom on her deathbed. Alone. And somehow convinced her to change the will. *No, Mom wanted it that way,* you said, when I accused you. *She always planned to cut you out, ever since you divorced Greg.*

"It took a long time, but I forgive you. Because above all, you're still my sister, Natalie. You held my hand through the toughest times—through my divorce from Greg, through Mom's death.

"You are mine, and I am yours."

The ceremony has ended, I read, from the glow of my

smartphone. *Wait for the deceased to find you, and make sure their body is free of spirit-inhibiting substances, such as salt and water...*

I didn't bother reading the rest. I stood up, blew out the candles, and waited.

Five minutes went by.

Then ten.

Then twenty.

That's when the tears started to fall. *If your loved one does not come to you within a half hour, it may mean too much time has passed since their death,* the text said, printed at the bottom. *If needed, please call a grief counselor at 1-800...*

I flung the phone into the dirt and began to sob.

But then I heard it.

A soft splash, from behind me.

From within the ravine.

"Natalie?"

Splash, splash.

It echoed up the rocks, off the trees. I scrambled to the edge. "Natalie!" I cried. "Is that you?"

Silence.

I retrieved the phone, and turned the flashlight on. The white light illuminated strands of grass and shards of rock, jutting out from the steep sides. The rest was in dark shadow. I shifted the flashlight, leaning over further, looking for something—anything—that seemed out of place.

But it was too dark.

I had to go down.

Turning my body, I lowered one foot onto a

protruding rock. I grabbed a thick root, caked with dirt, to my right. And, slowly, I began the descent.

It seemed like forever before I felt the cold water, the smooth rocks underneath my feet. I wiped my forehead, and shone the flashlight around me.

Yes.

There, standing in the stream, was a dark figure. A white dress hung off her bony figure, dirty and crumpled.

"Natalie!"

She didn't turn around.

"Natalie!" I ran towards her. The water splashed out around my feet, hitting me with cold spray. I flung my arms around her and began to sob.

She didn't hug back.

"I missed you so much," I choked.

She didn't reply.

"Natalie?" I pulled away.

She gave me an unblinking stare. "It's so cold down here," she said, her voice empty and hollow.

I took off my jacket and wrapped it around her. "I know. But we'll get you out of here, and get you warmed up back at home, okay?"

"Why did you do it?" she shouted. But her gaze was focused over my shoulder, somewhere slightly behind me. "It hurt so much."

"Natalie—I'm so sorry—but you're safe now. Come on, let's get you home."

"No, please!" she whimpered.

And then she broke away from me. She ran downstream, kicking up icy water behind her, wailing and moaning.

"Natalie!" I ran after her, slipping over the rocks. "Come back!"

But she didn't get far before she fell to her knees, right there in the middle of the stream. "No, please, it hurt so much," she cried, her face tilted up towards the sky. "Don't put the fire on me, please, I beg of you—"

A gut-wrenching scream. She convulsed and spasmed in the water. I ran over, throwing my arms around her—

But I jumped back, with a yelp of pain.

Her body was hot.

Scalding hot.

Tendrils of steam rose up from the water. She thrashed and convulsed, shrieked and screamed. I was sobbing, crying her name—

"Demon!" she screamed. "Get away from me!"

And then I realized.

You might bring the body back, but not the soul.

Her soul wasn't here.

It was in Hell.

Splash!

And then she was still. Quiet. Cold. I collapsed in the water beside her. "I'm so, so sorry," I said, tears rolling off my cheeks and dropping onto hers.

She didn't blink.

I pulled her slowly out of the stream, and onto the dry shore. I smoothed my jacket over her, and cradled her head in my lap.

And then, on top of the pain, a terrible fear settled in me.

Because I knew, whatever hell Natalie was in...

Was the same place I'd end up.

"When you told me about the will…" The tears fell hot and fast. "I knew I'd never be able to pay off my debt. Never give Brady the life he deserved."

Come over here, Natalie! Look!

Oh, wow!

Can you see the stream at the bottom?

Yeah, I think—

Thud.

My hands collided with her back.

Thud.

She hit the floor of the ravine.

Thud.

My feet hit the dirt, as I ran as fast as I could.

"I was just so mad." I rocked her slowly in my arms. "I didn't think it through. I didn't realize… life without you would be so hard. I didn't know I'd miss you so much."

I let out a shuddering breath.

"I didn't know how much I loved you."

The stream gurgled. A soft breeze blew through the forest, rustling the trees high above. We both lay there, on the river bank, still and cold as the water dried off of our clothes.

And then she blinked.

Looked up at me, with those beautiful blue eyes.

"Natalie?"

She broke into a smile.

"I'm so, so sorry—please, I—"

She pulled me into a tight hug.

"I've already forgiven you, a long time ago."

THE LITTLE MAN

By Gemma Amor

"So," said Louise, rubbing her hands together in glee and taking a deep drag on a rolled-up cigarette.

"Anyone got any scary stories?"

It was late on a summer's evening. In England, this means that it's warm enough to be outside if you're armed with booze and a big padded jacket. It was August, but this was no guarantee of balmy weather. The only thing guaranteed about English weather was that you would always be dressed inappropriately for it.

Eight people sat around a campfire, myself amongst them. We'd been outside all day walking, and our faces had that rich red glow, the glow of exposure to wind and sun, heightened by our proximity to the fire and the beer we'd been drinking since sundown.

Louise exhaled in anticipation, her thin knees jigging up and down with the cold. She hadn't eaten a lot throughout the day, but then she didn't eat a lot on most days. Unless you counted the fifteen cups of coffee she got through, each one brewed until it was as stiff as tar, strong enough to stand a spoon in and accompanied by a rollie. No wonder the woman never sat still. Her insides were probably black as night, coated in an egregiously thick layer of sticky, midnight goo. I shuddered, thinking about it.

The rest of us groaned, although secretly I was delighted by the suggestion. I love scary stories, and within seconds of the idea being mooted, I was transported back to my childhood when, as a girl guide, I'd stay up late on camping trips. Torch held under my chin as prescribed by that unspoken law of telling scary stories, I'd regale the most disgusting, twisted and sordid tales I could think of to my fellow tent-mates. In those days we camped in large canvas ridge-pole tents, the sort where the guy ropes had to be at perfect ninety degree angles to the roof ridge, or the heavy u-frame would topple and collapse, with you inside. The shadows you could make with a torch against the canvas walls around you were truly ghoulish, and I found that I was good at scaring people.

"I like the one about the disembodied hand!" a woman shouted after a few moments of indecision, as we all battled against our repressed eleven-year-old selves. I looked across the fire to see June, waving her arms about in excitement.

"Never heard of it," someone else muttered, but I nodded encouragingly.

"I have," I said. "It's a good one."

June suddenly realized that she was now responsible for telling the story, and clammed up. Between you and me, she wasn't the sharpest tool in the box, and she probably wouldn't have understood what that meant had I said that to her face. She was artless, pretty and almost devoid of personality, but that suited the rest of us just fine. She was a welcome respite, a pocket of calm in a circle of larger than life characters.

I looked around at all the faces gathered, faces that shifted continuously as the shadows of flames licked across their features, and wondered, honestly, why we kept having these reunions. Every year it was the same: a flurry of emails and texts, a last minute decision, finding space at whichever campsite wasn't already booked. The arrival, the hugs, the jollity, the sizing each other up after a year of not seeing each other.

We enjoyed the first few hours, but a whole weekend camping always turned out to be too much. We grated on each other. We knew which buttons to press, understood all too well each other's personal idiosyncrasies, tics and foibles, and had no qualms about using that knowledge whenever we could to gain the upper hand. Was it habit that drew us together, year after year? Or a stupid sense of duty? A misguided loyalty that no one enjoyed feeling, but everyone felt bound by? Either way, it was as predictable as a Sunday before a Monday: we'd arrive, full of false cheer, and leave without casting a backward glance.

Before that, there would always be a trek, upon which we would always argue over the map, get lost, and get rained on. Every year, without fail. Sometimes the rain would coincide with us getting lost, as if to add insult to injury.

Then the drinking would start, and a campfire would be built. The men would collect wood, talk about "green sticks" and "tinder" and "kindling" as if they knew what they were talking about. The women would cobble together some sort of canned supper: soup, or bean stew, or tinned fruit. I would always pretend to enjoy it, whilst quietly putting away as much alcohol as I could to make the situation socially bearable.

And then someone would start telling stories.

Maybe this was the reason I still came to these abominable weekends: for the stories. Or maybe I was a sadist, and I secretly enjoyed torturing myself by being in close proximity to a group of increasingly obnoxious human beings who all still referred to each other as "friends".

Or maybe, just maybe, there was another reason.

Whatever it was, I was here once again, another year older, another year wiser, and my ears were cocked, ready to receive.

"Well go on then," said Max, not unkindly. He and June had been a thing for a while, although I never really got why. He'd constantly cheated on her behind her back, and yet couldn't seem to ever let her go completely, as if, despite not really wanting her himself, he didn't want anyone else to have her either. He'd string her along for a week or two, find someone new, forget all about her until he found himself single again, then re-ignite the relationship. I could only assume it was ego at play: I have fucked this woman, ergo no other man may fuck her.

She chewed nervously on a strand of mousy blonde hair, and tried to remember the story.

"I don't know," she said hesitantly, fervently wishing she'd never spoken up. "I can't remember the whole thing. But there's this couple, and... for some reason... there's this severed hand. Which is alive. And it, you know, follows them around."

"Cool." Louise stubbed her fag out on the floor and immediately began rolling another one. I could literally smell her lungs necrotizing inside her ribcage.

June gathered some confidence from this, and sat up a little straighter.

"One night, they are lying in bed, and they wake up suddenly. They can hear something crawling and thumping up the stairs. Then there's a knock on the bedroom door, and when the husband gets up to open it, the hand crawls inside, just, you know, like, dragging its bloody wrist stump across the floor." June mimed the scene using her own arm, and shuddered. "Then it jumps at the woman and strangles her. Someone told me that one when I was a kid, and I had nightmares about it for years."

I smiled, and gazed at the fire.

It was a pitiful thing, this campfire, poorly stacked, no real space for air to flow beneath the logs that had been haphazardly dumped into the earthen pit instead of arranged in a wigwam shape that would have burned longer and brighter. It gave out just enough heat to keep the cool night air at bay, and crackled and snapped lazily, little sparks flying up into the dark sky, panicked fireflies racing away from a blazing death.

When the fire died down I would rebuild it, properly, and the thing would burn brightly until the dawn. I shook my head: three men and four women present, myself not included, and not a single one of them could build a fire for shit. What was the world coming to? What would these people do if there was a global event, an apocalypse? Would they be able to feed themselves, build shelter, keep themselves warm?

I shook my head again, a tiny gesture, but Anna, who was sitting across from me, spotted it and latched onto it, as was her way.

Secretly I called her Anna-tagonistic, which I thought was rather clever. The nickname also happened to be accurate. Because antagonistic she was, right from the first moment she met a person. If ever anyone's status in the group was to be challenged or called into question, she was the one to do it. She was bullish yet educated, swore profusely yet had an elegant bearing, and was possessed of a deeply ingrained sense of superiority that carried her through life and leant her an aura of entitlement that was hard to argue with. Her wit and her tongue were both sharp. I had learned from bitter experience over the years that it could be hard to stand up to her.

I bristled as her eyes, glinting with miniature reflections of the flames, met mine.

"What's your story, then?" she barked, mistaking my smile for a sneer, and casually chewing on a fingernail in an effort to distract the others from her bossy tone.

"Well..."

I hesitated, swigging at my beer and marveling as the

cool, gentle fizz washed over my tongue. Nothing beats a cold, sweating bottle of lager next to a campfire. Nothing.

The beer fortified me. "Actually, why don't you go first?" I threw the gauntlet back at her, but she calmly shook her head.

"Oh no," she said, her voice suddenly reasonable and her expression demure. "I'll be the first to admit that I'm useless at this sort of thing. Never had much interest in fairy stories or urban legends." A small smile now played at her lips. It was a condescending smile, but no one else seemed to notice. They never did: collective blindness, for as long as I could remember.

I shrugged, sighing and breaking eye contact, bored of her games and the poisonous subtext that lurked beneath everything she said.

Then, I noticed her feet. I saw that, absurdly, she was wearing slippers on them.

I paused in disbelief.

Slippers.

Actual, real, furry fucking slippers.

With bunny ears on them.

At a campsite.

In the middle of the fucking woods.

I started to chuckle, studied my beer bottle, and realized it was nearly empty. I raised it up as a signal to Keiran, who was sat closest to the cooler box we'd loaded with booze.

"Fine," I acquiesced, in good humor once again. "I'll need another one of these, though, to wet my whistle first."

"Why do you always talk like you're from the nineteenth century?" Max said, grinning at me from across the fire. I ignored him.

Keiran heaved himself out of his fold-up camp chair, lunged at the cooler, grabbed a beer and performed his party trick of popping the beer cap off with the heel of his hand. It spun across the circle, and somehow landed right in the fire. He bowed as we applauded: it was a good party trick, I had to give him that.

He handed me the beer. "Next time I'll do it with my teeth," he said, sincerely. I believed him. I'd seen him do it before, seen him use it to pick up women. It was a neat trick, but boy, did it get boring after the millionth time. I rolled my eyes and motioned for him to sit down. He was stealing my show.

"As it happens," I said, letting more deliciously cold lager slide down my throat first, "I do have a good camp-fire tale. It's about a woman called..." I scrunched my face up and hummed, making a show of coming up with a good name for the leading lady.

There were impatient rumblings around the fire, and someone muttered something that sounded like "Get on with it!".

"Ellie. My story is about a woman called Ellie," I decided out loud, although of course, I'd already known what her name was.

Now it was Anna's turn to roll her eyes. "Great," she said flatly, crossing her legs and flaunting her feet with those ridiculous, offensive slippers on. I had a sudden thought: had she put them on deliberately, just to piss me off? It's the sort of thing she would do.

"Ellie's obviously feeling like she's not been the center

of attention enough this evening." Anna looked at me with a pitying expression.

"Let me guess," she continued, "The heroine of your story is called Ellie, she's about thirty years old, roughly your height, has brown hair the same length as yours and terrible taste in men?" She cocked an eyebrow spitefully at me. I remained unprovoked. Ignoring her attempts to rile me made me feel quite powerful, it turned out.

"Quite right," I continued, nodding my head and smiling around at everyone as Anna suppressed a scowl. "Terrible taste in men." I made a point of looking at Max, Keiran and Dan in turn. Each one of them refused to meet my eye. Did they all know about each other? Had they swapped stories about me, compared notes? I felt something ugly stir in the pit of my belly. A friend was only your friend until you took her to bed: then she was no longer your friend, but something to be embarrassed about.

I shook my head ruefully, and kept spinning my tale.

"About ten years ago, Ellie moved from her small village in the country to a big, scary city in the West.

"The move was not good for her. She was young, she lived alone, had no job, money, or friends, and not the smallest clue as to where her life was headed. She had just enough rent money to cover the next few months, and then she would be homeless."

"What about her family back home?" June may have been stupid, but she had a heart, a fairly kind one at times.

I shook my head. "Home was not an option. Things back there were... untenable."

Anna yawned. "Sorry, but this story isn't exactly

scaring me."

I nodded, motioning for her to stop being impatient. I was getting to it.

"Then, two things happened in quick succession. First, Ellie got a job. A good one, enough to pay the bills and leave enough spare to have some fun."

"And the second thing?" Keiran, like Anna, was tiring of my story. He heaved himself up once more, handed around more beers. I realized my own bottle was empty again. I was five bottles down, and didn't feel even remotely hazy. I accepted his offering graciously: sixth was a charm.

"Well. The second thing was that Ellie met someone."

Max cocked an eyebrow salaciously. "Oh yeah? Who?"

"Ellie met the Little Man."

Louise snorted in amusement, and laughter quickly rippled around the campfire, followed by lewd jokes about my new boyfriend's small dick.

I barely heard them, lost in thought as I suddenly found myself. Every detail of that first encounter was burned into memory in the most precise detail. For a moment I had second thoughts about carrying on with the story. Why bother? None of them would understand it, appreciate the special relationship the Little Man and I had.

Then I shook myself, aware of multiple sets of eyes on me. I decided to stick to the original pan. I'd better make this good.

"It happened one night not long after she'd gotten her first pay packet. She'd taken it straight down to the local bar, and made a huge, beer-shaped hole in it.

"Then she dragged herself home to her lonely studio apartment above the Indian takeaway, picking up a greasy takeout she ordered from them as she passed the front door. She sat there in her lounge in silence, drunk, with nothing to watch as her TV had packed up and her internet was no longer working. She was too tired and pissed to read, and too maudlin to listen to music."

I stopped, swallowing a lump that had formed in my throat. Fuck, those had been dark days. I looked about me for any signs of sympathy, but the faces of my friends were unreadable.

"Interesting fact. Did you know that loneliness kills more people now than obesity? I saw that in a newspaper not so long ago. Apparently, social connections are 'crucial' to human well-being and survival, and isolation is health hazard." I could feel an unbearable sadness surging through my veins, and I struggled to keep a lid on it.

June bit her lip and had the good sense to look sorry for me.

"Anyway, there she was, sat there on the floor of her apartment, covered in spots of grease and crumbs and splashes of beer, thinking about how alone she was, when she heard a tiny, insistent knocking at her door."

"Thank Christ for that," Anna sighed, predictably. "This is the most uneventful scary story in the history of scary stories."

"Fuck off, Anna," I said, bluntly, and enjoyed the look of shock on her outraged face.

"Now, come on Ellie, there's no need for..." Keiran began, looking at me in disapproval.

I spoke over him.

"To begin with, the knocking was so faint, she thought she might have imagined it. She stood up, and moved over to her door cautiously, wobbling slightly as she was still full of booze. She stopped and waited to see if the knocking would occur again. It did, louder this time, and curiously, it sounded as if it were close to the ground, as if someone incredibly short, or, absurdly, someone who was lying down, were rapping against the door.

"Now, Ellie was cautious, living alone as she did, but she was also curious. And lonely, as we've already established. So she waited some more, wondering whether or not to call out, and trying to decide what to do. When the knocking began for a third time, she took a deep breath, unlocked the door, and pulled it open.

"Whereupon the Little Man strode into her apartment, and closed the door behind him."

There was a more peaceful atmosphere in the camp now, as my audience became reluctantly engrossed in my story.

"The Little Man was just that: a perfectly proportioned, slender, pale, ageless man who stood no more than a foot above the ground.

"To begin with Ellie thought he was a doll, a cleverly animated simulacrum, or animatronic, and not real at all.

"But then he began to move around the apartment, picking things up, putting them down, looking around him, and she knew she was being absurd. The Little Man was as alive and real as she was, and she didn't have the slightest fucking idea of who he was, or what he was doing there.

"She studied him carefully, trying to decide whether or

not to be afraid of him. So far, he'd made no threatening moves towards her, and he'd said nothing to her either. It didn't take long to figure out why: the Little Man had no mouth.

"On closer inspection it transpired that he also had no ears, and no nose. He did have eyes, of sorts, but they were staring white orbs that looked like ping-pong balls. There were no eyelids, or pupils either. Just these solid, white globes stuck to his otherwise blank face."

"Cool," said Louise again, like a moron.

"The Little Man was totally featureless in all other senses of the word. He wore no clothes, and didn't appear to have any genitals. His skin was so pale it was almost translucent. She could see what looked like his blood moving through the veins beneath the delicate skin—it was blue-black blood, and pumped slowly, as if he were asleep.

"He had small hands with pearly, smooth fingernails. He was also totally hairless.

"Despite his androgynous appearance, Ellie could tell he was a man, because, despite having no mouth, he eventually spoke to her. Not in the conventional way, but in a much more personal way. His voice popped up inside her head: soft, sibilant, like a snake.

Hello.

"Then he sat down cross-legged in front of her."

I rubbed a hand over my eyes, overcome with emotion for a second. I remembered how he had moved: like an alien thing, in slow motion. He had shifted so fluidly his bones looked molten. His greeting had rolled around inside my mind like an echo in a cave.

"Before Ellie knew what she was doing, her own legs had folded beneath her, and she sank to the floor opposite him.

"The Little Man held out his hand. Ellie took it, and shook it. She asked him who he was.

"I am your friend, he said, and before she knew what was happening, she was crying.

"She'd never really had a proper friend before now."

"Oh my God, Ellie, we get it!" Anna stood up, angrily. "You had a shitty childhood! You had no friends! Daddy probably beat you with a tire iron when you were eight years old, blah blah blah. We've all had stuff happen to us. This story is *weak*."

"I want to hear it," said June, quietly. It may have been her only moment of defiance in the history of our acquaintance, but I was grateful for it.

"Me too." Surprisingly, this was Max. Was it possible he was feeling guilty? "Stop being such a bitch, Anna." She shot him a look of pure rage. It was unusual for Max to take sides against her.

Keiran drew forth one more beer. There weren't many left. He opened it, carefully this time, with no flair or drama, and handed it to me. "I could keep listening," he said, grudgingly.

I sensed the tide turning in my favor, and thrilled to the feeling.

"The Little Man turned out to be a good friend. He took up residence with Ellie, and lived in the small space under her bed, where it was darkest, because, he said, his eyes hurt in the light and his skin was sensitive to it. When she awoke in the morning, he was there, perched on the end of her bed, waiting for her to move and start the day. When she came home from work, he sat crossed-legged on the living room floor, waiting to greet her, to ask her how she was.

"He never ate, or drank anything. He never went out, never seemed to sleep. He was just there, ready to listen, ready to talk. He took nothing from her, and gave himself completely.

"At night, when she was falling asleep, he would lie next to her, his head resting on her pillow, and whisper in her ear. It was always the same thing, a mantra he used to get her to fall to sleep:

"The Little Man is by your side

The Little Man has you in mind

Let no one harm what belongs to him

Not a single hair, or hand, or limb,

Those who do will disappear

For The Little Man is always near.

"Meanwhile, life moved on for Ellie. She began to make friends outside of her relationship with the Little Man. She started getting invited to parties, nights out to the pub, shopping trips, cinema trips, even the odd date. She began to feel more confident. The years rolled by, and Little Man was a reliable constant in her life, even as other friends, boyfriends, jobs and apartments came and went. When she needed him, he was there. When she didn't, he was there anyway.

"And then one day, she woke up and felt... wrong."

I drew a breath, my voice growing a little hoarse from overuse.

"The Little Man was gone. He no longer sat at the end

of her bed, waiting for her with those blank, white eyes. Ellie called out for him, worried, and scrambled to look underneath the bed. He wasn't there either.

"She checked all the cupboards and drawers. Nothing. She ransacked her apartment, feeling sick with panic and fear, but found no trace of him.

"The Little Man was gone.

"She didn't go to work that day. She sat at home, opposite the front door, and waited.

"The Little Man didn't come."

A tear rolled unbidden down my cheek.

"Are you okay, Ellie?" Dan was looking at me with a strange, wary expression. I fixed him with a cold stare and dashed the tear away with the back of my hand. "I'm fine," I said, my mind moving on to what was coming next. "I'm almost done." I looked at the campfire, checking to see what sort of state it was in. It had burned low, and we were growing cold as a result, even me, fortified as I was with my beer jacket.

"Ellie stayed at home for the rest of the week, watching and waiting for him, her heart slowly breaking. How could he have come into her life for so long, been a part of it for so many years, only to leave without warning, without a backward glance? Wasn't he supposed to be her friend?

"She felt her mind crumbling to pieces in her skull as each day passed, and each day, the Little Man remained lost to her. She was plunged back into the loneliness, even surrounded as she was by people at work, despite her busy social calendar which she kept to as a means of distraction from the grief pulling her heart to shreds. She realized she could still feel desolate and lonely when she was standing in a crowded room, surrounded by people she knew. She half-heartedly tried a few relationships, but no one understood her like the Little Man had understood her.

"Then, one night, sitting at a table in a trendy restaurant surrounded by young, fashionable people, she decided she just couldn't take it anymore. She quite literally couldn't bear the emptiness any longer." I paused for dramatic effect.

"Couldn't take what anymore? I'm lost," said Molly, mournfully, as she said everything. I'd almost completely forgotten about Molly. She was the only person I'd ever met who was more of a high-functioning depressive than me. She'd kept a low profile so far this evening—in fact she'd barely said a word all day. No doubt she hated these things as much as I did.

My voice hardened.

"*It*. All of it.

The bullshit.

The indolence.

The rampant obsession with buying crap that people didn't need, the stupid, private jokes her friends all shared and re-shared amongst themselves, pathetically convinced of their own cleverness. The sleeping around with each other behind everyone's backs, and then the gleeful gossip that arose from the simple, moronic act of fucking someone else's boyfriend or girlfriend, especially when that someone else was a supposed friend, someone who would never suspect that anything was wrong."

My eyes flicked to Max once more, and he dropped his

head, looking sheepishly down at the bark-strewn ground.

"She began to feel violently sick inside every time she sat amongst them, every time she listened to them drone on and on about their mundane, unimportant, ugly little lives."

An almost complete silence reigned around me, and only had the gentle noises of the trees and the crackling of the campfire dared to interrupt.

I swigged again, sweeping my hand back through my hair and feeling an energy awake in me, pushing away the sadness. Surreptitiously, I began to flex and clench the fingers on both hands, working and loosening the joints, cracking the knuckles, limbering up.

"The worst thing about these people, you see, is that they just didn't think there was anything wrong. They assumed that this was how all people lived. They went around high-fiving each other in public, and plunging knives deep into each other's backs the second they were turned. They complained about the price of property, and how they were being pushed out of the market, and they moaned about the government and how ineffectual they were, how down the politicians were on the hard-working man, and then they complained about the next election, how it was such a drag to have to vote again.

"They walked past homeless people sleeping rough in the freezing winter, and told themselves it would be useless to give them anything, because they'd just spend the money on drugs, or piss it up against the wall instead of finding shelter. Yet they thought nothing of buying designer label clothes, convincing themselves that an Armani suit was 'an investment'."

I moved my head from side to side, cracking my neck, feeling my shoulder muscles tense up.

"They ate, and consumed, and lied, and cheated, and stole, and fornicated. They came up with their own skewed moral codes and a complicated set of life instructions and ideals which they then failed to live up to. They woke up with clear consciences every day, and went to sleep feeling the same way. That they were untouchable."

Anna now lit a cigarette, leaning into the fire to do so. She blew a column of smoke above her head as a dragon would, a thick pillar of swirling white that vanished in seconds. She inhaled again, languidly, and looked at me, and her eyes were as black and hard as coal.

"So she woke up one day and realized her friends were all horrible human beings. Then what did she do?" she asked, and I think that perhaps she was beginning to understand, because I could see that underneath her calm poise, she was tense, her jaw muscles working in tiny circular movements. I smelt a worry and fear on her, and I liked it. I sucked it in along with the night air and the cigarette smoke and the combined reek of my so-called "friends," who all sat there looking at me as if I'd grown horns from my head. For a moment I was tempted to lift up my hand and feel my hairline, check myself. The urge passed, but it left me with a tingle on my scalp.

I spoke, holding Anna's gaze.

"Well, then one day, as I said, she grew tired of it all. So, she devised a plan: she concocted an excuse to go camping."

"An excuse?" Max interrupted, raising an eyebrow, an infuriating mannerism that he nurtured because he thought it was ironic. "It's your birthday, isn't it? Isn't that what this whole trip is about?" He waved his arms at his surroundings, as if the pine trees and fir trees were somehow my fault.

I leaned forward, deadly serious for a moment. "How long have you know me, Max?"

He thought about it, then said with certainty: "About ten years."

"Then you should know that my birthday is in November, not August."

"Shit," he breathed, and started laughing. "Really?"

I nodded. "Really." I made up my mind then and there, on the spot: he would be first.

Dan shifted uneasily. "You're not doing much to help our cause here, buddy," he said half-jokingly to Max. He gave him a meaningful look, one that was meant to convey a single message: be careful. Ellie's gone bat-shit crazy.

The shadows growing around Anna's eyes as the fire died, and the light with it, were enormous. "And?" she asked me, softly. "What did she do then?"

"Well, if you must know, she lured them out into the woods... and then killed each and every one of them with a hunting knife while they were sitting around the campfire."

More silence. June looked confused. Molly half stood, looking around her for reassurance. Dan, Kieran and Max gaped at me, mouths hanging open. Louise narrowed her eyes and watched me through her cigarette smoke.

Anna stayed seated, staring at me with her dead, block-of-coal eyes.

"I don't like your story," she said eventually, breaking the tension.

"Never mind," I said, fumbling in my hoodie pocket for the hunting knife I'd had concealed there throughout the evening.

I drew the wide blade out and turned it over several times in my hands, twisting the sharp, serrated steel edge so that it caught and threw back to me the crimson glint of the fire. I heard a series of sharp breaths being taken, muttered curses as my friends looked at me in pure disbelief.

"It's only a silly story," I continued, and rose to my feet, smiling from ear to ear.

None of them thought to run, so convinced were they of their immortal, godly status on this earth. Invincible, that's what they thought they were. Well, they weren't. Their screams echoed around the woods as I cut my way through them like a hot knife through warm butter.

I was fast, and lethal. I'd trained for this moment for years, practiced for hours in the privacy of my own home, the Little Man, my only true friend, egging me on, showing me how to move, twist, thrust, jab, eviscerate.

As promised, I began with Max, gutting him efficiently with a few swift, sure movements. He collapsed to his knees, and for a moment, as I looked at his agonized face turned up to me pleadingly, a handsome face that displayed such a tender vulnerability I almost regretted what I'd done, I had a flashback to an earlier time. A time when he'd kissed me, told me that it would be okay, that

233

we could just "regret it in the morning". That we would still be friends. Then he'd bedded me, and afterwards, grew instantly cold. He'd refused to speak to me for nearly a whole year, to really drive the message home. I had served a purpose, and was now no longer required. My hurt and shame was still a raw red wound: I sliced a crimson arc across his throat, so that he had a raw red wound too, and watched him choke on his own deceit.

I lost myself in the movement and rhythm of death. All the while, the pale moon sat there high up above me, coolly observing, not unlike Anna, a thick halo wrapped around its perfect shape, a great big silvery eye in the sky.

Speaking of Anna, I left her until last, and I couldn't resist a final, fond fuck-you, so I cut out her vicious tongue and threw it into the fire pit. The noise it made as it met the heat was indescribable, a noise I will remember, and savor, for the rest of my life.

Then, I removed her slippers, splattered now with blood and ash. The ridiculous, furry bunny ears sagged and curled from the heat of the blaze. I slipped them onto my own bare feet, wriggled my toes to make the ears move around like real bunnies. I giggled. The slippers were rather cute, actually. I decided to keep them.

When I was finished, I fed the pieces of my friends to the fire. It flared and roared, popped and spat at me as the fat and the meat and bones within the flames charred, bubbled, diminished, slowly. I stayed with them, cutting more wood, fanning the embers, pouring petrol, feeding and coaxing the blaze for hours, until it became a huge pyre, so hot I could hardly face it, so hot my cheeks burned and my hair rose up and floated around my face, carried by scorching eddies of wind. The noise was immense. Have you ever stood near a bonfire and listened to the sheer chaos of sound that happens when things burn? They don't just burn: they roar, and shriek, and pop, and crackle, as if it were not a fire at all, but an orchestra playing out a concerto. I swayed in time to the music the fire made, my slippered feet tracing patterns in the earth around me.

When it was over, it was dawn. I'd kept the fire burning until morning, as I'd promised.

Exhausted, I stopped dancing, and closed my eyes, letting the first traces of light brush against my eyelids.

I heard a faint crackle behind me, the sound of twigs snapping under tiny feet. I turned, and the Little Man moved out from behind a tree.

He stood for a moment, and then moved slowly towards me. A pale sun broke through the trees, sent fingers of light through the thick smoke that hung in the air, and lit the Little Man up as he walked. The light also broke through the heavy grief in my heart, and I sank to my knees.

He stopped before me, somehow larger, somehow no longer a Little Man, but a human-sized man. I trembled with longing, overwhelmed with joy at seeing him again.

He gripped my blood-smeared cheeks in his delicate hands, and bent down to whisper something in my ear.

I closed my eyes again, and a thick blanket of calm and peace descended on the maelstrom in my heart.

"Well done," he said, and touched me gently on my forehead. "Well done."

CAMP CREDENCE

By Grant Hinton

THE SMALL WHITE BUS SKIDDED TO A HALT, AND BRICK-colored dust whirled around like a magician exiting his stage. Mrs. Hart's seat squeaked as she rose, all corduroy and white blouse like she remembered the sixties and had apparently got stuck there. Her skinny hips eclipsed the driver's face as she stood in the aisle.

"Pay attention please, before we disembark I want you all to be on your best behavior. A few other schools will be joining us this year, and I will not have Sedgehill secondary school's good name dragged through the mud."

A greasy-haired boy sniggered in the back seat. The kid next to him covered his mouth with his hand to suppress his laughter.

"And that means you too, Scott and Lee. If you take a step out of line, I will send you back faster than you can say stickleback."

Her vivid green eyes went wide to emphasize her point; the two boys puffed out their cheeks and tried to hold their breaths.

"Now, gather your things and..."

The boys burst into silent giggles. A blonde girl in front turned in her seat.

"You fucking ruin this trip for me and my brothers will fuck you up."

Scott poked his tongue out at Jessica when she sat back heavily in her seat as Mrs. Hart prattled on.

"...outside move to the left and stand by the doors, Mr. Welbeck will give us the tour."

Scott and Lee scampered down the aisle, pushing past Mrs. Hart. She bumped into her colleague and sighed with an exasperated look.

"It's gonna be a long three days, Steve."

Steve Thorne, head of Geography at Sedgehill ruffled his paper and looked up distractedly.

"Sorry, Harriet. Did you say something?"

Mrs. Hart rolled her eyes and shook her head as she continued to count off the five teenagers descending the steps. A tall, middle-aged man in faded jeans, blue shirt, and a brown hunting vest approached with a raised hand.

"Hellooo campers, welcome to Camp Credence. You're the first ones here."

Mrs. Hart stepped off the bus and extended a hand.

"Good evening, Mr. Welbeck."

"Please, call me John, and that goes for everyone."

The assembled group chorused his name. After a brief discussion with Mrs. Hart and Steve, the bus driver unloaded the bags. John turned to the small group.

"Right-o, we have a few to wait for so just make your-self... ah, here they are now."

Four vehicles rattled down the dirt path and came to a stop by the white bus. A canopy of noise erupted as doors slid open, bags hit the gravel floor, and swarms of children assaulted the camp. After a few minutes of waving and shuffling, the assembled crowd waited for John to speak.

"Okay, quiet down now," he said.

The congregation fell silent, although the underlining excitement buzzed through them.

"Hello and welcome to Camp Credence. My name is John Welbeck, and I'm your host for the duration of your stay. Sally, my colleague, will be joining us at some point tonight, she's just running a quick errand.

"In a few moments, I'll be showing you where you'll be sleeping. These..."

He jabbed a thumb behind him.

"Are the bathrooms, this is where you'll shower and use the toilet. Unless, you want to use mother nature which is also fine. Ladies, yours is to the left, gentlemen, yours is to the right. Under no circumstance am I to find you entering the opposite bathrooms."

John glared around at the innocent eyes. He knew he would catch at least one curious boy in the girl's bath-room before camp finished. He always did, and some-times even a girl would go where she shouldn't.

"Okay campers. Follow me."

The group followed John down a path that led to an open space of grass surrounded by a vast forest. A large number of orange tents ringed the field in two decreasingly neat rows. A recently prepared campfire sat at the center with round logs surrounding it. Their surfaces polished shiny by generations of bottoms rubbing at their bark.

Soon the camp was bustling with activity as teachers and children alike unloaded their bedding and things into their tents.

Later that night, when small tongues of yellow flames licked at the dry branches, the kids and teachers came shuffling down after dinner at the camp kitchen. John sat on a tree stump by the fire, his face painted white with chalk, feathers sticking out of his hair at weird angles, and his knees clamping a bamboo bongo, which he hit at irregular beats.

The children huddled in their class groups down the narrow path; some girls giggled and glanced back at the boys as they approached.

"Come, my friends."

Bong.

"Come and sit."

Bong.

As they neared, John struck the drum faster. Driving an urgency into their strides until they all scampered onto the logs, some falling over each other in the process.

The last beat of the drum echoed around the campsite and died. John looked up to the black sky with closed eyes and held his arms out wide. Slowly his chin sunk until it touched his chest. He started to speak in a whisper that steadily grew stronger.

"His name was Credence, and this was his family's

land. Until a night just like this, when young Credence went missing."

John's eyes flashed open, and a girl with ruby red hair gasped. The white paint made John's dark eyes pop in the firelight.

"Credence liked nothing more than to splash about in the lake and play in his father's fields, just like you. But one day his father returned with blood on his hands, and Credence was no longer allowed out. There had been an attack on his cattle."

Scott and Lee both growled low in their throats until Jessica punched them on the arm.

"His father had noticed large prints surrounding the dead bodies of his cows. After another attack, he went out to catch the beast. But the creature was too quick, too sneaky. Until the one night he awoke to the screams of his herd. He jumped up."

John jumped onto the log, and a few girls screamed. He smirked and spoke down to them as the fire lit his face from below.

"He picked up his rifle and shot wildly into the field. A man stood up in the middle of his cattle. Taller than I am now, only he wasn't a man. No. He had the head of a goat. The beast looked at him with beady eyes and gnashed its pointed teeth. Credence's father watched in horror as it jittered and jerked. The air started to feel clammy and charged with electricity. The smell of copper and dried blood hung heavy in the air."

The kids sniffed eagerly hoping the air would change and John paused as if waiting, before carrying on.

"The Goatman charged with razor-sharp horns, but

thankfully Credence's father jumped on his horse and turned in the saddle. He fired at the beast, and the Goatman fell with a wound in the shoulder, Credence's father kicked at his horse and rode away."

John waved his arms and looked far off into the forest; an owl hooted in the distance, and the crickets came to life in the silence.

"He couldn't stop the killing, even when the beast came for his family."

John played the crowd like a fiddle; each kid hung on his every word.

"One night Credence woke up to a sound unlike any he had heard before. He crept downstairs and opened the door to the porch. There at the entrance to his home was the Goatman kneeling over his mother's body with bloodied horns. His father's voice sounded upstairs, calling out his mother's name. Before Credence could call his father, the Goatman snatched at him with wicked claws."

John jumped off the log and made a snatch at a girl huddling next to her friend. They screamed and shied back as he danced around the circle of faces. A moan sounded off to the right of the tents, and everyone looked about wildly.

"Credence's father barreled down the stairs, shotgun in hand only to see his dead wife at the door; Credence cried into the night as the Goatman carried him off, but his father only fell to his knees losing himself in the grief of his dead wife."

The fire crackled and spat as if it too wanted to hear more. The hollow moan sounded again.

"No one ever saw Credence again, and Credence's father aspirated—after years of neglect—sold the farm. We named the camp after Credence to remind us that something else lives in the forest."

John swept his arm around.

"And every month we leave something for the Goat-man, to keep our family and campers safe, but..."

He looked about wildly. "We forgot to do it last week."

A figure barreled through the clearing with a sickening moan. Its goat head jerked from side to side; big black beady eyes made the kids jump and scream. A few of the teacher engrossed in the story didn't see past the blue jeans and brown hunting vest and lost themselves in terror. After a few erratic moments of flaying bodies, Sally pulled off the goat head, and her blonde hair and white laughter sparkled in the firelight.

"Haha, got ya."

She clutched the goat head to her stomach laughing until she reached John's side. Sally put a hand on his shoulder as the kids, especially the boys looked up at her with open mouths. She smiled and raised the goat head as her golden skin shone in the firelight.

"It's an old hunting trophy of the camps. I think it used to belong to old man Welbeck."

A small red-haired girl off to the left raised a hand.

"Wait, you mean the story is true, you know about the animal attacks and Credence?"

John waved a hand and chuckled.

"Well yes and no. Yes, this was Credence's farm, and yes he did go missing, but no, the Goatman is just a story we tell to frighten you."

"So," said Sally. "The real reason you're all gathered around the fire is..."

Sally bent behind the log John sat on and pulled out some sticks. Then she reached into the goats head and pulled out a large bag of marshmallows.

"Dessert!"

SCOTT SAT on his sleeping bag long after the camp lights had shut off. Lee shuffled his cards and placed a Marshadow Pokémon down on the canvas between them.

"Do you think the girls will want to come and sleep with us in our tent?"

Scott shrugged and placed a Jolteon Pokémon card down. He adjusted his head torch and looked at Lee. A giant shadow dwarfed the tent.

"Lights outs boys!"

Scott snatched at the light and switched it off.

"Sorry, Mr. Throne," chorused the boys.

They held their breaths for what seemed like ages until they heard the sound of a zipper. Scott reached up to switch back on the light, but Lee clutched his hand stopping him.

"What?" he whispered.

"They'll see the light."

"So, we won't be able to see the cards."

"Shhh, listen."

Scott strained his ears, footsteps outside, slow and steady. Someone or something was out there.

"You don't think it's... you know?" Lee said swallowing.

Scott swallowed too and followed the noise around the tent; each step sent sharp stabs of fear to his heart. Lee shuffled away from the zipper, fighting Scott to the back of the tent. A nail dragged along the fabric as a second pair of footsteps came around the tent. The boys clutched at each other as the zipper slowly fell.

"Ah, got ya." Jessica squeezed through the zipper giggling, and a brown-haired girl the boys didn't know fell in after her. Scott quickly dragged the Pokémon card out of sight before the girls could notice.

"What ya do that for? Damn." Scott pushed Jessica as she laughed harder. She nodded to the girl.

"This is Mary, she's from Boney Bastards, um sorry,"— she smiled at the girl—"Bonus pastors."

Scott and Lee smiled and watched as Jessica pulled out a small bottle of vodka. She unscrewed the lid and lifted it to her rose-colored lips. Scott watched as a small trickle rolled down her cheek into her neckline. He didn't stop until he was looking at a shiny embroiled star on her pajama top.

"Want some?" she offered.

Scott jolted and accepted the bottle; the liquor burnt and soon his head started to feel dizzy and stupid.

LEE TRIED to follow the spinning bottle as the tent turned with it. The neck slowed and stopped on Jessica. She reached out, and French-kissed Scott. After some time the pair parted. He grinned, and she laughed.

"You're next, Mary." Jessica handed her the bottle, and

she twirled it. Jessica laughed again as it stopped on her. Mary looked shyly at her but didn't break eye contact. Jessica shrugged and leaned in as the boys pulled their sleeping bags over their laps.

A noise outside interrupted the kissing, and everyone froze listening until the crickets started up again. Jessica leaned over to Scott and whispered in his ear. Scott grinned and unzipped the tent. Jessica followed him out into the night. Lee smiled weakly at Mary.

"Do you want to play some more?"

Mary half shrugged and feigned a yawn.

"I'm tired." She crawled out the tent flap on all fours and disappeared.

Lee felt a little hurt, but his head was spinning too much anyway. After a moment of fumbling, he zipped the tent up and fell on his sleeping bag.

THE SUN SPIKED through the forest canopy like the fingers of God. Each ray spread out across bracken and crunching autumn leaves. The map wafted in Scott's hands as the students of Sedgehill school tried to navigate the forest. Lee, Dean, and Jessica trudged behind him as Natasha dragged a stick leaving a slight trail in the forest floor.

"What you doing that for?" Jessica rounded on her, and she stopped dead.

"Well if we get lost we can find our back can't we."

Her singing voice echoed through the forest of vast trees. Scott twisted the map again and again before humming and passing it to Lee's waiting hands. Lee screwed up his face with concentration; after a few minutes he huffed and passed it to Dean who seemed delighted. He stuck out a tongue as he twisted the map right side up.

"I've got no idea where we're going," said Scott. "Stupid maps just got lines and dots. Where's Google maps when you need it. I can't believe they wouldn't let us bring phones on this trip."

Jessica blanched and reached into her jeans' pocket.

"What, like this?"

The sunlight sparkled off the bejeweled back of her iPhone. She swiped at the screen before moving it in the air.

"Arg. No reception."

A loud hooting echoed through the forest, and they all fell silent.

"Can you make out where to go Dean?" asked Lee as he glanced over his shoulder. Dean traced a line with his finger and nodded.

"Yeah, I reckon we're about here, and the last marker is this little green dot here. So..."

He lifted a finger and waved it from left to right.

"This way."

The group continued through the forest as the wildlife spoke around them.

"Don't get us lost Dean, this place is freaking me out." Natasha brushed at a low branch and tripped on the exposed tree root falling to her knees.

"I heard the teachers saying a girl went missing last night," said Scott. "Apparently, she got lost going to the toilet or something, her teacher said the girl was there for lights out, but she wasn't in her tent in the morning."

"How can someone get lost going to the toilet? The light is constantly on, you can see it from our tent. That's just ridiculous," Lee said screwing up his face.

Natasha brushed dirt from her jeans and looked up into the branches of the tree. She screamed and pointed her finger at a brown sack hanging high above them. Lee ran around the giant trunk shielding his eyes from a spike of sunlight.

"Is that a person?" said Lee.

"Maybe it the Goatman," joked Dean.

"Don't be stupid Dean; it was just a story," Jessica said nervously.

"Well, there's only one way to find out." Scott took off his pack and started to climb. The wind blew, and the sack twisted and turn until something dirty fell to the ground. Jessica screamed this time.

A bloodied T-shirt lay crumpled on the forest floor. The hanging sack swung round again. A pale brown-haired girl hung limply from the tree branch. A distance moan echoed through the trees.

"What the fuck was that?" Jessica searched the forest in despair as Natasha clutched at Dean. The moan sounded again.

"Whatever it is," said Dean. "It's getting closer. Scott, get down."

Scott stretched out across the open space and pushed the body with the tip of his finger; a girls face slowly swung round. Her glassy eyes looked through him, purple veins struck across her face, and her swollen tongue hung out her mouth. Scott retched.

"It's Mary," he whispered. "It's Mary," he called down to the group, but something else caught his attention, something moving fast through the undergrowth.

"It's coming!" he shouted as the gawking faces turned to see where he pointed.

"Get down!" the girls screamed at Scott as he lowered his foot to the branch below.

The bushes before the group exploded as a horned man emerged. Twisted black-green horns protruded from a dark leather helmet covering its eyes and nose. Spittle flew from a lipless mouth with a savage roar. The skin stretched taut over its sharp, stained, crooked teeth. A tiny waist gave way to an enormous chest—each rib looked like a skeletal finger as it heaved with each disgusting breath.

The Goatman roared at the kids and grabbed for Jessica. She screamed and bolted away. Scott clung to a branch, too frightened to move. Dean trip backward and the beast tore toward him snatching at his leg with dirty, broken fingernails. They bit deep into his leg, and he screamed in pain. He kicked at the Goatman's claws and finally broke free.

Suddenly the beast twisted its horned head. Even without eyes it seemed to be aware of its surrounding. The girls raced away as its sightless head swung around and twisted up to the canopy of branches above and Scott. It barreled to the tree, hitting it hard.

"Run!" Scott's frightened voice shocked the group as the Goatman clawed at the tree trunk.

The girls looked back at Dean across the ground and froze, whimpering. Lee sucked in a huge breath and ran towards him, Jessica paused a moment and then followed. Between them, they managed to get Dean to his feet and with a shoulder each hobbled away.

They half ran, half hopped through the forest hoping that the Goatman wasn't following. Scott's deep cry suddenly echoed around them, and they knew exactly where the Goatman was.

THE BEDRAGGLED GROUP fell into the clearing. A small fire crackled in front of the entrance to an adapted Native American teepee, and a white and grey husky that lay next to it watched them approach. An old white man with a bald head and glasses ducked out from within the folds.

"Ah ha, the last group, we were starting to worry you'd gotten lost in there wasn't we, Rumpole." The dog looked at its owner and wagged his tail unenthusiastically. Then it stopped and stood up on tired bones. The heckles on its back stood on ends, and it started to growl deep in its throat.

"Woo Rumpole, these are friends."

The man took in the ragged group of four. The girl with blonde hair and a dirty puffy face. The dark girl with torn clothes. Both had been crying. One of the boys held another boy with a bloodied leg. His vacant stare went through him like he wasn't there. He didn't need to know that something was very wrong.

"What happened?" He took a step towards the group and took Dean under one arm.

"Something came at us. It had horns and... and—" Natasha broke down in tears and collapsed to the floor by the husky. The old man's face turned white.

"What do you mean horns?" His right hand started to tremble. He reached down and pulled open the tear in Dean's trousers. A deep wound leaked blood down to his ankle and dripped to the floor.

"What did this?" he asked.

"The Goatman. Or that's what I think it was," said Jessica.

The man's eyes grew wide with fear.

"Quickly inside, before it comes back."

He ushered them inside his tent, closing the door behind him. Then he brought down a thick fabric that blotted out the light from the window sending the interior into darkness.

"Quiet, don't breathe, don't make a sound."

The group huddled together not knowing if the old man was insane. A series of thumps echoed through the clearing. Rumpole whimpered and scurried under a bench by the wall.

"Shhhh."

Footsteps reached near the tent. Heavy snorting made the girls whimper. Each clamped hands over their mouths to suppress the sound. The breathing and footsteps crunched around a few times and then got quieter as it moved off.

"That was close, was that...?" whispered Lee.

A match flared in the darkness, and slowly a shuttered

lantern lit the small teepee.

"That," he looked over his glasses at the kids, "Was something that shouldn't be here. Come with me."

The old man moved a seat at the back and pulled at the fabric of the tent. A hole the size of a small human opened to darkness.

"Where's that go?" asked Natasha.

"Back to the campground, you'll be safe there."

AT THE CAMPFIRE, John and Sally gathered everyone around to congratulate them on navigating the woods. One team still hadn't arrived, and a seed of dread was creeping up John's spine. Suddenly the stump next to him toppled, and a shiny head popped out.

"Warren, you old devil. You nearly scared me to death." John's face went from mock surprise to genuine surprise when four more heads followed him out of the hole. A murmuring went through the crowd.

"What's happened Warren?" John's said concerned.

"Something attacked them, and by what they've told me, it's got two kids."

Sally quickly spoke to a teacher, and in a few minutes, the rest of the teachers were leading the children back toward the administration building. Steve, however, came round to face John.

"What the hell is happening? And where's Scott?" He looked at Lee and the others, but they dropped their eyes to the floor.

"Lee?" Lee looked up.

"We found the girl," he said sniffing. "We weren't looking for her, honest. But some monster thing came out the trees. It had a big horned head and went for Scott; he was up the tree seeing if the girl was Mary, you know the missing girl."

Sally reached over to a crate and flipped the lid. A second later she handed a shotgun to John and another to Warren.

"You," John pointed to Lee. "You're coming with us. I need to know where you saw it. You lot go quickly and catch up with the others. Go!"

"Wait, who's got who?" asked a confused Steve.

John turned to Steve and handed him a shotgun as the old man opened the hatch again.

"I don't know, but it's got your kids," he said.

Twigs snapped underfoot as they passed Warren's teepee. John stopped to survey the area before waving them on. He pulled Lee by the arm and spoke into his ear.

"Which way?" Lee glanced around nervously and pointed ahead.

Steve nudged Sally and spoke in a low tone. "What sort of operation are you running here? Allowing a man mad to run loose around your camp?" He hissed the last part to emphasize his displeasure.

Sally's eyes never left the forest.

"It's only happened once before, about seven years ago," said Warren out the corner of his mouth as Steve's eyes flicked between the old man and Sally. "We never caught the guy then, but we will now."

"And how do you know it's not this Goatman you talk about?" asked Steve.

"Pfff, that's just a ghost story John tells the kids," spat Sally.

Steve turned to Warren and continued. "We don't know who or what this thing is. We don't even know if it's the same person who... Well, Look we've got to get to the kids before something bad happens again."

John moved the group forward.

"Happens? Again? What happened last time, did someone die?"

Warren nodded sharply. "Yep, yep, a girl got killed. We nearly got closed down too."

John shushed them and spoke to Lee again. The boy pointed a trembling finger off to the right. John cocked the shotgun, and the rest followed.

Suddenly a loud howl sounded behind them, and they turned as one. The horned man barreled toward them with his head bent like a bull. Steve let off a shot but only managed to scare everyone. The Goatman plowed toward John as he lowered the weapon, but at the last second, he lifted the barrel.

A horn ripped through John's midriff, flipping him up into the air. Steve let off another shot and managed a partial hit to the Goatman's back. It howled with pain and took off through the trees.

"What the fuck was that?!" Steve turned to the group; Warren laid flat on the floor, Sally likewise by his side. John's crumpled form twitched in front of them.

Sally crawled desperately to John's side and pulled up the bloody shirt. A jagged wound exposed his ribcage; a few ribs poked through the torn flesh. Torrents of blood coated Sally's hands as she tried to stem the bleeding.

"John, John, hold on. No, hold on, please. We'll get help, just stay calm, stay with me."

John reached up and stroked a strand of hair behind her ear as Steve and Lee knelt beside them.

"It's not his fault. He doesn't understand." John coughed, and blood coated his teeth.

"Don't talk, just stay calm," she pleaded.

"It's ok, it's ok. I'm sorry; I didn't tell you the rest of that story. When Credence woke up that night, he came and woke me up too."

John coughed up more blood.

"I watched from the stairs as my little brother opened the door, too scared to come down. The monster stole Credence, and I froze." A tear rolled down his cheek. "Until our father pushed me out the way to get to my mother."

Sally's tears fell onto Steve and mingled with his blood.

"He came back though, but I knew he wasn't the same brother I lost. He stood in the fields never coming close to the house. My father saw him too, once. I knew it was Credence, so I fed him when I could. Left cattle tied to a stake in the fields for him. He's a good boy; he's just... just... just."

Sally pressed the shirt into the wound, desperately trying to stem the flow of blood as John's eyes fluttered and closed.

Steve touched her shoulder.

"He's gone."

Warren pulled her into a rough hug and looked up at Steve.

"We've got to get that bastard before he kills anyone else."

Lee picked up the fallen shotgun and cocked it.

"Now young man, I don't think it's right for you to..." Steve started to protest but stopped when Lee shot his teacher a dirty look.

"My dad takes us hunting all the time. I know how to use this." As if to emphasize the point he swung the gun around like a movie hero and pointed it towards the trees.

"This way."

It wasn't long before they spotted drops of blood on the leaves below their feet. Quietly they tracked them to a fallen oak tree.

"Do you smell that?" Sally sniffed and looked around.

"Smell what?" asked Warren.

"Smells like copper, and is it me or has it gotten hotter all of a sudden?" she said, pulling at the neck of her top.

A wet slapping sound echoed around them.

"Ssssh," Steve whispered.

Slowly they crept forward. Lee spotted Credence before the rest in the bowl of a fallen tree and motioned them to stop. No one needed to be told to stay quiet.

Credence's horned helmet lay in the dirt by his feet. One horn was still covered with gore. Pieces of white fatty sinews hung from the end. Credence ripped a hunk of flesh from a bloodied bone with his teeth. His lipless chew made the wet smashing sound they had heard. An unrecognizable body lay feet away. Mangled limbs splayed out in the dirt. Bones and tendons poked out with giblets of fat hanging to them.

Lee gasped at the deck of Pokémon cards that lay scattered by the body.

"Scott."

Lee felt the anger burning away the fear and aimed the shotgun at the back of its head. Although none of them made a sound, something made Credence stop and slowly turn around. Lee lost his nerve.

It was hard to believe Credence was once human by the sight of his face. The creature before them snorted through the jagged punctures of taut skin across a flat boneless nose. The skin continued up and across its eye sockets rendering it blind. But, still, it knew they were there. The punctures vibrated with every exhalation making a small whirling noise.

Lee felt a presence enter his mind and probe behind his eyes like the beginning of a headache. The barrel of the shotgun dipped and then swung around to face his teacher.

Kill.

"Lee, what are you doing?" Steve hissed as Lee's face contorted.

"It's not me," he said. The gun continued to dip and rise, dip and rise as Lee fought whatever was making him do it.

Kill. Kill. Kill.

"Stop being stupid and aim at that thing." Steve pointed the gun at Credence, but Lee's face fell into a stoic stare. Credence snorted, threw the gnawed bone against the tree trunk and roared. The shotgun in Lee's hand quivered.

"Kill, kill, kill, kill," echoed in his mind.

"Lee!"

The gunshot rang through the trees, and a spray of blood covered Lee's face. A flock of birds disturbed by the shot took off with loud squawks. As the bang died around them, Steve hit the floor clutching a bloody wound in his stomach. Credence's head jittered to the left, and Lee's gun moved down the line. Sally raised her hand. The blast took off three of her fingers before hitting her in the chest. Lee looked on with a glassy stare. Another shot rang out, and Warren screwed up his old pockmarked face.

Credence jittered again as a spray of dirt showered him from the blast, and then he stepped forwards. Lee felt the pressure in his mind move the gun; he didn't resist it anymore, it made sense. The voice spoke to him with visions and feeling.

Kill.

Lee saw himself standing in a field; corn spread as far as he could see. A large white house cast a shadow over him, and a man stood on the porch with a shotgun eyeing him wearily. But he didn't fear him. He loved him.

Kill.

The vision changed, Lee felt the man lying by his horse, he couldn't see anymore, not with his eyes at least. A smoldering fire kept the darkness at bay as the first rays of sun rose over the tree in the distance. A cow too engrossed in her feeding wandered too close to him and screamed. The man woke with a jolt and snatched at his gun aiming it wildly into the fields.

He spotted him as the cows bolted away, Lee heard the loud bang and felt the pain in his arm. Scared he ran, he didn't know where to; the pain was like nothing he had ever felt before, he couldn't concentrate on his surroundings. Another loud bang deafened him, and another bright flare of pain erupted in his mind.

Kill.

Lee's mind swept along with the sea of visions, a picture formed in his hands, one of himself a few years younger than he was now, a lady in a scarlet dress hugged him tight as she pointed to the other person in the picture. The man who he had seen on the porch and laying by his horse.

"That's your daddy right there. You listen to me now Bobby. He's remarried, so you can't go looking for him, you hear, not like he can do anything for us anyhow. The medical bills are too high for your treatment. But we'll get by though." Her smile made all his fears go away even though he had a thousand questions.

"Okay, Mumma." She hugged him again.

Kill.

Lee's vision blurred and a white door formed in front of him. He pushed the door open with a creak. A lady in a white nightgown startled at the moving door. Before she could scream, he snatched at her. His dirty fingernails tore at her dress, but she managed a scream and pulled away. Lee/ Bobby hit her hard on the head and felt her hit the floor. She was the one who had broken up his family.

Even if his father didn't want to know him, she would still pay.

Lee felt the presence of a small boy treading lightly down the stairs; he fell back into the shadows of the porch. As the boy drew near, he studied his features. So this was his brother then, a bastard brother, but a brother he didn't know he had.

"Credence? What are you doin—Martha!" Lee/Bobby snatched at Credence before the man—his father—reached the foot of the stairs and tucking the screaming boy under one arm and ran off into the night.

Kill. Kill. Kill. Kill. Kill.

Lee squeezed the trigger and Warren fell to the dirt. The shotgun clattered out of Lee's hand and fell amongst the carnage. Bobby snorted and roared, as another slightly smaller horned man emerged from among the tree roots. Lee slowly turned and stumbled along the trail and stood before Bobby. Bobby placed his face inches from his and sniffed; the skin vibrated with a tiny squeal.

Bobby reached down and picked up the discarded limb he had been feeding on before and gave it to Lee. He raised it to his mouth and tore off a strip of bloodied flesh, his eyes turning white.

OUTBACK OBLIVION

By Grant Hinton

THEY SAY EVERYTHING IN AUSTRALIA CAN KILL YOU, BUT what they don't tell you is there are things far worse.

I went looking for gold in the outback of Australia because I heard it's the richest land in the world for the precious metal, apart from South Africa, and I didn't want to go there, as it's too dangerous. The problem was that I went in search of a fortune and lost something more important. It happened the second day I arrived. Like so many before, I'd heard about the gold fields and thought I'd like in on the action. I even got myself a map with a little X on it and felt like a true pioneer with my pickaxe, compass, and other equipment.

Once I was set, I hired a car and drove to the place marked on my map. It took me a while to get to there as the terrain wasn't easy going, if you know what I mean, and the 4x4 wasn't the best either. The truck overheated at one point; I must have hit a rock or something or maybe it was just bad luck. I don't know, but rather than turning back I thought what the hell, I'm here now, I might as well try and make it on foot. I shouldered my gear and opened my map, pulled out my compass and corrected my course, then started out toward the mark.

After about an hour I rechecked the compass. But when it didn't read, it just spun back and forth, not settling on any direction, I thought I must have broken it. Not wanting to stay out in the blistering heat I found some shade under a tree and assessed the situation. By my calculation, I wasn't far from the marking of the mine I was heading towards, maybe an hour tops. Again, I just thought, what the hell, and kept on walking.

After what seemed like hours in the unrelenting sun, I came across a broken signpost that read "Murdoch's Mining Co." The landscape before me opened up to a deep, wide hole with smaller holes riddling the sides; like this quarry had been extensively mined. As I took in the warren of holes and burnished red rocks I noticed a little shack up on an overlook. Because my compass was still useless, I set the broken sign down on the ground, pointing the way I came. I thought it best that I had a way to find my way back.

The sun was well on its way to the horizon and all the hiking had done a number on me, so I headed to the shack. As I walked over the rocks I noticed a pile of dust-covered clothes. Then I came across another. When I looked around I saw loads scattered around the quarry. It didn't make sense, and the shack—that was the weirdest part. I knocked and when no one answered, I pushed the door open and stepped inside. It was like someone had just got up and left.

It was so damn weird. A small table in one corner had a plate with half-eaten food on it next to a glass of water and a coat hung over the back of the chair. The sight of the food sent a pang of hunger through me, but seeing as it wasn't my food and the person might have just stepped out, I thought it best to leave it. That's when I noticed a few piles of dust-covered clothes on the shack's floor. I really didn't know what to make of it, but as it was getting dark I thought I'd bed down and wait to see if anyone came back.

But no one did.

I got up the next morning and excitedly went down to the mining floor with my eyes full of money signs. There were so many holes I didn't know which one to choose. So I dipped until I settled on a big one to my left. The hole in the side of the rock was big enough for five grown men to stand side by side, and deep too. So I strapped on my head-torch and shouldered my pack and started to explore.

Within five minutes the sunlight cresting through the hole was almost a pinprick and the darkness drew in. I must have walked down that shaft for thirty minutes before I started picking out signs of life with my head-torch. Although there wasn't anyone in the mine, there were signs that work had taken place. Numerous old oil lamps hung on the walls, and mining tools scattered the floor like they had been discarded haphazardly. I even came across an old generator, but I didn't know how to work it so just carried on.

As I got deeper and the darkness became absolute, I heard what I first thought was wind, but something about it unnerved me. I don't know what it was about it, but it seemed to have the quality of words. Yet, I didn't recognize the language and thought maybe it was just the wind. Do you know that feeling when something is on the edge of your hearing and you strain to try to make out what it was? That's how I felt; the more I listened the more it unnerved me.

At some point, I realized that my light wasn't the only thing illuminating the tunnel. I turned off my head-torch and saw another pinprick of light further down the tunnel. When I turned my torch back on and it shone on the wall, I couldn't believe my eyes. I had found it.

Gold.

Not enough to fill my fingernail. But gold nonetheless, and it was all mine. I carried on wanting to see if there was more lacing the wall. The tunnel narrowed quickly and I had to hunch over. It got even tighter, and I had to surrender my gear. I took out my hand-pick and pushed on until I came to the source of the light.

As I wiggled through the small opening I fell into a chamber that bore a striking resemblance to the world outside. It too looked like whoever had been working there had just stepped away. There were a few boxes of mined gold laid against a wall, and piles of dust-covered clothes lying in heaps on the floor.

A pinprick of sunlight came through a hole overhead and it shone on a drink container in one of the piles. That's what was lighting my tunnel. There were a few more large passageways littering the wall, but all were dark. I looked into each with my head-torch but didn't see anything worth exploring, not with the gold in boxes within arm's reach.

But what was better than those crates were the walls: gold and other precious gems filled them, I couldn't believe my luck. Still stunned at my findings I turned to a wall that didn't have any passageways on it and stopped.

A large, crude picture of a creature with long arms and legs loomed over me. The more I looked at the thick lines of the creature's body the more I swear it fucking moved. Like it was a snake charmer weaving its magic and I was its snake. I couldn't tear myself away from its red eyes gleaming down at me. I saw my hand reach out like I was in a dream and touched the wall; then all of a sudden I was back on the mining floor, and it was night.

I couldn't explain what had happened, sure I knew I had been underground for quite some time, but to not remember coming out? For some reason, as I pondered what had happened I drew up to the stars above. Have you ever been to a place that has no electric lights and looked up?

It's an incredible thing.

I looked at the heavens, for the first time truly seeing what it offered. More gold and jewels than the mine held sparkled in the heavens above me. I felt truly insignificant and empowered all at once. After a while, I forgot what I was doing standing in the middle of the mining floor, so I went back to the shack and fell asleep.

There are some things you can never remember even when you try your hardest, and sometimes there are things you wish you could forget.

The next morning I noticed the food again, but didn't feel hungry despite not eating the day before. It was like I had already eaten and didn't need the nutrition. I went back down to the mining floor, picked another tunnel and set out again. This time I found stuff a lot sooner. Not gold but the crude drawing of the elongated man scattered on the walls. The pictures showed the same long-legged, long-armed being, only smaller than the one in the last tunnel and amongst them, I saw the effigies of people being tortured.

Have you seen Da Vinci's divine man?

Well imagine that, but with his skin pinned around him. Like someone had opened him up to take a look inside. And the worst part, there were hundreds of them. Hundreds of splayed figures pinned to rocks and trees. Although the marking underneath held no color, I knew the smudges were the blood pooling around them into a river that flowed down the tunnel away from me. The more I saw the more revolted I felt.

At one point, what I had been taking for random strikes on the wall turned more organized, and it dawned on me that what I was seeing was writing, although it wasn't in any form I had seen before. I carried on following the pictures and writing until I realized I had reached the same chamber as yesterday. The large creature loomed over me again. I felt kinda weird looking into its eyes, like spaced out and present at the same time. I saw my hand reaching out to touch it again and bam. I was right back on the mining floor in the dark of night.

I knew I had only just gone down that tunnel. Maybe two hours at best.

But, there I was standing in the pitch black with only my head-torch lighting the dusty floor. I figured I lost about ten hours. My watch stopped working some time ago, so I'd no way of truly knowing. I didn't know what to do as anger swelled in my belly. I wanted to get some gold. I hadn't actually harvested any and that was the whole fucking reason I was there. I decided to go down another tunnel and get what I had come for.

I think that was my last bad decision. Maybe I should have walked away there and then, but I didn't.

I went down every one of those fucking mines; every time I came back out in that chamber, and every time I saw myself touching the creature until I woke up outside. It wasn't until the last time when I knew something was really wrong.

I had forgotten my name.

I wandered around the site trying to find what I was missing. Trying to remember why I was there. Why I was standing in this barren place with nothing but a head-torch and a broken compass. I don't remember how long I had been in that godforsaken mine, it could have been days or years by that point. It wasn't until I stumbled over the signpost that I had a flicker of a memory. I thought the position of the signpost was strange, kinda out of place, so I followed where it pointed.

The further I went, the more I remembered. Little things at first, like my name.

Danny.

Also why I was walking under the blistering sun with no provisions. I don't know how long I walked for, I stopped when I had to rest, drank when I found water and ate whatever I could find. I was eventually saved by an aboriginal guy named Brian. I owe him my life.

It's been hard since I first set foot in Australia and now I can't even go home. There's nothing left for me.

Remember I said I lost something far more important than gold? I went looking to change my fortune just after my fortieth birthday on March 24th, 1918. I don't know how, but I think I was stuck in a time loop. That's what I think the clothes were. The people who worked there. I think they stopped remembering. I think they found that creature, whatever it was, and it kept them prisoner there. Kept them forgetting, forgetting to eat, forgetting who they were, why there were there in the first place until they became the dust that covered the place.

Sometimes when I sleep I have dreams of that mine, like it's never left me and will be a part of me until I die. I'm in those tunnels, searching for something, when the creature reaches out and grabs me, pulls me into the walls of those mines. I feel like I become one with it, with the walls, with the mine.

I went in search of gold, and what I found I can never be rid of.

FOR SERVICES RENDERED

By Kyle Harrison

THERE WAS SOMETHING SPECIAL ABOUT SUMMER DONAHUE. Everybody who ever met her said so. All of us girls envied her during middle school and junior high. She was smart, she was sassy, she had boyfriends, money, and a good life.

While the rest of us had to work hard for what we wanted, it seemed like everything always fell into place for Summer.

She also destroyed everything I ever cared about.

It started when we were able to arrange a senior trip to Europe for our marching band.

Because Summer was our captain she got to pick where we were going to go, and according to our band director the sky was the limit.

While most of us wanted to visit Barcelona or Paris, Summer insisted on a quieter locale, amid the tranquil countryside of Romania. She said she wanted to enjoy a good old fashioned camping trip.

So of course, given the fact that it costed a lot less and we could stay longer; the band director agreed with her choice.

We all got our parental consent and packed our bags to leave a week before spring break.

I didn't know it at the time, but that was when my boyfriend Todd had started talking to her.

There was tension between Todd and I already, thanks to an argument we had had at the Valentine dance.

Todd said I had trust issues, I was sure he was already cheating.

Still I wanted the trip to be our chance to rekindle our relationship.

It was about three days after we got to our destination that I found out that they were doing a lot more than talking.

When Todd confessed to me, all I could do was cry and run off to the woods we were staying close to. I didn't care where I was going, so long as it was far away from him.

There I was, literally thousands of miles from family, in a small secluded forest, walking in circles and crying my eyes out. Wishing all the perfect people in the world could be knocked off of their pedestals.

That was when I saw him.

I had been zoned out watching the clouds rolling over the mountains. Then my gaze strayed to the end of the tree line where this ancient oak stood, and I found myself staring at a handsome muscular young man.

He had to be no more than two or three years older than I, andbut something about the way he sat there and slowly smoked on a strong cigar made him alluring.

He was dark- haired, tall, and had perfect green eyes that twinkled with a hint of mischief hiding behind them. He sported a dark fur coat and a fitting leather jacket, well- ironed slacks and mountain boots that had recently been shined.

As he tossed the cigar to the ground, I realized he had noticed me and I turned away in embarrassment.

Before I knew it he had moved across the clearing to where I was and shot me a charming smile.

""Care for a smoke?"" he asked.

He had flowers pinned to the lapel of his coat. They smelled like dirt, which instantly set turned me off.

There was something attractive about his confidence though, so I responded in a flirtatious way, "I'm probably too young for you." "But old enough to know how to have a good time?" he responded as he leaned against the oak beside me.

"I should be, but instead I'm here with you," I said.

"Tell you what, let's share a cig and a conversation. I get to know you and you me. You don't like what you hear, then we go our separate ways. No harm, no foul," he responded.

There was something special about the way he said things. It made me feel comfortable.

"Okay, one smoke," I conceded and then checked my watch, "And you got fifteen minutes until my curfew."

Not that I had really anything to be running back to camp for.

He smiled broadly and I saw he had yellow ugly teeth;, then he waved his hand in front of my face and made a cigarette appear.

"Local magician?" I asked him as I took it nervously.

"Something like that,"he said.

"A small town like this probably doesn't get many tourists huh?" I said, suddenly feeling like the air was getting colder as we spoke.

He shrugged and answered, "Sometimes. I don't come near to town that often though. But tonight is special. So you should feel thankful."

"Oh really?" I smiled back. I was enjoying the playful banter. But I didn't like the idea of being here in these woods alone with a stranger.

"You came to Romania to learn about the culture right?" he asked.

"Eh... it's a long story," I said and checked my watch again. "It's getting late. Thanks for the smoke though."

"Leaving? We haven't even made proper introductions yet," he said.

"Look... you seem like a nice guy. But honestly I doubt this is going to go the way you're hoping dude," I said. I was starting to wonder why I was even lingering there, arguing with him.

Maybe he reminded me of those people that could always get their way.

"What if I told you that it could go the way you wanted though?" he asked.

I snickered at him and stood up to leave. "That isn't how life works," I said.

I stepped away from him ready to get away before

things got any stranger. I was halfway toward the edge of the clearing when he spoke again.

"Tell that to Summer Donahue."

I froze in my tracks.

I turned toward him and blinked for a second.

"How do you know about her?" I asked.

"I know a lot of things. Like I know if you keep walking you will leave an ordinary life the rest of your days," he answered.

"And if I stay?" I asked as I moved toward the center of the grove again.

"Then we get to know each other a little better," he explained as he passed me a professional business card that was written in Romanian.

"I don't understand," I admitted as I kept feeling like he was staring at me. "Hmm, I thought for sure I had it right; check again," he remarked with a sly grin.

I looked at the business card again to see that the words were slowly fading, and changing from Romanian to English.

"Martolea Julihov, private entrepreneur; professional handler; available every Tuesday and Thursday night to the weary and weak," I said reading it aloud and then tossed it on the ground. It faded away into the earth.

"That's a pretty neat magic trick," I said, laughing nervously.

"You don't believe in things you can't explain, but you will," he said.

He paused and raised his coat up to cover his face for a moment. Then he dropped it and I found myself staring with my mouth wide open.

I was looking at the visage of a hag, her face was covered with sores and warts. Her teeth were misshapen and her hair long and grey, her eyes nearly grey from blindness.

I found myself stumbling to get up at the shock of the sight and mumbled, "What... what are you?"

"I have many names, dearie; many names that you will forget. the one on my card will suffice for now," she said.

I wanted to run, to scream at the top of my lungs. But something in its gaze prevented me from doing so.

She whispered softly to me, "There is no need to fear, dear child. I told you already that I am here to help you."

"To... to help me how..." I asked.

"First you must listen to my voice... and hear my words, and forget this place," sheit responded.

It felt so easy to slip away. I didn't know why but I accepted his calling and soothing voice.

"Forget.. this... place.....," I repeated.

"Your friend, Summer. She has everything that you do not. What would you give to take it away from her?" Martolea asked.

I thought about it for a moment. I knew it was offering me some kind of bargain so I asked, "You would hurt her?" It sounded so enticing.

"I would make her pay the way that you feel she deserves. As you can see, I'm a professional. And my services are well known here in this country," the thing explained.

"And the price?" I asked.

I knew there had to be one. No offer like this could

possibly be free. The wind had stopped as the two of us stood there in the clearing.

"For taking a life, one must be given. An eye for an eye. But I'm not unreasonable about this. It will be the death of a stranger, someone you have never even met. I will find them and the price will be paid," Martolea said.

I couldn't resist thinking of the possibilities of what Summer had in store. The more I thought about it the more I realized this was really what I wanted.

No one would ever know, I told myself. I shook her hand and felt a sharp burn on my palm. I looked at the small mark she had made, and then found myself alone amid the forest again.

I strolled back to the campsite and started to wonder if any of it had even been real. I saw Summer and Todd near the mess hall acting like love birds and felt rage. Maybe I had imagined the encounter simply to get revenge?

Then as I settled down to sleep for the night, I heard the screams.

They were coming from the cabin across from me where the other girls stayed. Where Summer was at.

I grabbed a light coat and followed the other girls outside and toward the other building.

The crowd made it difficult at first to know what had happened but then, as our band director cleared the room, I could see the carnage. It was Summer Donahue, of course.

Blood stained the floor, leading up to the edge of the bed where bits of flesh and bone were hanging loosely. Her body looked as though it had been shredded from the torso down, and her entrails hung against the back wall with nails staked into them, wrapping around her neck and choking the life out of her.

There was no sign of what happened to her lower body, but it wasn't hard to imagine that the Martolea had made quick work of it as well.

I ran outside into the darkness as the girls spoke of a strange animal that had entered their room and attacked Summer. I felt my heart beat out of my chest as I looked toward the forest. I wondered if the Martolea was watching me as I stood there and tried not to vomit.

The cold air crept around me.

Our trip was cut short after the incident, and on the way home my boyfriend and I made amends with each other. At first I thought he was just feeling sorry for himself but eventually our relationship grew stronger.

I went on to get married to Todd, and last autumn we decided to start planning to have a family together. As time went on I forgot about Romania and I forgot about Summer. I was soon pregnant with our first child.

I have to admit those first few weeks I was in complete shock.

Then tragedy struck us a few weeks later when we went for our latest ultrasound.

The doctor called us the next day to tell us that the baby would not live beyond my first trimester. I remember listening to the dead static of the phone and trying not to cry.

The doctor explained that I was at risk as well and needed to come to the hospital for an emergency surgery to get the baby out before what was killing it caused the same effect on my body.

We drove that night to get the procedure done, and I remember squeezing Todd's hand as I prepped for surgery. I was more scared than I had ever been.

I asked them to put me under and it felt like an out of body experience that some people sometimes talk about. I could see the surgeons working on me as fast as possible to save my life.

Then I saw a shadow cross over the room and I heard laughter. In between the darkness I saw sharp gleaming green eyes.

The air grew cold again.

The demon's hands transformed into claws as it began to tear open my belly. His mouth shaped and opened wide to reveal sharp rows of jagged and rotting teeth.

I heard a cry, like that of an infant, and watched helplessly as the creature took the baby from my womb. Then as the darkness covered us both on all sides it began to devour my child. I could only watch helplessly.

I screamed and kicked and cursed. I wailed at the top of my lungs as he ate my baby, his smile becoming smeared with its blood.

Then I woke up in my hospital room, I found myself surrounded by family and friends coming to offer their support and care for me.

I was too paralyzed to say much of anything except a few simple words.

As the night wore on they lingered until at last it was just me and Todd in the room alone. I thought about the dream I had, and then woke my husband up. I had to confess everything to him. I cried as I found the words to say.

I started at the beginning and as I went on with the story he at first thought that it was beyond belief. Then as I explained the price that the demon asked for he got quiet.

The death of a stranger.

He stood up and walked over to the nightstand where many of our guests had stopped by to offer us condolences and small gifts and picked up a bouquet of flowers.

He brought them to my side and showed me the note that went along with them.

For Services Rendered—- MJ

They smelled like dirt.

UNCLE HOWARD'S CABIN

By Kyle Harrison

WHEN I WAS A LITTLE BOY, MY FONDEST SUMMER MEMORIES were spending time in the north woods at my uncle Howard's. He had this rustic old cabin that was surrounded on all sides by nothing but pure nature.

The local hunters called it Howard's Hideout. Every time my brother John and I would visit a new adventure would await us.

But as you grow up those things fade and you find yourself focusing on the adventures of adulthood. They aren't nearly as fun, and you can't just wiggle your nose and change the story.

I wish I could change this story. But this isn't about me. It's about my uncle and the legacy he left behind.

Howard died last June from a massive heart attack. I remember when John called me at work to tell me the news. He knew I was always particularly close to our uncle.

A rush of memories flooded over me after I got off the phone. Fishing down at the creek, setting snares along the property line, listening to old westerns as he popped a bag of kettle corn over the open stove.

What stuck out the most was the ghost stories Uncle Howard would tell.

That evening John and I went out for drinks and I asked him what his favorite campfire story Howard told us was.

"Gee, bro... I don't know. He told us a lot of crazy things," he said with a laugh. I prodded him for a moment longer and finally he gave in and said, "That one about the bear."

I sat there and drank my own whiskey, remembering the story quite well.

Uncle Howard had had a way of making the monsters extra vivid in his stories and none of them were more frightening than the entity that John recalled.

According to our uncle, the creature was about as large as a seven-foot tall man with massive claws that could tear a person into twelve pieces all at once.

Papa Bear is what he called it.

Apparently despite being so fearsomely large Papa Bear was actually not all that dangerous or so Howard reassured us.

"He's a protector of these woods, keeps the good in and the bad out. That's why you boys are safe here, Papa Bear is watching out for us," he said.

Apparently Papa Bear decided who was and wasn't

welcome in the woods and eliminated any threats to keep the forest secure and magical. Though I knew that somehow John and I were spared, I recalled every detail of what happened to its victims.

Those who trespassed were not simply killed. He made sure to tell us that the victims became slaves to the abomination, tasked to clean the forest that they had defiled. I knew even as a young boy Uncle Howard was trying to make sure we kept nature clean, but still; it scared the shit out of me.

Especially at night when the wind would whistle through the old cabin and it would make everything sound so loud, like a groaning noise or a wailing. I remember vividly hiding under the covers one night when the sounds went on for hours, I didn't even get up to go to the bathroom and instead peed on myself just to stay safe.

"Who do you think will get the cabin?" John asked me. I had to admit I really didn't know, considering that my uncle and aunt had divorced quite some time ago.

"It seems a shame to just let it sit out there," I said.

Later that same week I spoke with his second ex-wife Denise on the phone. (Our aunt, Rena, died around the time I went to college.)

Denise admitted she didn't really have any idea about the last will and testament or if it even included anything about the cabin, but promised she would look into it.

That Saturday my dad and I went to hear the reading of the will. A few of our other relatives I hadn't seen in a while were there. I even saw Howard's estranged son Walker show up.

"Wasn't he in prison?" my dad whispered to me when he walked in.

"You're the cop, not me," I said back as Walker sat down a few rows ahead of us.

"You know what, I think I remember now; it was just a misdemeanor on illegal possession but they always thought he might have been involved in the Cooper case," my dad whispered back.

If you have lived around this area long enough, then you would know what my dad was talking about. For those of you who don't, about six years back a family went missing on the north stretch of the interstate near the Stateline.

The investigation into their disappearance revealed that they had been planning a fishing trip for the family into the woods, husband and wife and two girls.

Shannon, the oldest girl, was the only body they ever found, around a year later.

Apparently she had somehow survived that long out in the woods and was trying desperately to reach civilization but ended up running into a meth lab.

The same meth lab that Walker had been busted for a few months after her body was found there.

I had never read the full report, but it struck me as odd that the timing of the two events was so close together.

A few moments after my dad made this comment the cabin was mentioned in the will, and to my shock and dismay it was Walker that had managed to get the property.

I followed him outside after the reading was finished

and found him leaned against the building smoking a joint.

He gave me a lopsided smile. "Brian! It's been awhile," he said as he offered me a smoke.

"I'm clean now, Walker. Pretty crazy about your dad, huh?" I told him. He nodded, not saying much. I knew that he had always been jealous of John and I.

Uncle Howard had always been much more of a father to us than him, and I was positive that had always rubbed him the wrong way.

"So whatcha need Brian, I know you didn't come out here to just chew cud with me," he said.

"You going to the funeral tomorrow?" I asked.

"Gotta pay my respects to the old man," Walker answered.

"I know it's probably an odd request... but I was hoping maybe I could handle the distribution of his remains..." I said.

"His ashes?" he asked with a nervous laugh.

"I was just thinking about his cabin out there and... and how much he loved it," I explained as I tried not to tear up.

I knew Walker wouldn't understand. But I was surprised when he agreed to let me have the canister.

"You can fling 'em all up and down the county for all I care," he said as he tossed his burnt cig down.

I talked with John about my intentions to head to the cabin that next weekend and my brother suggested we make a camping trip out of it, a final way to say a final goodbye to Uncle Howard.

We drove up that Saturday morning in the late June

heat. We took John's pickup truck and I remember having to keep myself cool by using a wet rag and some ice because he didn't have AC.

By the time we had arrived I was sweating so badly I decided to head down to the creek for a swim.

"You ain't getting out of helping me get this shit inside," my brother told me.

Even though we both felt like we were going to have a heat stroke, I helped him carry our luggage inside and set it down on the couch.

"It still looks like it's still in good condition," John said.

I had to admit I was impressed with the cleanliness of the cabin and I wondered immediately how long it had been since Howard had been here.

"He really loved this place," I realized.

We looked around at some of the hunting trophies that he had hanging on the wall, and I remembered Howard teaching me how to skin small birds to prepare them for the stuffing process.

"Remember that all things on this earth are created to serve men, boy. You don't want to hurt God's creation, and you want to respect life," Howard told me.

I saw one of the geese I helped to preserve and reached up to touch the feathers. It was amazing how after all these years it still seemed in perfect condition.

The woods made everything feel even more inviting, like we were taking a trip back in time and experiencing everything for the first time.

We followed the western trail, listening to the gentle singing of the birds and looking at some of the old snares of Howard that were still set up.

Once the trail came to an end we relied on memory alone to reach the creek. The water looked as clear as it had when we were kids.

I didn't take a moment to hesitate and tossed my shoes off and let my feet relax on the right side of the stream.

John took off his shirt and jumped into the deeper portion of the creek, howling excitedly. It felt so good to be here. We stayed down at the creek for about an hour and then John suggested we do a little bit of hunting.

Back at the cabin, I walked down to the basement to find any of our uncle's guns.

The basement was in a bit more disrepair than upstairs, but I recalled that Howard kind of used it as a spare closet, storing all his junk there.

Near the back of the room I found a small locked cache where he kept all his rifles and then rummaged through the other drawers nearby for the key.

A gentle sound like a whisper seemed to slowly creep into the room and it made me pause in what I was doing. Then the noise grew louder.

It sounded like the noises we heard when we were younger.

A gentle muffleding wail.

I took the keys and grabbed a few guns, leaving the basement behind and feeling a little unsettled.

As we walked out toward the woods, I told John about it.

"We're barely here a few hours and you are already hearing things? Man I can't wait for tonight," he joked.

I laughed it off as nerves or just my imagination.

We followed the other trail behind the cabin up

toward the mountains. I had brought our uncle's ashes along, remembering that one of his favorite spots was along this path.

It was a scenic overlook of the forest itself and nearby lake, Uncle Howard usually wouldn't let us come up there as kids cause of the precipitous slopes. There was one time we did though. We were going up to bury a deer there which was unfit for eating, and Howard showed me a pit where other hunters also disposed of animal carcasses.

"This keeps the bears happy," he explained.

I found the pit again after a little trial and error and decided this would be a perfect spot to release Howard's ashes.

I held a handkerchief over my mouth and opened the canister, watching as the wind carried the ashes away.

Then my attention was drawn toward the pit itself and I noticed something out of the ordinary. It took me a minute to realize what it was.

"Holy shit," I shouted out as I took a few steps back from the ledge. John was there in a second and I wordlessly pointed down the slope to where the littered remains of a few bones were at, along with a human skull.

"Jesus," John said.

He decided to climb down and examine the bones. A few minutes later he was back up on the slope with me, looking concerned.

"We should probably call dad. I can't tell for sure if that was an accident... or something much worse," John explained.

Neither of us said anything as we returned to the

cabin. I almost felt like we were being watched. But once we got there I decided I wasn't going to let it ruin the weekend.

I searched through Howard's freezer and found some thawed deer meat at the top to cook.

John was walking around the cabin trying to get reception on his phone and then finally admitted, "This is what I get for switching to T-Mobile."

I checked mine and noted I had a few bars so I passed it to him, and he walked outside to make the call.

I walked to the back of the cabin where the propane stove was at and turned on the gas to get everything heated, and paused as I listened to the soft whistle of the ignition light coming on.

Beneath that noise I was certain I was hearing the same wails I heard earlier. And a repetitive thudding noise.

It made me feel very uncomfortable as I cooked and tried to ignore the sound.

When John came back in he told me dad would be there first thing in the morning to examine the body. The noises had stopped for the moment but I was becoming more convinced than ever that the cabin was actually haunted.

That evening, as the sun went down, John searched through the second story closets for blankets and we both agreed to sleep in the living room.

"If this place really is haunted, we'll know tonight won't we?" he said.

I stayed awake until almost one in the morning

listening for anything. Then at last the noises returned. It sounded like gentle footsteps.

Then there were voices. I couldn't make out what they were saying but I instantly woke up John.

He switched on the lights in the living room and listened as well.

The noises were growing louder.

"What the hell...?" John said as he felt something under him. But neither of us could see anything on the floor. Then I felt it too, like a low vibration.

Nervously we moved to the second floor. The noises became more subdued and somehow we found a way to get back to sleep.

In the morning dad got there and we guided him to the ridge.

"Should we... tell him about the other thing?" I asked John as we trekked up the mountainside.

"Tell me what?" dad asked. He had always had excellent hearing.

"This is probably going to sound crazy... but Uncle Howard's place... it's got ghosts," John answered.

Dad looked at us both skeptically but we insisted he come back to the cabin and see for himself.

We all headed inside and John and I tried our best to explain what we had heard.

"It felt like something was moving around under our feet," John added.

Dad was trying to not roll his eyes. Then the noises returned, soft and subdued like before.

He pulled out his firearm and looked about muttering, "What sort of prank is this?"

"It's for real dad," I said as we walked around the cabin listening to the strange moaning noises.

Dad made his way toward the stairs, walking carefully to the basement.

The thudding got louder as we looked around the basement. and then dad gestured for all of us to be quiet and still. I was too scared to move a muscle.

Then he walked toward Howard's old tool cabinet and started to push it aside.

I watched silently as he revealed a large wooden door hidden behind it with a metal lock. The noises were coming from the other side.

Dad pointed his weapon at the lock and shot it off without hesitation. and all of us stood there in fear as the door creaked open.

A thin, skeletal woman collapsed onto the floor in front of us. Dad rushed over to help her, quickly glancing at the bruises on her legs and arms, like she had been chained.

"Don't just stand there! Call 911!" dad shouted to us. John took out his phone immediately as I took a few steps toward the door.

There was a dark tunnel beyond that curved into the solid earth, and I found myself stepping forward to see what the darkness hid.

As it curved around I found myself standing directly under the living room in a wide open den, where more chains were latched to the ground as though meant for animals.

The place reeked of the smell of urine and feces.

I held my mouth closed as I looked across the room to

see the decaying corpses of at least two other women and at last I understood.

John had followed me down there and then found himself running back up and vomiting.

I found a large cabinet on the west side of the dungeon filled with photographs.

I cannot begin to describe the things that Howard made them do while they were trapped down here.

The woman that dad rescued turned out to be the youngest of the Coopers that had gone missing six years ago.

She only lived for another two days due to bladder failure.

It's been almost eight months now since I went to the cabin.

I've tried not to think about the horrors I found there, but lately they've consumed my every thought.

And John... he handled it the worst. Once he realized the true depth of our uncle's depravity, all those times we spent summer there... giggling when we listened to the low wails that whispered their way through his cabin.

The guilt made him take his life.

I've returned to the cabin now, with one singular mission. I doused the entire first floor with gasoline and then activated the stove on a low setting.

I sat outside in the pickup truck and watched as it burned. It sounded like the cabin was screaming as it fell apart into shambles, like it was in pain.

But the pain I felt will always be greater.

THE TREEHOUSE

By Kyle Harrison

THERE ARE SOME STORIES THAT YOU CAN'T GET OUT OF your head, no matter how hard you try. They are like the roots of a tree, working their way deep into your subconscious.

This is one of those stories.

It didn't start out this way of course, because most things never do. Like a young sapling it flourished until finally producing foliage. And then it becomes time to pluck the fruit.

The only way it can be harvested and release you from its unyielding vines is if you tell it and purge it from your soul. So that's exactly what I intend to do.

Before my husband Leon and I got married and had our daughter we used to take a lot of romantic weekend getaways in and around the four states area. We both lived in Idabel, Oklahoma back in 2012, so planning a trip to somewhere like Queen Wilhelmina wasn't all that hard.

After saving up our money for about four months though we decided to do something different, and head towards the rustic scenery of the Ozarks.

Leon insisted that the entire thing be planned by him because we hadn't gotten a chance to celebrate our one year of dating anniversary. And even though I felt like I could predict where he would take me, I let him have his fun.

We grew up as childhood sweethearts, and during high school developed a relationship. What really drew us together was our mutual love of camping.

He knew more than anything I dreamed to experience the great outdoors every day if I could.

So when he announced he had found isolated cabin for us to stay at I was ecstatic. And that excitement only increased when I realized the private lodge was designed like a tree house.

Valleyview Treetops got about three-and-a-half stars online; not bad for a place that apparently was only three years old. The pictures showed that it was a secluded park-like area with about eight or nine lodges available, and a few more under construction.

Ours, suite #11, had a majestic view of the expansive forest that covered most of the eastern horizon.

When we arrived I was pleased to learn Leon and I were pretty much the only guests booked for the next four days, so we would have the campsite to ourselves.

It reminded me of one of those tree houses you might

see on the DIY channel, with an elaborate staircase rising from the ground for us to reach our private lodge.

While Leon was unpacking our bags I took a minute to walk around the spacious interior and open the blinds.

When I opened the window near the back of the cabin I was a bit surprised to see another treehouse a little deeper in the southeast ravine.

It looked far older than any of the models we had driven past, with the large branches of the hickory pines almost swallowing it whole. The construction of the tree-house looked like it was meant to resemble one that a child might build, with a solitary window and a rope ladder used to climb inside.

With the windows boarded up and the foundation clearly decaying, I figured it was probably some idea the lodge had concocted to draw in more customers but one that had never grown popular.

When Leon had finished bringing the bags upstairs I pointed it out to him and he gave it a curious stare.

"Huh, kinda spooky looking isn't it?" he commented. I gave him a smile but didn't have the guts to admit it made me feel uncomfortable to have our window open, so I closed it and then fell into his arms.

I wasn't about to let some weird abandoned tree house ruin our trip.

After a round of love making, I took a shower and walked back down to the car to get my camera gear, wearing nothing but a shower robe. I figured since we were the only ones out here it wouldn't hurt.

But my hopes were dashed as soon as I got to the car,

when I saw a group of men step out of a white van parked adjacent to the hill.

They didn't seem to notice me observing them, so I stood there for a minute and watched as they set up all sorts of equipment like they were about to film something.

My curiosity got the better of me and I grabbed one of Leon's coats out of the trunk and walked over to them.

One of the cameramen spotted me and gave me a friendly smile; I don't know if he was nervous cause he found me attractive but he seemed surprised to see anyone else here.

"Good afternoon, ma'am," he said as he adjusted his ball cap.

"What are y'all doing out here?" I said as a soft chilly breeze flitted through my wet blonde hair.

Before he could answer another man, shorter and fatter, approached me and smiled broadly before speaking.

"Howdy! Franklin Dean is the name, did you come to try and brave a night at the Valleyview Tree of Terror?" he asked with a laugh.

I looked at him in puzzlement and then saw that the cameramen were adjusting their equipment to point towards the abandoned tree house just beyond where we were staying.

"I'm... not sure what y'all are talking about..." I admitted hesitantly. The chubby older man smiled at me and gestured toward the strange decrypted lodge.

"That there is the reason we came here sweetheart. My team and I are expert paranormal investigators and we explore the active sites offor spirits in this area including mountains, swamps and well, well this!" he explained as he gestured toward the treehouse again.

"Y'all think it's haunted?" I asked skeptically.

It certainly looked like it could be.

"We got several reports from folks who stayed here reporting they heard ghostly screams in the night," another camera man said as he strolled by with his equipment and added, "And they said they heard the sound of scratching against their windows."

I wanted to call their bluff, knowing that I had seen far too many faux reality shows with a similar premise. They were just trying to cash in on this rundown treehouse, probably without any permission to probably even be there.

But I lost interest in with them and went back upstairs to tell Leon about our new neighbors. He was flipping through the channels on the TV while I watched the five of them carefully climb the rope ladder to get inside the abandoned cabin.

As it drew darker I noticed that they still hadn't come out and I commented dryly, "I bet they set up some kind of sound booth in there to make ghostly noises. We probably won't get any sleep."

"Don't worry, I'll protect you," Leon teased. I rolled my eyes and kissed him before tucking in.

Sure enough, about an hour later the noises I had predicted started to slowly wind their way through our cabin walls and woke me up.

These guys are pretty hardcore, I thought as I felt my hair stand on edge.

It's not real, I kept telling myself as I heard the whispers and the sounds of wailing.

Then the noises intensified and I heard scratching on the outside of the cabin.

"Seriously??"

Leon fumbled out of bed and raised the window to get a good look at the treehouse. It looked pitch dark inside but we could still hear the sound of the screams.

They were distant, almost old and echoey, like you would hear in a typical haunted house.

"This is annoying. I should go over there and give them a piece of my mind," he insisted.

"Oh let them have their fun,"

I told him as I yanked him toward the shower, "Besides, there's other ways that we can distract ourselves."

With the water hitting our naked bodies and our loud moans we were able to drown the noises out for a minute.

The rest of the night we watched television, since it seemed their film shoot wasn't going to be over until morning.

The next day Leon decided to go talk to them anyway, despite my efforts to convince him to let it go.

"They probably weren't planning on bothering us anyway," I said as I followed him toward the ravine.

He ignored my protests and walked carefully down the side of the pass to reach the rope ladder even while I followed behind.

The ladder creaked It as he went up to the top and then he started banging on the door to get their attention.

"Leon! Stop!" I told him once I reached the top.

"I want to see how they like it when they are disturbed," he commented as he tried to look past the boarded-up windows to catch a glimpse of the five men.

"It doesn't look like anybody is here," he said.

"Maybe they went out?" I suggested, feeling even more uncomfortable in this strange place than I did a moment ago.

Before I had a chance to again tell him again that we should leave, Leon used his elbow and knocked out one of the boards to get inside.

He pushed himself through the small passage and I waited for only half a second before following him inside.

The dark and dank space made it difficult to see anything, but it was clear we had stepped into some sort of living space.

Dust and decay covered the whole room and Leon covered his mouth and nose. A few seconds later the odor hit me as well, and I realized it smelled like something had died here recently.

"It doesn't look like anybody has used this for a while," he observed and used his phone to shine a light toward the ceiling.

Roots were growing in from the tree.

We stepped into the kitchen.

When we got there I saw something shimmer near the kitchen table and when he focused his light on it, both of us stood still as we looked at the strange ensemble of vines that covered what seemed to be a human form slumped over on a plate. As we got closer and I examined the man's face, I realized it was one of the camera men I had seen.

"Leon, he's been dead awhile," I said my heart racing as we looked about the strange open space.

Next was the master bedroom, where Leon was staring at the paintings on the back of the wall. I looked as well and I saw what seemed to be more strange dark roots encasing four individuals in the bark.

"They died here, they all died," he muttered as he scrambled to leave.

"How did it take their bodies so quickly?" I asked looking toward the table again and seeing what appeared to be a toppled over camera near the man's foot.

I couldn't help myself and propped the camera up, surprised that it still had battery life. Leon was tugging at my arm to leave but I simply had to press play.

The video came to life, filled with the sound of static, and I saw the five men standing in the dining room smiling at each other excitedly. They were getting ready to set up their other cameras and film the strangeness events of the tree house.

One of the camera men focused on the odd roots that we had seen entangling the roof and said, "Seems like every minute we stay here they move."

The video clipped and became distorted as Leon and I watched the men experience a phenomenon I can't even describe. The tree house was coming to life, ensnaring them in its grasp.

One of them was meshed into the wall before he could run away, another felt the roots tighten around his body as he filmed.

"Help us, please, we're stuck here," Franklin, the director, shouted to the camera.

As though he knew we were there, like he was speaking to us directly.

"We need to go," Leon said. I felt the tree house watching us, like it was coming to life as we hurried to leave.

But I couldn't resist. I took the memory card out of the camera out and raced toward the exit alongside him and down to safety.

The soft screams were whistling through the vines as we hurriedly climbed back down.

Leon caught his breath as we stood there and I looked up toward the strange enclosure, trying to make sense of what we had just seen.

"It's a trick. They set this all up to just scare us. Cause otherwise we would be dead too right?" I muttered softly. I flickered the memory card in between my fingers, desperately wanting to see the rest of the video.

He said nothing as we walked back to our own cabin, and it always felt like the abandoned tree house was watching us.

That night, as he took a shower to calm his nerves, curiosity got the better of me and I inserted the memory card into my own digital camera.

I watched in silence as the video showed one of the men laughing madly, and then roots springing out from his mouth and eyes.

Until it covered his body like a second skin.

Then it changed perspective as though some unseen force was guiding the imagery.

And I saw myself. Kissing Leon, pushing him toward

the shower. Making love to him while this ethereal force watched on in silence.

I closed the camera and tossed it toward the ground in horror. I ran toward Leon and told him I wanted to leave immediately.

He tried to reassure me it was all a trick of the camera as we walked toward the car.

But then we looked toward the east ravine and the tree house was no more.

Swallowed up by the forest.

We did not ask for our security deposit back.

POLICE SUSPECT FOUL PLAY

By P. Oxford

I WAS WORKING ON A LOCAL HISTORY PAPER FOR A COLLEGE class, flipping through microfiche of the local newspaper, when a headline caught my eye. After a series of articles about how a big storm would ravage, did ravage, and had ravaged the small coastal community, it stood out:

"Unidentified man found dead, police suspect foul play"

I skimmed the article. There weren't a lot of details, but he had been found in the same remote area that I used to live. Why hadn't I heard about it? I leaned back in the squeaky office chair, and stared up at the white library ceiling. I remembered that storm; it had been the most dramatic storm of my young life. I closed my eyes as hazy memories fit themselves together in my mind. I had seen a man outside the cabin, hadn't I? And I sat for a police sketch?

It all came rushing back.

I WAS CURLED up on the old armchair in front of the fire-place in the cozy living room of the old cabin. The wind was howling, the rain drumming on the window, and the many little streams that had appeared since the rain started were gurgling outside. The heavy rain made the mountainside behind us come alive with water, the newborn streams gathering into larger flows before they hurled themselves over the steep rock face in spectacular waterfalls—while I was safe and warm between the timber walls.

I stared intently at the page I was trying to read, attempting to ignore the conversation in the kitchen. My parents were talking in low, tense voices again.

"We're out here in the middle of nowhere," mommy let slip in a slightly louder voice. "That little girl needs friends!"

I reached out a hand to turn up the radio to drown them out, but daddy hushed her. I didn't need to hear, I knew why they were arguing. The little farm house in an isolated part of a deep Norwegian fjord used to be our cabin, and we had moved here after daddy lost his job. I didn't know why it bothered mommy so much, I loved having the forest as a playground. I turned the page of my book, and stared intently at the next page, willing it to come alive and distract me.

"...The storm is hitting small coastal communities hard," a newscaster read from the radio. "We have reports of several large landslides along the S—fjord. A slide has blocked road 6—, likely isolating the small community until the cleanup work can be finished. In other news..."

"Did you hear that, Jon?" Mommy's voice rose. "Did you hear that? The goddamn road is gone! We're stuck here! What if there's an emergency? We're trapped until they drag their asses out here to fix it!"

I couldn't make out daddy's answer, but it was probably something about keeping her voice down. The wind howled, drowning out the rest of the conversation in the kitchen.

The sky darkened further as the sun set, and I moved closer to the fire. I finished a particularly scary story in the horror collection I was reading, and delighted in the chills that ran down my spine.

Something scratched the wall.

I jumped in my seat, heart pounding. Something had come out of the woods, something was scratching at the far wall of the house, it was gonna come in, it was gonna break down the wall, I knew it! Werewolves? Monsters? A cry for help rose in my throat, but I swallowed it at the last second. I didn't want another stern lecture on the danger of reading horror stories. And it was probably just a branch.

The wind howled again, with an eerily human quality. I shuddered, and put the book on the wooden coffee table next to the chair. I glared at it, before glancing towards the kitchen door. I could still hear soft voices out there. My parents were still there, in the next room, I thought with relief. Well, for now, but they slept all the way at the other end of the hallway... I shivered. Stupid me, why did I read those stories?

A muffled thud rang through the room. I sat up straight, looking at the flowery curtains that covered the view of the woods behind the cabin. Branches don't do that. Had the wind gotten strong enough to fling logs around? I considered tiptoeing over to the little window, to peek out through the gap in the curtains to the dark tall firs that surrounded us. Immediately, I pictured a man pressing his face against the window.

God, that stupid, stupid book. In the story I just read, a boy sees the ghost of an old sailor peer through his little window. The illustration that accompanied the story would come to haunt me for years and it kept me from looking out the window as surely as if I had been shackled to the chair.

Instinctively, I pulled my feet up onto the chair, disturbed by the idea of someone grabbing at them. I quickly promised myself I'd never read another horror story. Another human-like howl from the wind made me pull my knees closer to my chest, and a low gurgling sound sent my heart racing.

It was definitely just the wind and a stream, though.

The door slammed open, and I jumped so I almost fell out of the chair. Daddy chuckled as he entered, saying something about children and horror stories before shooing me off to bed.

I brushed my teeth as slowly as I could, before walking hesitantly down the hallway to my room. Had it always been this long? I couldn't stop myself from glancing out the little window in the front door, and jumped as a flash of lightning illuminated the tree outside. I couldn't shake the image of the fisherman with his face pressed against the window.

In my room, the sounds of the woods seemed louder than ever. I tugged at the curtains, making sure there was no gap between them, no little opening for someone to peek through. Breathing in deeply, I bent down so that I could jump into my bed, keeping my ankles out of reach from anything that might be hiding in the dark abyss beneath it. Then I curled up under the huge down duvet, pulling at the corners so that every part of my body was covered, leaving no limb dangling over the edge for anyone or anything to grab at. Daddy came in, kissed my forehead, and told me to sleep tight, before closing the door and leaving me all alone in the little cave of darkness, miles and miles away from the safety of my parents at the other end of the hallway. After a few uneasy twists and turns I drifted off to sleep.

I awoke with a start, the outline of a nightmare fading, leaving me with a feeling of dread. I sat up, quickly turned on the bedside light, and pulled the duvet up to my neck. Could I stay awake until morning? Leave the light on? … run into my parents room? No, I decided, I'm too old for that. The wind howled, and I whimpered, pulling the duvet up even higher. And then I heard it.

Footsteps.

Right outside my window. I looked around wildly, but the heavy curtains saved me from having to see anything outside. I pulled the duvet up to my eyes. Lighting flashed, and thunder shook the room. I squealed, jumped out of bed, and was halfway down the hallway before I remembered the window. The window in the front door didn't have curtains, it was exactly the same size as the window in the story, with just enough room for a face, and I had to pass it to get to my parents' room.

My heart beat faster, but I couldn't turn back now. Just three more steps, and I'd be safe. I didn't even have to look, I could just stare straight ahead, and then I'd be safe. I retreated a few steps back towards my room, and turned on the hallway light.

Two steps forward, pause, deep breath, run, don't look.

But I did look.

The world froze.

There, in the little window, lit by the light in the hallway, was a face. A man, wild-eyed, hair plastered down the side of his face, a strange sneer on his lips, was staring back at me.

The world unfroze, and I screamed. Footsteps rushed towards me, warm arms hugged me, and I screamed until I had to gasp for air.

"There was—there is—there's a man! Outside! Out there!" I stuttered, pointing at the dark square in the door.

But there was nothing but darkness in the window.

"Aw, honey, there's nothing there!"

"No, he was theeeeeere!" I started sobbing.

"Shh, honey, it's just the storm, it's scary, I know."

"No," I sobbed. "Someone was there!"

Mommy bent down, holding my shoulder.

"It's ok sweetie, daddy will check if someone is outside. Don't worry!"

Daddy got up, and walked over to the door. He looked

out the little window, and went to open the door. The moment he pushed down on the handle, the door slammed open. A gust of wind brought the rain all the way into the house, and I was soaked in a second. I screamed again at the sheer shock of the natural force out there. My dad, ever my hero, poked his head outside and looked around. He jerked back, and slammed the door close. When he turned around, he was pale as a ghost.

"Nothing there," he choked out, doing little to reassure me. "Nothing at all!"

"Daddy, I saw a man!"

"Sweetheart, there's nothing there," he tried again in a calmer voice, locking the door behind him. "But know what? I think you should spend the night with mommy and daddy!"

"Why did you lock the door?" I asked suspiciously. Scared? My dad was never scared, what was happening? I cried even harder.

I heard him take a deep breath, saying: "Nobody is out there sweetie, I told you so!"

But then he switched to English so that I wouldn't understand, and spoke quickly in a low, tense voice. I had my head buried in mommy's shoulder, so I couldn't see their expressions, but I noticed mommy's sharp intake of breath.

"What?" I sobbed, "What is it?"

"Oh, nothing sweetie, just something wrong in the garden, you know, the water..." he trailed off.

Another terse exchange in English.

"Ok, hun, right now, you and me are going to bed, and

daddy will call some people about the—about what's wrong in the garden."

"What's wrong in the garden?" I asked suspiciously. "The man is still there, right? He is! I know it!"

"Nonono, baby, nothing serious. Come here, we'll sleep in the big bed together tonight! Won't that be fun?"

I scowled at her, furiously wiping the tears in my eyes. I knew they were hiding something. I knew it. She led me into the living room, closing the kitchen door behind us. I could hear my dad talking on the phone.

"…days?! No, we can't wait for days, there's a—"

"Jon!" mommy yelled, "We can hear you!"

He lowered his voice, and the rest of the conversation was lost to me.

The storm raged for three whole days—the three most boring days of my life. My parents decided to board up the windows, claiming they were worried about the wind, so I couldn't even look out. And I wasn't allowed to leave the house. It wasn't fair, all my life I had been told "there's no such thing as bad weather, only bad clothes," shoved into rain gear, and pushed out the door to play. And now, when I wanted to, I wasn't allowed. They wouldn't even let me listen to the radio. I just sat in my chair reading, while mommy paced up and down the living room, and daddy cleaned his shotgun even though hunting season was months away.

Three whole days of this. I was sure I would lose my mind.

I didn't notice the wind dying down. But on the morning of the fourth day, I heard a new sound, one I had never heard before. It was far away at first, but approached rapidly. A rhythmic succession of thudding sounds, like a flag flapping in strong wind. But the flag wasn't up?

"Moommy?" I yelled. "What's that sound?"

"Sound?" she said. "I can't hear—Oh, that's a helicopter! Oh thank the lord, they're coming for us. Jon!"

"Who is?"

"Oh. Well, erm, the police, sweetie. Because of—well, the road."

"We get to ride in a helicopter?" I said. "A real one?"

"We'll see honey."

A couple more hours inside the house, and then I really did get to ride in a helicopter. I craned my head around as mommy led me across the lawn; the police had strewn stuff all over, and part of it was covered by a big tarp.

I had to sit down with a sketch artist to draw the man I had seen. "It was probably just a nightmare," my dad assured me, "but just in case it wasn't and someone misses him, the police want to know what he looked like. Don't worry about it!"

And I never did. It's amazing of what you can convince a child.

I LEANED BACK in my chair. The memory had left a bad taste in my mouth. How had I never questioned these events?

I started flipping through the newspaper faster and

faster. For every new day, there was another horrifying headline, as details became known to the press.

"Unidentified male victim's death ruled a homicide"

"Murder victim was found decapitated"

"Head of murder victim not found"

"No leads on murder—police claims storm washed away evidence"

I shuddered as the sketch of the man I had seen in the window rolled across the screen.

"Eyewitness rendering of man likely connected to murder case"

A bit more hesitant now, I scrolled on. The next headline that hit me like a punch to the gut:

"Family trapped for three days due to storm, decapitated corpse in their garden, murderer still on the loose."

A quick Google search gave me all the details of the case.

The man in the sketch had never been identified, neither was the victim. Not a single clue ever turned up. All they knew was that two men had walked through the storm, through the woods and up—or down—the steep hills surrounding our house, and, once practically at our doorstep, one had cut the head off the other, taken it with him, and disappeared forever.

NORTHERN LIGHTS

By P. Oxford

I NEVER WANTED TO GO ON THAT STUPID HIKE IN THE FIRST place. Yet there I was, allegedly enjoying nature and getting healthy exercise while hiking from cabin to cabin in the Norwegian mountains with the devil spawn commonly referred to as "my classmates." Wohoo, right? For a misanthropic misfit like myself, it was a nightmare.

It just took half an hour of struggling along the uneven path over the heather for me to end up at the very back of the group.

"Hey man, how's it going there?" Nils, the teacher, asked in a cheery tone.

"Fucking amazing," I growled.

In spite of the cool wind, sweat was beading on my forehead, and my breath was growing short. I glared at Peter and Jon, who were bouncing along at the front of the group. Of course the most popular guys in my class would also be the best hikers. Assholes.

"So, Anders, do you go hiking often?"

"Do I go hiking often?" I said. "Look at me, teach, do I look like I fucking go hiking often?"

I gestured to my pudgy body, glaring at him.

"Then what do you like to do?"

"Computer stuff," I answered curtly. "So is this temporary, or are you gonna try to make awkward small talk the whole time?"

"Well, I didn't think it was awkward, but if that's how you feel..."

I looked up to find Peter and Jon out of sight—damn soccer players and their mutant lungs—and I used the opportunity to take in the scenery. Misshapen, warped birch trees were scattered over the alternating yellowing grass and purple heather. Mountains cascaded towards the sky on both sides, towering over us. It was quite breathtaking.

Now that the devil spawn was out of sight and lame ass Nils had shut up, I found myself almost enjoying it. In fact, I realized the whole experience would have been quite pleasant if all those fuckers would just go ahead and die. I kicked at a rock, and tripped.

"Hey there, be careful, buddy!" Nils said, catching my arm to steady me. "Don't wanna go and get injured on the first day, do we now?"

I sent him a death glare, and we kept walking in silence.

By the end of the third day, I was not just at the rear, but pretty much in a whole other hiking party then the rest of my class. My body ached from the strain, and Nils had long ago abandoned any attempt at small talk.

When the last cabin was finally within eyeshot, the sun had disappeared behind the mountains, and we were hiking by that gloomy, blue half-light that lingers long after the northern sun sets. The cabin loomed in the distance. What we called a cabin was really a set of small, red cabins, an empty campground, and a rather large main house. It could easily house a hundred people, probably way more with the campground open. It looked out of place there, in the middle of the bare mountains.

I was completely exhausted when I finally managed to drag my fat ass to the front door of the main house. As I pulled it open, I was immediately hit in the face with the laughter, shouting, and all the other sounds of general youthful tomfoolery. Damn devil spawn. A sour feeling spread though my guts; I was missing out on all of this. I had no idea how to socialize with these people. God, I wished they'd all just die, maybe then I'd get some peace and quiet.

"So, Anders, it seems the rest already finished dinner, I guess it's just you and me now!"

I groaned at the prospect. To add insult to injury, the dining room was at the other side of the common room. I looked down at the linoleum floor as I walked through the room, face burning as I endured the laughter of my peers. They were clever enough to not directly mock me, but I knew what they were thinking.

Nils and I sat down at one of the long tables in the empty dining room, and I stuffed myself full of the cold pasta as he chatted easily. A friend of his ran this place, it was technically closed for the season, but he had gotten us in here as a favor. That's why there weren't any staff around; they'd dropped off food earlier that day, and now we had the whole place to ourselves. So there we were, thirty kids, two teachers, and the vast, empty space that stretched between the mountains.

"Eerie when you think about it, right?" he said, winking. It was.

I got up from the table as soon as I could, with every intention of going straight to bed. I took a deep breath to steady my nerves enough to walk through the common room again. Laughter rang through the door, filling the dining room, taunting me with happiness and camaraderie I was sure I'd never experience.

I opened the door, and felt their eyes on me as I shuffled through the room. "You can't even look at us," they mocked. "You can't even keep up on a hike." "Fat loser, go home, we don't want you here." Nobody actually said anything out loud, but I knew they were thinking it.

I walked quickly to the room I was sharing with Peter, Jon and another kid. The assholes had left me a bottom bunk, like they were such nice people. Probably too scared to sleep below fatty, I thought bitterly, glaring at the pine bunk. They'd probably laughed about it, too. I wanted to be in bed, asleep or believably pretending to be when they got here; they didn't need to see my pudgy pale tummy, or smell the sweat that had permeated all my clothes. And anyway, the place was completely outside cell range. Without my trusty internet I had little to live for, let alone to stay awake for.

I curled up under the duvet, and the exhaustion

drowned out my usual self-depreciating internal mono-
logue. I was asleep in minutes.

I woke up in a panic in the middle of the night. The
room was pitch black, and I just knew someone was
standing over my bed, looking at me. My heart was
pounding in my throat, as I lay there for what felt like
hours. Nothing happened. Of course nothing happened, I
tried to tell myself. I was being silly, I was safe, there was
nothing but miles and miles of empty woods around here
where anything could be hiding, could have followed us,
could have seen us, defenseless, alone, NO! You're safe,
don't be silly.

How the hell had they made the room this dark?
Where was the crack in the curtain, the red standby lamp
on a device? I wanted to turn on the light, to see what was
there, but I didn't want to wake up the others. Guess I was
more scared of their taunting eyes than I was of the crazy
axe murderer that definitely was in the room. As a sort of
compromise I decided to go to the bathroom. I sat up,
swung my legs off the side of the bed, and felt around for
my shoes. I snuck out the door, flicked the switch in the
hallway, and glanced back into the room. Nothing there,
of course. I just had to make sure.

I padded down the hallway, the ugly red wall to wall
carpet muffling the sounds of my steps. I shuddered as I
opened the bathroom door; it was freezing. Some idiot
had left the window open. I did my business, and shuffled
over to the window to close it while rubbing my arms
with my hands. I stretched out an arm to grab the handle,
and froze.

The night sky was visible through the window, and I

had seen—it couldn't be, not this far south, right? It could be, of course, but... really?—soft green light spreading across the starry sky. It was the first time I saw them: northern lights.

I bounced down the hallway, and snuck into my dark room. I grabbed a coat and my phone, and was halfway out the door before I thought to wake up the others. They'd probably love to see the lights as much as I would.

Screw them, not like they'd wake me up if the tables were turned.

The grass crunched as I walked across it, the frost that now covered the ground glittering in the strange green light from the sky. A green blob stretched across the darkness, flickering slightly as if there was a strong wind up there. The lights weren't particularly strong or defined, but I don't know anything else that can turn the night sky green like that. The fear I had felt when I woke up had drained from my body, and I was mesmerized by the pure beauty of the natural show. I stood there for hours, not moving until my whole body started shaking violently and I realized I was in danger of hypothermia.

I shuffled back to the door, and cast one more glance at the sky before I opened it. My eyes had adjusted to the darkness outside, and I snuck down the hallway without turning the lights on. I didn't want the grim, fluorescent light burn out the beautiful memory of the Aurora. The little light on my phone was enough to identify my room. I paused outside the door, sighing, and quickly slipped inside. I curled up under the warm duvet, and fell asleep.

I woke up, stretched my arms over my head and yawned loudly. I groped around on the floor for my phone, and closed one eye as the bright screen blinded me.

10:37

Immediately I was wide awake. Shit, shit, shit, breakfast at 7:30, hiking by 8:30, why the hell had nobody woken me up? I jumped out of bed, almost hitting my head on the bunk above me in the darkness. The blinds were down, the room dark. I flipped the switch on the wall, but nothing happened. I groped around for my clothes, struggling briefly as my head got stuck in the sleeve of my sweater. I opened the door. The corridor was dark too, the place dead quiet. A chill ran down my spine.

Had they left me behind as a prank? No, Nils would never have agreed to that. Would he? I pictured his flustered face as I shut down his every attempt at small talk. Maybe he would. A slow burn of worry started in my gut as I thought of the miles and miles of empty wilderness surrounding me. All that empty space, the long lonely road. The road! Yeah, someone would have to come get me, I wouldn't have to hike anymore. Maybe this was all for the best. Actually they had probably just cancelled the hike, and all the kids were in the dining room now.

I set off to find people or food, preferably both.

The common room and the dining room were both empty. They looked so much bigger today, when it was only me in them. I crossed my fingers that I'd find some leftovers in the kitchen. I pushed open the door with the "staff only" sign, shuffled across the linoleum floor, and opened the fridge. A big smile spread across my face as I took in the sight in front of me. Is there anything more beautiful than a fully stocked fridge?

I made myself a sandwich, and munched on it while trying to decide what to do next. I went to make a second one, and paused, staring at the packed fridge. Enough food to feed thirty kids and then some. Hadn't anyone else eaten? Again, the image of the vast heather, the lonely road, the cabin that looked like it had been copy-pasted into the wilderness. Anything could be hiding out there, in the mountains, in the rooms—oh god, the rooms. There were so many empty rooms, empty cabins, closed doors. Closed doors with god knows what behind them.

I should have checked the rooms. Why hadn't that been my first move?

Panic spread again; I had to do something before I was completely paralyzed by it. I took a deep breath, got to my feet, and left the kitchen. My footsteps rang through the cavernous dining room. My heart was pounding in my throat when I snuck down the long hallway, past door after door, the only light what seeped in from the window at the far end. The gloomy sky outside did little to provide light, and even less to assuage my fears. I stopped in front of my room. It felt like a safe place to start.

I pushed the handle, and the door slid open without a sound. The room was as dark and quiet as ever. I crossed the room in two long strides, and groped around for the string to the blinds. I tugged at it, and jumped slightly as the sound of the curtain rolling up rang through the room.

I turned around, and to my great surprise found Peter sleeping peacefully in his bed. Relief flooded through me. I wasn't alone.

"Peter!" I croaked. I cleared my throat. "Peter!" I repeated a little louder.

No response. I stared at him, wondering why he was still there. And why he looked so oddly... still.

I took a step toward him.

"Peter..." I whispered, heart pounding in my throat.

I reached out, grabbed his arm under the covers, and shook.

No response. He seemed totally dead.

The thought hit me like a ton of bricks. Dead? No. No way. Absolutely not. I forced my shaking hand towards his neck to check for a pulse. My fingertips made contact with his icy skin, and I knew. He must have been dead for hours. My knees buckled under me, and I crashed to the floor. Peter was dead? He was just lying there, he had been lying there for hours. Right next to me, and I had walked in and out of the room, I had eaten breakfast, I had slept there, right next to his corpse. Oh god.

I threw up.

I scrambled to my feet, I needed to get out of this tomb. I steadied myself on the upper bunk, and jumped back in shock when I saw Jon, just as still as Peter, in his bunk. I stretched a shaking arm, I had to make sure. I shuddered as my fingers met his skin; he was as cold and dead as Peter.

Slowly, I turned around. I screamed as I looked right into Jacob's open eyes. His dead, cold, stare burrowed into me, and I backed away. I hit the bunk behind me, and the force made Jon's arm fall over the edge. It hung there, swinging.

I couldn't take my eyes off the arm as I backed out into

the corridor. I slammed the door shut, and continued my desperate retreat until I crashed against the door across the hallway. My knees grew weak again, and I started sliding down the door. My arm connected with the handle, and the door swung open behind me. I staggered backwards, overbalanced, and fell, hard, on my back.

The fall knocked the air out of me. As I gasped for breath, I spotted an arm out of the corner of my eye. Still trying to swallow air, I turned my head. Lisa, beautiful, blonde, Lisa, lay there, not moving. I poked her arm. It swung in the air just like Jacob's had, and I stared at it, hypnotized. I turned my head. The girl in the other bottom bunk had rolled up against the wall. I steadied myself with my arm, and pushed myself up. On my feet, I saw two more bunks. Two more corpses.

I stumbled back into the hallway, looked side to side, and froze.

So many doors.

I only remember bits and pieces from what happened next. Running wildly down the hallway, pushing desperately at locked doors, slamming the doors that opened closed after revealing another tomb.

They were all dead.

I collapsed in a heap outside Nils' room. My throat was aching from the screaming or the vomiting; I couldn't say which. Tears rolled down my face, and my body shook convulsively. I curled up in a little ball, face on the rough carpet, sobbing like a baby.

Eventually the part of my brain that was still running some sort of script managed to take over.

Can't stay here. I peeled myself off the floor, and sat

up, leaning against the door. I should probably get out of here, I thought in a detached manner. The fear was gone, in its place numb coldness. After all, if I were in danger I'd be dead already.

Call the police, I thought, pulling my phone out of my pocket. It had 16% battery, and no signal. I pushed myself to my feet, leaning my back against the door. I needed to find a high point, but would the battery last?

I scrunched my eyes up, took a deep breath, and walked back into Nils' room. His phone was right there, next to the bed. I picked it up, pressed the button on the side, and watched it as nothing happened. I held the button for ten seconds before I released it. Still nothing. The phone was as dead as everyone else. I forced myself to go into the next room. Kristian, Thomas, Kristoffer, Lars. Three phones lay on the little table by the window, all plugged into their chargers. First phone? Dead. Second phone? I sent a little prayer to a god I had never believed in as I pressed the button as hard as I could. Dead. Third phone? Nothing. I threw it angrily at the wall, making a satisfyingly loud bang as it hit the wooden panel.

Gotta start hiking and praying, then. When I pushed open the front doors, it felt like I was emerging from a grave. I took a deep breath, and walked towards the hill behind the cabin at a fresh pace. A path revealed itself, and I marched resolutely along it; it twisted up the hill, and would—it had to!—lead me to a signal.

At first I checked the phone every five meters, but as the battery level fell, I forced myself to wait longer and longer between my checks.

The path twisted between small pine trees, back and

forth across the hill. My face burned with exhaustion and frustration. Every time I checked the phone, the battery was a little bit lower. 10%, and the phone sent an angry message. Do you want to turn on battery saving? Fuck yes! 9%. 7%. 5% and the screen dimmed the lights. A raindrop fell on the screen—or was it sweat? 4%.

3%. 2%. A single bar blinked, and I shrieked. With shaking hands, I pressed 1-1-2, and waited, praying.

"Police, what's your—"

"No battery! Need police at the—goddamn, the B—cabin, they're dead, they're all dead, I need help, please!"

The line went oddly quiet, and I lowered my hand to see a black screen. I hovered my thumb over the power button for a moment before I pressed it. That stupid opening graphic flashed across the screen, I frantically typed in my pin, pressed the phone icon, and watched in disbelief as the screen turned black again. I stared at it until the cold wind made me shudder. I was soaked with sweat, exhausted, and freezing.

Only then did it occur to me to wonder why they were all dead.

You'd think that would be the first thing on my mind, but it wasn't. Up there, on the narrow path between the dark fir trees, my last avenue of communication gone, was the first time my mind asked the question that would haunt me for the rest of my life: What happened?

Serial killer? No, why would I be alive. Poisoned food? Again, why would I be alive. They looked like they had died peacefully in their sleep. Airborne poison? Carbon monoxide! That made sense. You hear these horror stories: busted heater, family dead. Why not school class? And I had spent hours outside, in the fresh air last night.

Relieved, I turned around to hike back down. In front of me, a gap in the pine trees revealed a perfect view of the field and the cabin below, and what I saw there shattered my rational explanation. Down there, on the ground surrounding the cabin, was a perfect circle of brown dead heather and yellow grass. The main building sat at the edge, the spot where I had been standing last night was right outside it.

The police was there when I got back down. Later, the deaths were ruled accidental carbon monoxide poisoning —I was told to let it go when I asked about the circle.

And the northern lights? They hadn't been visible anywhere over mainland Norway for weeks.

THE LAST BUS

By P. Oxford

WHEN BRITTANY DECIDED TO TWIST HER ANKLE LESS THAN an hour before the last shuttle left from the trailhead, we were sure we'd be stuck in the woods overnight. Brittany refused to give up hope, claiming that sometimes buses are late, so we pressed on. And lo and behold, when we got to the trailhead the bus was there, seemingly waiting for us.

I wriggled out of the straps and dropped my backpack on the dirt next to the bus. I pulled at my T-shirt to unstick it from my sweaty back, and delighted as the cool night air touched my bare skin. There was no bus driver in sight, but the bus was open so I tossed my pack into the gaping luggage compartment. I took a last long look at the hulking fir trees that surrounded us, breathed in that earthy smell of warm, wet woods, and climbed onto the bus.

"Oh hey, we're the only people on here!" Lisa said from behind me. "Nice!"

I chuckled, plopping down on a seat near the front, while Lisa grabbed one across the aisle, stretching her long legs over the seat next to her.

The stuffy smell on the bus made me wrinkle my nose; I already missed the fresh air of the trail. Lisa nodded in agreement, before casting a longing glance outside. A shower and a bed was going to be nice, but if we could we'd have stayed on the trail forever.

"Uh, girls? Could one of you help me?" Brittany called from outside.

I looked at Lisa, who rolled her eyes. She had been doing that a lot since Brittany had latched herself onto our little hiking duo two days earlier, and I couldn't blame her.

"Can I hike with you girls for a bit?" Brittany had asked, flipping her long blonde hair over her shoulder, all puppy eyes, when we ran into her standing in the middle of the path. She was wearing old hiking boots, jean shorts and a T-shirt, and her little backpack did not look like it contained sufficient gear for a multi-day solo hike.

"Ran into a weird dude, got a super non-chill vibe from him, and I was like, not down with that, like, at all!" Thus she invoked the unbreakable girl-code: you must help other girls escape from creeps. We were stuck with her.

"Sure," Lisa called out. "I'm coming."

It was only fair, I thought, I had practically carried Brit the last hour, ever since her alleged injury. It was Lisa's turn. She took three slow steps towards the front, and sighed before she jumped down the steps.

"Here," I heard Lisa say, "I gotcha."

She managed to pull Brittany up the steps, and they walked down the aisle, Brit following with one hand on Lisa's shoulder the other on the seats she passed. Lisa slumped down on the double seat next to mine, no doubt hoping that Brit would take another double seat so we could all lounge. Brit, however, happily plopped down next to Lisa, tossing her small backpack on the seat in front of them. Lisa sent me a wide eyed look, and I snorted at her annoyance, not quite able to hide my amusement.

"Ohmigod, you're so nice, Lisa. Isn't she Mary? Isn't she the best? Like, she's so nice, right?"

"Yeah, sure, Lisa's the best," I chuckled.

"Ohmigod, I know right!" Brit said, while Lisa turned to face the darkening window, no doubt trying to conceal the fact that she was trying not to laugh. "And you're, like, so pretty Lisa."

Brit picked out a strand of Lisa's hair, and let it run through her fingers. I could see Lisa try to suppress a shudder—Lisa liked her personal space, and Brittany seemed to have no knowledge of the concept.

"Mary, don't you agree?" Brit turned to me. "Isn't she like so pretty?"

"Sure," I nodded, feeling the corner of my mouth curl upwards even as I fought the urge to smile. "She's pretty pretty, that one!"

Brit wasn't wrong. Lisa's long blond hair cascaded down her back in soft waves, her long, tan legs muscled by hiking and climbing. She looked like a model with her soft red lips, high cheek bones, and strong jawline, all of which had contributed to me realizing I was gay when we met in middle school.

"God, I wish I had your face, Lisa, literally. Like, literally I want your face. But, like, you too Mary. Like you're pretty too."

I nodded, still trying not to laugh. I'm not bad looking by any means, but next to the Amazonian Lisa, I looked like a hobbit. It had bothered me back in high school, but these days I not only accepted it, I had grown quite fond of my freckled face and unruly curls. Besides, my girlfriend thought I was hot, and Lisa's succession of shitty boyfriends had left me thinking that maybe I was better off being slightly less breathtaking. Ann never seemed to like Lisa, though I never understood why. Lisa really was so nice. As Brittany kept gushing over Lisa, I thought I should get her to talk to Ann—maybe she'd manage to convince her that Lisa really was, like, so nice.

"And you're like the nicest person." Brit continued. "Like, you're just like, helping a total stranger you don't even know. Like, that's so nice. Like, I think you might be the nicest person I've ever met, like, really, you're so nice!"

I made eye contact with Lisa, who was trying to keep herself occupied with picking at what remained of her red nail polish, and lifted an eyebrow. Lisa immediately turned away, coughing unconvincingly to cover her laughter.

"Thank you." I chuckled.

The bus driver climbed up the stairs, briefly glancing

back at the three of us. His eyes lingered a little too long on Lisa—eyes often did that—nodded at Brittany, and ignored me. The bus sputtered to life, and we were on our way home.

"Bee tee double-u, girls, I totally got your water bottles for you!" Brittany said, leaning around the seatback in front of her to pull them out of her backpack. "I was like, maybe they'll be thirsty on the bus, and like, it's so important to stay hydrated, right? Right?"

"Uh, ok, thanks," I said, glancing over at Lisa. Lisa rolled her eyes again.

"Here, Lisa!" Brit said.

"Yeah, thanks, I guess." Lisa said.

"Don't you want water? Like, it's important to hydrate!" Brit said, wide eyed. She turned to me, adding: "Dehydration is bad, right?"

"Right," I said, taking a deep sip from the bottle. "Hear that Lisa?"

"Shut up, Mary."

"But you gotta, like, hydrate!" I teased, adding a slight valley girl inflection to my tone, stopping short of blatantly imitating Brittany.

"Shut up, Mary, you know I don't like peeing on buses." Lisa snapped. Brit looked heartbroken, and I felt like a dick. Was my imitation too much? Did she realize we were making fun of her?

"I'm like, so happy I met you girls," Brit continued unfazed. Lisa closed her eyes, mhm'ing as Brit continued showering her with compliments. The bus bounced down the gravel road, and I soon started to feel drowsy. I never could keep my eyes open on long bus rides; I used to love closing my eyes just to wake up at the destination what felt like moments later.

"I'm gonna go nap in the back, girls." I said, getting to my feet. Lisa shot me look, clearly trying to tell me that I couldn't just abandon her with Brittany. I shrugged.

"'Kay! Night night!" Brit said cheerily, no doubt ecstatic about two hours of uninterrupted one on one time with Lisa. I made my way to the back, already half asleep, as Brittany prattled on.

I curled up on the seats in the back, checked my phone —confirming we were still outside cell range—and promptly fell asleep.

When I woke up, it took me a moment to realize where I was. I looked around. Oh right, the bus. It wasn't moving, and the engine was off. Were we at the terminal already? Nice!

I caught a glimpse of myself in the window, turned into a mirror by the contrast between the darkness outside and the lights on the bus. I chuckled at my messy hair. Even Brittany wouldn't be able find something nice to say about it in this condition. The bus was dead silent; Lisa had finally shut her up. I sat up, stretching my stiff body, letting out a groan. My neck cracked as I rolled my head, looking around. Something was off. I froze mid neck crack.

The bus was empty.

I got to my feet, and walked slowly down the aisle, checking all the seats on my way to the front. Nope, the girls weren't hiding, they were definitely not on here. I looked around again, a vague feeling of dread building. Silly, I told myself. Nothing scary about an empty bus. We were probably at the bus terminal, where Lisa had gotten annoyed that she couldn't wake me up, and left me. She'd probably texted me.

I pulled my phone out of my pocket, rolling my eyes at the empty triangle where the bars indicating a connection should have been. I shook it, trying to convince it that it should have service by now, but nothing happened. Piece of shit.

I walked to the door, and pushed lamely at it; it didn't budge. For a moment, my claustrophobia reared its ugly head. I took a deep breath and walked resolutely over to the driver's seat, where I quickly found a lever that looked promising. I pulled it, and the door slid open with a jarring screech.

The weak light spilled outside and down on the grass outside.

Grass?

I shuffled down the two steps, and peered outside. The smell of wet earth and rotting undergrowth hit me before my eyes adjusted.

I was still in the woods.

My stomach squirmed, and I swallowed to push my pounding heart back down into my chest.

I took a hesitant step backwards, retreating into the safety of the bus. The spinning wheels in my head ran through a million horrifying scenarios before arriving at a plausible one: The bus must have had engine problems, the others had gone for help, leaving me to sleep.

I looked around, trying to think while my heart started beating faster, my confused face staring back at me from every window. Just like two way mirrors, I thought, if someone is outside in the darkness, they'd see me perfectly. Don't think about stuff like that! I scolded myself. Nobody's out there watching, that's crazy talk!

A strong feeling of déjà vu washed over me; I had said the exact same thing before.

It was right after Brittany had joined us, and we were sitting around our fire. Lisa had been staring into the dark, and I asked if something bothered her.

"No, nothing," she had said. "Just, I thought I heard something, and then I started thinking about how someone could totally be watching us right now. If they just stay outside the light from the fire, we wouldn't see them, you know?"

Brittany had looked around wildly, anger or anxiety flashing across her face.

"Don't talk about stuff like that!" I had scolded. "Nobody's out there watching, that's crazy talk!"

I repeated the line in my head as I retreated further into the bus. I wanted to go find the girls, but I had no idea where they'd gotten off to; the only sensible choice was sit here and wait for them to come back, no matter how little I liked it.

I plopped down on the seat where Brit had been sitting; Lisa's seat had a nasty brown stain on it. For all her beauty, she sure wasn't overly concerned with hygiene.

Idly, I let my eyes trace the pattern on the seat back in front of me. The coarse, woolen material was worn, and I noticed that there was something that looked like scratch marks across it. Aimless vandalism, probably. I looked closer, more to distract myself from the mounting fear

THE TREES HAVE EYES

and loneliness than any real interest. Something was stuck in it. I leaned in, trying to get a better look. My head cast a shadow over the seat, so I moved a bit, trying to get the right angle. I picked at the thing, and it came off in my hand.

A fingernail.

A whole, bloody fingernail, ripped out of a finger desperately clinging to the seatback.

Nausea rose in my throat, and I jumped to my feet, shaking my hand desperately. The nail landed on the seat. For a moment, I couldn't breathe. The chipped red nail polish was unmistakable. It was Lisa's fingernail.

My whole body went cold with panic. I gasped, frozen to the spot. Three heartbeats, and something clicked. The brown spot was blood.

I got my phone out with shaking hands, and took a picture. Still numb with disbelief, I didn't move, I just stood there, phone in my shaking hand.

A sharp ping rang through the bus, thrusting my out of my trance. What the hell was that? Fear shot through me like electricity. A rock? Had someone thrown a rock at the bus?

I dropped to my knees, my instincts screaming at me to hide. I shuffled backwards awkwardly, trying to wedge myself into the space between the seats and the seatback in front of them. With shaking hands, I unlocked my phone screen, where the gray triangle stared back at me mercilessly. I dialed 911, heart in my throat, and sent off a quick prayer as I hit call.

One ring, two rings. It was going through! Beep. I stared at it in disbelief. The complicated piece of technology was about as useful as a brick. Less useful, a brick could be used as a weapon. I looked around, the darkness of the windows taunting me; I was blind as a bat.

Think! I yelled at myself. Think!

Another ping.

I instinctively jumped backwards, only to slam against the wall of the bus. The side of the seat dug into my ribs as I pushed myself as far into the safe little corner as I could.

An image of a giant, hulking man walking onto the bus flashed through my mind. There was one door on the bus, and if that was blocked, I was trapped. I had pressed myself into my coffin, not a safe corner.

I whimpered as a third ping rang through the bus, but I had to get off. I slid out from between the seats, and stayed low as I made my way to the front. I'll go slowly down the steps, I thought, and then make a run for it. I took a deep breath, and moved across the open space next to the driver's seat.

Another ping, and panic took over. I stumbled down the two steps half-blind in the darkness, fell on my face, scrambled to my feet, and ran.

"Aah!" I couldn't stop myself from screaming when something hit me in the back of the head. I whipped around, but I couldn't see anything in the darkness.

I stumbled again, but regained my balance in time, and bolted...

I ran until my breath burned in my throat and I had to slow down. I looked behind me, down the dark tunnel the fir trees created around the road. Empty. I stopped, holding my breath as I tried to listen. A hooting owl made me jump, but other than that not a sound. I wasn't being followed. In fact, I thought, maybe it had been nothing but pine cones falling on the bus.

The fingernail, though, I thought, getting nauseous. Next thing I knew I was spitting bile at the side of the road, head spinning.

I kept moving at a slower pace, shuddering as the cold night air made my sweaty T-shirt feel like a sheet of ice. I briefly considered going back to the bus for my pack, but felt bile rise in my throat as an image of the bloody fingernail flashed across my mind again. They say freezing to death is quite comfortable, anyway.

As the adrenalin receded, I became acutely aware of the pain in the back of my head. I gingerly ran my fingers across the spot, and they came back bloody. A really sharp pine cone? I glanced behind me down the road again, making sure it was still empty.

I kicked at a sapling that grew on the grassy road. If trees had started growing on it, I couldn't expect anyone to drive by me. The darkness gave way to a gray half-light, and I prayed I wasn't walking deeper into the woods. Around noon, the sun pierced through the clouds, warming me, and still I walked.

My steps got shorter, and my head started pounding. Dehydration, I thought. Like, it's important to hydrate. God, what happened to poor little Brit? At least she was with Lisa, I thought. If they were together, maybe it was less scary. I tried 911 for the millionth time.

Ring, ring, beep.

Stupid fucking useless piece of shit.

I stopped, staring at the phone in my hand, as a

graphic played across the screen and then it went black. Tears welled up in my eyes.

My dry tongue was glued to the roof of my mouth, the cold was stuck deep in my bones, and every part of my body hurt. Overwhelmed by hopelessness and exhaustion, I dropped to my knees, and then just rolled over. I'd just take a little nap, then I'd keep going. Just as I let my eyes close, something heavy hit my face. I jumped to my feet, the adrenaline surging through my body, giving me new strength. Spun in my spot, ready for fight or flight, when I spotted the pine cone next to me. Just a damn pine cone. Lucky, I thought. I would've died if I fell asleep.

The shadows grew long, and the cold spread back around my body. I wrapped my arms tightly around myself, as I forced myself again and again to take one more step. Just one more step.

"Dehydration is bad, right?" Brit's voice rang through the woods.

"Brit?" I croaked. "Brit, are you there?!"

Not a sound. "BRIT?"

"You're, like, so nice though."

"Brit, where are you?"

"Like, I literally want Lisa's face, but you're pretty too, Mary."

I yelled for her, looking around wildly. I needed to find her, to save her, to save Lisa. No reply. A horrifying thought made its way through my sluggish brain, as I shuddered again.

Severe hypothermia leads to confusion, and can induce hallucinations.

I am dead.

Not yet. Walk. When I finally saw a gray crash barrier in the distance, the sun had disappeared behind the trees, and the sky was a bright pink. If I was less dehydrated, I might have cried.

I made my way to the spot where the logging road met the asphalt, and collapsed in an exhausted heap. I just needed a little break, I thought. I looked around, and spotted a narrow ditch next to the road. I needed to be in it, it would be warm and comfortable. Not fall asleep, no, just close my eyes, just for a moment. I rolled into the ditch, tugging at my uncomfortable shirt, too hot now.

"Don't fall asleep!"

Blackness took over, and I was gone within seconds.

When I opened my eyes, I had to blink at the bright white light. Thoughts moved through my head like molasses. Am I dead?

A loud beeping sound made me turn my head, and as my eyes adjusted to the blinding light, I saw the heart monitor. Am I in the hospital?

Why?

"H—," I croaked, triggering a coughing fit.

The door slammed open, and a nurse ran in. Still in a daze, I let my eyes slide close, and only heard the steps of the next person entering the room. An eyelid was pulled up, and a bright light shone right at me. I tried to jerk away, but strong hands held me.

"Can you hear me?"

"Y—," coughing.

More tests, more questions, more coughing.

"I need to talk to her now!" a man said loudly.

"She's barely conscious, you have to wait."

"Listen, doc," a female voice interjected calmly. "A girl's life is on the line here."

"I know, that one in there. And she's my patient, so you'll have to wait."

"L-Lisa?" I managed to choke out. "Wh—where is Lisa?"

"That's what we're trying to find out."

"I—" I wheezed. "I want to help."

In a haze, between coughing fits, I forced out what seemed like a coherent version of what had happened. I showed them my picture, and they disappeared with my phone as I slid into a fitful sleep.

The next time I opened my eyes, I looked right at my mother's puffy face, streaked with tears.

"Oh honey," she exclaimed. "You're OK!"

"L—Lisa?" I stuttered. My mother broke down in tears, reaching out to clutch my hand in hers.

"They—they don't know, honey."

It all became a blur of doctors, police, my crying mother, and not a single thing that made a lick of sense; I slipped in and out of consciousness. More doctors, more police, whispers outside the door, a pounding headache, drugs, sleep.

The third time I woke up, my head felt clearer. Within minutes, a woman in a dark pantsuit walked into my room, shooing my mother outside.

"Special Agent Keller, FBI" she said, pulling up a chair next to my hospital bed. "We're trying to find your friend."

"FBI?" I said.

"Yes. Look, we really need to know exactly what happened. Can you help me with that?"

"Yeah, I guess, I—But I told the cops everything, why—Shouldn't you be out there looking for them?"

"Every piece of information matters. I'll walk you through what you told us so far, please stop me if anything sounds wrong."

"Yeah, of course."

"The evening of the 12th, you boarded a bus at the trailhead in Oregon, at ten past nine. The real shuttle had left ten minutes earlier, as scheduled. Between 24 and 36 hours later, you wake up—"

"What? No, maybe a few hours." I interjected.

"You told us you walked along the road for what seemed to be around twelve hours, right?"

"Right."

"A 911 call about a girl sleeping on the side of the road was placed at 11 p.m. on the 14th. An ambulance picked you up in a remote, forested area close to the Canadian border a little after 1 a.m. on the 15th."

"What? How?!"

"Your tox-screen showed traces of sedative in your system. You were drugged."

"I—" I choked, adding in a small voice: "What?"

"I'm sorry if this is hard for you, but we need your help to find Lisa."

"No, of course I'll help, I'll do whatever, just—" I paused, stomach dropping when I realized the implications of what she had said. "Wait, just Lisa? What about Brittany? Did something happen to her? Is she safe? Where is she?"

"Well, we're looking for her too. But this isn't the first time this happened..." She trailed off, rubbing her forehead. "What we really need to know is how you ingested the drugs. Did anyone have access to you water bottle? Food? Maybe you left them with the bus driver?"

"No, nothing like that, I specifically remember Brittany taking them out of our packs, the bus driver never touched them."

"Okay," the agent said. "And then—"

"Wait," I said, horrifying realization spreading in my gut. "Wait. Wait. Brittany took them out of our packs, Brittany... Holy fuck it's her! She did it!"

"Is there any other way you could have ingested the sedative?"

"No!" I almost yelled. "That fucking bitch! After all we did for her!" Then the first thing she had said hit home. "Wait, wait, wait. What do you mean this isn't the first time this happened?"

"Well," she sighed. "Lisa happens to be the third young blonde woman going missing along the PCT in the last two years. The two first were solo-hikers, the cases closed on the conclusion that they simply got lost after having left the trail. One went missing in Oregon and the other in California, so the cases weren't linked before now."

"How—" I stopped. "What happened to the other girls?"

She shrugged. "Never found."

My head started spinning, and I had to grab onto the side of the bed. I had walked through the wilderness for hours. There must be miles and miles of forest around the spot. Anyone could hide out there, could stay hidden for decades, forever. If Brittany didn't want to be found, she never would be. And neither would Lisa.

I was sent home with the assurance that I'd be the first to know when they found something, but they never did. No trace of Lisa, or Brittany. No trace of Brittany anywhere; no permits, no witnesses, no sightings, no nothing. When the police searched the logging road, they didn't find a bus. It was like the forest had swallowed all of them. Weeks went by, and nothing happened.

Until about two months after I had checked out of the hospital, when I came home late from work one evening to find an envelope in my mailbox. It didn't have a stamp, or an address, just my name on the front in big, black letters.

It contained three black and white photographs, looking like they had been developed in a home lab. The first was of my face, as I slept in the back of the bus. The second of the bus from the outside, me clearly framed in the middle of one of the windows, looking terrified. The third was me passed out on the side of the road, in a ditch between the logging road and the asphalt.

They slid out of my limp hands, and as they fluttered to the floor, I saw that something was written on the back of one. It landed face down, the words screaming at me:

"I'm sorry you're not my type, but I still had fun playing with you.

Xoxo,

Brit"

DON'T FOLLOW THE FIDDLER

By P. Oxford

WHEN I WAS A CHILD, I WOULD SPEND MY SUMMERS IN MY grandparents' old cabin in the woods, deep in the valleys of eastern Norway. My grandmother grew up in the area, and would tell me horrible tales of the underground people, to scare me from breaking the rules and keep me safe when I played alone around the cabin.

This is one of the stories, just like my grandmother told it.

I WAS YOUNG, then. Very young. And it was long before I ever met your grandfather, I want you to remember that when you hear the story, okay?

The day it happened, I was all alone at the farm. Did you ever see the farm? Did we sell it before you were born? I can't remember. It was in the next valley over from this one. The woods were the same as here though. Those tall, dark, fir trees that that throw the undergrowth into eternal dusk. You know how easy it is for someone to hide between them. And just as it's easy for you to hide, it's easy for something else to hide. And they do hide there, the somethings. Fewer and fewer of them, I'll say, at the rate we cut them old forests down, but that may be for the best. Oh dear, where was I? Oh. My parents were very poor, as you know. Back then we rented the little piece of land, and grew some potatoes and owned some hens. Later, a few cows. It was nothing like these huge subsidized farms we have these days, oh no. What my father could have done if someone only helped him. Well, that's not the story I'm tellin', so just forget about all that.

I was all alone on the farm, my parents had gone to the market. My brothers had gone to America to try their luck, as poor people did in those days. Died over there too, but that's neither here nor there. I was alone on the farm. Stop me if I start rambling again, will you?

Well, I was out on the marsh, picking cloudberries. Those days we couldn't afford exotic things like chocolate, or oranges, or those green whatchamacallits. But berries we had, and we had plenty. These days there are fewer of those too, but when I was young the fall would cover the marshes in delicious, sweet, orange cloudberries, like thousands of little suns. That day had been one of the rare sunny days in fall, and I was out there on the marsh as the day drew to an end. My head hurt from the sunshine, and the cold marsh water had started leaking into my left boot. I couldn't help but long for the cool, dry shade under those fir trees.

Maybe the forest could tell.

I was standing there, the marsh gurgling as I shifted my weight, the easy wind whooshing between the trees when I heard it. Faint, far off, but clear as day. I paused, listening. It couldn't be—but it was, wasn't it?

A fiddle.

Now, I have always loved the sound of the fiddle. I didn't get to hear it very often, though, music was a luxury back then. Every once in a while, a fiddler would come to our little village, and if your great-grandfather was feeling generous, I'd get to go to the dance. That's how I met your grandfather, but that's a story for another day. In this story, I was standing in the middle of a field of cloudberries, hearing the sounds of a fiddle as it called to me from deep in the woods.

At first I was simply intrigued, curious about what kind of person would be playing the fiddle with only trees as an audience. The next thing I knew, the music had seeped into my very soul. It thrilled, jumped, gurgled and laughed, just like a stream. It roared like a waterfall, it flowed like a river. It coursed through my veins and flooded into my heart.

Now, I've been alive for many a year and heard many a fiddler play, but nothing ever came close to what I heard in those woods. Without thinking, I followed. I had to see who it was who could create such beauty.

At first I walked, slowly following the ebb and flow of the sound. The further into the woods I got, the louder the music, and the more urgent my need to find its source. I started running. I dodged between trees, jumped over rocks, and slipped on moss.

All the time, that sweet, sweet sound was getting louder. It washed over my body, flooded my whole mind. It didn't leave room for any other thought; no misgivings, no suspicions. I was filled with singular purpose: find the well from which the music sprang.

Suddenly, I was at the river. For a short second, I paused, looking around. Then the fiddle let out a long, wailing note full of longing, and I heard the sound of the waterfall. The rushing sound of the water provided a deep bass line as the fiddle picked up speed again. It became an orchestra, a whole symphony. The clucking stream, the rushing waterfall, the fiddle soaring above it all. I walked reverently over the soft green moss towards the waterfall. I was close, the rush was gone, but the need—oh, the need!—grew stronger with every step. If you could only have heard that music, you would understand. I took three more steps over the soft moss, closer to the point where the forest floor gave way to a cliff, and the stream hurled itself into the deep pool beneath.

The music stopped. My head snapped up, and I froze. My heart stopped, my breath caught in my throat, because there he was. Right in front of me, close enough that I could touch him if I reached out my hand. The most beautiful man I have ever seen. His blonde, beautiful hair flowed down past his chin. His young face was smooth, no hint of stubble, not a single blemish. High cheekbones, a strong jaw, a soft mouth curled into a wild smile. His bright blue eyes had a dark, hungry look in them. I quivered as he fixed me with his gaze. Never have I felt less

343

safe, but never have I felt so alive as I did in the moment our eyes locked. I couldn't have moved if I wanted to, but I didn't want to. Ten wild horses couldn't have made me budge.

He put the fiddle down on the soft moss, never looking away from me.

"Anna…" he whispered my name. The word moved through my whole body, stirred parts of me that had never been stirred before. It was electric.

"Come." His voice was smooth, melodic. It sounded like the first stream in spring, after the long winter. Like a lazy river on hazy summer eve. You smile, I see it, but you'd understand if only you could hear it. He held out his hand for me. As I moved to take it, a gust of wind blew my hair aside, exposing the silver crucifix I wore around my neck. He flinched, anger flooding his face. He pulled his hand back, shaking his head. Then he turned around, picked up the fiddle, and walked straight into the water. He was gone.

I stood there, shaking all over. The spell had been broken, and my longing turned to fear the moment I realized what he was. What he was trying to do. That was the Nøkk. I knew the stories, of course. He'd spellbind young girls—sometimes young men too—with his music, and in their desperation to hear more they'd follow him into the water and drown there. I said a quick prayer, holding the crucifix. They don't like things of Christ, things of silver, things of steel. As long as you have that, you are safe. As long as you're strong enough. Remember that.

I know I almost wasn't.

I said my longing turned to fear, but not all of it. Still I had half a mind to throw away the crucifix and jump into the waterfall, just to see if he would play again.

But I didn't, and he didn't.

For weeks I longed for that music. For weeks I tried convincing myself that it was dark, wild, evil. As the days passed, and the memory faded, I became stronger in my convictions. I was a child of the Lord, the wild things in the woods would not make me stray from my path. I would be strong.

But then, on another sunny afternoon much like the first, maybe two weeks later, maybe three, I heard him again. I was alone on the farm, leaning against the timber wall of the little house as the sun warmed my face when the fiddle rang through my soul. All my resolve faltered, melted away like snow under the spring sun. I wanted— no I needed—nothing else than to go with that man, that beautiful young man who could play the fiddle like the devil himself. Even if I knew what he was. Even if I knew he wasn't one of God's creatures. Oh, what he made me feel wasn't of God. But that music, that voice; all I wanted was to be with him, if only for a brief moment. Maybe an eternity of damnation would be worth if I could just hear that voice, if I could just feel his touch. Just for a moment.

I got to my feet, and took a slow, hesitant step towards the woods. Another step, and I stumbled. I landed face down in the dirt, and the sharp pain in my hands pulled me out of my madness. I crawled into the house, slamming the door shut behind me before the music took over again. I bolted the door, and stuffed my fingers in my ears.

It did nothing to drown out the music. That beautiful, dark, wild music. Music that made me want to run into

345

the woods, rip my clothes off, and be carried off by the river. Music that made me want to turn my back on the Lord himself. Desperately, I searched for a way to fight the temptation.

My eyes fell on my mother's bible, and I picked it up, hugging it to my chest. I went into the kitchen, closed the door, and put a chair against. I prayed, I pleaded; I fought with every fiber of my being. I spent an eternity in there. I stuffed my fingers in my ears, sang hymns in a loud voice. I screamed, I whispered forgotten curses and prayers, I read scripture in a loud voice. All the while, the music rose and fell, the music pleaded, persuaded, and pulled at me. Made me feel things I never felt before. Made me feel alive and dying at the same time.

I gave in. I tossed the Bible aside, got to my feet, and ripped the chair from the door. Three long steps, and I was at the front door, pulling at the bolt, desperate to get outside.

I slammed the door open, and it hit the wall with a loud bang.

Silence. I stood there for a long while, listening for the fiddle, but heard nothing but my breath and the birds singing.

Never again did I hear that beautiful, wild music. I know I should thank the lord above for not leading me into temptation, but a part of me will always be longing for that song.

A few days later, I realized how lucky I had been.

You see, something else happened that day. The day I heard the fiddle was the last time Gertrude from the village was seen alive. She was found floating face down in the lake under the waterfall a few days later. They said she drowned herself because of a broken heart. Word around the village was that she had taken quite the shine to the fiddler at the last dance. Evil tongues whispered that she was carrying his child.

The fiddler at the dance, they said. That hack was like a boy playing with his little toys next to the fiddler in the woods. Oh no, I knew exactly what had made her go into the water. I would have done it myself if he only played a little longer.

But if he hadn't gotten her, Anna, sweet little child, I don't know if either of us would be here today.

So child, listen to me carefully. Stay away from the river, stay away from the waterfall. Never go alone into the woods. Never go with them, even when they call for you in their loveliest voice. Because they really are out there, the wild things in the woods.

THE CALL

By P. Oxford

WE HAD STRUGGLED UP THE GRASSY HILL FOR MORE THAN an hour, and I was hungry, sweaty, and in an increasingly bad mood. The weak smell of cow dung hung in the air, and I could see the woods in the distance, above which the peak loomed ominously.

"Are you sure we're on the right path?" I asked, panting. "Feels like we've been walking really far."

"It said an hour's walk from the sign, it hasn't been an hour yet," my boyfriend said, seemingly unfazed by the climb.

"I just feel like we're kinda in the middle of nowhere. Can't we go back down and just take a cab like normal people?"

Ike turned around and gave me a disappointed look. We had reservations at this apparently "super-cool" restaurant that was in the middle of the forest, halfway up a goddamned mountain in the Swiss Alps. I was out of breath and sweaty already, and didn't really feel like a fancy meal at an expensive restaurant anymore. We were nearing the edge of the woods, and I didn't want to go into the dark shadows unless I knew we were going the right way.

"The hike is half the point," he said. Gesturing down towards the valley where the village we started in lay, he added: "This is beautiful!"

He wasn't wrong. The tall mountains towered towards the sky, the light dusting of early fall snow turning pink in the sunset. The jagged peaks continued as far as the eye could reach. I sighed.

"Yeah, sure, now it is, but it's getting dark, and once we're in the trees we won't be able to see anything!"

"But we'll know it's there!"

I just shook my head, I knew that I wasn't winning this argument. I had agreed to the hike, after all.

"That's fine and all, but are you sure this is the right path?" I threw a furtive glance towards the dark path that snaked itself up between the trees. It looked very narrow.

"Pretty sure!" he said, turning around.

I sighed, and followed. To be fair, he usually was right about where we were going. I guess I just didn't want to walk on the narrow path between the tall, dark trees— there was something claustrophobic about it. The open fields that dominated the lower part of the valley were much more my type of terrain.

"And look, there are people in front of us, they're probably going there too!"

I squinted in the half-light. At first I couldn't see what

he was talking about, but then I caught a glimpse of three shadowy figures moving about 200 meters in front of us.

"That's weird, where do you think they came from?" I asked, a slight tremor in my voice.

"I dunno, I guess they walked here?" he answered, not looking back at me.

"Yeah, but wait," I tugged at his arm, stopping him. "Wouldn't we have seen them before if they walked up from the village too?"

"I guess not, 'cause we didn't!"

I bit back a sharp retort, not wanting to start a fight. After a moment's hesitation, I tentatively added: "But don't you think that's odd?"

"Why?"

"I dunno, just like, you know..." I shuffled my feet awkwardly, not wanting to admit that I was actually a little scared of the whole situation.

"Oh my god, I'm never letting you see another horror movie!"

"It's not because of horror movies, I just think it's weird! I'm not always scared just because I say I think something's weird!" I said, eyeing the shadowy figures suspiciously. "I just think we're on the wrong path!"

"Maybe they took a break, I don't know!" he said, gently pulling his arm out of my grip. "Come on, or we'll miss our reservation."

I sighed, and continued walking. I kept my eyes fixed on the backs of the group we were following, hoping I'd catch them doing something weird so we could turn around. Had they really taken a break in the dark, creepy forest? Why would you take a break inside the forest, when you could have done it just a couple of hundred meters further down and enjoyed the incredible view?

I voiced my doubts to Ike.

"Maybe they were peeing? I don't know! Why?"

I mumbled something about weird forest people, and he chuckled.

"Honey," he said in an exaggeratedly condescending tone, "We're in Switzerland. Literally nothing bad ever happens in Switzerland."

"People sometimes disappear in the mountains though!"

"Yeah, in the real mountains. Not in places like this, on an actual path between a village and a restaurant!"

I looked down. He was right, of course. I got creeped out the moment we entered the forest, but it was probably just because I don't like the dark. I mean, narrow paths in lonely, dark woods in the evening do tend to invoke images from horror movies, it doesn't mean they're dangerous. There were even other people here. We kept walking.

As we walked deeper into the woods, higher and higher, we didn't gain on the group in front of us at all. We kept the same distance the whole time while we walked, over fifteen minutes or so. It was odd, usually you either overtake someone, or you lose them. I would have been suspicious of their motives if they seemed at all interested in us, but my close scrutiny had not revealed any of them looking back at us once. Well, maybe they didn't hear us; we sure didn't hear a single word coming from them.

We kept walking, until the light was almost completely gone.

"Hey Ike?"

"Yeah?"

"Aren't we gonna be late for the reservation now?"

He glanced at his phone. "Oh shit, yeah, it's seven now! Wow, I did not realize we had walked for that long!"

I didn't repeat that we were probably on the wrong path, but I was sure gonna ask the restaurant.

I pulled my phone out, and quickly found the number to the restaurant.

"Gueten Abig," a cheery voice answered in Swiss German, followed by a string of sounds in the indecipherable dialect uttered far too quickly for me to pick up on.

"Uh, sorry, do you speak English?"

"Yes, of course, how can I help you?" he continued in perfect English, accented in the bouncy Swiss way.

"Yeah, so we have a reservation, but we're a bit late. We wanted to hike up, you see."

"Jaa, that happens, of course. We hold the table for you, no problem! Where are you now?"

"We're in the woods, I guess, on this little path. We've walked for about twenty minutes since we entered the woods."

Silence.

The line crackled with static, and a strange scraping sound followed.

"Uh, hello? Are you there?" I asked, slightly unsettled. "Did we take the wrong path?"

"Is it a narrow path of dirt?" a female voice asked.

"Uh, yes? Wait, who's this?" Maybe the man had to run

suddenly, and gave the phone to a coworker, I mused. Strange though.

"You followed a family into the woods?" the woman continued. I swallowed, trying to keep my panic under control. How did she know?

"Wait, what? Who's this?"

"Did you follow a family into the woods?"

"Uh, I dunno, there are some people in front of us, but I dunno if—"

"Nein, listen to me, really! Turn around at this moment, and do not turn on your flashlights. And do not talk to the people."

"Okay, but—"

" Listen, please! Walk straight back where you came from, and Do. Not. Turn. On. Your flashlights."

"I—" Was she joking? What the hell was this?

"Please, you have to trust me!"

"Okay, but I..." The line crackled again, and then the call was dropped completely.

I looked up, searching for the shadowy figures in front of us. I couldn't see them at all. Panic surged through me. They had either stopped, or kept moving ahead from us.

"Okay, so we're definitely going the wrong way," I told Ike, trying to lay a plan for how to retell the phone call in a way that would convey the urgency. "And she basically told us to get the hell out of here and not turn on the flashlights."

"What?"

"Yeah, she sounded super serious about it too. Maybe there are weird mountain people here."

"Should we tell the people in front that they're going the wrong way?"

"No!" I shook my head frantically. "No, she said to absolutely not talk to them."

"Wait, what the hell? That's like the weirdest thing ever, right?"

"Yeah, but we're 100% listening to her."

"Why?"

"Because I do watch to many horror movies, and if you love me at all you just trust me and the weird phone lady on this. Not listening to the mysterious phone lady is literally how you die!" I said, my voice increasing in pitch as adrenaline surged through my body. If he didn't listen, I didn't know what I would do.

"Okay, sure," he said. I could hear the eye roll in his voice. "But she's probably just messing with you."

"Not taking that chance!" I grabbed his arm, and pulled led him down the hill.

I walked quickly, Ike one step behind me. My heart was beating fast, and I had to fight the urge to run. Winding roots crossed the path, barely visible in the half-light.

A loud bang filled the dark forest. A gunshot?

I caught my scream before it left my mouth.

Someone else screamed. A long, wailing, high pitched scream, half panic and half deep sorrow.

I turned to Ike, wide eyed. He stood slack-jawed, staring into the darkness.

Another shot rang out.

I broke out of my trancelike fear, and started running,

darkness be damned. I glanced back, only to see Ike still standing there, motionless.

"Ike," I yelled, "Come on!"

I took a few steps towards him, grabbed his arm, and pulled him with me. He immediately started running. I tripped, fell, skinned my knees, and was back on my feet before I even registered what was happening. We just ran. My breath grew ragged, that metallic taste in my mouth. How far had we walked? The forest stretched on forever. As we ran, the darkness fell, forcing us to slow down. A root caught my ankle, and I was on the ground again. This time getting up was harder.

Ike stopped a couple of meters ahead of me, panting. "You okay?"

"No," I groaned, "I twisted my ankle."

He was by my side in a second, and turned on the flashlight he had in his hand.

"No!" I yelled.

"Don't be silly, we need to see!" He shone the light on my ankle, and felt along the bone. "Don't think it's broken, let's keep going."

As he got up, the light from his flashlight illuminated the path behind us. I didn't see what was there, all I saw was Ike's face transforming into a mask of terror.

"Oh god, oh god," Ike muttered, bending down to grab my arm. "Get the fuck up and run."

"What is it?" I yelled, panicking, "What?"

He pulled me roughly to my feet, and half dragged, half carried me onwards. I gritted my teeth against the pain, and pushed on.

"Don't fucking look back, just run!"

And we ran. Pain shot through my leg with every step, but the adrenaline surging through my veins kept me going. The woods seemed never-ending. Breathing got painful, and my leg threatened to buckle under my weight. Just as I was about to give up, we were out of the woods. Ike turned, looking back into the dark.

"I think we're good," he whispered. "I think we're good."

"We're not fucking staying here." I said, struggling to stand up. "We're going back down to the village."

"Hell yeah."

And we started on the decent, me leaning against him.

A shrill tone rang out, and we both jumped.

"Isn't that your phone?"

"Oh, shit, yeah, totally," I said, patting myself down. I found the phone and pulled it out, trying to calm my shaking hands enough to hit the answer button.

"Yeah?" I said to the phone, voice still weak.

"Hello!" A cheery male voice greeted me. "I am calling from Berghaus U—. You had a reservation here at 7, it's now 7.15 and we haven't heard from you. Did you get lost on the way here?"

"Uh, yeah, I..." I frowned. 7.15? It had felt like hours passed since that phone call. "But I called you?"

"Ah, ja, I remember, but the call dropped out," he said, still just as cheery. "But that's fine, we were just wondering if you're still coming? Someone else wants the table, you see."

"Uh, yeah, no, I don't think we'll make it, just give up the table." I said. "But the call didn't drop, I talked to a really—" I cut myself off before I could say nice lady, and continued, "I talked to some woman, she didn't tell you?"

"No, we don't have any woman working here tonight."

"No, really, there was some static on the line, and then this super Swiss woman, picked up—"

"Well, that's odd, we haven't had a female Swiss employee here since—" he paused. "Well, since Petra."

"Well, maybe it was Petra? It was a little while ago!"

"No, Petra is dead—it's—I—it's, uhm," he trailed off. "Sorry, no, but maybe the line got connected to someone else? Ja, oder? Doesn't matter, I just needed to know if you still want the table!"

He didn't explain further, and I didn't ask.

Except I did some digging on this Petra when we were back in the village, and my leg was all bandaged up. It really wasn't hard. The village was small, and her grisly death was the only tragedy in as long as anyone could remember. According to the story, her husband had lost his job, and subsequently his mind. He had taken their children into the woods, tied them up, and shot both of them in the head. Then he had walked up to the restaurant where Petra was working, and convinced her to come with him into the woods. Nobody knows exactly what transpired in there, but both parents were found dead, shot at close range. Both sets of fingerprints were on the gun.

Apparently the local kids are saying that sometimes you can still see him in the woods, right around sunset.

And Ike, well, Ike never told me what he saw in there.

THE SIREN AND THE HOUND

By Jazzmin Moysey-Forrestall

THE OVERCAST SKY HUNG LOW AND DREARY OVER THE English moors. The grey clouds seemed to drain the color out of the already dull landscape. The rolling hills seemed to stretch infinitely toward the horizon, making me feel even more lost. Why had my car run out of fuel here of all places? I knew I had filled the tank before I left. Maybe it had a leak? That was just my luck.

My friend, Carlos, lived alone in a substantial house on the moors. He had recently called me in a panic, telling me about something large he had seen roaming the hills at night. He had not gone into much detail, but the things he told me were enough to send a chill down my spine. I had come to the moors to visit him and quell his fears of the thing. I intended to prove that he had nothing to fear in the dark.

I recall thinking back to his words as I trudged through the thick, sucking mud. The night was fast approaching, and the sky threatened to open up and unleash a storm at any second. I tried to walk faster, but the sameness of my surroundings caused me to question every step. Was I going the right way? I had heard horror stories of travelers becoming irrevocably lost in this disorienting plane. They had walked in circles until death eventually dragged them deep into the mud, never to be seen again. I looked over my shoulder; my car was but a tiny speck of silvery white on an otherwise grey and brown horizon. I debated going back, but no, I pressed onward.

A gust of wind howled across the planes, carrying down the first drops of the deluge to come. Lightning lit up the clouds in a flash, and as if on cue, the rumble of thunder was accompanied by the roar of torrential rain hitting the mud. I was instantly soaked through with water so cold it felt like it was burning me. I fell to my knees in the quickly deepening mud, my muscles stiffening up with the sudden and horrible change of temperature. I closed my eyes for what felt like an instant, and when they reopened the world was fully dark.

I scanned my surroundings, searching for anything that wasn't rain and darkness. Nothing, not even my car could be seen. It was as if I had fallen into another world. I stumbled to my feet, the mud trying to hold me in place. It wanted to keep me like it had so many others. It wanted me to stay with it forever, cold and lifeless in a tomb of ever-shifting clay. I had to find shelter fast, or it would have me. I took a few clumsy steps, seeking the dirt trail that I had previously followed. It was nowhere to be found. The rain had already washed away any trace of a path. I had no idea where to go.

I plodded through the ever-worsening storm, my steps growing weaker as the mud deepened around me. The world was entirely dark until I saw it. There, out of the corner of my eye, flashed a tiny pinprick of bright red light. I focused on it, taking a step in its direction. Could it be a house?

My heart skipped a beat when I saw that it was moving. It shook and bounced as if it were alive. It was moving too quickly to be a light held by a person, and too erratically to be the light of a car. The only other explanation could be a four-wheeler or an ATV? That didn't make sense, though, who would ride one of those on a night like this? My mind returned to the words of my friend. "Glowing red eye," he had said. That was all the convincing I needed to quicken my pace, to try to get as far away from that light as I could.

I tried to run, my stiff legs becoming stuck and twisted in the muck. The mud once again embraced me in its excruciatingly cold arms. I struggled and flailed, trying to escape its grip. My heart pounded in my chest as I attempted to crawl away. Each breath I took sucked in water and debris. I coughed, only for more muck to take the place of that which I had expelled. I dragged myself up, only to see that the light had grown brighter. No, not brighter... closer.

A new panic burned through me like a wave of fire, as a flash of lightning served to confirm my fears.

Lumbering towards me was a dark shape, red eye flashing as it approached. I ran like a panicked animal. My legs propelled me at a speed I had never imagined. I lost one of my shoes in the haste, but I didn't care in the least.

Lightning lit up the sky, casting the muddy expanse in a light brighter than day, showing me the lone house that stood on a distant muddy hill. The ensuing thunder left my ears ringing.

I dared to glance over my shoulder, seeing the thing's red eye cresting the nearest hill. I turned back, and I could just barely see a tiny golden light. The house. I looked over my shoulder again, and a flash of lightning lit up the world in blinding white light. I only saw it for a moment, but that image shall remain burned into my memory for as long as I live. The monster was at least the size of a fully grown horse, and its fur seemed to absorb all light. Its long, disturbingly red tongue dripped with tar-like saliva as it licked knife-sized silver teeth.

My feet slipped out from beneath me and I rolled down a particularly steep hill. I scrambled in the sudden mudslide, my clothes drenched in mud as thick as wet cement. I lost my remaining shoe in the battle to get to my feet, and the sudden river carried me to the bottom of the steep hill faster than I could have run. I got to my now bare feet in record time; the rain almost instantly washed the mud from my clothes as I resumed my desperate run for the house.

I didn't look back as I ascended the hill on which the lonely manor stood. My bare feet seemed to catch every sharp rock on the hillside, but I ignored the bleeding and pressed on. The door opened and a tall figure stood in the entrance.

My blood heart stopped as I heard a deep, reverberating howl sound out. It was at the bottom of the hill. I let out an impotent cry that was drowned out by the rainstorm. I was so close. My aching legs felt as if they had been pumped full of lead, yet I refused to give up. I could feel the beast's breath on my neck as I leaped for the open door, letting out a shriek of desperation.

The stranger slammed the door behind me as I lay sprawled out on the hardwood floor of the entry hall. I felt as if I had been hit by a bus. Every muscle in my body hurt. My vision swam as I frantically tried to catch my breath. The last thing I saw before my world faded to black was a pair of royal blue velvet shoes.

I woke up to a sweet smell, like lilac, with a faint hint of the sea. There was a woman shaking me. Her lips were moving, but it took me a moment to realize what she was saying. "Please don't be dead.... please don't be dead... wake up... I can't get you to a hospital in this weather... so just wake up." Her voice was like honey, with the slightest hint of an accent I couldn't quite place.

I let out a groan of pain. My eyes watered as her face came into focus. I gasped slightly; she was the most beautiful woman I had ever seen. Her eyes were the dark blue of a calm evening sea. Flecks of gold and green danced across her irises like the last lights of a sunset. Those sapphire eyes held my focus as she spoke. "Are you alright?" she asked kindly.

The pain seemed to fade away the longer I stared into those eyes. I felt as if I were sinking beneath their calm blue waters. A wave of bliss seemed to flood my body with a warm euphoria as I stared into those infinitely deep pools of wisdom. I felt ten years younger, as if I were twenty again. Those eyes were my fountain of youth, and I would gladly drown in their depths.

"Yes," I said, not sure what else to say. I no longer felt the burn of my physical exhaustion; it was as if she had renewed my life force.

"Thank goodness." she smiled, and her angelic voice was the most beautiful thing I had ever heard. I found that I wasn't cold anymore, as her very presence seemed to warm me to the core.

I smiled stupidly at her.

"Let's get you some dry clothes and a hot bath, lest you catch your death of cold!" she said, "I'll make you a hot meal while you get ready, for I wouldn't be as good a hostess if I let my guest starve!"

"Yeah," I said, following her up the dark oak stairs to a lavish bathroom where a hot bath had been drawn. A folded set of silk men's pajamas lay on a chair beside the deep marble bathtub. I didn't bother to question why they were there.

I peeled off my drenched and muddy clothes, discarding them in a pile on the floor. The water was perfect, blissfully hot and scented with something like lavender. I sank into the water, my eyes slipping shut. Once I had finished scrubbing off the mud that still clung to my body, I toweled off with one of the decadently plush towels that rested near the tub. I dressed in the pajamas and went back downstairs.

I couldn't help but notice that the floor of the hall and

stairs was now entirely free of mud. My host must have mopped it up. The entire place had a bright, new feel to it, despite the house's apparent age. I caught a whiff of something cooking, and my stomach growled. I had not realized just how hungry I was until then. Whatever it was had a rich, savory aroma, like perfectly prepared meat.

The kitchen door stood open, spilling a warm orange light into the hall. When I entered, I saw my hostess stirring a pot of some aromatic stew on the stove. My mouth watered; I could practically taste the sweet and savory meat.

The lady turned, smiling warmly. Her eyes twinkled like stars, she was so beautiful. "Hungry?" she asked. I could feel the warmth in her voice, warmth which spread throughout my entire body, bringing with it a sort of sleepy bliss that I had never felt before.

"Oh yes," I said, my vocabulary seemingly reduced to the most basic of words in the presence of this woman.

For the first time, I noticed her attire. Why was she wearing a leather apron? Weren't those for butchers? How did she keep her pristine white shirt so clean? Her black jeans looked to be brand new. How was her hair so perfect? I felt some of the euphoria leave as I asked these questions. She stiffened as if she were reading my thoughts.

"Why don't you go wait for your food in the dining room for me?" she asked sweetly. Her voice swept all doubt away like a wave. What had I been thinking about? "Nothing but my beauty darling," her voice whispered in my mind, "You know you love me, don't you pet?"

"Yes!" I cried. I needed to please her; it was my reason for living. She smiled, making me giddy with sheer joy.

I found my way to the elegant dining hall. The room was exquisite, its high ceiling held up by grand pillars. The long table appeared to have been carved of a single piece of marble. Intricate patterns were carved on the legs and sides of the massive stone table. These patterns were accented with gold and silver. I sat in one of the comfortable dining chairs and looked closely at the carvings. They were bizarre to say the least. One of the broad legs depicted a sailor being pulled underwater by a mermaid that looked oddly like my hostess. Above her flew birds with human faces, which looked as if they were singing. The carvings were so detailed that I could almost see the sleepy joy on the man's face as he was dragged beneath the waves.

"Beautiful, isn't it?" I almost jumped out of my seat. The lady was standing directly behind me. "It is an old family heirloom, crafted by the best sculptors in the ancient lands to appease my ancestors." She pointed to a portrait on the wall, "That is my great grandmother," she said with a smile.

The painting was magnificent. It depicted a beautiful woman standing in front of the sea. The lady had a warm smile and kind eyes, but something seemed off about her. Were her teeth really that sharp?

"You must be famished!" my hostess said suddenly, drawing my attention away from the picture. She held out a plate of rice topped with hot stew and a glass of deep red wine. "Eat up, you need your strength," she said as she left the room.

The stew was the most incredible thing I had ever tasted. The meat was tender and succulent. The vegetables seemed fresh, despite how late in the year it was. The whole dish was sublime, and it was paired perfectly with the deep red wine. The whole meal left me feeling more satisfied than I had ever been.

"You must be tired dear," my strange hostess said as she walked through the door to the dining room, "Allow me to show you to your bed for the night."

I followed her like a lamb to the slaughter. She was my world. The woman leads me to a lavish guest room. I fell asleep quickly on the silken sheets of the king-sized bed.

I dreamed of a great ship. I sat upon the bow and stared out at the seemingly infinite sea around me. The inky black water was as still as glass, not a breath of wind blew across its eerily tranquil surface. The water perfectly reflected the night sky above; I don't think I've ever seen so many stars. The utter stillness felt wrong as if my very existence in this silent dreamscape were disturbing something ancient and powerful. The feeling was so profoundly unsettling that the sound of my pulse began to sound disgusting and wrong. I felt as if I had no right to disturb that silence, and that by doing so I was committing an unforgivable and heinous act.

A distant ripple caught my eye. I felt nauseous with dread. No no no. This was disastrous. I had woken it up. It was coming for me. I began to cry with utter terror. A primal fear gripped me; my every instinct told me to stop my racing heart. I needed to be still. Everything depended on my complete stillness. It was watching me. It knew I was here.

Something pale rose from the still water in the distance. It was tiny, just a dot in the sea of night, but it frightened me more than anything I had ever experienced. It shot back beneath the waves, making a tiny splash that sounded like cannon fire in the silence. A bright red light crested the horizon, making the stars above bleed together into the crimson light of some terrible dawn. A cold, slimy hand rested on my shoulder, and I screamed, the sound tearing apart the stillness and drawing the gaze of the red light. I realized then that it was not the sun, but some great eye. As I felt my sanity beginning to shred and bleed into the red of the world around me, I shut my eyes and surrendered to the madness.

The world went silent, and all I could hear was the thundering of my heart. I dared to open my eyes, seeing the stranger looking down at me with concern etched into her lovely features. I looked down at myself, embarrassed. I was drenched in sweat, and I had kicked all of the fine bed covers to the floor. I felt my cheeks grow hot. I didn't want her to see me like this.

"It's all right," she said smoothly, her voice sympathetic, "We all have nightmares."

Though her face was etched with sympathy for my situation, I briefly saw something else glitter behind her eyes. It was a malicious sort of humor. It writhed behind the mask of concern, like a snake hiding in a bouquet of flowers. As quickly as I had seen it, it was gone. My hostess lead me downstairs, where she had prepared me a full breakfast, though that look had already planted the tiniest seed of suspicion in my mind. I was only then

367

beginning to question the strange effect the woman had on me.

"The phone lines are down due to the storm," she told me after I had finished eating, "I do not have a cell phone, so I shall go into town and call someone to come and fetch you." She paused, smiling at me, "I would much rather have you stay here, I hate to leave the house unattended." She met my eyes, "I hope this will not be a problem for you." Beneath her kind tone there lurked a firmness that told me that if I protested, she would be far less kind in the future. So no, I would not have a problem with this.

I gave her Carlos's home phone number so that she could call him. Something deep down told me she wouldn't, but my conscious mind firmly told me that I was just being paranoid. It made me feel horrible for doubting this kind woman's word. It shamed me for being suspicious and ungrateful after all my hostess had done for me.

I watched her jet black car drive away over the muddy hills from the library window. Seeing her leave made me feel even more isolated than ever. I felt like I was back on the ship, trapped in the middle of a silent black sea, without hope of escape or rescue.

I spent the day exploring the great house. The mansion seemed endless, with countless rooms branching off from every hall. It was beautiful and impossible all at the same time. It instilled in me a sense of great awe and a lingering dread that clung to my mouth like a bitter aftertaste.

At around noon I decided to take a shower. The

memories of the dream made me feel dirty as if it had coated me in cold chicken grease. I found my way back to the first bathroom I had visited. Somehow, despite the alien nature of the house, this bathroom, in particular, felt familiar and comfortable. The bathroom had a separate steam shower. I had never used one before, so I looked forward to trying it. I got in and turned on the steam and water. The shower fogged up quickly, and the hot water and steam washed away the cold, slimy feeling that the nightmare had left me with.

I got out and wiped the condensation from the mirror, staring into the eyes of my reflection. Something caught my attention, chilling me to the bone. There, on the shoulder that the cold thing had touched in my dream was a dark, bluish handprint. It was faint but clear. I could see that where the thing had touched me, it had left a mark the same color as its abhorrent flesh. I felt suddenly nauseous. That thing had been real. I barely made it to the toilet before hot bile surged up my throat. I looked down to see that the vomit was the color of ink, and reflective. It looked as if I had vomited crude oil. It smelled and tasted like seawater. Disgusted and confused, I flushed it.

Stumbling downstairs, I retrieved a bottle of fine whiskey from the library. I returned to the shower, where I stayed for the rest of the day. The hot water never seemed to run out, even though I was in there for hours. When the whiskey ran out, I went downstairs to find that my hostess had already cooked supper. She was nowhere to be seen, but there was a succulent roast set out for me. It was like no meat I had ever tasted, and it was garnished with carrots and potatoes that tasted almost too fresh for the season. It was perfectly paired with a medium-bodied red wine. The whole meal left me relaxed and sleepy, and no matter how hard I tried, I could not remember why I had ever mistrusted my hostess.

I went to bed to find that it had been tidied up in my absence. I felt a pang of guilt for ever thinking that the generous woman who had treated me so well could have any ulterior motives. Blissful fantasies of staying with her forever guided me into sleep.

I was in a well-furnished lounge. I sat on an ancient velvet armchair. The only sound was the muffled ticking of an ornate clock upon the mantle. The sound felt out of place in the silence. Any sound did. I stood, cringing as the chair groaned. All had to be silent. The floorboards creaked beneath my feet as I walked toward the clock. It seemed to tick faster as I approached, the minute hand moving faster and faster towards midnight. Somehow I knew that I did not want that hand to touch the guided number twelve. I grabbed the clock and threw it to the floor, the sound of it shattering felt like a drill penetrating my eardrum. I stood still, the clock broken at my feet, listening to the cold, oppressive silence.

There was a splash from outside the door. The sound of the shattering clock had alerted something to my presence. I ran outside, against my better judgment. I was back on the infernal ship.

The pale thing was standing gracefully upon the bow. Its head was downcast, its face shrouded in a veil of dark hair. I tried to look at it, but my eyes didn't want to see it. From the corner of my eye, I discerned that it was naked and sexless, but vaguely feminine in shape. It had an air of deliberate confidence to it. A lump swelled in my throat as it took a step towards me. Trying to picture the way it moved makes me nauseous, but I'll try to describe it. It moved like ink in water, but also with the purpose and determination of a predator stalking prey. It was simultaneously fluid and solid in a way that made my head hurt.

The sheer surreality of the situation must have subdued the terror I felt at the time because the monster was halfway across the deck when it hit me. Sheer terror punched me in the gut like a steel baseball bat. All the air left my lungs as a tight, fiery pain exploded in my chest. I gasped for air, falling to my knees. I felt lightheaded, and fainted.

I woke up in a cold sweat. The first rays of dawn were beginning to burn crimson on the horizon. My skin felt cold and greasy, and my head hurt. I stumbled into the bathroom and vomited up torrents of the reflective black gunk. I looked at my reflection in the mirror. I looked haggard and pale, with deep rings around my eyes that were almost as dark as the inky vomit.

I got into the shower, wanting to wash off the slimy remnants of my dream once and for all. The heat and steam cleansed my body and mind of the foulness of that ship. It was an incredibly cathartic experience, and I left feeling almost normal.

Breakfast was waiting for me downstairs, though I simply dumped it in the trash. I remembered how unnaturally complacent supper had made me the night before, and I didn't want to bend to this woman's will any more than I already had. I suspected that she had drugged the food.

The woman's car was missing, so I searched the house for my old clothes. I had left my wallet in my coat pocket. My wallet held my passport, money, and identification. I couldn't leave without it. I searched my room from top to bottom, but there was no sign of them.

I checked every room in the house until I found a laundry chute tucked away into a walk-in closet. I tried to find a door to a basement where the chute might lead, but my search was fruitless. I decided that the only way I could get down was to go down the chute. The incline was just gentle enough for me to maneuver my way down.

I squeezed into the opening feet first. The chute was just barely big enough for me to fit. I was sliding for a long time. The further down I got, the colder the metal became. Soon I was shivering in the dark, claustrophobic space. With no warning, the chute opened up beneath me. I landed with a thud on a pile of clothing. The space smelled damp and moldy, like a cave. The dampness and smell were quite shocking when juxtaposed with the freshness of the air upstairs. It was entirely dark, and I had to feel my way around the pile of clothes. Sure enough, I found mine. They were still damp and caked with mud. It was surreal to find anything dirty anywhere near the lady's immaculate house.

I found my wallet and began blindly feeling my way away from the clothes heap. The smooth stone floor was damp and uneven. I had to crawl so I wouldn't lose my footing. As I crawled, I could faintly make out a salty smell. It was like the sea but somehow corrupted. My hand splashed into a puddle of icy water. I gasped at the cold and wetness catching me completely off guard.

When I brought the hand to my nose, it smelled salty. I crawled faster. I don't know how long I spent in that tunnel, but eventually I saw a faint light up ahead.

The light was coming through a tiny crack in the ceiling. I stood up, touching it. The crack was long and strait. I pushed up on the ceiling, and it moved. It was a trapdoor.

The trapdoor lead into a furnished basement, with wooden flooring and plain white walls. The walls were lined with freezers. They smelled of the sea. I stumbled over to the one directly in front of me, my knees aching from their time on the cold cave floor. I placed my hands on the lid.

I stopped, hands resting on the cool metal of the freezer. The hairs on my neck stood on end as I looked at my hands. The hand that had landed in the puddle was coated with an inky black substance. It had just started to dry, and it clung to my skin, thick and sticky. It was reflective, like tar. What was the hell going on in this house?

I flung open the freezer lid. A wave of cold, pale mist shrouded its contents. As the mist dispersed, I could see more and more of the horror within. A wave of nausea rolled over me, but I forced down the bile threatening to spill out of me. Before me, in the freezer, lay the naked, headless body of a man. I put a hand over my mouth to stifle a scream. Had the meat been human? Dear god, had I eaten people?

Then I smelled it, lilac, with the faintest trace of a smell I now recognized as that wrong salty stink.

"They aren't for food," said a familiar voice behind me.

I whirled around to see my hostess standing there, looking as beautiful as ever. She was smiling wickedly. "That would be so much better than your situation," she laughed, it was a deep and genuine laugh. "You aren't the first who assumed that I was a cannibal," she said through uncontrollable giggles. "The reality of your situation is so much more complicated than that."

I was dumbstruck. "What?" I asked. That was all I could think to say. I could feel the effect of her presence starting to slow my thoughts, pumping a warm happiness into my brain. It made me docile and harmless. "No!" I screamed at myself internally. I felt like I was sinking into a pool of warm honey.

"Oh sweetie," she said, her voice was sharp and condescending, "That isn't going to work." She smiled wickedly. "Now, you are going to follow me. I have much to show you before the leviathan has its supper."

My body moved against my will, and the part of me that wanted to obey her beat down my rational mind.

"I like to show my guests how I do my little mind trick before I sacrifice them." Her voice was chipper and bright, like a kid at show and tell. "The look on their faces as I show them how I pulled their strings is the best part of what I do!" She turned around and grinned. "Heck! It's even better than the immortality and eternal youth!" She grinned, "Oh, and my name is Calypso, by the way, but you can call me Caly."

"Calypso, you are a monster," I growled.

The smile retreated from her face in the blink of an eye. "You will call me Caly," she said, her voice cold and sharp. She strode towards me, gripping my chin. "Call me

Caly and tell me how much you love me, you pathetic worm!" Her breath smelled like seaweed and salt. It was cool and almost refreshing, like an ocean breeze. "I am a goddess to you, you puny mortal!" she shouted, spittle flying. It hit my face like cold ocean spray.

"I am so sorry Caly!" I cried, losing control of my whole body. I fell to my knees and kissed her foot, "My goddess! Oh my goddess! Please forgive my evil tongue! It lies! It lies! Please cleanse me of the evil that would dare insult your all-powerful beauty!" The words disgusted me, but I had no way to stop them.

Calypso grinned, "Good boy." She chuckled sadistically. "Now follow me." She hummed a tune that sounded like Greensleeves as she slid open a panel on the wall that I had previously missed. I stumbled after her as she led me into a modest, but immaculate laboratory. "This," she indicated the lab equipment surrounding her, "is where I make the compound that makes you men so obedient. I won't bore you with the science of it, but this is where I make a drug with effects similar to devil's breath, except that it only works on male subjects, and rather than turning you into a sort of 'zombie', it makes you want to please me, even if you consciously don't; it bends your subconscious to my will. It is derived from the water in the leviathan's home plane of reality. It is an ancient recipe used by women in my family for centuries. I wear it like a perfume, that's why you are so attracted to me. Those affected suffer from what they think are nightmares, when in fact their consciousness is simply existing in the leviathan's reality briefly."

I was dumbstruck. I asked the only question in my mind. "What are the bodies for?"

She smiled sweetly. "Those?" she said, "Oh, those are just for bribing the hound." She saw my confused expression. Rolling her eyes, she said, "The hound that chased you here could have caught you if he wanted to, but all it did was get you where you needed to go. He's like my little sheepdog," she said endearingly. "I love my little puppy so much!"

I couldn't help but smile at this monster's show of humanity. "Cute," I said dryly.

"Yes, he is!" she smiled, ignoring my sarcasm.

She leads me to another panel in the wall, which opened into an elevator. I followed her in. The doors shut behind us and the elevator began to descend.

I don't know how long we were in the elevator. The farther down we went, the more the place smelled of the leviathan's home world. At some point, the lights went out. They stayed out after that.

We stood silently in the metal box. I don't know why I wasn't afraid. Maybe it was the drug; maybe I was a point where I could no longer feel fear. I had surrendered to my fate under the mighty hand of the woman's drug.

After a long time, Calypso spoke. "It's funny," she said, "you're the first person who ever managed to insult me." She sounded almost regretful in the dark. "Most people just silently followed me." Even in the dark, I could tell that she had turned her intense eyes on me. "How did you do that? Resist the drug, I mean?"

"I don't know," I said.

"Okay," she replied, sounding somewhat disappointed. "We're almost there."

"Yeah," I said numbly. "I know."

The doors opened and I saw the ship. The pale thing stood on the bow, regarding me through a curtain of dark hair. I calmly left the elevator, walking towards it. On the horizon, the red light crested the ocean, swallowing the world in its bloody glow. The thing extended a hand, and I took it. Together, we walked into the red.

THE SUNSET DOORWAY

By Kelly Childress

WHEN I WAS A CHILD, MY GRANDMOTHER TOLD ME SOME tidbit of wisdom that I took for fiction. She told me that in the moments before the sun rises and sets, our world is vulnerable. If we aren't careful and we go into the dark alone, we can wander into other dimensions without even knowing what we've done.

That's why I'm writing this. I didn't take her seriously then (I mean, who would?) but I should have. I'm hoping somebody can tell me anything, anything at all, that might help explain what happened to me two years ago. Just to get it out of the way: I wasn't drunk or sleep-deprived and had only taken a few hits off a joint that day. And I know the weed wasn't spiked with anything, because I'd been smoking it for days before this happened.

When July 2016 came around, and I hadn't really been

on any vacation yet, I decided I needed one. I made plans with my parents to stay at their rural home, about five hours away from the city where I lived. They were going to be out of town on a cruise and were happy to have someone checking in on the property.

I couldn't get on the road until Friday evening, but that was fine by me. I like watching the sun set while I drive; there's something indescribably calming about it. The wind in my hair, my favorite music playing, and the swelling hills flying past, dotted with cows and bales of hay. The way the rugged landscape becomes softer in the final light, everything tinged with the warm gold of the dying sun. Like a mother's hands affectionately smoothing wrinkles from her child's bedspread, the fingers of light cede the countryside to the growing shadows.

As the light loses its grip on the land, some animals and insects come out in earnest. Like well-behaved children who turn raucous once the final dismissal bell rings, they come alive. The lazy hum of cicada rises to a cacophony. The tremulous (yet persistent) song of the whippoorwill warbles over it. Thousands of leaves, made invisible by the darkness, rustle in the sporadic breeze. Occasionally, the drone of wildlife is punctuated by distant pops. Gunshots, fireworks, or falling rocks, I can't tell.

Once the sun goes down in earnest, things do get a little creepy—but I always liked that. Way out in the back-woods, the roads aren't lit. Sometimes the only things illuminating your path are your own two headlights, and it looks and feels like you're driving along the edge of the world.

The light glides along the road and rises when it hits the guardrails, but then it's absorbed completely by the thick, dark trees that swam the hills. When I was little, I used to think it was like driving on Rainbow Road in MarioKart. Just you and your little U-shaped bit of light on the road... and the utter nothingness that surrounds you both.

The sun had set around forty minutes earlier, and I was driving and enjoying the slow descent into full darkness, when suddenly it happened. All the boisterous sound of nature disappeared.

Everything was quiet, except for a low, far-away rumbling—like I was near an active volcano.

I immediately went from relaxed to alert. I slowed down and listened, hard. Absolutely nothing, aside from the rumbling. No animals. No bugs. No nature. I furiously dug my pinky into my right ear, and then left, terrified that my hearing had spontaneously gone. Nothing.

Shaking, I drove a bit further until I finally hit a part of the road with a decent-sized shoulder. I pulled over. Convinced it was my body and not the environment, I continued to dig in my ear, then gently wiggling my earlobes, then leaning from one side to the other.

As I was becoming increasingly more panicked, my knee brushed up against the car keys and I realized I could hear the jingling. I paused, and then clapped. The sound rang out in the car as it normally would.

I put the keys in my pocket and stepped out of the car and onto the shoulder. Trust me, I didn't want to leave the safety of my car, but I had to get my flashlight out of the trunk and couldn't do it from inside.

I retrieved the flashlight and hesitantly shone the piercing beam over the guardrail and down the hill.

At least, there was supposed to be a hill there.

The land sloped down, and then just…. ended.

In confusion, I shone my flashlight around. Nothing. I could see the hill, studded with rocks and boulders, maybe ten or twelve feet down. Then, only darkness my flashlight couldn't penetrate.

I stared for a few minutes, wondering whether I had gone crazy or not. I picked up a rock, and, keeping the light on it, dropped it. It bounced down the hill and into the black. I could still see it once it had passed that threshold, but not for long. I never heard it hit the ground.

I pushed myself away from the edge in terror. Running to the other side of the road yielded more of the same. I looked at the road behind me and in front of me—no other taillights or living things, no reassurance. As far as I could see, the road existed, but the world around it had fallen away. The only difference between the sky and the earth, that I could see, was the presence of stars. I kept turning in disbelieving circles in the middle of the road, willing another car, another person, to come down the road towards me.

The rumbling was growing louder. I reeled inwardly as I realized, among the rumbling, I could discern individual moans—human voices.

I jumped about six feet in the air when I saw something move in my peripheral vision. Stepping back, I aimed my flashlight at the road's left shoulder. It was a human hand, with raw red flesh showing underneath caked layers of dirt.

Any sense of wonder or comfort disappeared in an instant. My boots pounding the pavement, I threw open the car door and locked myself in. There was an arm attached to the hand, and it was pulling itself on to the asphalt. There were more hands around it. As I twisted the car key in the ignition, cold horror flowed through my veins as I saw the entire road was lined with wriggling hands and limbs. Even with the windows shut, I could hear their moaning and gibbering—growing loud enough to drown out the rumbling.

My quiet whimpering turned into a full-throated scream when the first of them jerked its body onto the road. It was a person, but all the flesh had been stripped away. Chunks of cartilage still clustered around the ears and nose, but everything else was gone.

Others followed, crawling up onto the road behind the first. I didn't wait to see what happened. I shifted into drive and slammed on the gas.

I picked up speed relatively quickly, and I was grateful for the V6 engine I didn't think I'd need when I bought the car. But the flayed people were faster than I thought, and I had only made it a dozen yards or so before I was running over them. My stomach turned with each meaty thump, as the wheels rolled across arms and legs and torsos. A few of them managed to stand and then run towards my car, shrieking as they bounced off.

By then, I was shrieking too. Even knowing how treacherous the hilly roads could be, I let my car reach eighty miles per hour before I let off the accelerator. At one point, the road curved and my headlights illuminated the way ahead.

Where the land ended, I couldn't see. But what had been only blackness upon first inspection was really thousands and thousands of bodies, skinned people, writhing and crawling just below the road.

White-knuckled, I drove past (and over) them, whispering rapidly to myself, "What the fuck. What the fuck. What the fuck."

From what I recognized, I was maybe thirty minutes from the nearest town. Keeping my speed as high as I felt comfortable, I pressed on. Every hair on my head felt like it was standing on end, and every bit of peace I'd felt from the drive had evaporated.

When the lights of Hollowfield, familiar welcome sign and all, came into view, I won't even try to make myself sound brave—I cried like a baby. I had to take deep breaths to stave off hysteria. When more familiar, totally ordinary things came into view (the old lodge with the restaurant connected to it! Family Dollar! The U-Gas, complete with normal, non-skinned people pumping gas!) this became a little harder.

And that's really all, except for one thing.

I made it through Hollowfield, and although I considered sleeping in my car there, I ended up pushing on to my parents' house. I ran inside with my bag as fast as I could, locking the door behind me. I locked the bedroom door, too. I even checked under the bed, half-sure in my delirium that a skinless person would be hiding there.

Suffice to say my relaxing vacation never happened. I kept everything locked and made sure I was inside well before sunset each night. When I returned to the city, I left early to ensure I wasn't driving while the sun set.

And the only tangible trace I ever found of what happened was embedded in one of the treads on my right rear tire—one brittle, blackened finger bone.

SOMETHING CREEPY AT MOSS GLENN FALLS

By Alanna Robertson-Webb

I'M TWENTY-SIX NOW AND LIVING IN PENNSYLVANIA, BUT when I was growing up I lived in Montpelier, Vermont. My summers were spent hiking mountains, swimming in lakes and exploring expansive forests. I knew that my state had bears and rattlesnakes in its more secluded, mountainous regions, but I never imagined that there was anything more terrifying than those out there.

When I was nineteen my friend Emily and I went to Moss Glen Falls for a day of swimming and picnicking, as it gave us a nice change of scenery from campus. The waterfall is located in Stowe, which is a remote town in Vermont that has a population of barely 4,000. Emily was from another state, and had never really seen much of the area beyond our college's campus, so I figured showing her some of Vermont's quaint locations was in order.

The day was perfect. We had packed plenty of food,

sunscreen and towels, and since it was a weekday afternoon there was no one else at the falls except for an
elderly couple who left not long after we got there. We
spread our towels out on a large rock by the falls and
alternated between climbing up the waterfall edges to get
to the swimming pools and relaxing in the late afternoon
sun. It was peaceful, and it was the perfect break after a
long day of homework and classes.

As the day wore on Emily wanted to explore some of
the trails near the falls. I was familiar with a few of them,
and tried to keep her on those. What I hadn't accounted
for was that she would insist on exploring some of the
more outlying trails, and that we would consequently get
lost. We spent nearly an hour walking in circles, our arms
and legs getting covered in mosquito bites and our
bathing suits drying uncomfortably onto our skin. We
had the flashlights on our phones to give us a little light
once the sun set, but they didn't do much to illuminate the
dense undergrowth shrouding both sides of the trail.

Finally we came across a blackberry patch that we
were pretty sure we had seen earlier, so by logical default
we started heading down the path closest to the bushes.
Emily kept asking me if I heard twigs snapping near us,
and I brushed it off as a city girl being afraid of deer or
rabbits. I didn't hear anything myself, so I figured she was
feeling paranoid due to it being her first time lost in
the woods.

Then I heard it. The noise came from somewhere
behind us, and it was too loud to be a small animal like a
rabbit. I figured it was another person out walking, or
maybe a herd of deer passing through. Stowe has never

been a populous town, and the locals could argue that there's more deer than people in the area. I ignored the uneasy feeling building in the pit of my stomach and kept walking, chalking it up to my friend's paranoia rubbing off on me, and I babbled senselessly about cute guys to keep Emily and I distracted.

After another ten minutes of walking we finally came in sight of the trailhead. There was a large boulder there with a plaque on it, dedicated to a young woman who had been murdered at the falls back in 1991, and right beyond that was my car. As we neared the boulder, relief evident on Emily's face, a weird noise came from the woods behind us. It sounded almost like a cat, but it was distorted and static, like it was coming out of an old radio. My first instinct was that the cat was wounded, or in danger.

I've always been an animal lover, and if there was a hurt cat I wasn't about to leave it to become a coyote snack. I turned around, ignoring Emily begging me to just get in the car, and peered back into the trail opening. I gave Emily the keys and told her to get our towels, now that we knew where we were, and I promised I'd be back momentarily. If I didn't find the cat right away I wasn't going to spend forever looking for it, but I couldn't just drive away either.

With the loss of the second flashlight the woods seemed a bit more eerie to me, and the darkness was nagging at my peripheral vision. I walked a little ways down the path as I called to the cat, hoping to locate it by its meow, but I didn't hear anything for several moments. I was about to give up when I heard a low, out-of-place laugh behind me. I spun around, my heart beating too fast, but all I saw was a large buck. I remember muttering something about stupid, sneaky deer, then I headed back to the trailhead. That was when the deer laughed again, and I froze.

The harsh sound was completely unnatural. For those of you who don't know, deer make sounds like grunts, bleats and snorts. They don't make any sort of laughter-like noises, and even if they did it wouldn't have the same cadence as a human's laugh would, and as this deer's did. This situation was weird and unnerving, and I kept hoping that someone would pop their head out from around a tree and tell me it was a prank. That didn't happen.

The deer took a few steps towards me, and then the odd cat sound came from it. I almost threw my hands up in a "nope" gesture, and I started walking away from it as quickly as I could. I was almost in sight of the end of the trail when I felt something snag my hair. I swatted it away, thinking it was a branch, since there were a lot of low-hanging trees along the trail, but the sensation returned instantly. I reached up to tug my hair free, but it wouldn't come loose. I turned to face the offending tree, my heart thumping in shock.

The deer, now on its hind legs, had my hair caught on one of its antler points. The snarls from a day of swimming and hiking were entangled around its antler, and I could feel its cold breath on my face. Not warm, not hot, but icy cold breath wreathed around me. I let out the most shrill scream I had ever heard myself make, and I violently yanked my hair off of its antlers. I sprinted for my car, screaming the whole way for Emily to start it. I heard the engine turn when I neared the boulder, and she didn't hesitate to floor it as soon as I was in the car. The tears streaming down my face were enough motivation.

She didn't question me until we were nearly five miles from Moss Glen. I told her about the weird noises and the deer getting up in my face. I told her it startled me, and that on top of the stress of being lost that was just enough to make me panic. She bought my explanation, agreeing that we were both super tired, and adding that my mind was probably playing tricks on me.

I haven't returned to Stowe since then, even though I've visited Vermont recently. I know there's probably some sort of rational explanation for what I saw and heard that night, but I haven't been able to find what that would be. What I never told Emily that night was that the buck had fangs, or how there had been blood on its mouth. I never shared that the huge animal was able to sneak up on me noiselessly, and I didn't bother telling her that it had the coldest breath I had ever felt.

She was my friend, but that didn't mean she would believe a crazy story. Emily, if you're reading this I hope you know I didn't want to lie. I was panicked, and in my nineteen-year-old mind I didn't want to get labeled as crazy or a liar. Please forgive me, and please never go to Moss Glen alone.

THE GOATMAN OF LAKE ELMORE

By Alanna Robertson-Webb

GROWING UP AMONG THE ROLLING, GREEN HILLS OF Vermont meant that I spent a lot of time outdoors. Even though I lived in the capital city of Montpelier, my activities of choice had always been camping, hiking and swimming. Most of my outdoors memories are happy, but there was one experience I had that almost made me never go camping again.

My cousin Cory and I were on summer vacation from high school, and we begged my mom to take us to our favorite campground for a few days. The next afternoon we arrived at Lake Elmore State Park where a ranger gave us a map with available sites circled on it, and after checking them all out we settled on a lean-to called Ash.

All of the lean-to sites at this park are named after trees, with Ash and Juniper always being our preferences since they were a little more private than some of the other sites. My family had been going to Lake Elmore since before I was born, and my mom and I both knew the grounds very well.

Our first night was uneventful. Since it was the middle of the week the park was almost deserted, which meant that Cory and I never had to wait for paddle boats to become available, and we got prime lake beach spots without having to get there early in the morning. The trip was perfect, until the second night.

My mom wanted to go home on the second day to check on my brother Nate, who hadn't wanted to come with us, so after dinner she left. We knew she wouldn't be back until around midnight, so we entertained ourselves by making s'mores and playing card games. After a while we got restless, and decided to walk down to the lake. From the bulk of the sites the lake is about a ten minute walk, and Mount Elmore, which looms over the lake, is always beautiful at sunset.

We made it down to the lake shore just fine, and we enjoyed the cool sensation of wet sand squishing between our toes as we built a sand castle. The sun was beginning to set in earnest, and we hadn't brought a lantern down with us so we headed back to the site to grab one.

I was ready to head back to the lake, but Cory suggested that we walk the trail that goes to the old fire tower at the top of Mount Elmore instead. I agreed, and we made our way to the outskirts of the campground where the trail started. An hour or so went by as we walked and talked, just enjoying the refreshing night air. The lantern gave us enough light that we didn't feel nervous, and we made sure not to go off the trail. There was only one path for most of the trek, so it was easy to follow.

At one point a herd of deer came bounding out of the woods near us, their appearance so sudden that I nearly dropped the lantern. Cory, now a bit spooked, asked if we could head back to camp. I wasn't really ready to, but I wanted him to be comfortable, so I agreed. We had been walking for about five minutes when we heard someone in the woods off to our right. It was clearly a person, since their rhythmic footsteps didn't sound like an animal.

It wasn't unusual for rangers to patrol the trails even at night, and if one of them had seen us they were probably checking to make sure we weren't doing anything illegal or destructive. We waited for them to appear, but the steps had stopped and no one entered the circle of light we were in. After a minute Cory called out a tentative "Hello?", his voice quivering slightly.

I thought it was a little odd that we couldn't see a flashlight by then, but I shrugged it off and kept walking. If some weirdo wanted to be creeping around in the woods at ten p.m. without a light then that was their business, not mine. It was probably someone sneaking away from their family to smoke or drink or something, which could easily explain why they weren't coming forward or greeting us.

As we walked I noticed that, since the appearance of the deer, the woods had seemed oddly silent. I can admit that by then I was glad that we were heading back to camp. We were about halfway down the trail when a voice called out to us, which we instantly knew was my mom's. The sound had come from behind us, and Cory and I spun around in unison. I shouted out a greeting, but got no response.

Cory looked at me, concern clear on his face. It made sense that it had been my mom in the woods, probably trying to get us back for all of the pranks we had pulled over the years, but it was weird that she suddenly wasn't responding after just having called to us. We waited for several minutes, occasionally calling out to her. I started to get mad, because by then her little prank wasn't funny anymore, and I was becoming unnerved.

A few more minutes went by, and I was finally fed up. I grabbed Cory by the elbow and began to march back to camp, grumbling about annoying mothers and stupid pranks. Cory hadn't said a word, but I noticed him watching the woods around us carefully. As we reached the last ten minute stretch of the trail my mother's voice once again rang out behind us. It sounded strange though, and I immediately thought she might be hurt.

I spun around, the swinging lantern casting distorted shadows. I couldn't see anything but trees, and I didn't hear anyone moving around. I was slowly becoming scared, and I just wanted to get back to the safety of the campfire. My attention was drawn to the lantern light reflecting off of something in a bush nearby. It was pair of green eyes, but to my confusion they were about eight feet off the ground. No animal around here could be standing that tall, even on back legs.

"What the hell?"

Cory echoed my confusion. We were both staring at this towering shadow, neither of us daring to move. After a moment it stepped towards us, and our feeble hope that it was just a deer on its back legs was smashed. To this day we still don't know exactly what we saw, but the word goatman is the best way I have of describing it. A pair of wooly legs and a fuzzy abdomen gave away to smooth, humanoid chest and arms. The face was horrifying, a mix of goat and man that still haunts me.

I watched as it opened its mouth, my mother's voice giving a cheery-sounding hello coming out of the creature, but it was warped and too deep.

"Hi baby girl. Good morning Lonnie!"

To this day I don't remember getting back to the campsite. I remember screaming, and running as fast as I could away from the creature, but that's it. I don't know if it followed us, or tried to communicate further, and I'm not sure that I want to know. We never did tell my mom or the park rangers about our encounter. We figured that they would tell us we were crazy, or chalk our experience up to the use of recreational substances, so it wasn't worth the hassle.

Cory and I have both returned to Elmore since then, but neither of us has ever seen anything like that again. I've often wondered if we imagined the whole thing, or if it was some sort of weird dream. People don't usually share the exact same dream though, right?

IMAGINATION

By AJ Horvath

MARY RAN INTO THE ROOM WHERE HER DAUGHTER, dwarfed by her new "big girl" bed, sat straight up shrieking in terror. Mary grabbed her screaming daughter and held her close, "Honey, it's okay. Shhh. Shhh. It's okay." It was like Lily didn't see her. She stared straight ahead at the foot of her bed. Holding her daughter at arm's length, she took in the small girl. Her blonde hair was mussed and cold sweat ran in rivulets down her face. She was pale and cold but the scariest part was her eyes. They did not see Mary; the blue eyes stared off as if in another world. They were wide and filled with fear. Shaking Lily gently, Mary spoke sternly, "Baby girl, wake up. It is just a dream." She tried this a few more times until finally the little girl rubbed her eyes.

"M-mommy, what are you doing in here? Is everything okay?" the small girl asked, her voice hoarse from the screaming that had been occurring for the past ten minutes.

"You don't remember, baby? You woke me up because you were screaming." Mary explained, gently stroking her daughters head.

"I just remember the two men." She answered leaning into her mother. "Two men?" she asked, her body jolted by fear.

"Yeah mommy. They were big and tall, they were all black like the shadows in Peter Pan, but they weren't funny like Peter's was," she told her mother nonchalantly. "I don't like them. They make me feel funny," she added with a frown.

"Well baby girl they aren't here anymore and mommy will protect you. Go back to sleep sweetheart. You have school in the morning," she said to Lily, who was already starting to fall back asleep in her mother's arms. Spending a few precious moments with her daughter was just what Mary needed to calm down from the strange turn of events of the past hour. With a four-year-old life didn't slow down very often. Gently repositioning her daughter in her bed, Mary kissed her softly on the forehead and made her way to the door. Turning at the doorway, she paused her hand over the light switch, hesitating, still haunted by the little girl's mention of the two shadow men. Kids, she chuckled to herself, trying to make herself feel better. The laugh came out strangled, but she hit the light switch and made her way back to her bedroom, exhausted from the long day at work. Hitting her pillow, she closed her eyes and fell into a deep slumber.

The alarm came too early for Mary as she dragged

herself from the warmth of her bed. Walking on autopilot she made her way to the bathroom, stopping in front of the mirror to take in her worn-out reflection. Her dirty blond hair showed a restless sleep and the bags under her eyes seemed to be weighed down more than usual. Rubbing her face, she walked over to the shower, turning the knob to warm up the water, the joys of third floor apartment living. Walking down the hall, she popped her head into her daughter's room to find the small girl still asleep, an angel if she had ever seen one. Smiling to herself, she made her way back to the bathroom, removed her clothes and let the warm stream of water ease her aching muscles. Being a single mom was tough, working double shifts at the local diner just to make ends meet. Her morning shower was one of the best moments of the day, topped only by the evening hour or two she got to spend with her daughter Lily before she had to go to bed. Breaking from her shower reverie, she quickly dressed and decided, after looking at the clock, that she would let her hair air dry today. Walking quickly towards Lily's room, she found the small girl awake and talking with her favorite teddy bear, Mr. Huggins. "Good morning baby girl. How are you feeling?" she asked, noticing the bags under her small daughter's eyes.

"I'm okay. Just sleepy. Mr. Huggins says he wants to go to school with me today to protect me," she responded, holding the teddy bear close.

"What a gentleman," Mary said, the dark memory of last night breaking through her morning haze. "Just for today, but he needs to stay in your backpack during school, okay?" Mary allowed. "Let's get you ready."

Allowing Lily to pick out her outfit, the two made their way to the bathroom to brush her blonde bed head. Finishing up their morning hygiene ritual, the two made their way out the door and into the busy city street. Mary kept a closer than usual eye on her daughter as they joined the constant flow of people on their way to their various destinations. The strange event from last night still fresh in Mary's mind, she kept Lily close. The two made it to Lily's school without incident, which also served as her daycare as Mary typically worked longer than the standard work shift. Lily ran up the stairs, turning at the top to give her mother a big grin and an exaggerated wave that filled Mary's heart with love and fueled her for the day. Watching her disappear behind the large oak door, Mary set her sights on the next three-block walk to the diner that she had called her second home for the past five years. Coming in the back door of the homey diner, she smiled at Tony, the large chef that cooked all the stick to your ribs comfort food that the locals craved.

"Hey Mary, looking good as usual," he called out, saluting her with his flat spatula. "You too Tony," she said laughing. She could look like hell and Tony would still compliment her; it was something she always liked about that sweet, teddy bear of a guy. Coming out of the kitchen, she saw Shari taking an order down the counter from a handsome young man with a scruffy beard. She turned after writing down his order and met eyes with Mary, smiling she fanned herself in reference to the handsome man down the counter. Mary laughed, "Hi Shari, looks like a good morning so far, huh?" She winked as she tied the apron around her waist and grabbed her order pad.

The day flew by and Mary's feet ached as she finished her shift. She tiredly removed her apron and set out to pick up Lily. Mary's eyes lit up as she saw her smiling daughter come out of the school. Her bright blue eyes were ablaze with youthful joy and love for her mother; Mary could feel it and it filled her with such happiness. The little girl skipped down the stairs and leapt into her mother's arms, embracing her as tightly as her four-year-old arms could. Reveling in the warmth of her hug, Mary put her at arm's length and said, "You ready to go home?"

"Yeah," Lily answered enthusiastically, "Can we have chicken nuggets for dinner?"

"We just had those this past weekend," Mary argued playfully. "Puh-lease" Lily begged with her eyes wide, lip protruding slightly. "I don't know," Mary said with a false apprehension. "Oh, come on, Mom. Please," Lily begged further. Sighing, "Oh I guess so," Mary relented. "Yay," Lily exclaimed, dancing in the sidewalk as they made their way home through the street.

Heading home, the sidewalks were much less crowded and Mary found herself letting Lily have a bit more freedom than in the morning. She enjoyed watching Lily spin and explore on the remaining two blocks to their small apartment. Lily raced up the stairs to their front door and Mary's feet slowed her down as she followed behind. "I wish I could bottle up some of that energy," Mary thought to herself.

Lily ran to the living room and turned on the television, the annoyingly catchy tunes of Daniel Tiger blared in the apartment. Mary kicked off her shoes and set her purse on the bench, getting up with great effort. Walking wearily, Mary opened the freezer and grabbed the bag of chicken nuggets and set the oven to preheat at 350 degrees. With a groan, Mary bent and pulled out the baking tray, the other trays clanking as she freed it from the cupboard. Dumping the rest of the bag on to the tray, Mary sat while she waited for the oven to indicate it was ready. She closed her eyes and tried her best to meditate and clear her mind. She was interrupted almost immediately by the beep indicating the oven was ready to receive the nuggets. Putting the food in, she set the timer for ten minutes and sat back down, hoping to relax for a few moments while dinner cooked. Her meditation was going well, her breathing slow and deep, but suddenly her chest tightened as the image of two dark man-like shapes entered her mind's eye. Already on edge, the sharp tone of the timer made her jump and she shakily retrieved the pan and set about getting the paper plates and ketchup for their dinner.

Lily ate with gusto, eating more ketchup than nuggets. Mary ate like a bird, barely finishing a handful of nuggets, her mind still plagued by thoughts of the shadow men. The rest of the night went by in a blur and bedtime came quickly for the two. Lily put up her usual fight and Mary hardly had the energy to get the girl through her night time routine. Teeth brushed and pajamas on, Lily ran and leapt into her bed, Mr. Huggins in her arms.

"Mommy, will you stay with me until I fall asleep," she asked, her eyes showing a slight fear. "Sure baby," Mary replied, gently stroking her head. Sleep came quickly for

Lily and Mary got up, joints creaking and protesting her every move. Like a zombie, Mary haphazardly got ready for bed. She was practically asleep when her head hit the pillow, all thoughts of the day forgotten.

Mary leapt up from her bed, her feet taking her to Lily's room before her brain really realized she was awake. The scene was exactly the same as last night. Lily, hair mussed and feathery, sweat dripping, mouth in an O of terror, eyes wide, screaming at the top of her lungs.

Mary's eyes swept the room, expecting to find the men her daughter had been screaming about, but there was nothing. After a few minutes, Lily calmed down enough and fell back into a deep sleep, her energy depleted from the trauma of this night's encounter. Mary went over to the windows, locked and secure, but she just had to check. The closet was also clear, well, as clear as one could be with a four-year-old. Her games, play clothes, and dolls covered the interior with her clothes hanging neatly above. Mary checked the window again, just to make sure, shaking it in its frame without the slightest movement. Slowly Mary made her way back to her bedroom, before turning around and setting herself up in the rocking chair that was left over from Lily's nursery set up. It wasn't comfortable but it gave her some comfort being right near Lily. She fell into a fitful sleep and awoke as the light of dawn peeked through Lily's window.

Calling into work, Mary thanked Tony for being so understanding and told him to get Jana, the waitress on duty for pulling a double. Lily was her first priority. Ever since Lily's father left them, Lily was all she had.

She had sacrificed everything to bring her into this world and she would do everything she could to keep her safe.

Mary set the phone down and took a sip of her coffee. She needed to call the doctor next, but needed to wait until they opened at nine. Lily walked into the kitchen, rubbing sleep from her eyes, Mr. Huggins hanging from her hand.

"Mommy...?" she questioned as she made her way towards Mary. "Yes, baby girl? How are you feeling?" Mary replied, pulling her daughter up on her lap.

"I'm just sleepy. Can we have smiley pancakes?" she asked with a grin. "Smiley pancakes!" Mary exclaimed, smiling at her daughter. "I guess so. Why don't you pick out your clothes while I make them? We're going to have a mommy-daughter day today."

"Really?" Lily exclaimed, her eyes going wide as she looked at her mother.

"Yes, we are, but you gotta get dressed first. I will get the pancakes started," Mary replied, watching her daughter practically race to her room, Mr. Huggins trailing behind her.

Going to the fridge Mary grabbed out the milk, butter, and eggs, setting them on the counter. The rest of the ingredients were easy to grab as pancakes were one of Lily's favorite foods. The smiley pancakes stared up at Lily as she settled into her seat. Her smile matched the one on the plate.

"Eat up baby girl," Mary said as she grabbed her phone and dialed the doctor's office. Luckily, they had an opening that afternoon, so Mary cleaned up the breakfast dishes and Lily squealed with excitement as they headed to the park to play before the appointment.

"All right Lily, open your mouth up real wide and stick out your tongue for me," Dr. Johnston said, shining the light down the little girl's throat. "Thank you, Lily, you have done awesome. Mommy and I need to talk, nurse Amanda will take you to the prize chest for being such a good patient, okay?" Dr. Johnston said to Lily's joy. She grabbed the nurse's hand and practically pulled her out of the room.

"Well she certainly seems healthy by the looks of that," Mary laughed, trying to lessen the tension that had been building in her chest.

"I would have to say so," Dr. Johnston said, looking down at her chart. "She appears completely healthy, no issues physically that I can find; however, I do think she may be experiencing night terrors. Night terrors are when a person may scream, have intense fear, or may even flail or sleepwalk unintentionally. They have no idea they are doing it, and like you said she wakes up with little to no recollection. I would recommend you take her to a psychologist just to make sure there isn't anything else. Many young kids get night terrors and then they go away after a period of time. My daughter had them for two years and then they just stopped. They are scary and I understand why you wanted to have her checked out. I will put a referral out to Dr. Miller and have her office contact you to set up an appointment tomorrow. Does that sound okay to you, Mary?" she asked.

"Oh yes, thank you so much. It has just been so hard doing this on my own since her dad left. She is all I got, and I hate to see her dealing with this even if she doesn't really remember it that much," Mary said shaking the doctor's hand.

Making her way to the waiting room, Lily smiled up at her mom with a small plastic ring on her hand. "Look at my new ring Mommy. I got it from the prize chest!" she exclaimed, waving her hand around frantically.

"That is quite lovely Lily. Why don't we head out and go home? I am exhausted. What do you say we order pizza and have a girl's night?" Mary asked as they headed out of the doctor's office.

"Pizza!" Lily exclaimed, "Can we watch Bambi, oh and will you paint my toes? Oh, and can we have popcorn," Lily rambled on and on. Mary just nodded and laughed at her daughter's antics. When they got home, Lily ran to her room returning with her arms filled with blankets, half of them trailing on the floor behind her. "Come on Mommy, let's cuddle while we wait for the pizza." Lily said, patting the couch. Never one to dismiss a cuddle request, Mary made her way over and burrowed into the blankets with Lily. After watching Bambi and finishing a medium pizza from Formaggio's, Mary had painted Lily's toes blue, her current favorite color. Lily's eyes drooped as she tried to convince Mary to watch just one more movie, but Mary didn't have to fight long as Lily passed out just minutes after. Mary carefully carried Lily and the mound of blankets back to her room. Laying her down gently, Mary laid the blankets over her, making sure she was properly covered. Mary thought about sleeping in the rocking chair again but her back was killing her and the doctor had said episodes like this were common. A niggling sense of fear ate at her, but her tiredness and sore back won out and she made her way to her room. She peeled off her clothes from the day and jumped into her pajamas. She was asleep before she hit the pillow, her last thought was of Lily.

Sunlight streamed in from the window as Mary's alarm rang out, waking her from her sleep. Stretching, Mary felt herself slowly coming to. Last night's sleep had been wonderful. Thinking about it Mary realized she hadn't heard Lily cry or scream all night. Maybe that was a good thing, she thought to herself. The doctor did say they can stop after a time, maybe Lily was one of the lucky ones for whom it stopped quickly. Deciding on letting Lily sleep in a bit more, Mary checked her phone and found a voicemail from Dr. Miller's office confirming a two o'clock appointment that afternoon. Smiling, Mary made her way to the kitchen, turning on the coffee pot and sitting down to read while the coffee pot filled with that magical brew. Lily typically awoke to the smell of coffee; it was almost a given that her little bed rumpled curls would come bouncing down the hall in a whirl, jumping right into Mary's lap, but today was different. She's just exhausted, Mary thought to herself, returning to her long-neglected book. After two cups of coffee and five chapters Mary began to worry that Lily might be sick. She set down her book and brought her mug to the kitchen sink. Mary padded her way down the hallway to Lily's room. The door stood open and the light coming in from the window shone in a long beam across the carpeted floor.

"Baby girl," Mary questioned, leaning in through the

doorway. Looking around, Mary saw the same room she had left the night before. To the right was a pile of princess dolls and the large princess castle Lily had begged her for last Christmas. Looking left she noticed the bed rumpled, blankets piled high.

"Are we hiding today, Lily," Mary said teasingly. "I wonder where Lily could be?" she said, creeping over to the edge of the bed. Pulling back the covers, she found Lily's pillows but no Lily. Clawing at the blankets frantically, she succeeded in making a mess as the blankets flew and landed all over the floor. Lily was not in bed. Mary frantically checked the closet, under the bed, the bathroom, her hall closet, her bedroom, and the kitchen and dining room. She was not there.

"Lily!" she cried, running up and down the hall of the apartment building. People began to poke their heads out of their doors, drawn out by the spectacle of a mother looking for her lost daughter. Violet, the little old lady from 3E called the cops and made her way over to Mary who was sobbing hysterically.

"Come here sweetheart," she beckoned. Holding the woman, she guided her back to her apartment and sat her down on the couch. "The police are coming dear, let me get you nice hot cup of coffee."

Busing herself, Violet found a mug and filled it with the hot aromatic liquid. Bringing it over to Mary, the woman accepted the cup with a blank stare. The mug shook in her hands and she wrapped both hands around it to steady it.

"Where is she?" Mary asked Violet, her eyes pleading for answers. Sitting next to the young woman, Violet just patted her back and rubbed her arm. "I don't know dear, but the police should be here soon. They will help us sort this out and find little Lily."

A loud knock caused Mary to jump, coffee sloshing on to the carpet, but she didn't seem to care. She set the mug on the floor and walked briskly over to the door. Two officers stood in the doorway. One stood at average height, had neatly trimmed hair and a baby face; the other was older, middle-aged with kind eyes and a bushy mustache. "Ma'am," the older officer said. "We are here in regards to the missing child. Can we come in?" he asked, gesturing inside.

"Yes, yes please" Mary responded, opening the door quickly and ushering them in. "Do you want coffee, water?" she asked, looking towards the kitchen.

"No thank you ma'am," the older officer answered. "I'm Officer Donald and this is Officer Strode. What can you tell us about this morning?" he asked. Mary began to tremble and tears rolled freely down her cheeks.

"I, I don't know. It was just a normal morning I mean, Lily hasn't been doing well. Night terrors the doctor had said. I had an appointment with a psychologist scheduled this afternoon. She had been waking up screaming and crying for the past few nights, it was truly frightening. She said the shadow men wanted to take her, but I never found anyone in the house. I figured they might just be a part of the dreams. This morning though, she didn't come out right away like she usually does but I figured she was just tired. It started to get later in the day so I went to go wake her up so we could get ready for the appointment with the psychologist. I thought she was playing a game

407

when I walked in, but then she wasn't anywhere to be found. Where could she be?" she asked. "You have to find her, she is all I have."

Looking at the mother's tear-stained face, Officer Donald's face softened. "We will do our best to get your little girl back. Do you have a picture of her we can use and something of hers as well?" he asked.

"Yeah, anything, anything you need," Mary replied. She left Violet and the officers in the living room and returned a few moments later with a 4 by 6 photo and her daughter's favorite blanket. Taking the items gently from Mary, Officer Donald nodded to Officer Strode, and the two turned to meet the rest of the team to start mobilizing the large canvass. Mary sat down next to Violet, large sobs wracking her body. The old woman held her close like one of her own children. Trying to provide what little comfort she could to the bereft young woman.

WEEKS HAD past and there was no word on Lily. Mary had been down at the police station every day since Lily had gone missing but they never had anything new to report. Mary had lost weight and the bags under her eyes grew dark, masking her beauty. She hadn't been to the diner since it happened and had no idea if she was going to have a job to return to when this was all over. Mary had taken to sleeping in Lily's bed each night, soaking in the smell of her daughter, hoping that when she awoke she would magically see her daughter there right next to her. Her bright eyes looking back into hers, a goofy smile spreading across her face.

Mary opened her eyes and was greeted with the opposite wall of Lily's room. Closing her eyes tightly, trying to stop the tears that never seemed to stop, she willed herself out of bed and made her way slowly to the kitchen. The phone rang and Mary's heart leapt. "Hello," she asked quickly.

"Mary, it's Tony. Are you coming in today? I don't want to be a dick but we really need you. If you can't make it in, we are gonna have to find someone else. You know we love you but we have a business to run. Shari's been running on empty for the past few days," Tony explained.

Mary sighed, "I don't know Tony. I don't want to be gone if Lily shows up. Do what you have to do. I'm sorry."

"Ah, Mary I'm sorry. I get it. Maybe we'll just get a part-timer. I really hope everything turns out okay. You know Shari and I are here for you if you need us, right?" Tony asked, his concern evident in his voice.

"Thanks Tony, I'll keep you updated," Mary said, "Tell Shari I said hi."

"Will do, bye Mary," Tony said ending the call. Mary spent the day cleaning the kitchen and trying to read. Officer Donald and Strode had been keeping her updated but their calls had become less and less frequent. Mary grabbed the phone and called the station; she had the number memorized by now.

Both officers were out but she left a message asking for an update as soon as they were back from the field. Hanging up the phone, Mary sat down on the couch and put on Bambi. The movie played but she wasn't really watching. In her mind she was imaging Lily: watching her daughter on the floor laying on her belly, feet swinging up in the air.

The movie had ended but Mary still sat on the couch staring at the blank screen. Mary had no idea how long she had been sitting there but she finally got up and made her way to the bathroom. Looking out the window she found that it was dark outside. It was much later than she thought. How long had she been sitting there, she wondered to herself?

Deciding she should just try to get some sleep, Mary made her way back to Lily's room. Lying down on the small bed, Mary felt overwhelmed with grief. It had been weeks; would they ever find her? She didn't want to lose hope but the doubts were threatening to overtake her mind.

Mary fell into a fitful sleep and awoke with a start. In front of her stood two tall dark shadows. They looked like large men but there were no significant characteristics. Her eyes darted back between the two figures and down their arms. Between them was a smaller shadow holding to the hands of the other two.

"Mommy," the little figure said. Mary didn't hear anything else as her screams pierced the night.

THE DEVIL'S CAULDRON

By Dustin Chisam

It goes without saying that your life can change on a dime. It may be for the best, but destiny barreling through your day like a freight train usually heralds a turn for the worst. But sometimes that train can hit you, and still leave you able to mill about in your boring, everyday life. All the same, afterwards your eyes are forever open to what you were once oblivious to, and though the change is entirely inside you, it seems that the world itself has turned inside-out. This happened to me at the most appropriate place.

The falls were our county's local secret. A 40-foot drop in a tributary seventeen miles off of the Platte River in Colorado. The pool lay in a perfect ring of stone with an opening which allowed it to continuing to flow. The dark grey of the stone around the pool, with the almost black stone behind the waterfall lent it an ambience that earned it the nickname "The Devil's Cauldron." To say nothing of the drooping tree branches that hung over the side of the fall, framing it in an almost macabre way. It was a popular hangout for teenagers to come drink or smoke. If a town troublemaker was unaccounted for, the adults expected them to be found here. But somehow, on Halloween of all days, we were the only ones here.

We were all slugging back some local lager around a small campfire at the shore atop the falls. I'd driven from the university where I was attending my freshman year to visit my two oldest friends on Halloween. All things considered, we hadn't been as scattered to the four winds like we'd feared as children. Kylie was attending a local community college, my school was only 45 minutes away, and Thorsten still lived in town. But there was a threat to our cohesiveness as a triad, and it was the tale he was regaling us with:

"That old bitch said it was all me," Thorsten growled. "Got a court date on the 15th—old man posted bail but said I'm on my own after that."

Can't say I'm too surprised. He had a long list of screw-ups that had earned him the entire medley of offenses a juvie could rack up and still be walking free. Fighting, stealing, drinking, and snorting. Add all those up, and it didn't look good for his trial. The judge was notoriously unforgiving for repeat offenders. The wild vandalism spree he'd been pinched for meant he'd probably be eating Thanksgiving dinner out of a divided cafeteria tray surrounded by glowering hard-timers. This impending separation had tinged everything about today with a melancholy I had expected to feel during graduation. And I knew it was because one of my best friends was slowly riding off into a sunset that foretold an ever-dimming future.

"Well, fuck it," Thorsten sighed. "Maybe I can serve it and walk out without my asshole wrecked." I knew Kylie's gratitude for the time, years ago, he'd kicked the ass of some kid who'd called her a dyke had worn thin after all of his problems, so she was glad at the obvious invitation to change the subject.

"Can you believe I've never been here before?" she asked. "Everybody I know made at least one trip before they could even drive, because they had an older brother, sister, or cousin to take them."

"But no parents?" I asked. We all chuckled at this—no responsible parent would take their kids here. It was a bit of a hike on a poorly maintained trail. Not too dangerous in and of itself. But there was another reason all the local parents discouraged us from poking around the Cauldron too much. Hell, I had never even tried to climb up or down the roughly carved steps not ten feet away that led down to the pool below.

"All the stories," Kylie nodded. "You know how weird you feel when you talk to other kids in other towns and they have to explain to you how weird it is how superstitious the adults in this town are?"

"I know all about that," I agreed. "How many times did you see someone do the horns gesture to ward off the evil eye by the time you were ten?"

"And it's all thanks to this place lying right in their backyard," Thorsten murmured. The campfire popped and crackled, but Thorsten's eyes remained in shadow as its light danced across his face.

The falls were gorgeous, of course. The tumbling water was soothing, and despite its forcefulness, not so loud that it threatened to overpower our conversation. I looked thirty feet down at the tree line that encircled the pool and flanked the stream it flowed into. Shining our flashlights on it, I had assumed it was the night time and power of suggestion that made it look like the darkest water I had ever seen.

"Would people think this place looked spooky if it weren't for all the stories about it?" I wondered aloud. "I mean, it's really pretty."

"I'm the wrong person to ask. I think it's pretty because it's spooky," Kylie chuckled. She wasn't quite a Goth, but she loved all things dark and mysterious.

"Some of 'em are pretty... intense," Thorsten replied. As he gazed into the fire, I saw the good cheer he'd tried so hard to keep up falter, as the future reminded him of its relentless approach.

"Why don't you tell us a few," I hurriedly suggested. And if he told me one I'd heard before, I knew I would keep my mouth shut. But it turned out I had never heard any of the stories he told. "First story I ever heard about this place was the 'Cries of the Broken Babe.'" He took a swig of his beer before continuing. "Chick has a hard pregnancy. Doesn't even have a midwife. I don't remember if this was the turn of the century, probably no later than WWII. Anyways, her husband dies in a freak accident—something he was fixing squished him flat. Now, he was the controlling type, and kept her inside all the time. She didn't have any friends to help with the birth—maybe she was too scared to go out at this point. So she pops the baby out by herself, and lo and behold, it's stillborn. It might have been days, or maybe even hours before she staggers her way here, and stands at the top of the falls. She screams to heaven above or hell below—she don't care, she'll take help from whoever's listening—and tosses her baby into the water.

"It was alive. But the fall had broken it. Kind of like those dogs with swimmer's syndrome. It cried, it bled, the whole time you could tell by looking at it that it shouldn't be alive. But nothing she did could end its pain, so she returned to the Cauldron, this time taking her and the baby under the water, and never coming back up. But you can still hear them both. The baby, crying in an agony that never ends, and the woman, for everything she'd lost. Some people even said they've heard crying from the pool —I mean, not just hanging in the air, but right out of the water like a goddamn speaker. Might be a baby. Might be a grown woman. There're a few who say they've heard both, in an eternal duet of agony."

We mulled that over for a long time, the small fire crackling as we finished our beers. A huge POP startled us out of our musings, prompting me to say the first thing that came to mind.

"Might be bullshit," I finally said, thought I was thinking More like definitely bullshit. "But still pretty goddamn spooky."

"Another one that's a little less crazy," Thorsten continued. "There was this religious group heading west, trying to find a place to settle out in California. Somehow they found this place. Well, the leader decides this'd be a great place to baptize a few new converts they'd made along the way. So he wades on in, and does the whole rigmarole with the first few. Then comes the two twin boys. They ask if he can dunk them both at once. This leader says 'Why not?' So he gets a big 'ol meaty paw on each head, and pushes them under. And a second later, he's freaking out. He starts frantically splashing and hitting at the water—because he lost them as soon as they went under. The second they disappear into that black water, it's water that's all he's holding.

"The whole entire flock starts panicking, and they all jump in, swinging and splashing the same as him. But there's no sign of the two boys. The group got out of town, post fucking haste.

"Funny thing is—this leader became known as a faith healer afterwards. He never stood in a pulpit again, but he'd come up during other services and lay the hands on anyone desperate enough. And once in a while—it worked. But he started to drink. He'd get in fights and lash out at people. One night he screams that he's a fraud, and that it's all from the forces of darkness. Then he up and vanishes for months. When he turns up again, it's right here in town. Nobody ever saw him. But he left a note on the front door of the sheriff's office, saying he'd returned to drown himself in the Cauldron, and that they should hurry up and pull him out before some poor kid finds him face down. But they never found him here, or downstream. Or anywhere else, ever again.

"Last one I know, I sort of believe. There was a rough couple of years—a long drought almost dried up the falls to a trickle. This was about a hundred years ago, and supposedly the mayor of our town waded into what was left of the Cauldron and slit his wrists. Same thing as the preacher—he left a suicide note in his office, and when they found it and went looking, they didn't find a body. Of course, the night before they found the note, the skies just burst open, and it rains for three days straight. Maybe his body just got washed away because the Cauldron got filled up again and hasn't dropped since."

There were similarities to all of the stories he'd shared. He didn't tell the story about how if you played a musical instrument at the edge of the pool on the solstice, you could supposedly hear your music played back to you during the next one. He never said anything about the supposed cave behind the falls that led to the subterranean ruins of a lost civilization. And not one word about how the Cauldron is supposedly the gathering place of a coven of witches, despite it easily being the scariest legend. He had grown steadily more somber as he went on, and a hint of bitterness creeped into his voice near the end. I think Kylie had the same thoughts that were welling up in my own brain, because she shot me an uneasy look when our eyes met briefly. I had never felt we were as far away and removed from the inseparable trio we had been when we were ten; when our parents joked about whether I or Thorsten would marry Kylie when we grew up. That was before Kylie and I found out we were gay and Thorsten anything but marriage material in our parents' eyes. I thought I could see some hint of the lonely little boy Thorsten once was as he pulled away from the fire, as if to hide incoming tears from us. But heavy, plodding footsteps that spared no branch underfoot surprised myself and Kylie—but Thorsten was obviously expecting them.

And there he was—the one who'd taken Thorsten's nascent rebellion and sculpted it into something tangible. I'd heard the phrase "walking hard-on" a few times in my life, but Jerod was just a walking scowl—a concentrated show of displeasure. Everything Thorsten dabbled in, Jerod did with gusto.

"What's he doing here?"

"Nice manners, queermo," Jerod snorted, seemingly not offended. Kylie's eyes flashed; when Thorsten had started to fall in with the wrong crowd, the time that he had fought a kid for calling her a dyke made us both think there was still hope for him. But this slur didn't seem to register with him now. He just trundled over to the log Thorsten was sitting on and sat his big-ass next to him, cracking open a beer from the cooler.

"He's here for my big sendoff, the pachyderm between four walls," Thorsten said diplomatically. "There's something I wanted to try, since I might not get another chance."

"You're not going away forever," Kylie said warily.

"This town won't look the same even if I bothered to come back," he spat. "So I'm not going to try."

"It won't miss you," Jerod agreed. "That's why I'm bailing too." He had gotten lucky—despite Mrs. Elkberg's testimony, the cops still only found enough evidence to connect Thorsten with the vandalism spree that had smashed the windows and bodies of six cars parked in the street.

Thorsten sighed, seeming to decide he could hold off no longer, and slammed back the last of his beer, and stood up. But he didn't say anything at first.

"And you're... planning on doing something about it?" I asked, not content to leave the subject hanging.

"Hey, you want me to be completely honest with you?" Thorsten sneered. "Yeah, we did it. We smashed up all those cars outside up and down that block. We were as careful as could be—we wore ski masks, and even used someone else's car that we had them report stolen, just so it could be 'found' the next day, completely unharmed. But somehow, old lady Elkberg was able to give the police every detail. There's something not right about her, never mind that she got me sent up the creek."

Ms. Elkberg seemed to perfectly typify every old woman accused of being a witch. Sure, she lived in a beautiful house and was impeccably dressed and groomed, but that didn't help. She was so aged and weathered that, combined with her sharp features, it made her look like one of the Weird Sisters from Macbeth trying to hide out plain sight in suburbia.

"Taking revenge on a monster ain't no crime," Jerod nodded. With that, he got up and went back to the edge of the clearing, and picked up something he had left just out of sight. We knew what it was before we saw it, with a cranky meow making it obvious. It was a small wire cage that just barely gave the black cat inside room to stand. Kylie and I gasped when we got a good look at it. I had seen these in the news, on social media—it had two faces. One was glaring at all of us through jade green eyes above a slightly askew nose and mouth, while a third eye lay closed above another mouth and nose. The second set of features all seemed so tightly closed they appeared to have been glued shut.

"This is her fucking cat," Thorsten said. "Never comes out of her house, but somehow she knew all about it. Only one who saw us was this freaky little shit, looking down atop that big wrought iron fence."

"These cats are supposed to die," Jerod said. "You surprised that old bat has a little monster like this? She probably dances naked around this same pool with all the other witches in town on the solstices."

"What are you going to do it?" Kylie asked nervously.

"Test a theory," was Thorsten's simply reply. He opened his backpack, and to our horror, amidst the knickknacks inside, was a large, silver, curved knife.

"Ever hear about how animal shelters won't adopt black cats before Halloween because they're worried Satanists'll sacrifice them?" Jerod said, the words rumbling forth from thick rubbery lips stretched into a predatory smile. Only physically pulling his mouth into the crescent of a fake smile would have looked less inviting. "If there was ever the right place, this is it. If there was ever the right night, this is it. And if there was ever the right sacrifice, this is it. This is like the seventh son of a seventh son in terms of currency in black magic."

A trembling yowl came from the cage, as if the cat understood their intentions.

"I was thinkin' about this place," Jerod said. "It has to have some kind of power. It takes, but it gives. That's what all the stories say. I figured, maybe if I give it something I might get something worthwhile back. Thorsten's gonna need all the luck he can get."

I tried to tell myself this was all a prank, but then Kylie acted. She loved cats even more than me, so she immediately dove at Jerod to try and wrest the cage from his meaty paw. He showed more restraint than I expected, merely keeping the much smaller Kylie at arms' length. But it turned out to be merely an obligatory gesture to his run-around buddy, before he got tired of struggling with her and slapped her across the temple, sending her sprawling into the grass.

He always told me I had more sense than balls—as if that was a bad thing—and I could not forget that Thorsten had about twenty pounds on me and Jerod fifty. The cat was quietly growling at them now. I suppressed similar rage and instead helped Kylie up. He spared her a glance, and then met my eyes. He looked alarmed for a second, before his face shifted into a completely passive expression as he set up the contents of his bag.

It was a dime store Satanic altar that he may as well have bought at a Spirit Halloween store. This wasn't a prank. He wasn't going to deal with his impending incarceration by simply freaking us out with an elaborate prank.

"Don't do this," Kylie pleaded as she held her head. "Those stories are all bullshit. There's nothing to them, you're not going to get anything out of this..." I was certain that if an innocent little deformed cat's life weren't at stake, she would have been long gone.

"The price of finding out is exactly one cat. Seems reasonable," Thorsten said, as he reached into the cage and grabbed it by the neck. It had seemed docile enough, but the second he got a grip the cat went berserk, turning into a snarling black blur in his hand. He was forced to slam it down on the chintzy faux altar he had set up, and as he raised the knife, the moment of truth came: Part of me, deep down, wanted to believe that Thorsten was a little afraid of Jerod, and that was why he had barely reacts to him hitting Kylie. But the moment I realized that I was afraid to get too close while he wielded that knife, I knew our friendship was over. Hell, I had been afraid of him for a long time, which was why I hadn't protested more. So it was the fear that made me watch helplessly, as Thorsten brought the knife down into the cat's side. The pitiful creature screeched, and we, the two unwilling spectators, screamed. The screech waned, petering off into a faint, throaty mewl as the expressive face went slack.

"This for anyone who's listening, who cares to hear my voice!" Thorsten called, before unceremoniously tossing the cat into the water below. I knew it was still alive. Sucks for a animal that hates water that much to drown, was the inane thought that rolled through my head. We all looked down after the splash for a long time, and when the disappointment set in, Thorsten took it out on me:

"Don't look at me like that. Nobody wanted to help me!" Thorsten screamed. "Dad didn't even care to look at me when we were kids—"

"Oh, shut it!" I snapped. "Nobody made you do anything. They didn't make you smash up those cars, rob all those stores—"

"Hey, wait a minute," Jerod said. "Listen!"

"Oh, fuck you, dirtball!" Kylie spat.

"The waterfall!" At that, I realized that as relatively quiet as it usually was, it sounded now like a trickle. But we could see plain as day that the water still flowed and fell as freely as always.

Thorsten's eyes instantly lit up, and he ascended those stone steps far more quickly than was safe, but he had the luck of the devil on his side. Poor choice of words, I know.

One careful walk down later, we found it quickly: the cat was crawling onto the shore, out of the pool. It was barely moving, and yowling pitifully as it pulled itself through the grass. Thorsten was kneeling a car's length away, fascinated.

"Fucking stomp on it!" Jerod called. Thorsten seemed not to hear him and kept his eyes on the cat. Jerod decided he had to be the one to take action.

"I'll just break its fucking neck. No big deal." And when he picked it up, our illusions about living in a sane world were shattered.

Seemingly out of nowhere, the cat's vitality returned with a screech as it slashed Jerod's wrist in a flash. We lost sight of it almost as soon as he dropped it, and Jerod grabbed the wound with his other hand.

"Been ten years since I've been scratched by a—" and he cried out in shock as a torrent of blood suddenly gushed from his fingers—this was not a normal cat scratch.

"Oh, god, oh god!" Jerod screeched. We pointed our flashlight, and clear as day, the scratches were unmistakably spreading, deepening. That burning sting of a cat scratch was usually only accompanied by the barest trickle.

And just like that, his forearm was reduced to a stump as all four scratches delved all the way through, causing it all to just drop off in four bloody pieces. Thorsten screamed as his friend fell backwards in a faint into the Cauldron, vanishing into the water as if he was a lead weight and not a buoyant human. We were all screaming then, but somehow we all managed to hear the sound over our cacophony and silence ourselves.

There was a baby crying. And a moment later, a woman. Both could be the quiet somber cries of one grieving on the anniversary of a loved one's passing. But it quickly escalated, swelling into an agonized din. What I saw next cemented the promise of horrific nightmares for years to come:

A woman was rising from the pool. Everything about her was a dull spectrum of black to light gray. Dark hair fell limply about her face, revealing only silver eyes peering through. In her arms, held against soaked and rotting clothes at least a century out of date, was something wrapped in a dripping, sodden blanket. She held it tightly against her breast, but as she stepped foot on shore, she held it out to Thorsten, opening it slightly. Despite himself, he shined his light into it, and promptly screamed at something that was obscured to Kylie and myself by the angle. And the wailing began, from the woman and the bundle.

Behind her, two boys in a similar state staggered out of the water. They looked to be no older than seven, and they sang a hymn in unison as they marched for the shore, hand-in-hand:

"Up from the grave he arose

With a mighty triumph o'er his foes!"

And last but not least, a tall stately-looking man wearing a fancy, out-of-time suit—albeit one similarly ruined as the others were. Some awareness in that mask of gray and black peered at Thorsten, one that the others lacked.

"It's about that time," he sighed in a wet and croaking voice, flipping open a rusted pocket watch. Atop the falls, the now-forgotten campfire flared up, drawing our attention for no longer than we dared look away from the horrors lurching towards us. It shot into the sky in a column worthy of the Old Testament before abruptly winking out.

"No—no, please—"Thorsten was always the fastest of us. He might have gotten away, if the black blur hadn't zipped past his foot, splitting his work boot open. The heel of his foot followed a moment later, as he toppled, screaming. Instantly, the swarm of wraiths were pulling Thorsten into the Cauldron—they seemed to flow over and wrap around him like water. I realized after a moment that they were— they were de-coalescing into the dark water of the cauldron, sucking Thorsten below. It hadn't been my imagination— Jerod's body was nowhere to be seen. Kylie and I made to pull him out, but the cat came between us, glaring a warning at us from three open emerald eyes. We stopped right there. That it was hale and uninjured was the least remarkable thing. Thorsten's screaming turned into gurgles as the black liquid gushed out of his mouth, his ears, and nose, before finally bursting out of his eyes. The ghosts finally lost their shape and collapsed back into the water with our friend, and the Cauldron was silent and still once more. We ran, of course, back to where we had parked our cars. We dared to think we were home free and ready to mourn our lost friend once we got inside and I put the key in the ignition, but there was quite the surprise waiting for us.

The cat was standing in front of the open back seat window of my truck, the eye from the dead face closed again. Kylie and I froze in terror as it took a quick glance at either of us, before letting itself in to curl up on the large armrest between us. We looked at each other, prepared to get out, to chance running home, when it laid its head down and started purring loudly.

"It wants to go home," Kylie said. Giving it what it wanted seemed like a good idea.

We were silent the whole way back to town. It was past midnight at this point. A few jack o'lanterns still glimmered their pulpy grins, but we both knew the occasional small hooded form staring at us from the sidewalk wasn't unusual for Halloween. When we arrived at old lady Elkberg's place, the wrought iron gate in front of the old Tudor was open. I knew we were expected, so we both headed out, hand-in-hand, a silent promise that this time, whatever happened would happen to both of us.

The front door slowly opened, as if pulled on a wire. Blackness was all we saw, and we didn't dare get any closer. The cat followed us from the truck and stood between us expectantly. We knew we were being watched, and spoke into the darkness at the same time:

"We—we have your cat. We didn't mean—"

"We didn't have anything to do with—"

"I know," came the matter of fact pronouncement from the blackness within. "Just let her in. Morrigan, come!" And the cat happily disappeared into the house. "There's a third kitten inside of her, you know. A second she absorbed in the womb. She's a fighter. A survivor. Tonight, of all nights, even more so. Take care to never forget that."

And the light of a passing car illuminated the living room. For a split second, we saw the decrepit woman still clad in a resplendent blue dress sunken into an easy chair. And on the armrests, the headrest, on every side, were at least fifteen more black cats scattered about. Fifteen pairs of green eyes scrutinizing us before the front door slowly pulled closed on its own, the locks promptly clicking and sliding into place.

I still wonder if it was the animal or the place. I don't have an answer. All I have is a lesson learned—to tread carefully when it comes to the ancient and arcane on All Hallow's Eve. If you can learn the same lesson, then I've done all I can.

THE ELEVATOR IN THE WOODS

By Adrian J. Johnson

THE LAST THING I REMEMBER HEARING ONCE I RAN OUT OF the school building were the excited shouts and screams of every student around me, trying to start their summer break right away. Many people are trying to push and shove their way through the exit doors, swarming out like flies, wanting less of the constant, boring school days and more of the exciting fun outside of school. It's insane, everyone is desperate to start their summer vacation like there is no tomorrow. To be honest, I don't mind school much, so I didn't really care if it were to be the last day of school or not. Probably the one guy that I know who's crazy about breaks from school, or basically any day without school is my best friend, Barry Amsterdam.

Barry is the kind of guy who got into detention count-less amounts of times for, well, a lot of reasons actually. Most of those reasons were because of slacking and not doing much of his school work. Some other reasons involve skipping classes by hiding in the boys' restroom, texting during class, and being disruptive for fun. Even though he does these things at school, he's actually a great guy once you get to know him.

I became best friends with Barry when I started middle school a few years ago; he sat with me at lunch for absolutely no reason and started talking to me. I was just flat out confused because he was talking to me as if he knew me, about what he did before school started. What happened was that he had brought a stray cat he said he found outside on his front porch, he had dressed it up in a skunk costume, and had let it roam free around the school. It had surprised a lot of students; they ran away thinking it was a skunk, teachers too had freaked out. The principal had found out and gave him a few weeks' worth of after-school detentions. I remembered that day, someone came up to me and told me there was a "wild animal" roaming around in the school, and it ran past us. It took me a minute to realize that it was too big to be a skunk.

It was a simple prank, but thinking about it more, it was a bit cruel to do that to an innocent animal.

Barry was in a few classes with me, so I actually got to hang out with him in school and after school. He was really nice to my parents when I first introduced him to my mom and dad, and we played some video games in my bedroom. My parents know about the kind of trouble he usually gets in, but Barry told me that he'd never act like himself around anyone related to his friends or family, unless he wanted to. Sometimes. I was introduced to his parents. His parents didn't care much about how they act in the house. His dad was a man who drank a lot and usually wore a white tank top and shorts that had a few stains on them—I wouldn't ask what the stains are though, but he's actually very welcoming once you get to know him, just like Barry. His mom was the kind of parent who was hardworking and tried to keep the house clean, usually drenched in sweat every time you'd see her, but she's also kind as well. It reminds me of the old saying, "don't judge a book by its cover", don't you think?

That's what Barry and his parents are like, but I'm the opposite. I live in a small, decent house that's always clean for anyone to come and visit with my mom and dad, and my little sister, Cassandra. You'd pretty much expect what they did for a living; both have great jobs, they have great well-behaved children, and are living a great life. As long as I'm doing well to make my parents happy, I'm happy with the way I am.

I'm out in the school parking lot, standing as I wait to see if Barry would come out and ride our bikes home. Most of the time, he would be in the principal's office, either about whatever shenanigans he got himself into, or about whatever dropping grade he has in one of his classes. I have a way of finding out if he is in there, by counting down from fifty, because he's usually one of the first people to come out of the school building. If he doesn't come out by the time I finish counting, he's obviously in the principal's office or in some classroom.

I decide to start counting down from fifty as I looked around for him, which was kind of hard since I'm surrounded by a big crowd.

50... 49... 48...

No Barry so far.

47... 46... 45...

Nope, still isn't here yet.

44... 43... 42...

He's still not here, so I keep counting. As soon as I got to zero, the parking lot was less crowded with students and teachers, so I run back into the school without coming across anyone. Getting to the principal's office, I saw Principal Horrace and you-know-who, slouching into a chair in front of his desk. I stand outside the office, waiting a few minutes for him to come out, which didn't take long at all. Barry came out with a disappointed look on his face, which is surprising. Usually when he's out of the principal's office, he seems to shrug it off as just a warning, but it was rare for him to look at me as if his whole world had turned upside down.

"What's up?" I asked him, looking down at his hands, which were behind his back as if he had something he didn't want me to see. Barry tried to avoid eye contact with me, so I tried to get his attention.

"Hey! I'm right here, now tell me, what did he say?" I asked him, snapping my fingers in his face. He finally managed to show me what's in his hands, which is a piece of paper that showed his grades throughout the eighth grade school year, which were bad, of course, but underneath all of that was something that almost made me lose my mind. This has never happened to Barry before, he would usually progress grades every year — but this time, he's being held back into the eighth grade.

"Yeah, I'm not going to the high school with you this year," said Barry.

I let out a loud groan and shove the paper into his face, moving it around as if I was smearing a pie into a clown's face as a joke.

"What have I told you about raising your grades a little? Always get at least—"

"—a passing grade in some of the classes," Barry and I said at once, him knowing what I said many times before. "I know, but school is just boring. If they made it more fun, then I would participate in learning a lot more. God, you're like my parents."

"I just want to be with you throughout the rest of school, then we're off for good! But then I would have to wait a year for you to graduate, or maybe a lot more if you're going to keep this up! Come on, let's get home." Then Barry and I walk out of the school and towards the bike rack, getting our bikes and heading home.

It was nighttime; I sat and ate some Italian food for dinner with my family, and I was about to stay up and quietly play some video games. My bedroom is dark, but I'm able to see some of my surroundings with the illuminating light from the television screen. I pick up my controller and turn it on, but then I hear a slight buzz come from my phone. Picking it up, I notice that Barry, of course, has sent me a message. He's the kind of person who would also nonstop text anyone, even if people are busy with something. Barry would still text them, mostly trying to start a conversation. I opened up my phone and checked out what Barry had to say, only to find a short message: "open ur bedroom wndow."

I slowly got off the bed, quietly walking over to the window and lift it open, only to see Barry with his bike, waving up at me.

"God, dude! What are you doing here? It's already dark out, my parents are asleep!" I whisper loudly at him.

"Come on, man. It's summer break, we're supposed to have fun! Now come and get your bike and let's head out," he said, patting his bike seat as if he wanted me to get on with him.

"To where?"

"I don't know, maybe get a slushy at the gas station and hang out at the park?"

"First of all, I'm not sneaking out with you when it's so dark outside, and second of all, I don't have any money."

"And that's why I always come prepared." Barry held up his wallet, showing it to me.

Yup, you might have guessed correctly, I went to sneak out into the night with my best friend, who kept pressuring me to go out. I had to grab my bike out of the garage without my parents waking up to see what's happening. Out in the cold night, the moon is shining bright, and the silence being broken by Barry's loud howling as we're pedalling down the empty streets on our bikes. I try to get him to quiet down, but he just ignored me as he had all the fun in the world, while I had to be dragged along when I would've enjoy a good video game and stay out of trouble.Don't get me wrong, Barry is a really great guy when he's not wild and crazy, but he can be a pain in the ass sometimes.

It only took us a few minutes to get to a gas station downtown, which is still open with the lights on inside.

The parking lot is empty, pretty much expected, except for a motorcycle that's parked on the side of the building, possibly belonging to the worker at the register. We walk in after we park our bikes next to the motorcycle, an even colder breeze hitting me like a brick.

"Hey," the worker at the register said in a casual tone. Barry gave a greeting nod at him, I doing the same as we both walk closer to the slushy machine on the other side. I got myself a blue raspberry flavored one, while he got cherry cola.

As we got to the register to buy our slushies, the worker, an older teen named Ray according to his name tag, smiled at us as he started scanning the cups.

"Starting your summer break fun, huh?" Ray asked us, handing us our slushies. Barry and I nodded.

"Hell yeah, we are!" Barry said, giving Ray a fist bump, followed by a mimicking sound of an explosion from the both of them.

"Man, I remember being able to sneak out and start doing whatever I want the moment I got out of high school, that was awesome. All right guys, have a great night," Ray said, chuckling. We went to head out of the gas station, but he stopped us before I pushed open the glass doors.

"Just don't do anything too crazy, okay?"

"Sure, yeah," I said, then we both walk out and head to the park.

The national park is closed for the night hours, but Barry pressured me into sneaking in. I went to drink my slushy as I sit on a swing while Barry went down a slide with his, some of it splashing out of his plastic cup. He is making as much commotion as he can, acting like a little kid on Christmas when waking up to find presents. Once he tired himself out, which was when I was halfway finished with my slushy, he walked over to sit next to me in another empty swing.

"Come on, why aren't you having fun?" Barry asked me, noticing how down I was. I didn't answer him for a few seconds, but then I say something.

"It's just that we're not going to be in the same grade together."

"I'll be in the high school with you, eventually. Come on, cheer up." He start poking me with his finger in my ticklish spots, trying to get me to smile. With each poke, he kept saying "huh" in the weirdest voice he could. I eventually let out a laugh, feeling a bit better.

"Yeah, you're probably right—"

I stop talking as I heard a noise coming from somewhere around us. I couldn't make out what it was, but I could tell Barry heard it too. He is looking into the forest that was by the park, focusing on looking deep through the dark trees.

"I heard it from those woods, let's say we check it out!" He drops his cup and runs off into the woods, leaving me alone in the park.

"Barry! Wait—" I got off the swing and ran off to go look for him. It's almost pitch dark out; I could only see outlines of trees. I stop running every now and then to see if I could hear any sort of noise, at least a twig or leaf crunch.

"Barry?" I didn't hear anything. I continue running, but then I see someone standing still, a few meters away from me. I try to be quiet, walking closer to inspect who or what it is, finally able to see that it's Barry, his back turned to face me.

"There you are! What in the hell were you doing?" I ask him, trying to get his attention, but he didn't even bother to face me or say anything.

"What are you looking at—" I stop to look at what appears to be some sort of an elevator, out in the middle of the woods. I walk up to touch it, expecting it to be a hallucination, but I actually feel cold metal once I place my hand on the doors. This really is an elevator, the kind you would see in any building, a nice one that would have the buttons you would press to go up or down any floor, but except taken out and placed randomly in this spot.

"What's this doing here?" I ask, both surprised and confused at the same time.

"Should we go in it? You know, to see if it works?" Barry asks, finally speaking. He runs up to the elevator and presses a down button on the side. A few seconds later, a loud ding rings out as the elevator doors slide open, revealing a nice interior. The elevator had a red carpet, white wallpaper, and a brass handrail, just an average looking elevator. What's not so average however is why it's here in the middle of the woods, out in a clearing.

"Yeah, it works," I say before the both of us go in. It feels a bit warm inside, but not enough for me to start sweating right away. Barry presses the down button, the others being the up button instead of 1st, then a 2nd, 3rd, and 4th floor button. The doors close and the elevator starts going down.

THE TREES HAVE EYES

"What do you think those other floors would lead to?" Barry jokes at me, chuckling.

"I don't know, man. What if it just leads underground in the dirt or something? What if this elevator is just abandoned here for no reason?" I ask him.

"Would it not work if it were to be abandoned? Besides, it's too weird to have something like this in the woods. It's obviously going to lead to somewhere."

It takes us a few seconds for the elevator to stop moving and the doors to open, only to leave us... where we first began? It seems like the elevator has taken us back to the woods, because the only thing we could see were trees, but there's no way it would take us back outside. It would be impossible to do so, since Barry had pressed the down button to take us to a lower floor.

"Yup, garbage. Let's get out of here," Barry said, walking out of the elevator.

"Barry, wait!" I went to catch up with him, noticing a disappointed look in his face. "You know there was no way it would take us somewhere, right? There's just no way something like this would be out here in the middle of the woods!"

"I know! But hey, at least it worked, right? Besides, I'm done having my fun, I just want to get back home."

We head out of the woods and out of the park, riding our bikes back home. I check my phone as I arrive, and it's almost midnight. We've been gone for about two hours. I'm glad to be back home so I can relax, but at the same time, I feel as if something isn't right. I look around, and at Barry, who is looking back at me.

"What? We're back to your house. Is this not it?" he asks me, groaning impatiently.

"I guess so, yeah." I set my bike on the side of the house and head inside, only to notice something really isn't right at all.

I check every room in the house, but my family is gone. Everything is here in the house, untouched and where it should be, but my parents aren't in the house. I'm alone. I run outside, noticing their car is in the driveway. They definitely didn't go anywhere.

"What's up?" Barry asked, starting to worry as he notices how terrified I was.

"My family is gone!"

"No way!"

"Yes way!"

"Not a joke?"

"Not a joke, I swear! Where have they gone?"

"I'm sure they're fine, even if they headed off somewhere."

I get out my phone and try to call them, but I have no service, so I can't get a connection. I tell Barry that we should go to his place and see if his parents know where my family went, and he thought it's a good idea, so we head off. As we get to his house, we notice that his parents are gone too. In fact, we went to look around town and noticed nobody here but the two of us.

"What is going on? Where did everyone go?" Barry starts hyperventilating, both of his hands on his head as he freaks out. "This is just too weird for words!"

"Calm down, man!" I slap him across the face to snap

him out of it. "Okay, so all of this happened when we got into that elevator, right?"

"Right."

"So, if we get back into that elevator and head back up, that probably would get everyone back!"

"Yeah, that sounds like a good idea!"

The two of us get on our bikes and are about to head off, but we stop as we hear a noise. Maybe it's just our imagination, I thought, probably a trick from the elevator, perhaps, if it has the ability to do things like that. We decide to ignore it, so we continue to ride down the hill to the park. Barry rode his bike to the gas station first. Wondering what he was up to, I follow him. By the time I get in there, he's already picking up a few items, a gallon of gasoline and a matchbox. He looks up at me as I stand at the entrance with the doors open.

"What are you going to do with those?" I ask him.

"I might use it for some sort of an emergency," he replied.

"Like what?"

"I'm thinking about burning the elevator once we're out of here."

"But you know it's surrounded by large amounts of trees, right? You want to cause a forest fire? But at least the fire could stop the elevator from working properly somehow."

"Eh, you do have a good point, but I'm still gonna take these."

The worker, Ray, is gone too, we both noticed. Getting out of the gas station and to the park, we pedal fast to the point where our legs are burning and we're sweating a lot.

A few minutes later, we finally get to the park, and are about to go into the woods, but then I hear the same noise from earlier again. This time, it was a bit more audible, as if the source of the noise is coming closer to us.

"You hear that?" I ask Barry, who is holding the gasoline gallon up to him like a shield, looking around. He only nodded, trying to stay quiet in case the noise would appear again, the sound of what I could make out is footsteps. The footsteps are getting louder, but we can't see anything in the dark. I keep looking around, and stop to see a dark figure standing far away from us. Barry noticed what I was looking at too, and took a step back. The outline of the figure moved a bit, getting a bit bigger as it got closer. Each time we step back, it would make the same movement as we did.

I thought we're alone? I thought. Feeling terrified, Barry and I start running away, the sound of footsteps now becoming rapid and loud. With every single piece of energy I have in my body, I keep running, dodging trees that were in my way. Eventually, I stop to see if we outran whatever was chasing after us, but I notice that Barry is gone. My heart starting to pound in my chest, I look around in the darkness, staying where I am.

"Barry?" I whisper out loud. Nothing happened, everything is quiet except for my heavy breathing from running so much.

"Barry!" I yell this time. At that moment, I feel something push me to the ground, knocking me over into the grass. I try to punch and kick whatever is on top of me, but I stop to see Barry, a few scratches and light bruises all over his face.

"We need to get out of here, now!" he said, pulling me up as we start to run further into the woods.

We eventually find the elevator. I immediately press the up button and wait for the elevator door to open. Then the same sound of footsteps, mixed in with the crunching of leaves and twigs on the ground, comes closer to us from behind.

"Come on! Come on!" I shout as I bang on the elevator doors, waiting for them to open. I turn around to see Barry, opening the gallon and pouring the flammable gasoline around us, then threw the empty container on the ground as he finished. He turned to look at me as if he wanted me to finish the task, and I knew what to do. I opened the matchbox and got out a matchstick, igniting it as the flame on the match head appears. I threw it on the ground, a circle of fire instantly surrounding us. It starts spreading fast, and yet the elevator door still didn't open. From over the fire, we see the light of the fire shine onto a blood-covered Barry, *another* Barry was coming closer to us. *Two Barry's? Why is there two of them? And was that what was following us?*

"What—"

"Don't! Just ignore it! Let's just go, now!" The Barry next to me said.

"Don't—" The other Barry from the other side of the fire ring mutters. I turn around to the elevator, noticing the doors opening. I feel as if good luck has hit me fast, grabbing Barry as we both got into the elevator. I press the up button inside the elevator, the doors closing a few seconds later. The last thing I heard from the other Barry before the doors close still leaves a stain my memory. It's something I can't stop thinking or hearing in my head over and over, the words being a painful scream that still terrify me to this day.

"Don't leave me, please!"

A FEW MONTHS LATER, summer break ended and it's time to go back to school. Barry and I had decided to forget about the elevator, and never dared to speak a word about it, even if it comes back up in our minds as an unforgettable memory that will stay with us for the rest of our lives. I still have a few questions about what the elevator was and what its purpose is, which I can't seem to figure out a reasonable answer. There were other buttons as well, but if they did lead to other floors, what would they be like? There was nobody in town when we went to that one floor, but what was with the clone of Barry? Did it have something to do with the elevator? Has anyone ever encountered it before? And especially, where did it come from? A lot of other questions kept coming into my head, but I just thought about letting everything about it pass. I had my first day of high school, which was actually better than I expected. I got to meet a lot of new people from different grades, I had great teachers, but it still wasn't the same without Barry. After school, I walk over to the middle school to wait for him. I start to count down from fifty.

50... 49... 48...

In those few seconds, I see Barry run toward me with a smile on his face.

"Hey, man! How was your repeating year in middle school?" I ask him.

"Great, I'm actually doing great in most of my classes! Who knew learning was fun?" he replies, giving me a few school papers of his. I look through each one, noticing all of them have good grades marked on the corner. Most of them are B's, one of them is an A, and it's rare for Barry to get a grade like that.

"Wow, you actually took my advice!" I said, surprised as I look through the correct answers he got on some of his work.

"Yup! I changed! It's almost as if I'm not who I once was anymore, the old Barry!"

Those words that came out of his mouth somehow has given me an unnerving chill, hoping it's nothing, but I couldn't help ask him the question I feel like asking.

"Um, Barry? How do I know if you're the real Barry?"

"What?" Barry was looking at me with a confused expression.

"... nevermind."

Ever since that day, I'm starting to question whether or not Barry is who he says he is. The clone from that strange version of our town seemed to be the only person, or thing, there was, and it took the form of my best friend. I am starting to notice a few differences in him, but just hoping for the best; that it's just a change he's willing to make to make himself a better person. For example, one time when he came over to my house for a sleepover, he actually had good manners at the dinner table, unlike him usually being a fast eater who would chew loudly and make a few messes. He also seems more nicer than usual;

he apologized to every one of his teachers for his behavior from before, which surprised me since he cringes whenever he's forced to apologize. I don't know, there's no way that the one Barry that was left out of the elevator could be the real one, the one I have been best friends with throughout my middle school years, but could it be?

DON'T GO SWIMMING IN LONG LAKE

By Nick Botic

AFTER WE GOT OUR THINGS PUT AWAY IN THE CABIN, WE SET out to do what we were most anticipating: swim. We got changed into our swimsuits and walked down the long pier at the back of the cabin, and we each jumped off into the water of Long Lake. The sun beat down on us as we waded around in the unbelievably refreshing lake. It was myself, my girlfriend Kimmy, and our friends Ryan and Alyssa. We swam around for nearly an hour and a half, and the time flew by. Only one thing sticks out about our time in the water, and it's only in retrospect that it does so. At one point, Ryan said he had felt like something bit him on his stomach. The pain went away almost instantly, he said, so we didn't worry or even think about it anymore.

After nearly an hour and a half in the water, we were all exhausted and hungry. We swam to the ladder on the pier and climbed up. When my foot touched the pier, I noticed there was a leech on it and I admittedly freaked out a little more than I should have. I got it off, and that was that. Ryan and Alyssa walked ahead of Kimmy and I, and it wasn't until we got to the cabin and I saw the front of Ryan that I was able to see the trail of blood coming from his naval. It wasn't bleeding profusely or anything, it just looked like a pin had poked him in his bellybutton. He wiped the blood away and that was that.

We cooked our dinner over the firepit, just burgers and hot dogs, and sat around listening to music and talking. It was too late to take out the ATVs, and we were all tired not only from swimming, but the seven hour drive it took us to get there as well. While sitting around the fire, Ryan began complaining of a sharp pain in his stomach. He put his palm over his navel area and gently squeezed. And as quickly as it had started, it stopped.

Throughout the rest of the night and into the next day, Ryan would intermittently comment on the same sharp stomach pain he'd felt at the fire. It was around noon of our second day there that Ryan got his first nosebleed. I say "first" because they would a mainstay over the following two days. We were sitting at the kitchen table in the cabin playing cards when, out of nowhere, the dark red liquid began *pouring* out of Ryan's nose. He assured us that nosebleeds were a regular thing for him, and that it would stop soon. He attributed it to the change in air quality from the city to the countryside.

Nothing truly gave us worry until the last day we were there. Ryan had had nosebleeds and complained of the strange stomach pain throughout the day before, but then, everything came to a head.

It started when blood began leaking from Ryan's left ear. I alerted him to it, and he just sort of stared at me blankly. I said his name, but got the same blank expression. Then his nose started bleeding again, but he did nothing to stop it. He just stood in the same spot, letting it pour down over his lips and chin, and drip onto the floor. Then his other ear began bleeding. Then, the naval area of his white t-shirt began turning red, spreading outward.

I ran to Ryan and lifted up his shirt, unsure of what to do. What I saw made me vomit. His bellybutton was much larger than it should have been, and on the edges of it were these leech-like things. I looked into the chasm in his stomach, and I couldn't see any organs; there were just hundreds, if not thousands, of these leeches squirming around inside him. He eventually dropped to the ground, landing on his back. The leeches began squirming their way out of his ears, his nose, his mouth, and worst, his eyes. They chewed their way from under his fingernails, and judging by the squirming bulges in his socks, his toenails.

We called 911 as the leeches ate their way through my best friend's flesh. He didn't bleed as much as one would think. I attribute this to the fact that leeches are bloodsuckers, and there were *so* many of them that they quelled the flow of blood from the lesions they were creating all over his body. From when I noticed his ear bleeding, it wasn't even 30 seconds before Ryan was dead. It wasn't a minute before his entire body was mangled and chewed through. He was unrecognizable, both as my friend, and as a person in general. The only thing that would give anyone the idea that the pile of meat on the floor was a person was the shape.

Normally, a completely ravaged human body would be a bloody, red and pink mess, but the thousands of black leeches that covered his cadaver made the whole scene a squiggling tarp of shiny black, and they all consumed the blood that would normally have made a mess of the entire area surrounding him. Me and the girls eventually ran outside to wait for the police and stay away from the leeches. A short time later, a single police car came up the cabin driveway, one officer got out, and retrieved a large bag from the backseat of the car.

Without introducing himself, he simply asked "You got any of them on you?"

We all replied in the negative. He cautiously walked to the cabin door, and we looked past him to see what macabre scene awaited him inside. He inched the door open, and leeches began making their way outside. The officer jumped back whilst simultaneously opening the bag he'd brought from his car. He began pouring out what looked like a white powder, that I soon deduced wasn't a powder at all, but salt, and covered the wayward leeches.

He then poured a trail of salt to the gnarled body of Ryan, covering all the leeches between it and the dead pile of them near the door. He proceeded to pour the entire supply of salt over what was left of Ryan. When he was done, he walked out of the cabin and up to the three of us, as we stood there dumbfounded.

"Someone'll come here to clean this up in the next few hours. Don't go swimming in Long Lake."

And with that, he got back in his car and backed out of the driveway. We took pictures as evidence of what had happened, and waited around for the ambulance to get there. They cremated what was left of Ryan and gave us the ashes, which we in turn delivered to his parents, who were devastated to hear what had happened to their son. A lawsuit was filed against the town of Long Lake for what had happened to Ryan.

And while I'm glad justice will be done to those that knew about the dangers that lurked within it and failed to warn outsiders of it, I'm even happier I noticed that leech on my foot when I did. It could have been me.

SEEKER

By William Stuart

TRISTAN BREWER STEPPED OFF THE BUS, HITCHED UP HIS pack, and lit a cigarette. After two days on the road, he was finally home. Tristan wasn't sure he was glad to be back in Spenser Springs. He and his father had moved here about five years ago when his parents had divorced, and his dad had taken a position with the forestry service. It had been the summer before tenth grade. He had been just getting seriously into high school, music, friends, and skateboarding when his father had announced they were moving, "not too far away."

For not being too far away, Spenser Springs was a tiny blip on the map in the middle of nowhere. It could be called a suburb of Houston if you were a very liberal real estate agent. Otherwise it was the actual middle of nowhere, a tiny town in Texas only visited by hunters and fishermen who wanted to get really far away from everyone and everything.

A few weeks after school let out he'd said goodbye to his friends and come out here, where the kids his age listened to country music, hunted and fished on the weekends, and spoke in a strange accent that seemed to him what someone would sound like if they were making fun of an accent. Yet, that was the way they really talked. Since he'd been in college, he'd caught some teasing for his own accent which he'd never thought was very pronounced, but was apparently hilarious to people in California.

There had been no fellow skaters, no record shops, and the nearest bookstore was a thirty-minute drive into the next town. Tristan had been quite miserable that first summer. Most of his time was spent rereading horror novels and going through the rule books for his favorite role-playing games. He'd left behind a couple of long-standing Dungeons and Dragons campaigns with his old friends, and he'd just gotten a guide for a new game called Seeker before everything he owned went into boxes. By the time school started in the fall Tristan had committed most of Seeker to memory. It was an intriguing game and he'd hoped beyond hope that he'd meet someone here who would want to play it.

Tristan gave his cigarette a final drag and tossed it. He dug in his pocket for another when the rev of an engine grabbed his attention. There they were, his two best friends, Rob and Jen Gooris. They pulled up in their battered old Ford Bronco, its brakes screaming as they stopped at the curb. "Would you look at that!" Rob called from the driver's seat as Jen hopped out and gave him a hug, "I was hoping you wouldn't come!"

"Up yours!" he laughed. Jen opened the back door and Tristan tossed his bag inside. Then Jen got into the back-seat and yanked the door shut, giving Tristan a cross-eyed middle finger through the grimy glass. He put his thumb to his nose and wiggled his fingers at her and then climbed in front. He'd barely gotten the door shut when Rob floored it and threw him into his seat. The tires screeched as the Bronco tore out of the parking lot and onto the interstate. Jen reached over and handed them both a beer, "You might want to wait a bit before you open it. Bo Duke here flung the cooler all over the place tryin' ta make you laugh."

Tristan held his can over Rob's lap and cracked the top. "Hey!" Rob laughed but the beer did not foam, and Tristan sat back in his seat laughing and gulped it down.

"Oh, Lone Star, how I've missed you!" he said, tossing the can out the window as the Bronco started pushing ninety. If the roar of the engine weren't enough, Rob leaned up and pushed the cassette into the player and the truck was suddenly full of the frenzied guitars of Megadeth. Tristan smiled. It was just like old times.

"So, nobody knows you're here?" asked Jen when the song ended.

Tristan lit a cigarette and shook his head. "Not till tomorrow. I told my dad I'd be home late Friday, but I wanted to see you guys and not catch any shit about not spending time with him, so I left a day early."

"You're so cool, Brewster!" Jen pantomimed before lighting a cigarette of her own.

Tristan laughed, "You know they're almost done making part two?"

"No shit?" Rob said.

"No shit. Read about it in Fangoria."

"Welcome. To. Fright. Night. Part 2," Rob said, "Has a nice ring to it. Can't be better than fuckin' Evil Dead 2, though."

"Nothing will ever be better than Evil Dead 2," Tristan agreed, "So what's the plan?"

The Spenser Springs City Limit sign sped by, barely legible by both the speed of the truck and the number of bullet holes in it. Tristan himself was personally responsible for at least a dozen of them. Rob began to slow down.

"We're going to party!" Jen announced, "Like we used to!"

"We gotta stop and pick up ice and more beer, then we're heading out to the spot!"

"No shit? Camping, huh? It's been a long time."

"We know, College Boy!" Jen said, her accent effectively masking any guile or sarcasm. She smiled brightly, "But since the weather's been nice and all, we figured you'd like a place where we could smoke and get high and loud and shit. Liz and Ryan are already out there setting up!"

"Got any good scary stories from that big-boy school of yours?" Rob shouted.

"Maybe so!" Tristan replied, "Maybe so!"Liz Rankin had actually been the first person Tristan had met that first day at Spenser Springs Senior High. He'd been doodling on his book cover as the teacher passed out calendars and reading lists. Tristan liked to draw and whenever he wasn't reading, skating, or playing D&D, he was drawing dragons and monsters and such. On this day he was sketching a hockey mask.

"Nice Jason," the girl sitting next to him had said.

"Thanks. Um, you watch scary movies?"

"I watch everything. My daddy owns the video hut down on Franklin."

"Cool. I'm Tristan."

"I'm Liz. I like your jacket."

Tristan's denim jacket had patches from different bands and brands that he enjoyed. It was emblazoned with the logos of Vision Street Wear, The Scorpions, Def Leppard, and Iron Maiden. It also had a few autographs written in marker along the bottom—friends of his from home. His jacket was sure to attract unwanted attention from the locals in this new burg, but he couldn't fathom parting with it. He missed his friends and the jacket was a piece of home he could carry with him. The fact that this girl liked it meant that he might not have too much to worry about.

"Tho you might get your ass kicked for wearin' it. Lots of the rednecks around here don't go for no faggy hair-spray bands."

At that she'd turned back to her papers, her dirty blonde hair falling over her face, and said no more for the rest of the class. Her statement came true when at lunch he'd been accosted by the Daltrey twins, Butch and Bubba.

"Well lookie what we got here!" said Butch, "Somebody done wrote all over this faggot's jacket."

"I'll get it," said Bubba who then spit into his hand and wiped it on Tristan's autographs. Tristan was petrified. These two were each at least six feet tall and two-hundred pounds of musclebound farm boy. And the way everyone moved, the way the cafeteria went quiet when they came in, told Tristan he was in for trouble.

"It didn't come off," Bubba called to his brother, "What do you think we oughtta do?"

Butch was just about to answer when a kid ran into the cafeteria, "Daltrey! Coach is looking for you!"

"Which one?" asked Bubba, "We're busy saying hello to the new kid."

"Both of you," said the kid, "He said it was important."

"You just got lucky, asshole," said Bubba, "Real lucky." He reached over and ripped a patch off the jacket. "The damn hell does 'def leppard' mean anyway?" He flung the patch into Tristan's face and walked off toward the door.

Butch followed his brother before turning back, "Hey, Fag! If I catch you wearing that fucking jacket in my school again, I'm going to make you eat it. Understand?"

Tristan nodded slowly, still too shocked and afraid to speak.

"Damn right you do," Butch said over his shoulder before going off to see what Coach wanted.

Tristan stood in the cafeteria trembling and fighting back tears. He looked around the room at the kids sitting with their friends. They didn't look so bad, but none of them wanted to get on the wrong side of Butch and Bubba Daltrey. Most looked at their lunches or at books or just their hands. Nobody looked in his direction. He bowed his head and skulked off to a corner to eat alone in his humiliation.

He'd been sitting at an empty table facing the window when a voice said, "You might want to take that thing off before the asshole brothers see you again." He looked up to see Liz and the kid who had told the Daltreys about Coach. "This is Ryan."

"Um, hi," Tristan said, uncertainly.

Liz looked at him a moment before holding out her oversized purse to him. "Best to shove it in here. I'm serious."

Tristan stared at the bag and then to Liz for a moment before slipping the jacket off and dumping it in. "I'll get it back to you after school," she said. "Butch and Bubba won't mess with me. Their mom works for my dad."

"Thanks."

"You can come sit with us if you want," Ryan said, "Liz says you can draw pretty good."

Tristan shrugged and nodded, still fighting back tears and feeling waves of relief that he was being offered even a little bit of compassion. The three of them stood looking awkwardly at one another until Liz finally said, "Come on then," and led him to a table on the other side of the room. Rob and Jen Gooris had been sitting there too, and for the next few years the five of them would be nearly inseparable.

"So, what's it like living in California?" asked Rob as they pulled up to the gas pump.

"Well, the weather is just about perfect all the time. But I've been so busy with class, that's really all I know."

"Oh come on. You've got a nice tan and everything!" Jen said, "I'll bet you're at the beach every day surfing and skating."

"I wish," Tristan answered, "I mean, I do spend a lot of time outside but that's just hanging out in the quad reading. You wouldn't believe how much reading there is."

"You've always been a bookworm. It can't be that bad," she said.

"Yeah, when it's Stephen King or something I want to read. Forty essays discussing why Moby Dick was white instead of gray is not exactly fun reading."

"They really make you read that stuff?"

"And write really long papers about it."

"Screw that."

Rob killed the engine and the three of them hopped out of the truck. Tristan lifted the handle on the pump and placed the nozzle into the car. "Fill her up?"

"Hang on," Rob said, lifting the tailgate on the Bronco, "Get these too." He removed two five-gallon cans and set them on the ground. Tristan reached into his pocket and pulled out a twenty-dollar bill. "I need four packs of Camel Lights and a Coke. The rest on gas and beer."

Rob took the money and went inside. Tristan leaned back against the truck and sighed. If nothing else, it was nice not to be studying. When the tank was full he filled the cans and hoisted them back into the Bronco. Rob and Jen returned shortly and the three set about loading beer and ice into the cooler. Within moments they were back on the road, screaming engine and heavy metal racing through the Texas backroads. A few minutes later, Tristan turned in his seat to talk to Jen, no longer being able to put off the inevitable question he'd been dreading since getting on the bus in Los Angeles.

"So, what do y'all do here?" Tristan asked. He had been nervous about asking the question, feeling it might be presumptuous—like these locals might not appreciate the new kid asking about them or assuming he'd be welcome doing whatever they did. These were not his friends. They were just a couple of sympathetic bystanders who had been nice to him in a painful moment.

Rob and Jen shrugged and looked at Liz, who was braiding a lock of her hair. She looked up and noticed that everyone was looking at her. "Not much. Go to school, go home. Watch movies, listen to music."

"What kind of music?"

"The radio only picks up the country station out of Houston, so that's pretty much it," said Ryan.

"Sometimes there's a rock station out of Austin that comes on. Michael Jackson, Hall and Oates, that kind of stuff," said Jen.

"How 'bout you? What do The Scorpions sound like?" asked Liz.

"Um, they're like heavy rock from Europe somewhere."

"Is it on the radio?"

"Sometimes. There was a station that played some heavier stuff late at night. Mostly I get tapes from my cousin, though."

"You're not in to all that devil music, are you?" Ryan asked.

Tristan laughed, "No, none of the stuff I like is about the devil. It's mostly love songs and stories with loud guitars."

"How do you know?" Ryan countered, "My dad said they hide all kinds of stuff in their lyrics and you can't even understand what they even say,"

Tristan thought for a moment, "Don't know. I mean, I don't have any of the real tapes, just copies my cousin made for me. But when I was at his house they have the words in the book that comes with the records. I've never even seen the word devil in any of them. They're more like, 'I'm gonna love you forever,' and, 'Make some noise!' Stuff like that."

"Maybe I can borrow one of your tapes and see if they talk about the devil?" asked Liz.

"Sure!"

"Bet you play Dungeons and Dragons too, huh?" said Ryan, a little less sure of the newcomer than Liz seemed to be.

"Um, sort of," Tristan lied. Things were going well, and he didn't want to scare them off. "I mean, I have before but just a little bit. It was too much. People get way too into that game."

"Because they're serving the dang devil, that's why," said Ryan, satisfied.

"Leave him alone, dorkface," said Liz, "Ain't nobody worshipping no devil. That's all just your mom reading them newsletters from the church."

"It's like, it never had any devils or evil or anything that I saw. Just monsters and dragons and junk. It's sort of like…" He tried to think of something they would all be familiar with and hopefully not afraid of. "Like He-Man. Y'all ever play with them?"

"He-Man has demons and stuff in it," Ryan pointed out, "Lots of 'em."

"Shut up ya dang Bible-thumper!" said Rob, "You used to have all the He-Man guys at your house! You even have some of mine that I never got back from you."

"So what? Don't mean there ain't no demons in it."

Liz and Jen looked at each other and rolled their eyes.

"I do have a new game," Tristan said, trying to change the subject. "It's called Seeker and it doesn't have magic or monsters in it at all."

"What's the point then?" Rob said, making a face at Ryan.

"It's like, weird history and science. Like, real stuff mixed with stuff from stories and legends." He reached into his bag and brought out the book. "Like, you ever heard of the Pied Piper of Hamelin and how he played the song and drowned the rats? Well this game is like it's true and you and your team are working together to solve clues and stuff to find the flute before your time runs out. It's pretty neat."

Rob took the book from him and started leafing through it. "So how do you win? I roll higher than you?"

"Not exactly. You're on the same team in groups of up to five people. When you solve a case, or find a clue or whatever, there's a 1-800 number you call to report it. If you're right and within the first hundred or five-hundred or whatever callers to get in, you get prizes and they send out new cases to solve."

"What kind of prizes?" asked Jen, taking the book from her brother.

"I don't know. I just got the book right before we moved. I haven't even played it yet."

"Maybe we should," Liz said, "You know, to see what the prizes are."

"Everybody can come to our house after school," Jen offered.

That afternoon, the five of them sat around the Gooris' breakfast table munching on Star Crunch cookies and drinking fruit punch. Tristan read the rules.

"'Seeker is a game of grand adventure and dark mystery set in the strangest place of all, the real world. For centuries, Man has tried to understand the world around him and shine light on the things that lurk in the dark. As Seekers, you will travel through time and across the world in search of the truth behind some of history's greatest mysteries and have fun and win prizes along the way.'"

"Cool!" said Rob.

"'How to play: The game is best played by at least three but no more than five players. In the index is a five-pointed star. Four of the points are labeled for the four elements: Air, Fire, Earth, and Water. Players roll for their position on the star and take the role of the Seeker at the allotted point.

The top point is reserved for the one called Malumesti (Latin for storyteller). The Malumesti will guide the other Seekers through the stories and lay out what needs to be done to win. The Malumesti should be elected by the other players. Make sure that the Malumesti you choose is comfortable explaining rules, telling stories, and following up with the results of each challenge.'"

The kids looked at one another. "Well, that's easy. It should be him," said Jen.

"Why him?" asked Rob, "We just met him and he's our leader now?"

"Duh, because he's played this kind of game before and it's his book you moron," Jen shot back.

"Hey, just because I had to repeat first grade does not make me a moron, moron."

"Jen's right," said Liz, "It is his book. Are you going to read that whole thing?" she asked Rob.

"Hell no!" said Rob.

Ryan shook his head too. "I'm not sure I even want to play."

"Then it should be Tristan." Liz said. All four nodded. "Read on, then Malmisti."

Tristan looked at each of their faces for a moment before continuing. "Uh, where was I? Okay, here: 'Once the Malumesti has been elected, each player will roll a single die over each of the points of the star, moving counter-clockwise from the top. Highest roll takes their point, and the process continues until each point has been populated.' Um, anybody have any dice?"

"I've got some," said Rob. He went over to the bookcase and shook two red dice from an old Monopoly box.

"Okay, hold on, this is going to take a while. Let me get through this last part. 'Once you have populated your star, tear it out of the book at the perforations. Write the name of each player at each point, then skip to Part Six—Registering for prizes.' Do we want to roll for positions or read about prizes first?"

"Prizes!" Rob, Jen, and Liz said in unison. Ryan simply shrugged.

"'Part Six—Registering for Prizes: Seeker is different from other role-playing games in that it rewards you for your time and effort. That's right, you get prizes for solving the mysteries in each challenge! Prizes range from in-game currency to high-quality replicas of artifacts described in the game.

To register your team with the Seeker International Network, call toll-free 1-800-123-4567. Please have the names, mailing addresses, and phone numbers of each Seeker on your team. Incomplete teams can add additional Seekers later. In addition, fill out the contact information on the Star diagram in the index and mail it in to the address below. Kids, get your parents' permission before calling.'"Tristan turned to the index and removed the five-pointed star. Each point had lines for name, address, and phone number which each of them filled out in turn as they rolled for their position on the Star. Liz rolled Fire. Next was Jen who got Air, Rob rolled Earth, and Ryan, Water.

"So, what's our first mission?" asked Rob, getting more excited as the formalities were ending.

Tristan turned the page. "Challenge One: You have been assigned your Elements. But do you know their history? Fire, Air, Earth, and Water are very important to many cultures around the world. Familiarize yourself with them. Each Seeker, except for the Malumesti, must discover and learn the word for their element in each of the four following languages: Latin, German, Arabic, and Hebrew. Learn to say the word in each language and call in to the network. Each Seeker will say the word for their element one time in each language before passing the phone to the next Seeker. When this task is complete, you are an official band of Seekers and your first prizes will be awarded."

"That's kind of weird," said Jen, "Where are we supposed to find out four different translations for this?"

"Maybe the school library?" suggested Ryan.

"Dictionary?" suggested Rob.

"No idea," said Tristan. "Maybe call a college?"

"That's not a bad idea," said Liz.

Ultimately it took three days for each Seeker to get the correct translation. All four were a bit weary of the game when they got together again.

"I don't know if it's worth it, but here goes," said Liz when Tristan handed her the phone. Liz said her lines, then passed the phone to the others. Tristan listened to the recorded message end and hung up.

He shrugged. "I guess that's it."

The five of them moved on from the game and watched a movie on the Gooris' big-screen TV.

Seeker was all but forgotten three days later. The kids, Tristan included, no longer cared for in-game currency or whatever trinkets the game makers had offered. The challenge had been difficult and seemed pointless. They sat together at lunch and talked and joked. Tristan was welcome at their table and had begun to feel comfortable being part of the group. The bullies left them alone as Liz had promised, and he settled into school.

Then the prizes arrived.

All at once, they were back in the game. The prizes were nothing short of amazing.

Tristan had his headphones on and was riding his skateboard in front of his house when the mail carrier dropped a box on his front step. He waved at the mail lady, kick-flipped his board into his hand, and walked over to get it. It was addressed to Malumesti and it was heavy. He carried it to his room and sat on the bed. He couldn't imagine any trinket from a game company being this large. He carefully peeled the tape from the box and opened the flaps. It had two books and a smaller box inside, as well as a letter. He unfolded the paper and read the script.

SALUTATIONS MALUMESTI!

Welcome to Seeker, the most exciting in interactive role-playing games where the game rewards you for playing. If you haven't figured it out by now, the first challenge was a test to see if your band of Seekers was willing to do what it takes to win. And win you did!

Each Seeker on your team has been sent a prize pack related to their point on the star. You, dear Malumesti, have been given a greater gift: two exclusive Seeker expansion packs. These are special previews for your team and will not be sold in stores until spring, 1985. You will also find the Malumesti amulet. Wear it when you play to enhance the realism!

Thank you for playing, and we look forward to hearing from you when you complete your next adventure.

P.S. You may skip straight to the expansion packs for exciting adventures today.

HE OPENED the smaller box to find an amulet with a five-pointed star on one side and a stylized 'M' on the other, which he put on before thumbing through the expansion packs and seeing several interesting adventures that had nothing to do with foreign languages. The phone rang.

"Is this real?" said Liz, "What did you get?"

"An amulet and two expansion packs. You?"

"I got a silver necklace with a dangle that has the Fire symbol on it. And a red leather diary, and a really nice pen, and a letter opener that looks like an old-timey dagger, and this weird looking thing that I finally figured out is some kind of lighter!"

"Wow!"

"I know! I'm going to call Jen. I'll call you back!"

Each of them called the others in time. They had all gotten similar bounties; some obviously related to their respective signs, others were not so easy to explain. All of them, however, seemed of quite high quality and value. All of them received amulets. And all of them wanted to play again as soon as possible.

Within mere days they had moved through most of the first expansion pack. The challenges were interesting, esoteric, historical, and fun. All of them ended up with one or more Seekers calling in and saying something in a different language, or backwards, or something just as weird. By now, however, the strange requests were more like a scavenger hunt. Where the first query was odd, the call-ins now felt like you were just proving you'd completed the challenge, most of them being somewhat unrelated to the actual story.

Sometimes they won prizes, sometimes they were informed that, sorry, the prizes went to the first one hundred teams and theirs was one thirty-nine. The prizes were never quite as large or as fine as that first package, but they were always very cool.

As Christmas break rolled around, all the Seekers could talk about was the next challenge. At this point, even Ryan had come around and was one of the loudest advocates for getting together for at least a little while nearly every day. All five kids' bedrooms were now adorned with books, maps, artifacts, and mazes related to the game.

Tristan and Liz spent a lot of time together reading, planning, researching, and keeping track of challenges. They spent hours going over stories and prize tallies. Liz had become enamored with all of Tristan's heavy metal bands and the two of them hung out together long after the others had gone home each night. Tristan realized one day that, with the exception of Seeker, Liz Rankin was all he thought about. He stayed at her house until there were no more reasons not to leave, then rode home on his skateboard thinking about the way she pushed her hair behind her ears when she was concentrating on something.

Before he had moved, there had been girls that he had liked, and who had probably liked him, but he'd been distracted by the daily trauma that was his parents' crumbling marriage to really pay attention or do anything about it. As far as he was concerned, he'd like to have a girlfriend, but if that was what it would lead to, he'd rather lose himself in books and games and music. Still, the feelings he had for Liz were undeniable and getting stronger every day.

One night, after an evening of Seeking, she leaned over and kissed him. He was both shocked and elated. His head went swimmy and he couldn't think straight. She took his confused grin as an invitation to do it again and this time he kissed her back. As he skated home that night with the scent of her perfume lingering on his shirt, he thought he was about as happy as anyone could ever be. Soon, they were spending entire "Seeker" sessions making out, making plans, and making Spenser Springs feel like somewhere he enjoyed being instead of somewhere he was waiting to leave as soon as he was able.

"How is she? How's Liz?"

Jen grimaced and rolled her eyes to the side. Then she shrugged and looked out the window.

Tristan was crestfallen, "That good, huh?"

Jen shrugged again and then dug in her purse for a cigarette. Tristan opened one of his new packs and lit one himself. "Damn."

"It's not like you didn't know," Jen said, "You broke her heart."

"Okay, yes, I did know that. And it broke mine too. But what was I supposed to do? Skip going to college?"

"We didn't go to college and we're doing okay," said Rob.

"Shut up, moron. We all know he wasn't going to skip college for a high school girlfriend. But you never called, never wrote, and you didn't even come home at Christmas."

"I couldn't! My parents, my very divorced parents who hadn't spoken to one another at all since they split up came to visit me at school in California. It was a really big deal for all of us. What was I supposed to do? 'Hey Mom and Dad, I know you just spent hundreds of dollars and took vacation from your jobs and you've chosen to be around someone you despise for several days just to make your son happy for the first time in years but instead I'm gonna catch a Greyhound to Texas?'"

"I didn't know that. Sorry. But you could have at least written."

"I called when I could. There's a two-hour time difference so when I was available, she was always working. I called her house and she was never there. I'd call the video store and I always got put on hold. And long-distance calls are too expensive to get put on hold while she's talking to customers about different movies for ten minutes. But yeah, I didn't write. Because the best way to fix a long-distance relationship that isn't working is to write, 'Dear Liz, how are you, I am fine.'"

Their eyes met for a moment and he saw true sorrow there. What had been going on since he'd left? When he'd broken it off with Liz, after almost a year of phone tag, missed connections, fights, and miscommunication, she seemed to have taken it rather well. Sure, she had been cordial and perhaps a bit curt, but he'd been fighting tears of his own so the less of a big deal she made of it, made it that much easier for him.

He had truly cared for her. She'd been his best friend, his girlfriend, his first real date, his first lover... But the college situation was untenable and after so much sustained misery on both their parts, he came to believe that they both knew it should end but one just needed to get up the nerve. He hadn't spoken to her since.

The Bronco slowed as Rob turned off the highway onto the dirt road taking them to their destination. The spot was a camping area that the five of them had claimed the year Rob got his license. Spenser Springs was surrounded on all sides by forests that were a mishmash of private property, government lands, and timber company reserves that amounted to thousands upon thousands of acres of woods that were perfect for a bunch of kids who wanted to avoid parental supervision or curious law enforcement officers. Tristan himself had found the spot using one of his father's forestry maps. It was a remote clearing, miles from the highway or any houses. There, they could smoke cigarettes, a habit that had seemed to sprout up overnight, and drink alcohol, a pastime that started when Rob had pinched a twelve-pack of Shafer from his father.

The freedom offered by the forest allowed them to yell and chant and bring a kind of manic realism to Seeker that they couldn't realize sitting upstairs in a bedroom. Here there were no prying eyes or shouts to keep it down. As the five of them entered their junior years in high school, the Seekers found themselves out at the spot nearly every weekend.

"What are we going to do when we graduate?" asked Ryan.

The five teenagers sat around their campfire drinking beer and smoking cigarettes. Rob's boom box played Master of Puppets as the wind sent swarms of crackling sparks spinning into the night sky.

"Drink beer every night? Because we don't have to be somewhere in the morning?" Rob suggested.

"Ever hear of a fricken job?" his exasperated sister asked, shaking her head.

"Oh right," he chuckled. "Damn."

Liz sat with her legs crossed. Tristan lay beside her with his head in her lap. "I'll be managing one of the businesses, I guess. Probably the video store," she said.

"Trophy wife," said Jen. She threw up her hand with the index finger and pinky extended and said, "Or Metallica groupie. Just as good."

They all laughed.

"No, I mean, with Seeker?" Ryan continued, "I mean, we ain't all gonna be together forever, and we can't break up the team either, so how are we gonna keep it going?"

"Where the hell you going?" Rob asked, "Other than church?"

Ryan flicked his still-lit cigarette at him, causing the front of Rob's shirt to explode in tiny embers. He hopped up and shook and dusted the fire from his chest. "Hey!"

"I'm serious! Do you know how much progress we'd lose if we tried to start over? If one of us left?"

Tristan sat up. "I mean, yeah, but it's not like we'll ever get to the end anyway. They release new expansions and revisions all the time. We'll have to stop at some point, eventually."

All of them were quiet now, alone with their thoughts, staring into the fire. It was something none of them had considered, apparently. Here they were, young and mostly free of responsibilities. It had not occurred to anyone that they might someday have jobs and families, that someday they would not be free to spend every spare moment in the woods getting drunk with their friends. That someday there may not be spare moments anymore.

Tristan got up and went to the cooler for another beer. He dug into his pocket for a cigarette and lit it, then leaned on Rob's truck, his face lit by the Coleman lantern hanging from the tree opposite the fire. "I wasn't sure how to tell you all this, but I've been accepted to USC in Los Angeles. My, um, grades are good enough that I even got a partial scholarship." He took a drag from his cigarette and looked around at their faces.

"Whoa," said Rob.

"That's wonderful!" said Jen, who hopped to her feet and came over to hug him.

Ryan stood up too and shook his hand. "Congratulations," he said. Although he was not smiling.

Tristan turned to Liz who still sat where she had been, a look of astonished bewilderment on her face. She noticed him looking, then got up herself and hugged him. "That's incredible news," she said, a slight hitch in her voice, "I had no idea."

He pulled her closer and kissed her. She kissed back, but there was hesitation, a resistance that he hadn't felt before. When he released her, her eyes were wet. She sniffled and wiped her nose and eyes with the sleeve of her flannel shirt. "Stupid smoke," she said.

Ryan looking more sullen than normal said, "So when are you leaving?"

It was near dark when the Bronco finally rolled to a stop at the campsite. Ryan and Liz had set up their tents in the corner and Tristan helped Jen and Rob unload their gear. He counted the tents and realized there wasn't one for him. He'd always simply slept with Liz in the one they'd shared. He continued helping to set up without asking. He didn't want to make things more awkward than they were already going to be. For their parts, Liz and Ryan had been busy. They had gathered and piled two rather large stacks of firewood, much more than they would need for just a night or two, and a third, smaller pile stacked on a pile of old ash, ready to be lit.

Ryan came out of the woods with another handful of firewood. He tossed it on one of the larger piled when he saw Tristan. He came over and shook his hand and then hugged him. "You have no idea how good it is to see you."

"You too, man! How have you been?"

Ryan shrugged noncommittally and looked up into the trees, "Okay, I guess. Workin' at the church with Mom. How's school?"

"They keep me pretty busy."

Ryan nodded, "Beer?"

"Sure."

Ryan slowly turned and went to the cooler. Rob put an arm around Tristan's shoulders.

"What's with him, is he high or something?" Tristan asked.

"If he is, I don't want any," Rob laughed, "Come help me with the tent."

Moments later, Liz emerged from the woods as well. She too was carrying a stack of firewood. When she saw Tristan, she dropped it and ran over to him. The two stared at one another for a moment, before she leaned in and hugged him. Tristan was relieved. He relaxed and hugged her back. He'd missed her terribly over the past year. In her arms is where he'd needed to be. When their embrace finally ended, there were tears in both their eyes. In the near dark, he glanced around and could see that Rob, Jen, and Ryan were all watching them. Ryan and Jen had tears in their eyes as well.

When it was dark, after they had all eaten and caught up on current events, the five of them sat around the fire smoking and sipping beers. "Hey College Boy, you said you had a scary story to tell us," said Rob.

"Oh yeah," said Tristan, "So, I've got this guy in my dorms whose dad is on the LAPD. He gets to hear about some really wild stuff. So, I don't know if you guys noticed that Seeker is no longer in stores. All the guide books and expansion packs and everything have been pulled?"

The other four glanced at one another, then back at him and nodded.

"Well, the official word is that they had copyright infringement issues with other games and books and stuff and ended up going bankrupt and just closing up shop. But that's not what really happened at all. Turns out that the main writer, Sammons, was this millionaire occultist guy who was using the game for some sort of giant ritual."

Ryan's face was lit when he took a drag of his cigarette and Tristan noticed that the kid looked absolutely spooked.

"It turns out that the whole thing was fake."

"What do you mean, fake?" asked Rob, "The books are real. The prizes were real. It was a game we played; that was real."

"But the competitions weren't. The prizes were bribes to keep kids playing. What Sammons did was line it up so that he was recording the voices of thousands of children saying all these strange words. They found this special room, like a combination of a recording studio and some sort of black church, under his house. He had taken all the words and chants and all the stuff we called in over the years and cut them together and layered the tracks together, so he had all these kids all over the world basically saying the words to spells and stuff. He was using us to try to summon demons."

All five stared deeply into the fire as it crackled in the cool night air. Nobody said a word for a while, each silent with whatever thoughts this revelation had left them. It was Ryan who finally spoke.

"Do you believe in God, Tristan?"

Tristan was caught off guard. "Uh, I don't know. I guess? We've never been too religious."

"We are. My family. Religious," Ryan replied. His wide, haunted eyes seemed strangely calm as he stared in the firelight. "The thing about faith? It's something you believe in even when you don't have proof. You know? Like, you know that God is watching. Just watching. But you don't really know. You only hope. You hope, and you try to believe in Him, even when things like books and songs and other people tell you he don't exist, you know? That's faith."

"Ryan, I don't—"

"I don't know what you call it when you believe in God because you have proof. I don't know if there's even a word for that." He looked up. "You know how I know that God is real, Tristan? You know?"

Tristan looked at the others for help, but they were all silent, just staring into the fire.

"Rya—"

Ryan leapt to his feet and screamed, "ASK ME HOW I KNOW THAT GOD IS REAL!!!"

"How do you know that God is real, Ryan?"

Ryan's rage seemed to dissipate. His shoulders slumped, and he sat back down in his seat, "I know because I gave my soul to Satan. He has me now. He comes to me every night and laughs about how he tricked us, how he got me to give myself to him and how I didn't even fight. How I said all the words. How I said them willingly. How I wanted to say them. He comes to me, Tristan. He comes to all of us. You delivered us to him."

Tristan was stunned.

"Knowing that God is real, but that he will never have me. Sitting in church with my parents, listening to Satan laughing at me in my head. I'm worse than lost, Tristan, I'm damned. We all are."

Tristan got to his feet, "Look, I don't know what's going on here. Is this some kind of game?" Suddenly, his body felt weak and he needed to sit down again. His head swam for a second before his vision cleared. He thought

476

nothing of it, as he'd been drinking all day. "Ryan, I'm sorry. I never meant to… He scammed me too."

"The Pied Piper," said Ryan.

"What?"

"That first day, back in school. You mentioned the Pied Piper. An outsider who comes into town with odd clothes and strange music that lures the children away. You remember that? You said it was like He-Man, these games. But when I played with He-Man, I never had dreams about demons slaughtering my parents and raping my little sister. Not once." He looked up at Tristan with wide eyes before staring back into the fire. "Now that's all I ever dream about."

"But nobody meant for you to promise your soul to anyone." Tristan tried to reason with Ryan, but he seemed too far gone. "I didn't know! It was just a game!"

Rob, who had been quiet the whole time spoke up. "You think the devil, or Satan or whatever… You think after you promise yourself to the devil hundreds of times a year for like five years he's going to just let you go because you thought it was a game? We did it over and over and over again in like seven different languages! He's got us, man. It's true. I ain't got it bad as Ryan but it's there. We're fucked."

"What do you mean? You're in on this too? Jen! Liz, come on! Tell me this isn't happening!"

Jen hugged herself and rocked forward on her lawn chair. "This… It's happening." She then put her hands to her face and began sobbing.

Tristan tried to stand again but found his legs did not have the strength. He fell backwards into his chair and went a little off balance before falling back into place. "What... What's happening?"

"We had to give you something to keep you here," Rob said, "So you can't run off."

"What the hell?" Tristan stammered. He didn't feel drugged or overly drunk, but his extremities refused to work correctly.

"Remember the Marie Laveau challenge?" Liz asked, "The Voodoo Curse? Turns out a lot of the stuff we learned about potions and poisons is true. Most of Seeker turned out to be true. The goal of the challenge was to gather the names of all these herbs that the Voodoos use in their rituals. Once I had the names, it was easy to get hold of them and mix 'em up."

Rob came to stand behind Liz, "Look man, I'm sorry about this. I love you man, you're my brother. But it's the only way." He stepped out of the shadows with a coil of rope in his hands. Jen sobbed harder. Rob shrugged. Ryan stared into the fire. Liz stared into Tristan's eyes. Her face blurred and everything went black.

When he awoke his head was pounding. It was full dark, and he could not see. His hands and feet were bound, and he was covered in some sort of blanket. The odor of wood smoke was in the air, so he knew he was not far from the campsite. There was another odor as well —gasoline. He dared not move. He had to figure a way to get untied and away from here. His friends had all gone insane. What were they planning? Whatever it was, he was terrified to find out. He moved his hands slightly, testing his restraints.

A bell rang above his head. Startled, his body jerked

and the bell rang louder. The bell was tied to him so tightly that any movement would alert the others. Tristan struggled to get up, finally getting his back against a tree and moving into a sitting position. He had some sort of hood or cowl hanging over his eyes, so he could not see properly, but what he saw made him shudder.

By the light of a lantern they came, four cloaked figures in procession. They walked in single file toward him, stopping ten or fifteen feet away, then spreading out and facing one another. Each had a candle in one hand and a small dagger in the other, except for the one who held the lantern. Then the lantern was extinguished, and then that figure lit a candle as well. They moved away from one another and took positions farther away. As one they dropped their candles and small fires erupted at their feet. Tristan watched in as one of them stepped away from the fire and knelt in front of him. The figure removed the hood and Liz's face was revealed in the firelight.

"The cloaks," she said, "Were the final set of prizes. They arrived about a week after you left. I don't know why I never mentioned them. It just seemed, improper somehow."

"Liz, please—"

She held a finger to her lips and shook her head. "Shhh. Now is not the time for talking. It's time for listening. It won't work if you are not fully aware of what is happening." She glanced up and let her eyes roam through the trees, "What, and why, and how. You have no idea how hard this is for all of us. If there was any other way... If it could be one of us, even. Tristan, you're my first and only love. I love you so much it hurts. I want you to know that. I want you to know that I never wanted to hurt you."

"But why? Please!"

"Because he demands it. Because we are beholden to him and cannot resist. Because he is angry with you, Tristan. He thinks you tricked him. He thinks you tricked him on purpose and because he is the father of lies, he will not stand for any of yours."

"Wha—"

"Shhh. Remember all the challenges, all the phone calls, the words, all of it? It was supposed to be you. Malumesti does not mean 'storyteller,' it means, 'Evil One.' Early on, you either didn't read it right or you missed something or, I don't know, maybe you were being sneaky. You were the elected leader of our little coven, yet somehow you never took the vows yourself. You never gave yourself to him. Not like we did. It was just a game to you, and still is. You gave nothing to him. And he is furious.

"After you left, the nightmares began. Night after night, my father's face, burnt, smoking and charred, begging me to save him as his melted eyes ooze from their sockets. Ryan already told you his. Robert and Jennifer don't talk about theirs but when it came to what needs to be done to stop nightmares, they agreed quite quickly. They'll do anything to make them stop.

"When I was finally able to contact Sammons, about the dreams, about the visions, about the voices in our heads, he explained it all. It was so simple, he'd said. So subtle. While the preachers and the parents railed against mazes and monsters, he was winning souls for his master.

The only way to stop the torture, he said, was to break the circle. One of us has to die.

"I offered myself. I want you to know that I did but he said no. It was our prodigal that would have to be offered. Our pure, white lamb. Our unblemished Malumesti."

"You're going to kill me," Tristan said, casting about desperately, looking for any means of escape. But he now knew it was futile. He slumped and looked up at Liz. "Please. Make it fast."

Liz's face cracked and tears streamed down her face. She shook her head and said, "I wish I could, my love."

One of the cloaked figures sniffled and bawled. Jen. "Jen, please! Rob! Don't do this!"

Liz stood and took her place near her fire. Tristan realized they were standing in a pentacle, with him at the top. "PLEASE!"

A cloak approached him and knelt. It removed its hood and he saw Jen's face, swollen from crying. She looked him in the eye and began chanting in Latin, then in German, then in Arabic, and finally Hebrew. She leaned in close and blew on his face. Air. She stood up and took her place on the star.

Each Seeker repeated the same words in four languages. Rob splashed him with water. Ryan dusted him with earth. When they were finished, Liz began her chant. As she spoke the words, Ryan and Rob walked into the woods. Each came back carrying one of the gas cans Tristan had filled earlier. As Liz finished her incantation, they poured the fuel over him. He sputtered and coughed as the gasoline entered his eyes and nose and his skin began to burn.

Liz Rankin stood up, walked away from him, then turned and threw a burning brand towards him. As the fire erupted all around him, as he watched his four best friends burn him alive, he could see a fifth figure standing behind them. He did not have time to wonder who the newcomer was before everything became agony and flame.

LUCIE AND SNAGGLETOOTH

"Where are they, Campbell?"

"I already told you, Sheriff, I don't know!"

"That's shit and you know it."

"It's not! I swear! I'd give anything to be able to help."

"You just tell me what you do remember."

It started with the lottery and it ended with a losing bet. I had to get that part down before any of the rest because it's important somehow. It's going to help me remember what I've already forgotten several times. I don't want to forget, I don't think. It's not my fault. No, that's not right. It's all my fault. I think. It's just... The forgetting is not...

Look, I'm doing the best I can here. I'm trying to cooperate but there's this thing. Like... a barrier to my memory. I can see in my peripheral but not straight ahead. There's something about playing cards and a stack of shingles. Roofing nails. I can see the box of nails and the leather of the boots of... someone.

Black leather. Old and worn. But polished. Well-kept. A bit of clay dried to the sole. Tan canvas pant leg. Frayed hem.

Sound of a voice. Sweet Creole accent. Musical. Sexy. Sexual. More than that... Pure lust. Offering refreshment. This is no servant girl though. And while I am almost painfully aroused by her presence, I am also frightened to my core. Still out of focus, indistinct, a hand holding a pitcher. The hand and arm are... white?

That's not right. The hand should be dark. Dark skin. Everything is out of focus and the harder I think about it, the more I lose it.

Stop. Relax. Focus on the pitcher. On the boots. On the clay or the wooden deck. Roofing nails. Shingles. What's with the shingles?

The pitcher. The hand holding the pitcher is white. That was right. The hand and arm belong to my wife, Becky. Becky is pouring me a glass of iced tea as I sit on the front porch, taking a break from fixing the roof. She's wearing jean shorts and a white and blue button-down shirt with the sleeves rolled up. She fills up my glass and refills her own and sets the pitcher on the table.

"How's it coming?" she asks.

"Coming along," I say before draining my glass.

"You think you'll finish today?

"Don't want to jinx it," I say, "But unless something happens, I should be done before dark."

"That's good. I know you're not having fun, but it needed to be done."

"I just feel, like if I can make my case, that as many times as I've patched the sombitch, it should be completely water tight by now. I mean, I've been tearing off more new shingles than old ones."

"Well, now that you found the dry rot, you'll fix it and it'll be the last time for a really long time. And who knows? There might be a little something in it for you later." She shoots me a sexy smile.

"Oh yeah?" I say before hooking a finger into one of her belt loops and pulling her close. She leans in slowly, then scrunches up her face and gives me a peck on the forehead before pulling away.

"Extra stuff comes after showers. And maybe a ceremonial burning of your clothes. Shoo!"

She turns and goes into the house, leaving me on the porch wondering about the shiny boots and the sexy Creole voice.

Without knowing why, I shudder.

I do remember winning the lottery. That part is not obscured in my mind. I had been coming home from somewhere. Rebecca had texted and asked me to pick something up, so I stopped into a convenience store and bought a couple of scratch-offs and a lotto for that evening. The scratch-offs were both losers, so all three tickets went into the console under the dashboard to be entirely forgotten until the following week. I almost threw the lotto away before I realized I hadn't checked it. Imagine my surprise when the "winner" music started playing. It said I had won ninety-four grand. After taxes and all other associated rigmaroles, it came out to be roughly sixty-three thousand dollars, which I was happy to accept.

Becky and I had long dreamed of owning a house in

the country; a place we could grow fruit trees and maybe have a goat or some chickens. But with incomes and economies the way they'd been, the, "Ranch," as we'd taken to calling it, was probably never going to happen. I mean, we'd even started a Ranch fund in our monthly budget. That's how serious we were. But of course, that had been the first thing to go when our son was born.

Our son.

My wife and I had a son, a little boy, and his name was...

Jim? No, that's not right. Jessie? Jacob? George? Something with a "J" sound.

I'll think of it in a moment. I told you, I can't remember anything.

Anyway, the kid needed diapers so our dreams of a little homestead out somewhere you could still see stars at night was impossible until this nice little lottery payout. As it stood, we were able to afford a much larger piece of property than we'd dreamt about. Given the combination of public auction and cash in-hand, we managed to grab a plot that was just shy of thirty acres with utilities and well water already there. There was even an older ranch-style house on the property. It was no Taj Mahal, but it was serviceable while we figured out our next steps.

"What do you want to do first?" Becky had said as we turned off the paved road onto the dirt one that took us up to the property.

"Let's get the keys first," I joked, "Else we won't get in the gate."

"We need to clean things, make a safe place for Jason (Jason! That's it!) to toddle around in."

"Of course! And we need to clean out brush and burn it and plant fruit and nut trees and make a few garden plots. I also want to get a deer feeder up before too long so maybe we can attract some game. So, we probably need to get a deep-freeze pretty soon."

Becky laughed. She was just as excited as I was about our new life and likely had just as many things on her wish list as I did.

We pulled onto the property after about ten minutes on the bumpy dirt road. As we parked, a car pulled in behind us and a Sheriff's cruiser behind it. The Sheriff get out of his vehicle and shortly after, a neatly dressed young woman got out of the other car. She was on her phone and held a stack of papers. She chatted for a moment more before ending the call and coming over to shake hands with us.

"Sorry, I tried to get out here before you, but I got a bit lost," she said, "Amanda Murphy, Murphy Real Estate Group." She handed us both business cards. "This is Sheriff Wood."

The uniformed man removed his sunglasses and shook hands with us as well.

"Mr. Wood comes with me on my remote meetings sometimes, just to be safe. Sometimes you have homeless people squatting on vacant properties. Always better to be safe than sorry. How was the drive?"

"It was nice," Becky said, "Pretty country out here."

"Oh, it is!" Murphy said as she made her way to the house. "Y'all planning to live out here full time?"

"We'd like to," I said, "As soon as we can sell our other house we want to build a new one."

"Well, let me know when you do. I know all the good contractors. This one ain't much. But of course, you've already seen the pictures. Three beds, one and a half baths, fourteen hundred square feet. So, not a lot of room. But it's solid construction so it ain't going nowhere. It'll get you through while you build your dream house. And let me tell you, it's so much nicer to live on property and monitor the construction day by day rather than having to live in a hotel for months on end."

Murphy unlocked the door. A stale, dusty odor assailed us as we crossed the threshold. The house was a wood-paneled, linoleum-tiled, orangish-brown and blue monument to mid-seventies home décor. The bathrooms were both tiled in a light, powdery blue that matched the threadbare and crumbling carpet running through every room but the kitchen. I laughed and made a comment about how it must have been a long time since anyone had lived here.

"It's been, oh, twenty years easy," said Murphy, "Old Mr. Johnson. He passed," she turned to the sheriff, "Ninety-six? Ninety-seven?"

Wood nodded, "Sounds about right. I was still in high school so you're pretty close."

"Passed away three days after his hundredth birthday, if you can believe it," said Murphy.

"And what?" I said, "It's just been sitting here since?"

"Well," Murphy explained, "Mr. Johnson didn't actually own the property. Colton Bradley gave him the plot and the house when he retired. Mr. Johnson had worked for the Bradley family his whole life."

She walked through the kitchen and opened the back

door. A screen door whined on its hinges as she opened it onto a rotting wooden deck. We all stepped carefully out into the back yard.

"The Bradleys used to own pretty much everything out here. The family still does own quite a bit, but as the kids grow, they've been selling off their stakes and properties and moving away. Anyway, Mr. Johnson worked for Colton and Mr. Colton 'gave' these thirty acres and this house as a retirement present. He built the house new for them, even. So, Mr. Johnson and his wife Miss Bernice lived here. Had a little garden plot and some goats and just did their retired thing. Miss Bernice passed away back in the mid-eighties. Old Mr. Johnson just stayed here and tended the garden and the goats.

"Well, when Mr. Johnson finally passed, his family started discussing what they were going to do with the land. That's when they found out that Colton had never actually deeded the land to their grandfather. Colton Bradley had been dead at least fifteen years, maybe more by then, so there was nobody even alive who knew what had been discussed. So, the Johnsons got a lawyer and the Bradleys had a few of their own and in the end, Johnson's lawyer found some old squatter's law that worked in their favor and they ended up winning the case. But God, that took something like ten years? The Johnsons ended up just selling it to pay the court costs and taxes. It was really a shame. Since then, it's been through a couple different property companies and two foreclosures. It finally went to auction because the bank just wanted it off their books."

We walked around the house and Murphy showed us

the well pumps, the septic system, and other things we would need to know about. There was an outbuilding with some rusty old tools hanging on rusty hooks, and here and there the remnants of a chain-link fence that had long since given up on its job. "It really is a pretty piece of property," she said again.

After a bit more exploring and signing some documents, Murphy handed Becky the keys to our new home. We said our goodbyes and moved toward the vehicles, walking with them as they left.

"You hunt?" Sheriff Wood asked me casually as he opened the door to his cruiser.

"On occasion," I said, "Haven't been in a couple of years."

Wood nodded, "I'd suggest you get a good pistol and learn to use it. Don't take to walking around out here without some kind of weapon and believe me when I say that the bigger you can get, the better. We got a feral hog problem, well, pretty much statewide but it's extra bad here. Bastards are big and have no fear of humans. They'd as soon cut you as look at you. And hog cut ain't no good way to go."

I looked around at the trees and took in the relative wilderness we were surrounded by. "Thanks, I'll definitely look into it."

Wood pulled out his phone and scrolled for a second. "Y'all come take a look at this."

Becky and I went over and looked. "Oh God!" she said.

On the screen lay a man with a huge gash in his side, and his intestines lay next to him in a black heap.

"This is... was, a local man by the name of Guillermo

Rivas. Hogs got him walking out to his truck one morning. This happened just three weeks ago about half a mile down yonder. Guillermo was no slouch. He grew up here. Did ranch hand work through junior high and high school. Hunted, fished. He knew what he was doing, and the hogs still got him. Hit him from behind and used their tusks to rip his belly clean out. He was probably alive for a bit while they chewed on his liver and kidneys. Hell of a bad way to go. You need to go from here to wherever it is you have your guns stored, or to a place where they sell them and get you one before you come back here and start stomping around the woods. Get one for the missus too.

"Now, I'm sorry. That photo sure is shocking, I know it. But it was just to show you how serious it is. If you see a hog, shoot it. There's no season, no bag limit. You can process all the bacon and ham you want. Bring your friends out and let them shoot 'em too. And when your freezer is full, feel free to drop 'em where they stand and let the coyotes eat 'em. I'd sure thank you for it."

As we pulled back onto the dirt road to head back to the hotel, I turned to Becky. "I guess Officer Wood helped us decide what we need to get first."

She grimaced. "I don't know. I never thought about animals before. Do you think it's safe? I mean with Jason and everything?"

"Honey, people live out here with their kids and have for hundreds of years. I'm sure it's safe enough. Or, at least it's no more dangerous than the city where we have to worry about crosswalks and child predators. We'll follow Woods' advice and get some firepower. We'll put a

491

fence up around the yard. We'll just have to keep an eye on the boy. But not any more than we already do."

"I don't know, Jim. I could have gone my whole life without seeing that picture."

"Yeah, it was pretty gnarly. I didn't realize they were so aggressive."

We rode the rest of the way in silence, both of us contemplating just how long Mr. Rivas had been alive while the hog or hogs stomped around in his guts, taking little bites as he slowly bled to death. How much did he feel before shock took over and he fell out of himself? I'd read books about soldiers who had been gut-shot or hit by shrapnel. Sometimes they would live for days, writhing in agony. I shook my head as the car bumped along the uneven road.

The next day, the two of us arrived bright and early to the sporting goods store in town. We spoke to the salesman and explained why we needed weapons and he set us up with what he said were the right tools for the job. "Now, these are going to be a bit bulky for carry pistols," he had advised, "But you want the knockdown power to take down a hog."

He sold us holsters and special ammunition as well. I wondered at the ammo. I'd shot plenty of times before, and I couldn't see what was so special about these cartridges over any other hollow point. Becky, however, was sold. She wanted any advantage the gentleman could offer. She was not going to risk a thing. While we were there, we signed up for the license to carry class, as it just seemed like the right thing to do.

Jason was staying with Becky's folks, so we had a

couple of days to explore and begin work on the new place. We arrived early with our shiny new guns in our shiny new holsters. The trunk was full of cleaning supplies, tools, gloves, and a cooler full of sandwich makings, soft drinks, and bottled water.

We began by opening all the doors and windows and tearing out the moldering antique carpet. We got it out in large chunks, setting it in a pile near the tire ruts that served as a driveway. We then swept and mopped the whole place corner to corner before rinsing out the mops and starting over. We cleaned the windows and counter-tops, and even the walls. Becky had picked up some color swaths and paint samples at the hardware store so while she set about marking walls, I removed the screen door from the back and started tearing out the rotten decking from the porch. This, too, I carried to the front and set on the pile of carpet. By midafternoon, the deck was almost completely demolished, the house was clean enough to work in, and we had the start of a pretty large burn pile.

"Want to walk up the trail, see what's around the bend?" I asked Becky as we finished off a bag of chips.

She looked at the woods and back at me and she looked worried. "I don't know. That guy really freaked me out with the hogs. You think it's safe?"

I pulled out my pistol and racked the slide. "I think we'll be fine."

She loaded hers as well and we walked from the back of the house to what appeared to be an old trail that had never quite grown over. The forest was thick and rather dark, but there was no sign of killer swine anywhere. After a short time, we reached a larger clearing. It was overgrown and littered with what appeared to be rubbish piles that nobody ever bothered to burn. I was going to have to rent a brush cutter to get a trail cut through here, but as I scanned the area, it looked like a great place to build the big house when we got around to it.

We headed back to the house and began shutting it down for the night. In the morning we would buy paint and schedule the carpet and flooring guys. We'd have power in a day or two, and once I found the right size filter, we'd have clean drinking water from the well.

That night, after a few drinks in the hotel bar and some much-needed ibuprofen for aching muscles, Becky and I made love to celebrate our good fortune and then we both fell hard asleep.

Guillermo Rivas lays in a pool of congealing black gore. His eyes are closed, his blood-flecked face locked in an agonized grimace. Occasionally a large hog, brown and bristled, trots over and nudges the body once or twice before walking away. A smaller boar walks over and sniffs at the man's innards. It leans in slowly and then snatches a piece of offal from the pile. As it tears its prize away, Rivas sits bolt upright and screams in agonized horror. His screams are cut short, however, as the larger hog runs over and knocks him back to the ground, butting the dying man with its uneven tusks again and again. Rivas' head lolls to the side and his open eyes stare into mine as the smaller pig chews and smacks its lips.

I woke in a cold sweat, the image of the hog chewing the man's guts fresh in my mind. It was dark still. I rubbed my eyes and found the clock. 2:45. Still a long way to go until morning. I played on my phone, scrolling through

Instagram, looking for mindless drivel to take my mind off the dream that had seemed all too real. It would be hours before I dozed again, and when Becky woke me the next morning, I felt drained and lifeless.

We spent the next two days painting the walls and cabinets, followed by placing contact paper in all the drawers. We ordered a refrigerator and a washer and dryer set and scheduled the delivery to coincide with the carpet installation. Becky was diligent about making lists of things we needed to buy or do before we could move.

"I want that deck put back together before we start trying to move furniture in here. That's a lawsuit waiting to happen," she said.

I had taken a few vacation days from work, so I was making my own lists and trying to see what I could do that would have the most impact in the shortest amount of time. "I'll take measurements and buy the lumber on my way back out here tomorrow."

When we finished up for the day, we would drive the hour and a half back to the in-laws and pick up our son. Then we would go back to our city house and start filling boxes. Becky stayed there with Jason and packed while I went back out to the ranch to continue working on making the house someplace we could live for a year or so as we had the new place designed and built.

The next morning, I put several boxes of miscellaneous housewares and a few power tools into the back of my SUV and drove back out to the property, stopping at the hardware store on the way to buy materials to rebuild the deck.

I'd never built a deck before but after a couple of YouTube

tutorials and several questions at the store, I thought that I was ready. I dug the post holes and mixed the concrete, then sunk the posts and set them level. Once I'd placed some braces to ensure they stayed that way, I wandered out to the front to do away with some trash. I wasn't sure if or when we got trash service this far out and I didn't have room in my truck to carry the carpet and other junk back to a dumpster. I stacked the pile a little better, then I threw in some kindling and some paper and set a lighter to it.

The fire was small at first and I waited for the inevitable burst of smoke that told me it had gone out. Instead, however, the carpet burst into flame and a very hot, very intense fire roared. I was caught off-guard by the raging inferno and had to step back several feet to keep from getting burned. I began looking around for a water source in case it spread. We had water to the house itself, but no hoses yet. This could be a disaster.

After a few minutes of angry flame, the carpet had been burned away. The pile of wooden planks and other refuse collapsed in on itself and the fire calmed down to a steady, contented burn. A plume of smoke replaced the wavy heat mirages that had been there before. I used a stick to poke at the fire and watched it consume the pile of garbage. I glanced around and realized there was plenty of deadfall and miscellaneous rubbish that could go into the fire today.

I went back and checked the level and the concrete. It was still wet to the touch and it would be another fifteen or twenty minutes before I could trust building on it. I gathered up the empty concrete sacks and threw them onto the fire. There were old plastic buckets and brittle plastic flower pots in the shed and I threw them on as well. After a time, I was walking back and forth through the yard looking for, well, anything I could add to the pile. I figured it would all be ash by nightfall and scattered to the breeze by morning.

I stood and watched the stuff burn, my mind on other things. Occasionally, the smoke would waft in my direction and I'd catch the odor of burnt plastic or rubber. I would move out of its path, but as smoke is wont to do, it would catch me again and then again. My eyes began to water, and I became light-headed. I moved away from the fire and went back to my project. The pylons were sticking out of the ground waiting for me to start attaching joists. But instead, I walked past them, past the house and toward the trail into the woods. I felt strange; not altogether well. Some combination of nausea and migraine. I needed fresh air, but the burnt plastic smell had permeated my nostrils and infected every breath I took. Poisonous plastic smoke hung in the air as well, as there was no breeze to carry it off.

I made it through the woods and into the larger clearing before my eyes began to clear and I could breathe again. All at once my head began to pound and I nearly stumbled into a strand of prickly pear. I needed to sit down, to clear my head, to breathe. I stomped through the high grass to the middle of the clearing. The grass was shorter here. I looked around for a moment to get my bearings and to make sure there were no ants around, then sat down in the grass. I was still quite dizzy, and the day was cool and bright, so after a moment I lay down on my back and closed my eyes.

I don't know how long I slept. I don't know if I slept at all or just zoned out listening to my pulse pounding in my head. But when I opened my eyes, my headache was gone. I squinted across the clearing as the late afternoon sun created a glare across my field of vision. The air was wavy with heat mirages. Then, something moved in my periphery and I turned to see what it was.

It was the ghost of a house. In the clearing. A house. It was bathed in what looked like heat mirages and it was very much and obviously there and not there at the same time. Had someone lived here before the Johnsons? It would have had to have been very long ago, considering the pedigree of the land as Murphy had explained it. And wouldn't prior owners or tenants have shown up in the records when the court cases were raging?

I took a few steps toward the wavy structure. I can't describe it now other than to say that it was very, most definitely there. Not structurally, but spectrally. It was right there. As I moved toward it, the grass got higher and I got wrapped up in some thorny vines. I stepped back and cut myself free and when I looked up, the house was gone. All I could see across the field were the trees opposite the way I had come. I considered moving forward, wanting to see if maybe there was some sign of an old foundation or something. But as I took another few steps toward where I thought the phantom had been, the ground became uneven and the thorn vines thicker. I stood still for a few minutes, trying to will the vision back, but it was gone. After a time, I became convinced that I had either dreamed or maybe hallucinated the specter. I had inhaled an unhealthy bit of polluted air, after all. It was then that I remembered the fire I had left unattended and the drying concrete and my desire to have the deck completed by the end of the day. I retreated to the forest trail and returned to my various home improvement projects, leaving ghost houses to be concerns for another day.

I returned to the yard and checked on the fire. It had burned most of the way down and had not spread anywhere. I breathed a sigh of relief. I had already been on the bad side of responsible for burning this stuff to begin with; leaving a fire that large unattended was plain reckless. I pushed the remaining material together to keep it burning, the fire now much smaller and easier to maintain, and retrieved a shovel from the shed so that I could cover the coals with dirt later.

The concrete had long since hardened and all my posts had stayed level. I laid out and attached the support joists, then the deck itself. The work went smoothly and by dusk I had most of the decking in place. A couple hours at most in the morning and this project would be complete.

At this point I decided it was time to get ready for the evening. I had brought some camping gear—a cot and sleeping bag, several flashlights, a propane stove, a lantern, and other miscellaneous items. I unloaded the SUV and brought everything into the house. I assembled the cot and bedding and put the cooler in the kitchen. I placed the lantern and the stove out on my half-completed back porch and set about getting ready for my first night in my new home.

After a meal of hot dogs and ranch-style beans, I broke the seal on a fresh bottle of Maker's and lit a cigar. I enjoy a cigar from time to time, finding that I usually don't have time to finish one. So, I look for the peaceful moments where I can. I sat on the porch smoking and sipping the whiskey and watching squirrels play in the yard, when I saw lightning off in the distance. I pulled out my phone to check the weather. The app said there were storms in the area, but they should be gone by morning, so I should still be able to complete my projects the next day. I set the cigar aside and moved anything that I didn't want wet into the house. I then called Becky and told her about all the things I'd accomplished. The first drops began to fall as Becky signed off and I stubbed out the cigar and took the Maker's inside with me. I changed clothes and lay on the cot playing with my phone. Within just a few minutes, though, my eyes became heavy and I felt fatigue overtake me. I slipped into a thankfully dreamless sleep; cradled by sore muscles and the oncoming storm.

I awoke to the sound of water dripping. At first, I was confused and couldn't figure out where I was. The house without power, the lack of street lamps, and a whisky buzz were not a comfortable combination. I found my pocket lantern and turned it on. The living room and kitchen were bathed in an ultra-bright pale white light. A light that, now that I think about it, is the same color and intensity they use in scary movies to amplify the dread effect. Drip. Drip. Drip.

I followed the sound to the kitchen. Drip. Drip. Drip.

I checked the ceiling for any discoloration then, finding nothing, decided it must be in the attic. The roof had leaked and was dripping onto the sheetrock. Not a good thing, but fixable. I got back into my bed and shut off the lantern, grumbling to myself about having to go into the attic to find the leak.

I woke up at dawn. It was dreary and grey, even a bit foggy from the storms. I rolled out of my cot, stretched, and found a bottle of water. Although I had only drunk two glasses of whisky, my head pounded and my throat was dry. I drained the first bottle and grabbed a second. I dug through my pack for the little bottle of aspirin I kept there and washed down three of them, finishing the second water bottle. I found my little percolator in my camping gear and went out onto the porch to start the fire on the camp stove, setting the kettle there to boil. In a few minutes I would have coffee and would be able to think straight.

Early morning mist hung over the yard and I took in the sight of my first true morning out in the sticks, my own place far from civilization where I could do my own thing. I went back in and slipped my boots on and wandered into the yard in my boxers. "This is freedom," I imagined as I took a long hard piss against a tree. I looked all around me and saw nothing. I was nearly naked, pissing where I liked and there was nobody anywhere who could say a thing about it.

That's when I heard the first grunts.

Startled, I pinched myself off and looked slowly over my shoulder. There in the yard between me and the house were about a dozen hogs snorting and rooting about. My blood turned to ice and images of a torn and half-eaten Guillermo Rivas sprung to mind as I also realized I'd left my gun inside with my pants. The largest of the hogs had tusks jutting out from its bottom jaw that I could only guess were between four and six inches long. Squeaks and grunts came from the bristly and nervous creatures. I stayed as still as I could, still facing the tree, looking back over my shoulder, watching the beasts nose around, sniffing, investigating. How long before they realized I was here?

I thought of Jason and of Becky and of this stupid idea we'd had. What business was it of ours to come out here and try to live like some sort of suburban pioneers? Nature had a name for creatures like us: extinct. The hogs rooted around and I realized as they spread that there would be no way for me to find shelter before one of them noticed me. I began to pray. I asked please God send something to distract the monsters. Please take them away. Oh God, please, don't let me get torn apart like Rivas. I'd do anything. I'd be anything. Just please God, please.

Off in the distance there was a woman's voice. "Hey! Hogs! You leave dat man be!"

The hogs all ran in different directions, their snorting mixed with squeals. They were maddened now and looking for a fight. They clustered in a group and ran off in the direction of the voice. I spun around, half expecting to feel a tusk in my belly for the effort, but the hogs were gone. I ran toward the side yard, then decided that whoever that was who called the hogs had helped me, but I couldn't help her any standing in my underwear. I ran into the house and snatched up my pistol, then came out the front door.

The hogs were gathered around a girl who was feeding them by hand from a sack of oats and corn. The maniacal squeals had turned to satisfied grunts and the swine rubbed against one another and jockeyed for position to receive the next handful. The girl was young, dark-skinned, maybe twenty-five years old. She wore an old-fashioned dress covered by an apron and her head was adorned with a wrap, like a scarf or a turban. She fed the hogs a few more handfuls of feed, then called to them, "Get on, now! Ain't no pesterin' our new neighbor. Go on! Git!"

And as one, the hogs ran across the dirt road and into the forest.

When the last of the beasts left her side, she looked up at me and smiled. "Well good morning, Monsieur" she said.

I was not sure what to think. Despite her strange dress, here before me was the most exquisitely beautiful creature I'd ever seen before. Her presence was absolutely spellbinding. In but a second, my fear of being mauled and ripped apart by animals gave way to an almost uncontrollable desire to impress this girl. I felt like I was twelve years old again standing on top of the monkey bars to impress Stephanie Walden, my junior high school crush. That had ended up with my arm in a cast and a lecture from my teachers and parents about not doing stupid things to impress girls. "Just talk to them," they'd said. But at the end of it all, Stephanie had signed my cast with a heart over the "I" in her name so as far as I was concerned, it had been worth it.

I stood there staring for a moment before the girl said again, "Good morning sir."

I shook myself out of the trance. "Uh, good morning. Um, thanks for helping with the hogs."

"It's not no thing," she said, "Jus gotta know how to talk to them."

I thought about the large herd and of Mr. Rivas and wondered if she was skilled or just lucky. "All the same, I appreciate it."

"You're fixin' up Ole Mr. Johnson's house."

It was a statement, not a question. I looked back over my shoulder, "Yeah, I guess. For now. Planning to build a house further back, maybe, in the future."

Her eyes swept the property and then landed back on mine. "You plan on wearin' clothes while you workin' so hard pluggin' dem leaks an all dat?"

I realized all of a sudden that I was still in my boxers and boots from earlier. My right hand hung heavy with the weight of the pistol. And as I took a step backward, I realized to my horror that I was erect and sporting out of the front of my shorts! I dared not look down. I dared not move. I didn't know what to do or say. Humiliated is too weak a word. Devastated? Maybe. Horrified—certainly. The girl, however, seemed not to care.

"Imma head on up the road now. Nice meeting you, Monsieur. I'll be seeing you again soon."

And with that, she wandered back onto the road, humming a little tune under her breath. As soon as I could be sure she wasn't looking, I spun around, shoved my cock back into my shorts, and ran back inside to put on my jeans. I walked to the back as I pulled my shirt on, thinking that this had been one of the longest and strangest mornings of my life only to see that the percolator had not yet started to boil, and it would still be several minutes before the coffee was even ready. I thought about the girl who had just saved my life. I tried to think of her fortuitous arrival and her almost hypnotic control over the herd of hogs. It was nothing short of amazing.

Not only that, but although she had been dressed as an extra from a History Channel show, the figure under her costume was... sublime. I couldn't remember a time when I'd been so overcome by such pure lust. I tried to shake off the thought because it just didn't make sense. She was just a girl. She did save my life, true. So maybe that had something to do with it. But even so, even now as the percolator boiled and I had so many things to do today, I closed the doors and leaned against a wall and stroked myself until I came so hard it hurt.

Afterwards, I felt as if a spell had been broken. I told myself it was just a matter of having been a few days separated from Becky and the combination of excitement, fear, and ah, fuck it, let's throw the whisky in there too because lord knows I need as many fucking excuses as I can get, right? Right.

I climbed into the attic to find the source of the drip. Sure enough, there was some wet insulation and I could see where the roof had leaked. I marked it and went to the hardware store to get some shingles to repair it. Luckily, it appeared to be a new leak, so there was no other damage. I finished the deck and began pacing off the yard for fencing when the carpet guys arrived. The appliances arrived a bit later and by midday we had power. When everything was finished, and all the crews had gone, I packed up the truck and drove home to see my wife and child.

Within days we had the house ready for the movers and listed with our realtor. Becky and I packed our most immediate necessities in our own vehicles, buckled Jason into his car seat, and hit the road. Upon arrival at the new place, we got busy. After the incident with the hogs, I ordered an eight-foot chain-link fence to be installed around the yard. The way they had come up on me without me even realizing they were there had scared me to the core. No way my kid was going to be playing outside without a barrier to protect him.

After that, we settled into our normal routines. I saw no sign of any hogs or mysterious neighbors and after weeks of getting used to the rural life, that strange Saturday morning had almost been forgotten. We'd had two solid bites and an offer on the house in the meantime and it looked as if we were going to have that business completed soon. I stood on the porch flipping burgers while Becky sat at the table sipping a glass of wine.

"So now that we have the house pretty much the way we want it, what do you want to do next?" she asked.

"You mean instead of patching yet another roof leak?"

"I said we should just get roofers out here, but you said no."

I rolled my eyed and huffed. "That was before I started an unending game of whack-a-mole with the fricken' drip monster."

"Monsters go RAWR!" said Jason from his spot on the floor.

"Yes, they do, little man, yes they do," said Becky.

"Sometimes they go DRRRRIP!" I said. Then to Becky, "Seriously, though—you really want to spend six or eight grand on a roof for a house that probably won't be here in two years? All we have to do is plug the leaks and limp this old hoss to the finish line. If everything goes right, we'll meet with the builder right after we close next week."

But that didn't stop the leaking; there was another one within a few days. Every time it rained, there was a new leak. Fair enough, the roof was probably original to the house and from patching it, I could tell that it really needed to be replaced. But economics and pure stubbornness kept me up there patching rather than replacing.

I happened to be on the roof one day when a man came up the drive and waved at me. He was a black man who looked to be in his sixties. He wore an old-fashioned western shirt with pearl snaps and canvas khaki-colored pants over black cowboy boots. He nodded and tipped his white straw hat at me.

I waved to him, placed my hammer in my belt loop and made my way down the ladder to meet him. "Good morning!" I said.

He smiled and nodded, "Good morning to you."

I removed my gloves and reached out to shake his hand. "Jim Campbell."

He nodded again and shook. "Mmm Hmm. You're fixing up Ole Mr. Johnson's place."

I looked back at the house. "Uh, yep. Uh, did you know him?"

The cowboy looked up at me with a strange gleam in his eye. "Yes sir, I did. I know, well, just about everybody." He raised his arms and looked around.

"You've been here for a long time, then," I said, "Seems like a nice place."

He nodded and smiled wide, as if he was holding onto the punch line to a joke that only he found funny. "It can be. Now, don't let me go off and forget my manners. My girl told me she come up here and saved a city slicker from gettin' tore up by some hogs. I told her I didn't believe it none as the Johnson place keeps getting stuck with the lawyers so much people think it's cursed. So, when I heard you hammerin' I grabbed my hat and come to see it for myself."

I looked back over my shoulder, "I don't know that it's cursed so much as neglected. But, it'll do until we can get the big house built next year."

"I wonder, can I trouble you for a drink? Maybe some sweet tea?"

"Uh, of course. Come on in."

We went inside and I offered him what was there in the fridge which was mostly bottled water and a couple cans of beer. Becky had taken Jason with her on a grocery run that morning and left me to work on the roof, so our stock would be low until she returned. The old man took a Coors and cracked the top. He looked at me and shrugged, "I stopped caring what time it was a long time ago."

I laughed before deciding I'd have one too. We went to

the back and sat on the porch and sipped our beers at ten in the morning. "So how long have you been here?"

His eyes rolled up a bit as if calculating, he then started counting off his fingers one by one. "Well, when it's all said and done we been here one hundred and sixty-one years."

"That is a long time. Your family must have been one of the first ones here."

"We were. You see, back then the world weren't no good place for no negros. One was either slave or freedman or..." He waved his hand around dismissively. "Aw hell. Even if you had papers that said you were free, sometimes they'd take 'em away and cart your black ass on back to the market."

"So, your ancestors found a way out?"

"Damn right. We pulled up roots and headed west. We come out here deep into Texas territory and found this little group of Germans trying to set up a town. We offered to be employed and things were good." He looked out toward the woods, "Till the war started, then them fool Germans run off and got themselves killed, leaving their wives and children behind. T'was a terrible mess."

"Oh wow. What happened?"

The cowboy looked at me and sniffled, "We jumped their claim, locked 'em in irons and made 'em pick our damn cotton, that's what!"

I sat there stunned. What had he just said? Did he really mean...?

"Got you!" He laughed and slapped his knee. Aw, y'all city boys just take it don't ya? I don't know how we come to be here anymore than nobody. I just like messing with folks."

I couldn't help but wonder at how strange this old fellow was. And even with the laughing and the gentle ribbing, I couldn't help but feel like the truth was buried somewhere in there. Like the story was mostly true with elements either changed or left out. I laughed a little nervously and my visitor stood up.

"Well, thanks for the laugh and for the drink but I gotta be movin' on. Got things needing my attention this morning."

"I understand," I said, relieved that it was his idea to go. We walked back through the house and out the front door.

"Well it was nice meeting you mister, uh, I didn't catch your name."

"You can call me Jack," he said with a grin, "It's as good a name as any."

"Okay Mr. Jack, you have a good day."

"Yessir, I will. Oh, one more thing. Old Mr. Johnson and I used to spend occasional Sunday evenings playing cards over a cigar and some sweet tea, if that's something that suits you."

I eyed this strange man standing in my driveway and admonished myself for being defensive. Here was an old man whose friend died more than twenty years before looking for someone to spend time with. I smiled and said, "You're on. Next week okay?"

"Next week jus' fine. You be careful up on that roof, sir."

"I will. See you next Sunday."

He was already walking toward the road and raised a hand to wave. Then he was gone.

Becky and Jason got home a couple hours later. We put away the groceries and played in the yard, enjoying one of the last tolerable spring days before the summer heat would kick in and send us running for our air conditioner. We sat in the grass rolling a ball to one another; Jason giggling happily as he toddled around trying to catch it. Becky went inside to get drinks and I caught and tickled my son. It was a good day.

A little while later, as Becky and Jason chased each other around, I glanced up and saw two hogs standing near the trail to the clearing. One was huge and sported almost comically large and uneven tusks. The other was smaller and stood next to its companion. They did nothing but stand still and watch us, but the way they did it put me on edge.

"Becky, get Jason inside," I said. I followed them in and retrieved my hunting rifle, a bolt-action 30-06 that had been my father's, and walked back outside. The hogs were still there. I raised the rifle to my shoulder and spotted the large one in my scope. As I steadied my aim, I realized that I had seen this animal before. The uneven tusks were a dead giveaway. But it was also impossible. These were the hogs I had seen in the dream I'd had about Guillermo Rivas being attacked. Yet here they were in my field.

I took careful aim and squeezed the trigger. The report was deafening, and I quickly worked the bolt to cycle another round. If I could, I would take the pair. But when I drew down on them again, they were both still standing there, casually staring back down at me. I lined up another shot and fired but again they stood unmolested. There was no way I could have missed twice! I cycled the bolt once more and aimed a third time, fired, and then watched as the two hogs walked casually back into the woods.

I went inside and told Becky that I'd missed and that there must be something wrong with my scope, but I didn't believe it. I had taken countless deer with this rifle and had never needed to adjust the scope more than a couple of clicks either way in over a decade. The worst possible shot I could make at that range should have still hit somewhere. To miss outright was impossible. I told her to keep her pistol handy when going outside from now on, just in case and I spent the rest of the evening researching hog traps and containment systems online.

That night, I had a dream. I was in the clearing and the phantom house I'd seen was whole. On one side, there was a plot with crops coming up and on the other was a corral with several horses. Whoever lived here was doing well. It was still some distance away and I began to walk toward it. When I took my first step, however, the hog with the uneven tusks ran into the path and blocked my way. I reached for my pistol, which in my dream was a toy cap gun from my childhood. I fired anyway but it had no effect on the animal as it walked toward me grunting.

"Best not let him bite you, Monsieur," said a voice from behind me. I turned to see the girl who'd saved me weeks before but this time she was nearly naked, wearing only a small linen skirt around her thin waist. Her head wrap was gone as well and thin dreadlocks fell about her shoulders. At once I was overcome by an almost panicked lust. I suddenly felt as if I was moving through very deep and warm water and I knew instinctively that this was all wrong—the setting, the company, and especially the seductress who licked her smiling lips and beckoned me to follow her to God-knows-where.

I took a step back and the hog grunted louder. I could hear it pawing at the ground. "You've had a hard day, Monsieur, come and let Miss Lucie feel you better, oui?"

Stepping away from the hog brought me closer to the girl who in turn took another step toward me with arms outstretched. I looked away from her and the hog to the house which now had smoke and flames pouring out of the windows. The hog stepped forward. I moved away from it. The girl wrapped her arms about my shoulders and chest and began kissing my neck.

Unimaginable pleasure ripped through me all at once. I could feel her breasts pressing against my back as her lips moved to my ear. All attempts at resistance fell away and my knees buckled as she pulled me to the ground. I lay on my back as she straddled me and traced designs on my chest with her long fingernails. Although I knew it was a dream, it was still just as real, or even more real somehow than reality. My mind recoiled as my body relented. I felt her touch hot on my chest, each kiss the most exquisite torture I'd ever felt.

Suddenly, Lucie's head snapped up and her countenance changed. Where before she'd had her head thrown back and her eyes closed in sexual abandon, now she was staring at me angrily. The hog squealed and snorted nervously as I felt a hand that was not Lucie's slide down my chest toward my crotch. Lucie hissed before fading.

The whole scene fell apart as I came awake to Becky slowly stroking me and kissing my neck.

"Sounded like you were having a good dream," she whispered, "Thought I'd join you."

I turned to her as she kissed me, then we made love furiously, quietly, in the tiny old house in the middle of the deep, dark woods.

Afterwards, as she slept quietly next to me, fear settled in. Something was horribly wrong here. Something horrible had happened here. Something horrible was still happening here. And we had moved in next door to it.

A week later I found the true source of the roof leaks. I had been in the attic trying to take some measurements. I had planned to lay down some plywood and make some flooring so that we could use part of the attic for storage. When I was up there, I touched a piece of the plywood decking and when I did, I came away wet. The wood had gotten dry rot and deteriorated to a spongy gray mass. I watched rivulets of water running in several directions at once, all ending their journey through the attic with an audible drip. Here was the ultimate culprit. Here, this would end.

I bought the plywood, tarpaper, and other supplies I needed and spent the whole day on the roof tearing out shingles and hoping that this would solve the issue once and for all. Occasionally I paused to look out toward the clearing and wonder what I might find if I walked to that back corner with a shovel or an axe. Might I find old tin cups and medicine bottles; signs that someone had lived in that spot before? Or might I find ancient cinders instead? Melted glass. Maybe charred bones; signs that someone had died there long ago? I turned back to my work and pushed the thought out of my head. The truth is, I didn't want to know.

I sat on the porch taking a break for a moment when Becky came out with a large pitcher of iced tea. She poured us both a glass and gave me a pep talk and a promise of some fun once I showered and burned my clothes. I was drinking to that suggestion when Jack came sauntering up the road and through the gate. He was dressed the same as last time except for now his hat was black instead of white and looked newer. I complimented him on the hat. He tipped it to Becky, thanked me for the compliment and then pulled a deck of cards from his shirt pocket.

"It too early to get up a game?"

Becky looked at me and frowned. I shrugged. I had mentioned to her that a neighbor may be stopping by for a while, but it was early and I was in the middle of a chore that could not be left undone.

"Actually," I said, "It is a bit early. I've got at least another hour or two fixing the roof. You want to come back maybe five or so?"

With nimble fingers, Jack cut the cards and flipped them over themselves. "One hand. You win, I'll come back at five. I win, we play now and I'll help you fix the roof my own self later on."

I stared at him for a second as he twirled the deck on one finger. This guy was good. I could tell that at some point in his life, Old Mister Jack had been something of a hustler.

"Uh, that's great and all but I really need to get this

done. It's supposed to rain later and there's a big hole in my roof that I need to have patched by dark."

Jack shrugged. "Have it your way then." He shuffled and cut the cards before pulling one and putting it at the bottom of the deck. "Burn," he said, then turned the top card over. "Jack of Clubs." He turned the second card over, "King of Diamonds. You win, I'll see you at five." He winked and walked back out of the gate.

"Ooookay?" said Becky as the gate banged shut behind him. "Your friends are weird."

I finished the roof and got showered and changed. Jason was up from his nap, which itself had been an amazing thing to have happened given I had been pounding on the roof all day. He sat on the floor playing with his trucks as Becky and I sat on the sofa enjoying each other's company, watching a movie on Netflix. At five on the dot there was a knock at the door. I was really not in the mood for guests and gave a groan as I hoisted myself from the couch. "I'll see if we can't reschedule."

"Be nice," Becky said, "Weird or not, we need to start getting to know the neighbors."

I nodded in agreement as I stretched and walked to the door.

Jack stood on the porch holding a paper bag. "What's your game, Jim?" He tilted the bag and smiled. Inside was a six-pack of Coors, a fifth of Maker's and a pack of cigars in cellophane. "Cubans. Best there is."

I waved him over to our patio table and went to find something we could use as an ashtray. He unpacked the bag and brought out two new decks of cards. "Your call, my friend."

"Well, it's been a while so let's go for an old-fashioned game of five-card draw."

"Sounds good to me."

He shuffled a deck and set it before me to cut. "Jokers wild. I like a little extra chance, don't you?"

I cracked the top on one of the beers and nodded. I enjoyed wild cards too. He dealt the first hand and I won with two pairs. He won the next with three-of-a-kind. Back and forth, up and down. He told me stories of the people in the area. Who got along with whom and more importantly, who didn't get along. He shared his opinion on local politics—"Ain't none of em ever gonna do nothin' worth a damn. Ain't worth the time it takes to get my ass out of bed." And the weather, "Only goldarned place it'll be colder'na witch's tit one day and hotter than the Devil's sack the next, but I can't leave."

The stories he told were interesting and the way he told them was warm and engaging. At some point we forgot to play cards and just traded stories and laughs. Becky came outside and joined us for couple drinks. He paid her several compliments that bordered on the flirtatious and made her blush. "One hell of a family you got here, Jim. Play you for them!"

I laughed, "You're on!"

Becky giggled as the cards were dealt and the bets and draws went back and forth and Jack won the hand. "Welp, honey, I guess go pack up, Mr. Jack won you fair and square."

"You wish!" she said playfully, "We just got the house the way I want it and you're sending me away? No way, Jose!"

Jack laughed, "Well it would be nice to have a pretty lady like you to keep me company and maybe pour me a glass of sweet tea from time to time, but not iffin' it's gonna make you sad. I suppose you can stay here if you want."

"I'm such a lucky girl!" she remarked before going back inside.

It wasn't long before Jack said he needed to get moving on and he'd see us next week. And shortly after, he was up and gone. Becky and I cleaned up and talked about how much fun we'd just had. I honestly could not wait until the next weekend to play cards with Jack again.

A couple of nights later, Miss Lucie appeared in a dream. I was standing in the clearing, near the trail through the woods. The white house was on fire and smoke was pouring out windows and doors. Horses were screaming in their corral and through the flames I could see figures moving inside the house. Were people trapped in there? I stepped cautiously toward the house when Miss Lucie came out the front door and walked up the trail toward me. She was not naked this time, but her outfit left little to the imagination as she sauntered toward me. "Bonjour," she said.

I didn't know what to think. She was moving slowly, swaying, showing me all that could be mine if I but wished it but despite a sudden, uncontrollable ache in my crotch, the feeling I had was almost paralyzing fear. I took a step back. She laughed.

"Come now, Monsieur, you gotta let Miss Lucie in sooner or later. You'll go mad if you do not."

"What do you want from me?" I said as I started to tremble.

She paused and considered, "Oh, Monsieur, I don't want nothin'. I ain't nothin' but a dream in that pretty little head of yours. You want me. You want this. You jus' dreamin anyhow. You oughtta let me work my magic for you."

I took another step backward when something muscled and hairy brushed by me. It was the snaggle-toothed hog, blocking my exit as it had before. I tried to step around it when it whipped its head around and knocked my legs out from under me. Almost as soon as I hit the ground, Lucie was upon me, tearing at my clothes and kissing and caressing me. For my part, I still felt drugged and slow, as you do in dreams, but somehow even deeper. I began thinking, moving, trying to wake myself up but it wasn't working. I turned my head and saw that there were, in fact, people inside the burning house. Someone broke a window from the inside and was trying to climb out when her head exploded, splashing red across the white washed timbers. The rifle report echoed through the field. I didn't know what I was seeing, what was real, what was not. I could not be sure, but the face of the woman who had just been shot looked like Becky's. Nobody else tried to escape the burning house. They simply screamed as the fire consumed them. I watched it as Lucie kissed and groped, and finally climbed off of me.

Had there been sex? I didn't think so but I could not be sure. Time and events move differently in dreams and I had been so focused on the house and the fire, I had totally ignored the witch woman who was trying to rape me. I remembered how angry she had seemed when Becky had pulled me out of the last nightmare. I looked around and Miss Lucie was gone. The house and the hog were gone too and instead of clear blue sky, it was dark. I was sitting on the ground near the trail and after a few minutes of very intense disorientation, I realized that I was awake. I was awake and sitting in the woods in the middle of the night. I got up, feeling rather sick, and walked back to the house in my bare feet and shorts. When I got back to my bedroom, Becky snored softly, and I climbed into bed next to her. I lay awake until dawn wondering what the hell had just happened. I was now sleepwalking into the woods at night.

This was not good.

For the first time since we'd lived there, we had a hard rain and the roof did not leak at all. It seemed as if I had fixed at least that while I felt my sanity slipping further and further away. How else could I explain giant dream hogs that refused to be shot? Or a spectral house that got clearer and more horrifying every time it appeared? Sexually ravenous dream seduction by my new neighbor's daughter; who, by the way, managed to tame a dozen feral creatures with a bag of feed and a song? My strange new neighbor himself whose last name I didn't even know but who would just appear on our doorstep when he wanted to play a game. I didn't know what to think. I didn't know anything anymore. The season moved in a series of good days, days when I was a stable, loving husband and father to my wife and son; and bad days, days when I was tormented by beasts and dreams and blasphemous seduction.

Jack arrived at five o' clock on Sunday each week. And while I had a lot of fun when he was here, more and more often, that little rapping knock sent shivers down my spine. Becky had started getting annoyed with the bizarrely strict schedule and with the fact that I spent every Sunday drinking and smoking cigars while she got left alone to deal with Jason's bath and bed time by herself. I mentioned this to Jack, suggesting we take a week or two off or whatever, but every time I did, he'd make a bet on it that I'd lose, and he'd leave that evening saying, "See you next week."

And those fucking hogs.

Every time I'd have a dream, of any kind, Snaggletooth and his buddy would show up somewhere. They were always snorting and squealing and either standing there staring at me or shoving me around. I'd come to see Snaggletooth as Lucie's pet, as she was never without him.

I continued to sleepwalk. I found myself in the clearing night after night, barefoot and confused. Becky was no longer sleeping when I'd come in after a weird walk. She was worried and upset and started to suggest I see a doctor if these fugues didn't stop. It came to a head one night when, in the dream, Lucie and Snaggletooth were coming after me. I pulled my pistol and shot at the mad hog. The pistol, of course, was the cap gun I got for my fifth birthday. I aimed and shot and came awake immediately in the woods holding my very real smoking gun in the middle of the night. Horrified, I ran back to the house to Becky who sat at the kitchen table, her countenance a mixture of fear and worry.

"I don't know what's happening," I said, "Something's not right. I'm sleepwalking; having strange dreams. Something's very wrong." I handed her the pistol, "I can't be trusted with this. I was asleep just now. I need you to take this and go, right now, and change the combination on the safe. Don't let me know what it is. Just... Don't."

She did as she was asked and then came back to me. "I want you to see a doctor, Jim. Maybe it's stress over the life changes? I don't know but what if it's something worse? I want you to get checked out."

I could say nothing. I agreed with her. I shuddered. All this time, I thought the experiences were external. What if, instead, there was something in my head that was causing the dreams, the breaks from reality? What if I wasn't haunted? What if I was sick? Jason woke up crying and Becky went to check on him. I sat at the kitchen table trying to make sense of what was happening to me, but sense could not be found. The next day was Sunday. I'd scheduled a Tuesday morning appointment with a doctor in Austin to get checked out. All I needed was to make it through the next two days and everything would be fine.

Jack arrived at five to play cards. Becky rolled her eyes and said, "Really?"

I got up to answer the door and tell Jack I wasn't well and we'd have to skip a week. When I opened the door, however, Lucie stood there instead. My heart leapt into my chest. Was this a dream? What was going on? Feelings of guilt and fear struck me and I stumbled backwards as the girl in front of me cocked her head and gave me a curious look.

"Are you okay, sir?"

"I, uh, I'm fine. I just, uh. I was expecting someone else."

"I know. My dad sent me up here to tell you he can't make it tonight. He's a bit under the weather."

"Who is it?" asked Becky.

"Uh, it's Jack's daughter. Uh, Lucie, right?"

She eyed me curiously. "Um, no, I'm Kara." She reached out a hand to shake. I hesitated and she narrowed her eyes, genuinely confused. "Are you sure you're okay? You look a little pale."

This was terribly wrong. This was Miss Lucie, the demon girl who had been terrorizing me since we'd moved in. I knew her too well. She could call herself what she liked but I wasn't fooled. Becky came to the door and took the offered hand. "Becky Campbell, nice to meet you Kara."

"Thanks. Anyway, Dad wanted me to let you know. He really has a great time playing with you. He hasn't had a friend to play with since Old Mr. Johnson died. And I was barely five then, so it's been a long time. I appreciate your kindness."

"Well, we like him too," said Becky, "Tell him we hope he's better by next week."

She thanked us again and turned to walk home. "Nice seeing you again," I said, waving.

She stopped and turned, "Excuse me?"

"Um, it's nice to see you again. It's been a few months."

"I'm sorry, but you must have me confused with someone else. I just got in last night."

I thought of the girl who had saved me from the hogs that morning. If this wasn't her, then this was her twin. "Maybe it was your sister, then."

"Uh, nope. There's just me and dad," she said, obviously uncomfortable, "Don't know who you saw but it wasn't me."

"My mistake, I'm sorry."

She gave us both a quizzical look as she wandered down the driveway to the road to Jack's place.

"Well, that wasn't weird or anything," Becky said, closing the door.

"I've met her before," I said.

"Well, she's never met you. You should go lay down, Jim. You're starting to worry me."

I couldn't argue. I was suddenly very tired and could think of nothing that would please me more than a good, long nap.

I came awake to a crash and a scream. I sat up in bed and listened as things slammed and glass broke outside my bedroom. I leapt to my feet and ran out into the living room. To my horror, Snaggletooth and the small hog were in the house! I stared at the two of them before the little one came at me and I kicked at him as hard as I could, my bare foot connecting with the side of his head. He squealed and shied away but his distress enraged Snaggletooth, who foamed at the mouth as he ran at me.

I spun on my heels and ran to the closet that held the gun safe. Of course, it was locked, and I did not know the new combination. I slammed the door in his face and held it shut as he slammed against it again and again. The wooden door began to splinter, and I looked for anything I could use against him when he came through. My hunting bag was on a top shelf and I reached for it, retrieving my knife. Seconds later, Snaggletooth's head poked through and I stabbed him in the snout. His flesh yielded and he let out a scream that sounded almost human. His head drew out of the hole in the door and the large animal went back to join the little one. Had I really hurt them? I had sent countless bullets at these beasts over the past several weeks and never so much as scratched one. Now Snaggletooth stood huffing and rubbing his bleeding snout on his leg. Where were Becky and Jason? Hopefully they got out or were locked in a bedroom away from the carnage.

I stood with knife in hand. Snaggletooth stood eyeing me madly. Each breath he took was a promise that as soon as he could, he would tear my guts out. He shook his tusks in warning as the little hog continued to squeal fearfully. Without taking my eyes off the animals in my living room, I took a step toward them. Each time, their squeals got louder and more nervous, but they did not attack. Another step. More grunts and squeals. The anxious hogs trembled as they backed themselves into the corner. Emboldened, I crossed the threshold toward them. Snaggletooth screeched and swung his tusks at me as he cowered. I was careful in my approach, keeping my eyes on the injured beast. Although it would be a terrible mess, I realized I was going to have to kill these animals in my living room. I took another step toward them, they moved away.

Suddenly, the small hog squealed and ran toward me, breaking to the side to get by me. I swung out with the knife and buried it an inch or so into the flesh behind his head. He screamed in pain and fury and ran into the wall, dragging a bloody stain down the newly painted surface. Then Snaggletooth came at me. He grunted and screeched as he charged, turning his head and tusking my hand, ripping it open from the base of my ring finger to my wrist. At the same instant I brought the knife across, burying it deep in his neck. The animal screamed again as blood poured from its neck and mouth. He then slowed down, his breathing heavy. He crossed into the kitchen and collapsed onto the linoleum floor. I walked over to him and drew my knife across his throat before turning my attention back to the small one. He was not as badly injured as his pal but was still squealing in panic. I quickly cornered him and brought the knife down again and again, finally ending the terror of the hogs, these unlikely beasts that had been haunting my dreams for months.

Dreams. I looked at my hand and realized that although it was torn open and I could see the ligaments exposed, it didn't hurt and it wasn't bleeding. The hogs still lay across the floor, bodies giving little spasms as they died. Blood was everywhere and the knife in my hand felt as real as anything I'd ever held. But why was I alone? Where were Becky and Jason? I checked the other rooms of the house but there was no sign of them. It was strangely quiet and I kept expecting to wake up any second. I then had an idea. If this really is a dream and I'd just faced down and destroyed my fears, maybe I could go outside and Miss Lucie would show up. Then I could put an end to that nightmare as well.

I walked outside barefoot and went straight to the clearing, knife in hand. As I stepped off the trail, the night turned to day and the house sat in the field. The horses trotted around merrily. There was a shot, followed by a scream and another shot. Moments later, smoke began to rise from the house. A window broke and a woman began to climb out, but someone shot her in the head and she fell across the window sill. I looked up to see a man on a horse holding a rifle to his shoulder. Another window broke and another shot rang out as the mounted rider shot at anyone who tried to escape the blaze. The rider turned and nodded down at me and I recognized Jack.

"Hell of a day, ain't it Jim?"

I tightened my grip on the knife as Miss Lucie appeared on a horse next to her father.

"My name is Kara!" She laughed. Jack laughed with her, both amused at something I didn't understand. I still don't.

"Thanks for playin' Jim, my boy, you've been a real sport," Jack said.

"I had a good time too, Monsieur. 'Hard to get' is my favorite pantomime," said Lucie.

Jack took aim and fired at another poor soul trying to escape the fire.

"Go on back home and get some sleep. Lucie and myself will leave you alone now. I'll even let you keep part of my winnin's, cause we're such good friends."

Lucie blew me a kiss, and then faded away. When I turned back to Jack, he too was gone. The house continued to burn out of control for a moment, then it too faded and the day turned into night. I began to start for home, then I heard the rumble of thunder from an early morning storm and I woke up in my bed.

I lay there for a moment, listening for any sign of Jason, who nearly always woke up and cried during thunderstorms. I opened my eyes and looked around. Whatever time it was, it was still dark outside. I remained still so as to not disturb Becky and listened to the rain. I dozed.

I woke up to a sound with which I had become angrily familiar. The sound of water dripping through a leak in the roof to splatter on the ground. It was light outside this time and I sat up, ready to discover the source of the drip. But the source of the drip was something else entirely. I have no words. I can barely think of it now. I still don't believe it.

I ran to the kitchen to find a phone to call the police and everywhere I stepped was covered in blood. Blood on the floor; bloody handprints stained the wall. In horror I remembered stabbing the smaller of the two animals. Jason lets out a scream and runs from me, his hand streaking blood down the hall. I suddenly relive the entire fight with the hogs.

I wake up to a crash and a scream. I walk out of the bedroom to see Becky picking up pieces of a broken vase that Jason has knocked over. Jason runs toward me, happily calling, "Daddy!" I haul off and kick my two-year-old son in the face. Becky shrieks as Jason falls.

"What the fuck!" she cries in shock, picking up a piece

of the shattered glass and coming toward me to retrieve our fallen son.

I retreat to the bedroom closet and find my knife. When I try to open the door, it's locked. The locks we installed on the outside as an extra safety measure to keep Jason away from dangerous things. I begin stabbing and kicking at the door. It splinters easily, and I break out of my prison to renew my assault. Becky is holding Jason and her purse and is trying to get out the front door to one of the cars. I am too fast, however, and immediately corner them. Becky screams at me to stop, waving her broken shard of glass at me desperately. She sets Jason on the ground and tells him to run out the door and hide. He takes a few clumsy steps and I strike at him with the knife and he falls against the wall, his tiny hands smearing blood across the newly painted surface. Becky manages to catch me with the shard, but the cut is tiny. I stab her in the neck and she collapses on the kitchen floor. I finish them both off before going outside to hunt phantoms.

On the dresser, set up as if on display, were the heads of my wife and son, apples shoved into their mouths. My knife was imbedded in the wood of the dresser between them, its blade and handle covered in gore. The drips were coming from their congealing blood as it seeped onto the floor. Drip. Drip. Drip...

Sheriff Wood keeps screaming at me, "Where are the bodies? What did you do with their bodies???"

And I guess that's what Jack meant when he said I could keep part of his winnings. It was a little joke. Something that the Devil might find funny.

And that's all I can remember.

PUBLISHER'S NOTE

Please remember to honestly
RATE THE BOOK!

It's the best way to support the authors and help new
readers discover our work.

Check out our other titles and download a
FREE BOOK:
TobiasWade.Com

Made in the USA
Middletown, DE
27 December 2020